HIGH DRUID OF
SHANNARA
JARKA RUUS

HIGH DRUID OF
SHANNARA
JARKA RUUS

TERRY
BROOKS

BALLANTINE BOOKS • NEW YORK

A Del Rey® Book
Published by The Random House Publishing Group
Copyright © 2003 by Terry Brooks
Excerpt from *The High Druid of Shannara: Tanequil* copyright © 2004 by Terry Brooks

This book contains an excerpt from the forthcoming book *The High Druid of Shannara: Tanequil* by Terry Brooks. This excerpt has been set for this edition only and may not reflect the final content of the forthcoming edition.

www.delreydigital.com

ISBN 0-345-43576-1

Manufactured in the United States of America

OPM 9 8 7 6 5 4 3 2

First Edition: September 2003
First Mass Market Edition: September 2004

For Judine, my favorite traveling companion,
at the start of another journey.

HIGH DRUID OF
SHANNARA
JARKA RUUS

ONE

She sat alone in her chambers, draped in twilight's shadows and evening's solitude, her thoughts darker than the night descending and heavier than the weight of all Paranor. She retired early these days, ostensibly to work but mostly to think, to ponder on the disappointment of today's failures and the bleakness of tomorrow's prospects. It was silent in the high tower, and the silence gave her a momentary respite from the struggle between herself and those she would lead. It lasted briefly, only so long as she remained secluded, but without its small daily comfort she sometimes thought she would have gone mad with despair.

She was no longer a girl, no longer even young, though she retained her youthful looks, her pale translucent skin still unblemished and unlined, her startling blue eyes clear, and her movements steady and certain. When she looked in the mirror, which she did infrequently now as then, she saw the girl she had been twenty years earlier, as if aging had been miraculously stayed. But while her body stayed young, her spirit grew old. Responsibility aged her more quickly than time. Only the Druid Sleep, should she avail herself of it, would stay the wearing of her heart, and she would not choose that remedy anytime soon. She could not. She was the Ard Rhys of the Third Druid Council, the High Druid of Paranor, and while she remained in that office, sleep of any kind was in short supply.

Her gaze drifted to the windows of her chamber, looking west to where the sun was already gone behind the horizon, and the light it cast skyward in the wake of its descent a dim glow beginning to fail. She thought her own star was setting, as well, its light fading, its time passing, its chances slipping away. She would change that if she could, but she no longer believed she knew the way.

She heard Tagwen before she saw him, his footfalls light and cautious in the hallway beyond her open door, his concern for her evident in the softness of his approach.

"Come, Tagwen," she called as he neared.

He came through the door and stopped just inside, not presuming to venture farther, respecting this place that was hers and hers alone. He was growing old, as well, nearly twenty years of service behind him, the only assistant she had ever had, his time at Paranor a mirror of her own. His stocky, gnarled body was still strong, but his movements were slowing and she could see the way he winced when his joints tightened and cramped after too much use. There was kindness in his eyes, and it had drawn her to him from the first, an indication of the nature of the man inside. Tagwen served because he respected what she was doing, what she meant to the Four Lands, and he never judged her by her successes or failures, even when there were so many more of the latter than the former.

"Mistress," he said in his rough, gravel-laced voice, his seamed, bearded face dipping momentarily into shadow as he bowed. It was an odd, stiff gesture he had affected from the beginning. He leaned forward as if to share a confidence that others might try to overhear. "Kermadec is here."

She rose at once. "He will not come inside," she said, making it a statement of fact.

Tagwen shook his head. "He waits at the north gate and asks if you will speak with him." The Dwarf's lips tightened in somber reflection. "He says it is urgent."

She reached for her cloak and threw it about her shoulders. She went by him, touching his shoulder reassuringly as she passed. She went out the door and down the hallway to begin her descent. Within the stairwell, beyond the sound of her own soft footfalls, she heard voices rise up from below, the sounds of conversations adrift on the air. She tried to make out what they said, but could not. They would be speaking of her; they did so almost incessantly. They would be asking why she continued as their leader, why she presumed that she could achieve anything after so many failures, why she could not recognize that her time was past and another should take her place. Some would be whispering that she ought to be forced out, one way or another. Some would be advocating stronger action.

Druid intrigues. The halls of Paranor were rife with them, and she could not put a stop to it. At Walker's command, she had formed this Third Council on her return to the Four Lands from Parkasia. She had accepted her role as leader, her destiny as guide to those she had recruited, her responsibility for rebuilding the legacy of the Druids as knowledge givers to the Races. She had formed the heart of this new order with those few sent under duress by the Elven King Kylen Elessedil at his brother Ahren's insistence. Others had come from other lands and other Races, drawn by the prospect of exploring magic's uses. That had been twenty years ago, when there was fresh hope and everything seemed possible. Time and an inability to effect any measurable change in the thinking and attitudes of the governing bodies of those lands and Races had leeched most of that away. What remained was a desperate insistence on clinging to her belief that she was not meant to give up.

But that alone was not enough. It would never be enough. Not for someone who had come out of darkness so complete that any chance at redemption had seemed hopeless. Not for

Grianne Ohmsford, who had once been the Ilse Witch and had made herself Ard Rhys to atone for it.

She reached the lower levels of the Keep, the great halls that connected the meeting rooms with the living quarters of those she had brought to Paranor. A handful of these Druids came into view, shadows sliding along the walls like spilled oil in the light of the flameless lamps that lit the corridors. Some nodded to her; one or two spoke. Most simply cast hurried glances and passed on. They feared and mistrusted her, these Druids she had accepted into her order. They could not seem to help themselves, and she could not find the heart to blame them.

Terek Molt walked out of a room and grunted his unfriendly greeting, outwardly bold and challenging. But she could sense his real feelings, and she knew he feared her. Hated her more than feared her, though. It was the same with Traunt Rowan and Iridia Eleri and one or two more. Shadea a'Ru was beyond even that, her venomous glances so openly hostile that there was no longer any communication between them, a situation that it seemed nothing could help.

Grianne closed her eyes against what she was feeling and wondered what she was going to do about these vipers—what she could do that would not have repercussions beyond anything she was prepared to accept.

Young Trefen Morys passed her with a wave and a smile, his face guileless and welcoming, his enthusiasm evident. He was a bright light in an otherwise darkened firmament, and she was grateful for his presence. Some within the order still believed in her. She had never expected friendship or even compassion from those who came to her, but she had hoped for loyalty and a sense of responsibility toward the office she held. She had been foolish to think that way, and she no longer did so. Perhaps it was not inaccurate to say that now she merely hoped that reason might prevail.

"Mistress," Gerand Cera greeted in his soft voice as he

bowed her past him, his tall form lean and sinuous, his angular features sleepy and dangerous.

There were too many of them. She could not watch out for all of them adequately. She put herself at risk every time she walked these halls—here in the one place she should be safe, in the order she had founded. It was insane.

She cleared the front hall and went out into the night, passed through a series of interconnected courtyards to the north gates, and ordered the guard to let her through. The Trolls on watch, impassive and silent, did as they were told. She did not know their names, only that they were there at Kermadec's behest, which was enough to keep her reassured of their loyalty. Whatever else happened in this steadily eroding company of the once faithful, the Trolls would stand with her.

Would that prove necessary? She would not have thought so a month ago. That she asked the question now demonstrated how uncertain matters had become.

She walked to the edge of the bluff, to the wall of trees that marked the beginning of the forest beyond, and stopped. An owl glided through the darkness, a silent hunter. She felt a sudden connection with him so strong that she could almost envision flying away as he did, leaving everything behind, returning to the darkness and its solitude.

She brushed the thought aside, an indulgence she could not afford, and whistled softly. Moments later, a figure detached itself from the darkness almost in front of her and came forward.

"Mistress," the Maturen greeted, dropping to one knee and bowing deeply.

"Kermadec, you great bear," she replied, stepping forward to put her arms around him. "How good it is to see you."

Of the few friends she possessed, Kermadec was perhaps the best. She had known him since the founding of the order, when she had gone into the Northland to ask for the support of the Troll tribes. No one had ever thought to do that, and her request was cause enough for a convening of a council of the nations. She did not waste the opportunity she had been given. She told them of her mission, of her role as Ard Rhys of a new Druid Council, the third since Galaphile's time. She declared that this new order would accept members from all nations, the Trolls included. No prejudices would be allowed; the past would play no part in the present. The Druids were beginning anew, and for the order to succeed, all the Races must participate.

Kermadec had stepped forward almost at once, offering the support of his sizeable nation, of its people and resources. Prompted by her gesture and his understanding of its importance to the Races, his decision was made even before the council of nations had met. His Rock Trolls were not imbued with a strong belief in magic, but it would be their honor to serve as her personal guard. Give them an opportunity to demonstrate their reliability and skill, and she would not regret it.

Nor had she ever done so. Kermadec had stayed five years, and in that time became her close friend. More than once, he had solved a problem that might otherwise have troubled her. Even after he had left for home again, his service complete, he had remained in charge of choosing the Trolls that followed in his footsteps. Some had doubted the wisdom of allowing Trolls inside the walls at all, let alone as personal guards to the Ard Rhys. But she had walked in darker places than these and had allied herself with creatures far more dangerous. She did not think of any Race as predisposed toward either good or evil; she saw them all only as being composed of creatures that might be persuaded to choose one over the other.

Just as she saw the members of her Druid order, she thought, though she might wish it otherwise.

"Kermadec," she said again, the relief in her voice clearly evident.

"You should let me rid you of them all," he said softly, one great hand coming to rest on her slim shoulder. "You should wash them away like yesterday's sweat and start anew."

She nodded. "If it were that easy, I should call on you to help me. But I can't start over. It would be perceived as weakness by the governments of the nations I court. There can be no weakness in an Ard Rhys in these times." She patted his hand. "Rise and walk with me."

They left the bluff and moved back into the trees, perfectly comfortable with each other and the night. The sights and sounds of Paranor disappeared, and the silence of the forest wrapped them close. The air was cool and gentle, the wind a soft whisper in the new spring leaves, bearing the scent of woods and water. It would be summer before long, and the smells would change again.

"What brings you here?" she asked him finally, knowing he would wait for her to ask before speaking of it.

He shook his head. "Something troubling. Something you may understand better than I do."

Even for a Rock Troll, Kermadec was huge, towering over her at close to seven feet, his powerful body sheathed in a barklike skin. He was all muscle and bone, strong enough to rip small trees out at the roots. She had never known a Troll to possess the strength and quickness of Kermadec. But there was much more to him. A Maturen of thirty years, he was the sort of person others turned to instinctively in times of trouble. Solid and capable, he had served his nation with a distinction and compassion that belied the ferocious history of his Race. In the not so distant past, the Trolls had marched against Men and Elves and Dwarves with the single-minded intent of smashing them back into the earth. During the Wars of the Races, ruled by their feral and warlike nature, they had allied themselves with the darker forces in the world. But that was the past, and in the present, where it mattered most, they were no longer so easily bent to service in a cause that reason would never embrace.

"You have come a long way to see me, Kermadec," she said. "It must be something important."

"That remains for you to decide," he said softly. "I myself haven't seen what I am about to reveal, so it is hard for me to judge. I think it will be equally hard for you."

"Tell me."

He slowed to a stop in the darkness and turned to face her. "There is strange activity in the ruins of the Skull Kingdom, mistress. The reports come not from Rock Trolls, who will not go into that forbidden place, but from other creatures, ones who will, ones who make a living in part by telling of what they see. What they see now is reminiscent of other, darker times."

"The Warlock Lord's domain, once," she observed. "A bad place still, all broken walls and scattered bones. Traces of evil linger in the smells and taste of the land. What do these creatures tell you they see?"

"Smoke and mirrors, of a sort. Fires lit in darkness and turned cold by daylight's arrival. Small explosions of light that suggest something besides wood might be burning. Acrid smells that have no other source than the fires. Black smudges on flat stones that have the look of altars. Markings on those stones that might be symbols. Such events were sporadic at first, but now occur almost nightly. Strange things that of themselves alone do not trouble me, but taken all together do."

He breathed in and exhaled. "One thing more. Some among those who come to us say there are wraiths visible at the edges of the mist and smoke, things not of substance and not yet entirely formed, but recognizable as something more than the imagination. They flutter like caged birds seeking to be free."

Grianne went cold, aware of the possibilities that the sightings suggested. Something was being conjured up by use of magic, something that wasn't natural to this world and that was being summoned to serve an unknown purpose.

"How reliable are these stories?"

He shrugged. "They come from Gnomes for the most part, the only ones who go into that part of the world. They do so because they are drawn to what they perceive in their superstitions as sacred. They perform their rituals in those places because they feel it will lend them power. How reliable are they?" He paused. "I think there is weight to what they say they see."

She thought a moment. Another strangeness to add to an already overcrowded agenda of strangenesses. She did not like the sound of this one, because if magic was at work, whatever its reason, its source might lie uncomfortably close to home. Druids had the use of magic and were the most likely suspects, but their use of it in places beyond Paranor was forbidden. There were other possibilities, but this was the one she could not afford to ignore.

"Is there a pattern to these happenings?" she asked. "A timing to the fires and their leavings?"

He shook his head. "None that anyone has discerned. We could ask the Gnomes to watch for it, to mark the intervals."

"Which will take time," she pointed out. "Time best spent looking into it myself." She pursed her lips. "That is what you came to ask me to do, isn't it? Take a look for myself?"

He nodded. "Yes, mistress. But I will go with you. Not alone into that country—ever—would I go. But with you beside me, I would brave the netherworld and its shades."

Be careful of what you boast of doing, Kermadec, she thought. *Boasts have a way of coming back to haunt you.*

She thought of what she had committed herself to do in the days ahead. Meetings with various Druids to rework studies that members of the order would undertake. Those could wait. Overseeing the repairs to the library that concealed the

Druid Histories—that one could not happen without her presence, but could wait, as well. A delegation from the Federation was due to arrive in three days; the Prime Minister of the Coalition was reputed to lead it. But she could be back in time for that if she left at once.

She must go, she knew. She could not afford to leave the matter unattended to. It was the sort of thing that could mushroom into trouble on a much larger scale. Even by her appearance, she might dissuade those involved from pursuing their conjuring. Once they knew that she was aware of them, they might go to ground again.

It was the best she could hope for. Besides, it gave her an opportunity to escape Paranor and its madness for a few days. In the interval, perhaps a way to contend with the intrigues might occur to her. Time and distance often triggered fresh insights; perhaps that would happen here.

"Let me tell Tagwen," she said to Kermadec, "and we'll be off."

TWO

They departed Paranor at midnight, flying north out of the Druid forestlands with a full moon to light their way, riding the edge of their expectations just ahead of their doubts and fears. They chose to use Grianne's War Shrike, Chaser, to make the journey, rather than a Druid airship, thinking that the Shrike would draw less attention and be less cumbersome. An airship required a crew, and a crew required explanations. Grianne preferred to keep secret what she was investigating until she better understood what it meant.

Tagwen accepted the news of her sudden and mysterious departure stoically, but she read disapproval and concern in his eyes. He was desperate for her to tell him something more, a hint of what she was about so that if the need arose, he might be able to help. But she thought it best he know only that she would be gone for a few days and he must see to her affairs as best he could. There would be questions, demands perhaps, but he couldn't reveal what he didn't know. She braced his shoulders firmly with her hands, smiled her approval and reassurance, and slipped away.

It went without saying that Tagwen would make no mention of Kermadec unless she failed to return; a visit from the Rock Troll was always to be kept secret. There were too many who disapproved of the relationship, and the Dwarf understood the importance of not throwing fuel on a fire already dangerously hot. Grianne could depend on Tagwen to use good judgment in such matters. It was one of his strongest attributes; his exercise of discretion and common sense was easily the equal of her own. Had he the inclination or the talent, he would have made a good Druid. That accolade bestowed, she was just as happy to have him be what he was.

The flight took the rest of the night and most of the following day, a long, steady sweep out of Callahorn and across the Streleheim to the peaks of the Knife Edge and the Razors, where the ruins of the Skull Kingdom lay scattered in the valley between. As she guided Chaser onward, the rush of air in her ears wrapping her in its mindless sound, she had plenty of time to think. Her thoughts were both of what lay ahead and behind. But while the former merely intrigued, the latter haunted.

Her efforts at this new life had started so promisingly. She had returned to the Four Lands with such confidence, her identity regained, her life remade, the lies that had misled her replaced by truths. She had found her lost brother Bek, whom she had never thought to see again. She had broken the chains that the Morgawr had forged to hold her. She had fought and destroyed the warlock with her brother at her side. She had done this so that she might be given a chance at the redemption she had never thought to find. The dying touch of a Druid, his blood on her forehead marking her as his successor, had set her on her path. It was a destiny she would never have chosen for herself but that she had come to believe was right and had therefore embraced.

Walker, a shade with a shade's vision, had reappeared to her at the Hadeshorn, and given her his blessing. Druids dead and gone passed in review, their shades materializing from the ether, rising out of the roiling waters, infusing her with their knowledge and a share of their collective power. She would rebuild their order, resuming the task that Walker had undertaken for himself and failed to complete. She would summon members of all the Races to a Third Druid Council and from it found a new order, one in which the dictates of a single Druid would no longer be all that stood between civilization and anarchy, between reason and madness. For too long, one Druid had been required to make the difference. Those few who had done so—Bremen, Allanon, and Walker— had persevered because there had been no one else and no other way. She would change that.

Such dreams. Such hopes.

Ahren Elessedil had talked his brother, the Elven King Kylen Elessedil, into supplying the first of the new order; two handfuls of Elves Ahren had led to Paranor personally. After Kylen discovered he had been tricked, that Walker was dead and the hated Ilse Witch had replaced him, he had sought to recall those he had sent. But it was too late; the Elves who had come were committed to her and beyond his reach. In retaliation he attempted to poison the minds of the leaders of the other Races against her at every opportunity. That did not prove to be too difficult with Sen Dunsidan, by then Prime Minister of the Federation, who already feared and detested her. But the Dwarves and Trolls were less easily persuaded, especially after she made the effort to go directly to them, to speak in council, and to insist that she would place the order at their disposal so far as it was possible to do so. Remember what the Druids were created to do, she kept reminding them. If you seek a source of strength in the cause of peace and goodwill among all nations, the Druids are the ones to whom you should turn.

For a time, they did so. Members of both Races came to her, and some from Callahorn, as well, for they had heard good things about her from the Rover Captain Redden Alt Mer and from the Highlander Quentin Leah, men they respected. Besides, once they learned that the Federation did not support her, they were inclined to think that was reason enough for them to do so. The war between the Federation and the Free-born was still being fought, mighty armies still locked in combat on the Prekkendorran, leaders still waging a war that had been waged since the passing of Allanon—a war pitting unification against independence, territorial rights against free will. The Free-born wanted Callahorn to be its own country; the Federation wanted it to be a part of the Southland. At times it had been both, at times neither.

There was more to it, of course, as there always is in the case of wars between nations. But that was the justification most often given by those involved, and into the breach left by the absence of any sensible attempt to examine the matter stepped the Ard Rhys.

It was a fateful decision, but one she did not see how she could avoid. The Federation–Free-born war was a ragged wound that would not heal. If the Races were ever to be brought together again, if the Druids were to be able to turn their attention to bettering the lives of the people of the Four Lands, this war must first be ended.

So, even as she struggled to strike a balance in the diversity of temperaments and needs of those who came to Paranor to study the Druid ways, she was attempting, as well, to find a way to resolve the conflict between the Federation and the Free-born. It involved dealing with the two leaders who hated her most—Kylen Elessedil of the Elves and Sen Dunsidan of the Federation. It required that she put aside her own prejudices and find a way to get past theirs. She was able to do this in large part not through fear or intimidation but by making herself appear indispensable to them. After all, the Druids were still in possession of knowledge denied common men, more so than ever since the events in Parkasia. Neither man knew for certain what knowledge she had gained from the Old World that might prove invaluable. Neither understood how little of that knowledge she actually possessed. But perception is often more persuasive than truth. Without the Druids to offer support, each worried that crucial ground would be lost to the other. Without her help, each believed he risked allowing the other a chance to grow more powerful at his expense. Sen Dunsidan had always been a politician. Once he understood that she did not intend to revert to her ways as the Ilse Witch or hold against him his temporary alliance with the Morgawr, he was more than willing to see what she had to offer. Kylen Elessedil followed along for no better reason than to keep pace with his enemy.

Grianne played at this game because it was the only choice she had. She was as good at it now as she had been when she was the Ilse Witch and manipulation was second nature. It was a slow process. Mostly, she settled for crumbs in exchange for the prospect of a full loaf. At times, brought close by promises made and fitfully kept, she thought she would succeed in her efforts, her goal no more than a meeting away. Just a truce between the two would have opened the door to a more permanent solution. Both were strong men, and a small concession by one might have been enough to encourage the other to grant the same. She maneuvered them both toward making that concession, gaining time and credibility as she did so, making herself the center of their thinking as they edged toward a resolution to a war no one really wanted.

Then Kylen Elessedil was killed on the Prekkendorran, the blame for it was laid at her doorstep, and in an instant everything she had worked for nearly six years to achieve was lost.

When they stopped at midmorning to rest Chaser, Kermadec reopened the wound.

"Has that boy King come to his senses yet, mistress?" he asked in a tone of voice that suggested he already knew the answer.

She shook her head. Kellen Elessedil was his father's son and, if it was possible, liked her even less than his father had. Worse, he blamed her for his father's death, a mindset she seemed unable to change.

"He's a fool. He'll die in the same way, fighting for something that to right-thinking men makes no sense at all." Kermadec snorted softly. "They say Rock Trolls are warlike, but history suggests that we are no worse than Men and Elves and in these times perhaps better. At least we do not carry on wars for fifty years."

"You could argue the Federation–Free-born war has been going on for much longer than that," she said.

"However long, it is still too long." Kermadec stretched his massive arms over his head and yawned. "What is the point?"

It was a rhetorical question and she didn't bother to attempt an answer. It had been a dozen years since her efforts at finding a solution had broken down, and since then she had been preoccupied with troubles much closer to home.

"You are due for a change of guards," Kermadec offered, handing her his aleskin. "Maybe you should think about a change of Druids at the same time."

"Dismiss them all and start over?" She had heard this argument from him before. Kermadec saw things in simple terms; he thought she would be better off if she did so, too. "I can't do that."

"So you keep saying."

"Dismissing the order now would be perceived as weakness on my part. Even dismissing the handful of troublemakers who plague me most would have that effect. The nations look for an excuse to proclaim the Druid Council a failure, especially Sen Dunsidan and Kellen Elessedil. I cannot give them one. Besides, if I had to start over at this point, no one would come to Paranor to aid me. All would shun the Druids. I have to make do with things as they are."

Kermadec took back the aleskin and looked out over the countryside. They were just at the edge of the Streleheim, facing north toward the misty, rugged silhouette of the Knife Edge. The day was bright and warm, and it promised another clear, moonlit night in which to explore the ruins of the Skull

Kingdom. "You might think about the impracticality of that before you give up on my suggestion."

She had thought about alternatives frequently of late, although her thinking was more along the lines of restructuring and reordering so as to isolate those most troublesome. But even there she had to be careful not to suggest an appearance of weakness to the others or they would begin to shift allegiance in ways that would undo her entirely.

At times, she thought it might be best if she simply gave them all what they wanted, if she resigned her position and departed for good. Let another struggle with the problem. Let someone else take on her responsibilities and her obligations as Ard Rhys. But she knew she couldn't do that. No one else had been asked to shoulder those responsibilities and obligations; they had been given to her, and nothing had happened to change that. She could not simply walk away. She had no authority to do so. If Walker's shade should appear to tell her it was time, she would be gone in a heartbeat—though perhaps not without disappointment at having failed to accomplish her task. But neither Walker's nor the shade of any other Druid had come to her. Until she was discharged, she could not go. The dissatisfaction of others was not enough to set her free.

Her solution to the problem would have been much easier if she were still the Ilse Witch. She would have made an example of the more troublesome members of her order and cowed the rest by doing so. She would not have hesitated to eliminate her problems in a way that would have appalled even Kermadec. But she had lived enough of that life, and she would never go back to it. An Ard Rhys must find other, better ways to act.

By late afternoon, they had crossed the Streleheim and flown through the lower wall of the Knife Edge into the jagged landscape of the Skull Kingdom. She felt a change in the air long before she saw one on the ground. Even aboard

Chaser, several hundred feet up, she could sense it. The air became dead and old, smelling and tasting of devastation and rot. There was no life here, not of a sort anyone could recognize. The mountain was gone, brought down by cataclysmic forces on the heads of those who had worked their evil within it, reduced to a jumble of rocks within which little grew and less found shelter or forage. It was a ruined land, colorless and barren even now, a thousand years later, and it was likely to be a thousand more before that changed. Even in the wake of a volcano's eruption, in the path of the resultant lava flow, life eventually returned, determined and resilient. But not here. Here, life was denied.

Ignoring the look and feel of the place, even though it settled about them with oppressive insistence, they circled the ruins in search of the site where the fires and the flashes had been observed. After about an hour they found it at one end of a long shelf of rock balanced amid a cluster of spikes that jutted like bones from the earth. A ring of stones encircled a fire pit left blackened and slick from whatever had been burned. When Grianne first saw it from the air, she could not imagine how anyone could even manage to get to it, let alone make use of it. Rock barriers rose all about, the crevices between them deep and wide, the edges sharp as glass. Then she amended her thinking. It would take a Shrike or a Roc or a small, highly maneuverable airship to gain access, but access could be gained. Which had been used in this instance? She stored the question away to be pondered later.

Guiding Chaser to one end of the shelf, they dismounted and walked back for a closer look.

"Sacrifices of some sort," Kermadec observed, glancing around uneasily, his big shoulders swinging left and right, as if he were caged. He did not like being there, she knew, even with her. The place held bad memories for Trolls, even after so long. The Warlock Lord might be dead and gone, but the feel of him lingered. In the history of the Trolls, no one had done more damage to the nation's psyche. Trolls were not superstitious in the manner of Gnomes, but they believed in the transference of evil from the dead to the living. They believed because they had experienced it, and they were wary of it happening again.

She closed her eyes and cast about with her other senses for a moment, trying to read in the air what had happened here. She tracked the leavings of a powerful magic, the workings of a sorcery that was not meant to heal or succor. A summoning of some sort, she read in the bits and pieces that remained. To what end, though? She could not determine, though the smells told of something dying, and not quickly. She looked down at the fire pit and read in the greasy smears dark purpose in the sacrifices clearly made.

"This isn't good," she said softly.

He stepped close. "What do you find, mistress?"

"Nothing yet. Nothing certain." She looked up at him, into his flat, expressionless features. "Perhaps tonight, when darkness cloaks the thing that finds this dead place so attractive, we shall find out."

She tethered Chaser some distance away, back in the rocks where he couldn't be seen, giving him food and water and speaking soothing words to steady him against what might happen later. Afterward, she ate a cold dinner with Kermadec, watching the light fade from the sky and the twilight descend in a flat, colorless wash that enveloped like smoke. There was no sunset, no change in the look of the land and sky save an almost rushed transition from light to dark. The sensation it generated in Grianne was one of possibility draining into despair.

She pushed such dark thoughts away but could not change her feelings for the place. It was wretched ground for living things, a wasteland in which she did not belong. The pervasive feelings of hopelessness and isolation gave notice that for some transgressions there could be no redemption. If she lived another thousand years, she did not think to see a rebirth of life in the Skull Kingdom. Perhaps, given the types of life that might find purchase in such a land, it was for the best.

"Sleep," she told Kermadec. "I will keep watch the first half of the night."

He grunted agreement and was asleep in seconds. She envied him a rest that came so easily. She watched him for a time, his rough skin looking smooth in the darkness, his hairless body and nearly featureless face giving him the appearance of a smoothly faceted shape hewn from stone. Sleek—that was the way he struck her. Like a moor cat, big and powerful and smooth. She liked him better than almost anyone. Not so much for the way he looked as for the way he was. Direct and uncomplicated. That wasn't to say he was slow-witted or combative; he was neither. But Kermadec didn't complicate matters by overanalyzing and debating. When something needed doing, he spent as little time and effort as was possible in getting it done. He had a code of conduct that served him well, and she did not think he had ever varied from it. She wished her own life could be as straightforward.

Time slipped away, and Grianne watched the moon rise and the stars paint the sky in a wash of white pinpricks. The rocks around her remained silent. The fire pit, its rings of rocks looking like hunched Gnomes in the gloom, sat cold and untended. Perhaps nothing would happen this night, the one night she was here to see it happen. Perhaps whoever built the fires and created the flashes had sensed her presence and would stay away. She wondered if she could force herself to keep watch another night if nothing happened on this one. She had no good reason to do so; her presence now was generated mostly by her instinctive reaction to the possibilities of what she feared might happen, not to what actually had.

Then, as midnight approached, the fire pit abruptly flared

to life. It did so without warning or reason. No one had appeared to tend it; no fuel had been laid or tinder struck. It burned sharp and fierce on nothing more than air, and Grianne was on her feet at once.

"Kermadec!"

The Rock Troll awoke and rose to stand beside her, staring at the phenomenon without speaking. The intensity of the fire increased and diminished as if the flames were breathing, as if the air were changing in some indefinable way, first lending strength to the invisible fuel, then leeching it away. All around, illuminated by tendrils of light, the jumbled rocks became ghostly spectators. Grianne eased forward cautiously, just a step or two at a time, eyes shifting back and forth among the shadows in an effort to find what was out there. Something had to be; something had to have initiated the blaze. But she could detect no life, no sign of anything living save Kermadec and herself. Someone had lit the flames from another place, someone or something that did not need to be present to work whatever magic was intended.

"Mistress!" Kermadec hissed.

Flashes of light appeared in the air above the fire, sudden flares of brightness that suggested small explosions. But they made no sound and left no residue of smoke or ash, as if giant fireflies in the darkness. They were moving in circular fashion, widening their sweep and rising higher as their numbers increased. Below, unchanged, the fire continued to burn.

Grianne reached out with her magic to explore this mix of burning air and flameless light, using the wishsong to investigate what was there that she wasn't seeing. She found other magic at once, concentrated and powerful, dispatched from another place to this one. It was as she had thought. She detected, as well, that something was responding to it, something that was able to find purchase in this ruined land where it might not have been able to do so in one less poisoned. It was not something she could put a name to, but it was there nevertheless, pressing up against the fire and the light.

A face in the window, she thought suddenly.

Perhaps not just from somewhere in this world, but from another plane of existence altogether.

She probed harder with her magic, trying to break through to whatever was out there, to generate a response that would reveal something more. Her efforts were rewarded almost at once. Something small and dark appeared at the edges of the light, like a wraith come out of the netherworld, not altogether shapeless, but lacking any clear definition. It slid in and out of the light like a child playing hide and seek, first here, then there, never quite revealing itself altogether, never quite showing what it was.

Kermadec was whispering hurriedly, anxiously, telling her to back away, to give herself more space. It wasn't safe to be so close, he was saying. She ignored him; she was caught up in the link she had established between the foreign magic and her own. Something was there, quick and insubstantial, just out of reach.

And then all at once it wasn't hiding anymore. It was there, right in front of her, its face turned full into hers, edges and angles caught in the light. She caught her breath in spite of herself. The face was vaguely human, but in no other way recognizable. Malevolence masked its features in a way she had not thought possible, so darkly threatening, so hate-filled and remorseless, that even in her time as the Ilse Witch, she had not experienced its like. Dark shadows draped it like strands of thick hair, shifting with the light, changing the look of it from instant to instant. Eyes glimmered like blue ice, cool and appraising. There was recognition in those eyes; whoever was there, hiding in the light, knew who she was.

Grianne lashed out at the face with ferocious intent, surprising even herself with her vehemence. She felt such loathing, such rage, that she could not stop herself from reacting, and the deed was done before she could think better of it. Her magic exploded into the face, which disappeared instantly, taking with it the flashes and the burning air, leaving only darkness and the lingering smell of expended magic.

She compressed her lips tightly, fighting back the snarl forming on them, consumed by the feelings this thing had generated. It was all she could do to pull herself together and turn back to an obviously unnerved Kermadec.

"Are you all right?" he asked at once.

She nodded. "But I wasn't for a moment, old bear. That thing radiated such evil that I think letting it come even that near was a serious mistake. If I didn't know better, I would say it lured me here."

Which it had, she knew at once, though she would not say so to him. It had known she would come, would respond to its advances, and would step close enough to feel it. It wanted her to know it was there. But why? What did it want? Where did it hide that she could not find it, and that it could not do more than it had?

"Do we stay here another night?" the Rock Troll asked cautiously.

She shook her head. "I think we've seen all we are going to see. We'll fly to Paranor at first light. I'll find better answers back there to what is happening."

THREE

"We've talked enough!" Shadea a'Ru snapped irritably. "How much more talking does it need? This is the best chance we'll get!"

No one said anything in response. No one cared to be the first to speak. She was a big woman, and she dominated with her size as much as with the force of her personality. Fully six feet tall, broad-shouldered and strong, she had fought in the front lines on the Prekkendorran for two years, and none of them had survived anything nearly as terrible as that. The contrasting hues of her sun-browned skin, smooth and dusky, and wind-blown blond hair, short-cropped and uncombed, gave her a look of good health and vitality. When she stepped into any room, heads turned in her direction and conversation slowed.

Here, however, the reaction was different. Here, they all knew her too well to be much more than cautious. She looked from face to face, her calculating blue eyes searching out signs of doubt or hesitation, challenging them to try to hide it from her. Their responses were as different as they were. Terek Molt disdained even to look at her, his flat, hard features directed toward the doorway of the room that concealed their secret meeting. Iridia Eleri's stunningly perfect features had a cool, distant look. Neither Dwarf nor Elf had ever demonstrated any hesitation in their joint endeavor. Either would have undertaken the effort alone long ago but for Shadea's insistence on unity.

Traunt Rowan and Pyson Wence glanced uneasily at each other. The problem lay with the Southlander and the Gnome. *Cowards,* she thought angrily, though she knew better than to say so to their faces.

"Act in haste, regret at leisure, Shadea," the former offered softly, shrugging.

She wanted to kill him. He was the only one of them who would dare to speak to her like that, and he did so for no better reason than to demonstrate that she could push him only so far before he would dig in his heels. He wanted this as much as she did, as all of them did, but he was too cautious for his own good. It came out of being the child of Federation functionaries; the fewer chances you took in that world, the better off you were.

"Please don't fall back on platitudes to justify your reluctance to do what is necessary!" she snapped in reply. "You're better than that, Traunt. Smarter than that. We can nose this matter about like a dog with an old bone for as long as you wish, but it won't change a thing. Nothing will happen to improve matters unless we make it happen."

"She smells out plots like ours," Pyson Wence said, his small hands gesturing for emphasis. "Step wrong with her, and you might find yourself down here for good!"

They were deep underground in the cellars of Paranor, gathered in one of the rooms used primarily for storage. The room smelled of dust and the air was cold and stale to the taste. Stone walls locked them away beneath tons of rock and earth, a safehold that few ever bothered to visit save to retrieve stores. It was the one place in Paranor where some degree of privacy was assured.

They had been meeting for almost a year, just the five of them. Shadea a'Ru had carefully selected the other four, discovering where their loyalties lay, then approached them one by one. Each shared her distaste for the Ard Rhys. One hated her openly. All wanted her gone, if for widely differing reasons. To some extent, they complemented each other, each bringing an attribute to the endeavor that the others lacked. The Southlander, Traunt Rowan, was strong of heart and body, more than a match even for Shadea—a warrior seeking to put right what he perceived as wrong. The Elven sorceress, Iridia Eleri, was cold of heart and hot of temper, but quick-witted and intuitive, as well. Her ability to stanch her emotions masked the dark truths that had set her on this path. The Dwarf, Terek Molt, while stolid and taciturn in the manner of Dwarves, was hungry for power and anxious to find a way to get past the Ard Rhys' rules and restrictions so that he could claim the destiny he so desperately craved. Pyson Wence, so frail and helpless-looking, was a snake trapped in a suppliant's body, a rare combination of treacherous instinct and decisive purpose. No superstitious tribal pagan, he wielded his magic in a cold and calculating fashion.

Had the Ard Rhys any inkling of their true dispositions when she accepted them into the order? Shadea a'Ru could not be certain. It was possible, if only because Grianne Ohmsford herself had been such a dark creature for so long—the Ilse Witch, the Morgawr's tool. She had found redemption, she believed, and so thought others could find it, as well. She was mistaken on both counts, but that was to the advantage of those gathered in this room, those who waited only on fate to provide them with the chance they needed to be rid of her.

As perhaps it did here, if their impatient leader could gain the pledge of support she required.

"You want her gone, don't you?" she asked Pyson Wence pointedly. "Dead or otherwise, but gone?" She looked around. "How about the rest of you? Changed your minds about her? Decided you like having her as Ard Rhys? Come! Speak up!"

"No one in this room and few outside of it want Grianne Ohmsford as Ard Rhys, Shadea." Traunt Rowan looked bored.

"We've covered this ground before, all of it. What keeps us from acting is the possibility of failure—a very real possibility, I might point out. Failure means no second chance. So before you start berating us for our reluctance, try to see the reality of the situation a little more clearly. When we act against her, we had better be very certain that we will succeed."

The weight of her stare settled on him and she did not remove it for long seconds. The others shifted uncomfortably, but they said nothing for fear her eyes would seek them out instead. Traunt Rowan, to his credit, held her gaze, but she could see the uncertainty mirrored in his eyes. She might do anything; that was her reputation. If you provoked Shadea a'Ru—something not at all hard to do—you did so at great risk. One who had tested her had already disappeared. Everyone suspected that she might have caused that disappearance, even the Ard Rhys, but no one could prove it.

"I would not summon you with such urgency," she said, speaking to Traunt, but including all of them with a quick shift of her eyes, "if I did not have a way to dispose of her that would pose no risk at all to any of us. I am aware of the possibility of failure. No matter how carefully we plan and execute, something can always go wrong. The trick is to make certain that even if that happens, no suspicion or blame will fall on us. But in this instance, I do not think we will fail. I think we will succeed better than we had hoped. Are you ready to hear me out?"

All nodded or at least kept quiet. Terek Molt never agreed or disagreed with anything. He simply stayed or walked away. Dwarves were given to physical gestures over words, which suited her fine. They were given to directness, as well, and it was good to have at least one of those among so many dissemblers.

"Wait!" Iridia hissed suddenly, one hand lifting sharply.

She rose from her bench, crossed the room to the door, and put her ear against it. The door was ironbound oak two inches thick and sealed with magic to prevent even the faintest echo of their voices from escaping. None of them cared to have even the smallest whisper drift beyond this chamber. The Ard Rhys already suspected they were plotting against her; what saved them was that others were doing so, as well. There was no time for Grianne to deal with all of them. Still, if she was ever to discover the particulars of this specific plot, they would be dealt with swiftly and thoroughly. The Ard Rhys might claim to no longer be the Ilse Witch, but she could revert in the blink of an eye. Not even Shadea a'Ru cared to go up against her if that happened.

That was a good part of the problem, of course. That Grianne Ohmsford was not simply the Ard Rhys, but that she was the Ilse Witch, too. It was not something any who had come to Paranor to join the Druid order could ignore. The past was the past, but it was always with you. She might claim to be a changed woman, having taken up the Ard Rhys mantle at the behest of Walker Boh, having been given the blessing of Druids dead and gone, and having pledged herself to reestablish the Druid Council as a viable force in the Four Lands. She might claim to be committed to helping the Races become strong, independent, and peaceful neighbors, to putting an end to the war between the Free-born and the Federation, and to reintroducing a mix of science and magic into the world for the betterment of all men and women. She might claim anything she wished, but that didn't change what everyone knew about her past. It didn't erase what she had done. In some cases, nothing could. It was too close, too personal—as with Traunt Rowan and Iridia Eleri, the two among these conspirators who sought vengeance for acts committed by the Ilse Witch and forgotten by the Ard Rhys. The others were simply hungry to employ their magic and sate their ambitions in ways that were forbidden. But for each, to realize desires meant getting rid of Grianne.

This tension didn't start and end with the five gathered in secret here. It manifested itself in other splinter groups, as well, all of them working to achieve something secret, all of them with goals and hungers that were in some way in conflict with the Third Druid Council as Grianne Ohmsford had conceived it. It wasn't a question of *if* she would be done away with; it was merely a question of *when*.

And a question of who would prove clever and bold enough to make it happen, of course. And then be strong enough to take charge of the order, once she was gone and a new Ard Rhys was needed.

Some part of Shadea a'Ru, some tiny bit of reason shoved far back into the darker corners of her consciousness, accepted that not all of those who had come to Paranor to begin life as Druids felt as she did. Some admired Grianne and believed her right for the position—strong, determined, tested, and unafraid. But Shadea a'Ru would not allow herself to think well of those because to do so might give credibility to their loyalty, and she believed that to be a weakness she could not afford. Better to see them as sycophants and deceivers and to plan for their removal, as well, once the path was clear to do so.

Iridia was still standing by the door, listening. Everyone was waiting on her now, watching silently. "What is it?" Shadea asked finally, irritated and impatient.

The sorceress stepped back and stared at the portal as if it were an enemy that needed dispatching. Her distrust of everyone and everything ran deep and unchecked. Even Shadea herself merited Iridia's suspicion. She was beautiful and talented, but deeply flawed. Her personal demons ran loose through her predatory mind, and someday they were going to turn on her.

"I heard something moving," she said, turning away, dismissing the matter. "I just wanted to be certain the warding was still in place."

"You set it yourself," Shadea pointed out.

Iridia did not look at her. "It could have been tampered with. Better to be sure." She returned to the bench and sat down. For a moment, she said nothing more. Then she glanced up at Shadea, as if remembering her. "What were you saying?"

"She was saying she has found a way to solve our problem with the Ard Rhys." Traunt Rowan picked up the loose thread of the conversation with his calming voice. "Without posing any danger to us."

"There is a potion I have a chance to obtain," Shadea told them. "Mixed with a spell, it produces a magic strong enough to work against anyone, no matter how well prepared they are. The potion is called liquid night. Together with the spell, it will dispatch the intended victim to another place. It doesn't kill them; they simply disappear. No blame attaches because there is no body. There isn't even a residue to tell any searchers what happened. Everything disappears in a few hours, victim and magic alike."

Pyson shook his head. "There is no such magic. I know most, have read about the ones I do not know, and I have never heard of liquid night."

"That is because it isn't from this world," Shadea said. "It is from the world into which I am sending the Ard Rhys."

They stared at her with a mix of expressions. "What world would that be?" Traunt Rowan asked finally.

She shook her head. "Oh, no, Traunt. I don't give you anything more until after I have your word that you are committed to me and to what I am proposing. I am the one who sought the potion out, and I intend to keep the particulars my own. All you need to know is that once I have implemented it, you will never see the Ard Rhys again."

"But she will not be dead," Pyson Wence persisted doubtfully. "If she is not dead, there is always a chance she can find her way back. She has more lives than a cat. You know her history, Shadea. She is not like anyone else. I like her no better than you, but I respect her ability to stay alive."

Shadea nodded in agreement. *Idiot.* "She won't be coming back from where I intend to send her, Pyson. No one comes back from where she will be going. Besides, she won't stay alive long enough to do much about her situation in any case. There are things there far more dangerous than the Ilse Witch. Once gone, she will never come back."

They were intrigued, interested, but still hesitant. Except for Terek Molt, who was nodding vigorously. "Do it, I say. If you have a way to eliminate her, woman, do it!"

"When will this happen?" Iridia asked.

"When she returns, two or three nights from now. I can have everything in place before then. It will happen while she sleeps, so smoothly and silently that she will not wake again in this world."

"If you have this all ready, or can make it ready, why do you have need of us?" Traunt Rowan asked. "This was begun as a joint endeavor, but it seems to me that you have taken over the effort yourself. We no longer have anything you need."

She had been anticipating the question and was pleased to know that she was still able to keep one step ahead of them. "It might seem that way if you didn't think it through carefully," she said. "This effort will not succeed if we don't look beyond eliminating Grianne Ohmsford."

"You would have us make you Ard Rhys in her place," Traunt Rowan declared softly. "Wouldn't you?"

She nodded. "I am best suited for it. I command the most respect among those who must be convinced of the necessity of choosing a new Ard Rhys quickly. But do not be fooled, Traunt. I do not see myself as another Grianne Ohmsford, a leader standing alone and apart, needing no one. This is exactly what set us against her in the first place. She isolates herself. She sees herself as wiser and more capable, better able to determine what is best for everyone. If I were to take that route, how would I be any different?"

"You oversimplify," Pyson Wence said. "Our dislike for the Ard Rhys goes well beyond the way she holds herself above us."

"Indeed," she agreed. "But inaccessibility and the appearance of isolation will doom whoever stands for the position of Ard Rhys, once Grianne is gone. I need all of you to support me if I am to succeed. You each represent a faction of the order—you, Pyson, of Gnomes; Terek Molt, of Dwarves; Traunt, of Southlanders; and Iridia, of Elves. Not all of each, by any means, but a sizeable number. You are among the strongest of your respective Races, and you can bring support to me as such. I cannot serve as Ard Rhys and achieve what we have decided upon without your help."

"Why should you be Ard Rhys?" Terek Molt snapped suddenly, his sullen features tightening.

She kept her temper. Speaking out like this was his nature. "Because the order would not have you, Terek. They might have Traunt Rowan, but none of the rest of you. And Traunt is not interested." She looked purposefully at him. "Are you?"

He shook his head, his lips pursing with disdain. "I have no need to be leader of the order—only to see it set upon the right path, one determined by someone other than her."

Grianne Ohmsford, he meant, but would not speak her name. In his own quiet way, he hated her most. If Shadea had found a way that would allow him to kill her himself, he would have accepted it without question. She often wondered what he thought things would be like for him after Grianne was gone. What would there be left for him to do after having burned so much energy and devoted so much time to seeing her dispatched?

"Where have you found this potion?" Pyson Wence asked. "Liquid night? If not from this world, if instead from this place you refuse to reveal, how did you come by it?"

She shook her head. "No answers until I have your commitment, Pyson. It is sufficient to say that it will do what is needed."

"Someone gave it to you?" he continued. "You have a secret ally? Another who serves our cause? Are you keeping other secrets, Shadea?"

She was, of course, but he would never find them out. "No more questions from you, no more answers from me," she told him, told them all. "I want your oath, your Druid oath, your word and your bond. Everything that you hold sacred stands behind it, and we all bear witness to what you say. If I do this, if I rid you of the Ard Rhys, then will you support my bid to be the new leader of the order? Will you stand with me to the death to see finished what we seek to do?"

Iridia Eleri rose, cold eyes sweeping the room. "You have my oath. Let her burn a thousand years in her own magic's fire!"

Terek Molt grunted approvingly. "She's earned banishment a thousand times over, and I care nothing for where she gets banished to. Get it done, Shadea. Put this creature out of our lives!"

There was a long silence. Traunt Rowan was clearly thinking, head lowered, hands clasped. Pyson Wence, sitting beside him, glanced over, then looked at Shadea, frowning.

"If you can do as you say, then I have no quarrel with your effort." His eyes shifted from face to face. "But if Shadea exaggerates in any way, if the power of the magic she proposes to use is less than what she thinks it is, then I want to be certain she does not exaggerate, as well, her certainty that nothing of this can come back to haunt us."

"How could it do that, Pyson?" she spit at him. "Would it

bear our names spelled out upon its liquid surface? Would it somehow speak them aloud?"

He shrugged. "Would it, Shadea?"

"It is a potion supplemented by a spell. The potion does not originate in this world. The spell is one familiar to dozens and available to all who care to read and study on it. Nothing of either attaches to us. Stop equivocating! If you want out of this business, there is the door that brought you in. Pass back through, and you have your release."

Not that he would ever live to reach it, she thought darkly, waiting on him. Not that he would take half a dozen steps before she burned him to cinders. It was too late for backing away. Too late for anything but going forward.

Maybe Pyson knew this, for he made no move to rise, showed no inclination to do anything but ponder her words. He was so settled in place, so loose and comfortable with his legs tucked under and his arms folded into his robes that it seemed to her, infuriatingly so, that he might be thinking of a nap.

"I'll give you my oath, Shadea," he said finally. "But—" He paused, cocking his head to one side, his sharp Gnome features thoughtful. "But I think my oath must be conditional on discovering where it is that you propose to send the Ard Rhys. If it isn't sufficiently far away or secure, I intend to tell you so and back out."

There were murmurs of assent to this, but Shadea ignored them, knowing that what she had in mind for Grianne Ohmsford would please them all. Once they heard, there would be no more mutterings. "What of you, Traunt?" she asked the Southlander. "You've said nothing."

"I have been thinking." He smiled faintly. "Thinking about how much we are entrusting you with. It seems to me that more than one of us ought to be involved in this effort— not just in the planning, but in the execution. It would require a stronger commitment, which is what you are looking for. It would give us all a sense of participation beyond what you have proposed so far."

"It would also entail a greater risk," she pointed out, not liking where his suggestion was going. "Two stand a greater chance of being detected than one. Whoever administers the potion and the spell must approach the Ard Rhys secretly. Stealth and quickness will determine success or failure."

"Two can move as quietly as one," he argued, shrugging. "Moreover, if one falters, the other can still act. It offers us a measure of protection."

"I don't intend to falter," she said coldly, openly angry.

"We'll draw straws to see who goes with you," Iridia said, siding with Rowan.

Both Pyson Wence and Terek Molt nodded in assent. Shadea knew when she was up against a wall. She was not going to get them to back off without arousing suspicion. "All right," she agreed. "But only one."

She rose and walked to a stack of crates containing serving ware packed in straw and drew out four strands. Breaking off three, she evened them between her fingers and offered them to the others. Terek Molt snatched the first. It was short. Iridia drew a short straw, as well.

The other two looked at each other, hesitating. Then Traunt Rowan picked from the remaining two straws. His was the long one.

"How fitting," Shadea sneered, "since taking part was your idea. Now give me your word, Traunt. Your oath and your promise as a Druid to stand with me no matter what."

He nodded, unruffled. "You always had that, Shadea, from the moment you told me what you intended and recruited me to your cause. I am as committed as you will ever be."

Perhaps, she thought. *But we will never know for sure because there is no way to test such a claim.* For her purposes it was sufficient that he was committed to support her as the new Ard Rhys after Grianne was dispatched. Once she held that office, and despite what she had told them to gain their support, they would all become expendable. Her plans were greater than they knew and did not include them.

"We are agreed then," she said, looking from face to face, seeking again any sign of hesitation.

"We are agreed," Traunt Rowan affirmed. "Now tell us where you intend to imprison the Ard Rhys. Where can you send her that she cannot find a way back to haunt us?"

Shadea a'Ru smiled at the looks on their faces when she told them.

FOUR

Sen Dunsidan was a cautious man. He had always had reason to be cautious, but he had more reason these days since he had more to lose. His life's accomplishments were impressive, but the price exacted in exchange had been severe and permanent. It wasn't the sort of price one could measure in terms of wealth. If it had been only money, he would not have been as cautious as he was. The price levied against him was a piece of his soul here and a part of his sanity there. The price was psychological and emotional, and it left him bereft of almost anything resembling peace of mind.

Not that he had ever possessed much of that in any case. Even in the days when he was only Minister of Defense of the Federation and in the thrall of the Ilse Witch, he had compromised himself in almost every way imaginable to advance his position and increase his power. Peace of mind was a benefit that did not accrue to those who lacked moral restraint. He was cautious back then, as well, but not nearly as much so as now. He saw himself as invincible in those days, too clever for anyone to outsmart or outmaneuver, too powerful to be challenged. Harm might come to lesser men, but not to him. Even the Ilse Witch, for all her disdain and aloofness, was wary of him. He knew how she saw him—how most saw him. A snake, coiled and ready to strike. He did not take offense. He liked the image. Snakes were not cautious. Others were cautious of snakes. It was beneficial to instill a sense of un-easiness in those with whom he was compelled to deal.

Caution came to him after he broke off his relationship with the Ilse Witch—betrayed her, in fact—and allied himself with the Morgawr, her warlock mentor. It was the smart thing to do. The Morgawr was the more powerful of the two and the more likely to succeed in their battle to destroy each other. Moreover, the warlock was the one who was willing to give Sen Dunsidan what he wanted most in exchange for his support—a chance at becoming Prime Minister. Two men stood in Sen Dunsidan's way, and the Morgawr had them killed in what appeared to be for one an accident, and for the other, natural causes.

But what the Morgawr claimed from him in the bargain was much more than he had ever expected to pay. The Morgawr forced Sen Dunsidan to watch as he turned living men into the walking dead, creatures without wills of their own, things that did only as they were told. Worse, he forced Sen Dunsidan to participate in the atrocity, to bring the men to him under false pretenses and to witness their destruction. When it was finished and the Morgawr had gone, Sen Dunsidan was a changed man. Even after becoming Prime Minister, even after gaining enough power that no one dared to challenge him, he never felt safe. Devastated by watching what had been done to those men, by being an accomplice to it, he could not regain the sense of invincibility he had once thought he would never lose. Worse, he could not take any comfort in what he had gained. He could not stop thinking about those men. He became obsessed with his own vulnerability; his need to protect himself against falling victim to what he had witnessed dominated his thinking. Emotions already blunted by his lesser crimes were turned to stone. His heart hardened and his soul shriveled. He no longer felt anything for anyone other than himself, and what he felt for himself was mostly fear.

With the passing of the years, he grew steadily more unsettled, responding to fears he could not control.

Tonight was one of those times.

He sat waiting impatiently in a reading chair that did not face the doorway of the room, but a blank wall. The room itself was in a place he had never thought he would visit. He was at Paranor, a guest of the Druids and, more particularly, of his onetime nemesis, Grianne Ohmsford. Twenty years ago, when she had returned from the airship voyage she had undertaken in search of a lost magic from another time, he had thought himself a dead man. She had destroyed his ally, the Morgawr, and would certainly have determined that he had supplied the Federation ships and men under the warlock's command. Had she been the Ilse Witch still, had something not happened to change her while she was away, she would have killed him at once. Instead, she had ignored him, retreating to the confines of Paranor, secluded with the shades of dead Druids, and had done nothing.

At first, he had thought she was playing a game with him and had waited stoically for the inevitable. But after a time, he began to hear rumors of a new Druid order and an Ard Rhys who would lead it. He heard that the Ilse Witch had forsaken her name and disclaimed her past, that she was no longer who or what she had been. It was too outlandish to credit seriously, the sort of rumor that invariably proved false. But men and women from all the Races were traveling to Paranor to seek a place in the Third Druid Council, and he began to wonder.

And then the impossible happened. She summoned him to a meeting on neutral ground to discuss their relationship. He went because he saw no reason not to. If she wanted him dead, she would find a way to make him so, and hiding in his compound in Arishaig, or anywhere else in the Four Lands, wasn't going to save him. To his astonishment, she told him that the past was behind them both and it was time to consider the future. There would be no more dealings of the sort that had taken place before. There would be no recriminations for what was done. She sought instead to open lines of communication between Paranor and the Federation that would facilitate a productive sharing of ideas and solutions to problems of mutual concern—like the war on the Prekkendorran, for instance. She would give him what help she could in his new position as Prime Minister, sharing knowledge that would aid the people he led. In turn, he would help her restore the credibility and effectiveness of the Druids throughout the Four Lands.

It had taken him a while to adjust to the new relationship, but in the end it gave him back the life he had thought forfeited and so he was willing to make that adjustment. There had been other meetings over the years, many of them, with visits to Paranor by him and to Arishaig by her. Discussions had been held and trades made and, all in all, they had gotten along well enough.

Which never once stopped him from trying to find a way to kill her, of course. It was impossible for him not to think of doing so. Whoever she claimed she was, Ilse Witch or Ard Rhys, she was too dangerous to be allowed to live; nothing prevented her from reverting at some point to the creature she had been, casting off her new guise, her new identity. More to the point, he knew he could never control her. If he couldn't control her, he couldn't control the Druids, and controlling the Druids was essential if he was to govern the Four Lands. That was his ambition and his intention, and he meant to see it fulfilled. Only the Free-born stood in his way, but eliminating the Free-born meant finding a way to subvert the Druids. They claimed not to be siding with anyone in the Federation–Free-born conflict, but it was clear enough that however the war on the Prekkendorran turned out, the Ard Rhys was never going to allow either side to crush the other.

Sen Dunsidan had decided long ago that crushing his enemies was the only way to survive them. Leaving them alive after you had defeated them only gave them another chance to come after you. If they were dead and gone, you had nothing to worry about.

So he was in Paranor for yet another meeting with Grianne Ohmsford, for discussions concerning the Prekkendorran and the war with the Free-born and whatever else she cared to talk about, and none of it mattered to him because the meeting would never happen. It was scheduled to take place in the morning, but by then the Ard Rhys would be dead.

Or would wish she was.

It had taken a long time to find a way to eliminate her, and it had come about in a most unlikely way from a most unlikely source. Assassination had always been an alternative, but her instincts were so acute that she could sense that sort of thing almost without making an effort. Her magic was formidable, the wishsong of the Ohmsford legends, passed down through the bloodline, stronger in her than in almost any other member of her family, made so by her training and her life as the Ilse Witch. You might try to catch her off guard and kill her, but you would have a better chance at growing wings and learning to fly.

He had looked for other ways to rid himself of her, but no other solution immediately presented itself. Employing another magic to overcome her own was the logical approach, but he didn't know any magic and wasn't equipped to wield it if he did. Finding an ally who could act in his place was the logical solution, but with the death of the Morgawr and the formation of the Third Druid Council, he no longer had direct dealings with magic wielders save for the one he wanted to eliminate.

Then help arrived from an unexpected source, not much more than a year ago, and he had not only his ally, but a spy in the Druid camp. The spy gave him a pair of much needed eyes and ears to monitor the Ard Rhys' movements. Sooner or later, he believed, he would find a way to get past her defenses, as well.

Now, he had found that way at last. Tonight, he would test it—without risk to himself, without danger of discovery. If it worked, Grianne Ohmsford would no longer be a problem. By morning, the world would be a different place.

Yet he was uneasy, not quite believing it would happen, afraid that his complicity in the deaths of all those men years ago at the hands of the Morgawr would take form somehow this night and devour him. It did not seem ridiculous that it might happen; it seemed almost inevitable. There was a price to be paid for what he had done, and sooner or later someone would appear to collect it.

He was thinking of that as the wall across from him slid silently open and Shadea a'Ru stepped into the room.

Grianne Ohmsford sat at the writing table in her chambers, making notes for her meeting with Sen Dunsidan, preparing herself for the bargaining that would take place. It was always a matter of give and take with the Prime Minister, a question of how much she was willing to give versus how much he was attempting to take. He had changed over the years in some ways but, when bargaining, still sought to extract more than the other party was prepared to give. A politician to the end, he remained outwardly friendly and forthright while inwardly thinking of ways to cut his opponent's throat.

Literally, in her case.

She knew how he felt about her. To him, she was still the Ilse Witch and that would never change. He was afraid of her, no matter how hard she tried to convince him that her time as the Morgawr's creature was at an end. She might be Ard Rhys of the Third Druid Council, but that was not how he saw her. Because he could not change old habits, she knew his fear would rule his thinking. That meant he would be looking for a way to eliminate her.

She didn't mind that. He had always been looking for ways to eliminate her, from the moment they had formed that first alliance, nearly twenty-five years ago. That was how Sen Dunsidan dealt with allies and enemies alike; he used them to the extent he could while searching for ways to render them ineffective, which often meant eliminating them altogether once they had served their purpose. In some cases he had been successful, but he had never posed a threat to her. He did not possess the tools to cause her harm, lacking both magic and allies to accomplish that end. Alone, he could do nothing.

Besides, he was the least of her worries. She had other, more dangerous enemies with which to contend, others with equally strong motives for seeing her dispatched, others living closer to home.

She didn't like thinking of it. So much hard work had gone into re-forming the Druid order, and now it was a nest of vipers. It wasn't what she had intended or envisioned, but there it was. Kermadec was right. Her position grew more tenuous with the passing of every day, and if the erosion of her authority continued, she would lose control completely. If that happened, she would have failed, and she could not bear even to think of that.

She returned her thoughts to Sen Dunsidan and the more immediate concerns of tomorrow's meeting. She was seeking a truce in the battle on the Prekkendorran, one by both Federation and Free-born, one that would result in a stand-down of both armies. And that might lead to a gradual reduction in forces and a chance at peace. But neither side was showing much interest in the idea, even though after nearly fifty years of conflict it seemed almost inconceivable to her that they could think of anything else. Most of the people who had initiated the struggle were dead and gone. Only the inheritors were left, men and women who probably didn't have any real idea of the circumstances that had triggered the war.

Not that any of them cared, she thought darkly. War was often its own excuse.

A knock at the door announced the arrival of Tagwen. She bid him enter. The Dwarf shuffled in under a load of books and papers, which he deposited on the working table to one side, where she could pick through them. They were the detritus of her previous efforts to persuade Sen Dunsidan and the Federation to her cause. Tagwen studied the stack forlornly for a moment, then looked at her.

"Is he settled in his chambers?" she asked.

"Quite comfortably. He should be. He has the best rooms in the Keep." Tagwen didn't like Sen Dunsidan, a fact he didn't bother to hide from her, though he was careful to hide it from others. "I left him to his ale and cogitation. More of the former, less of the latter, unless I miss my guess."

She smiled in spite of herself. She rose and stretched. "Everyone is advised of tomorrow's gatherings?"

He nodded. "You meet privately with the Prime Minister after breakfast, then he addresses the full council, then he meets with a select few—you know them all and they know one other—and then you sit down for some serious bargaining, which will once again probably result in nothing much being decided."

She gave him a hard look. "Thank you for your optimism. What would I do without it?"

"I prefer reality to fantasy," he said, huffing through his beard as he met her gaze squarely. "Better for you if you did the same now and then. And I am not talking about your meeting with the Prime Minister."

"Have you been trading opinions with Kermadec again?"

"The Maturen sees things far more clearly than some people. He doesn't waste time on looking for ways to smooth things over when he sees it is a waste of effort. You ought to listen to him."

She nodded. "I do. I just can't always follow his advice. I am not in a position to do so. You know that."

Looking back at the stack of documents on the table, then at the half-eaten dinner sitting cold on the plates he had brought earlier, Tagwen didn't say anything for a moment. "He wants to know if you've decided yet when you are leaving." Tagwen looked back at her.

She walked to the window and looked out at the moonlit sky. Her rooms in the high tower were so far above the forest that wrapped the Keep that the trees seemed a black ocean stretching away to the Dragon's Teeth. She had decided that she would go to the Hadeshorn to seek the advice of Walker's shade about what she had seen in the ruins of the Skull Kingdom. Shades did not always give direct answers to questions of that sort, but they sometimes revealed insights into what was being sought. Someone or something was behind those fires that burned on air and in those strange flashes of light, and the magic invoked had come from a source she did not recognize. Walker's shade might at least be willing to tell her about it.

Wanting to see the business through and to make certain she stayed safe in the process, Kermadec had offered to go with her. She was happy for his company.

"As soon as the Prime Minister departs," she answered. "I would guess he will not stay after tomorrow night. Everything will have been said by then."

"Everything has been said already," Tagwen said.

"Perhaps it just needs saying again."

The Dwarf gestured toward the door. "Traunt Rowan is outside. He wants to speak with you. I told him you did not have time for him tonight, but he was quite insistent."

She nodded. Another thorn poking at her from the Druid bramble bush. She liked Rowan, admired his determination and willingness to work hard, but she knew that he did not like her. Sometimes she wondered at the source of his dislike, but she had never broached the subject with him. If she started asking everyone who disliked her why that was so, she would not have time for anything else. It pained her to think that so many in the order could not get past their bad feelings toward her. On the other hand, it said something about their resolve that they had come to study with her anyway.

"Send him in, Tagwen," she said. "I can give him a few minutes."

Tagwen went without a word, but his parting look suggested he thought she was making a mistake. She smiled. It wouldn't be her first.

She glanced at herself in the mirror that hung by the door, reassuring herself she was still presentable so late at night. Or maybe to reassure herself that she had not faded away into her thoughts, become a ghost woman.

Traunt Rowan knocked and entered at her bidding. He was tall and broad-shouldered and in his black robes looked less a Druid than a warlock. His strong features had a calm, distant expression that belied the intensity he brought to every meeting. She had been fooled by it at first, but knew better now. Rowan never did anything haphazardly or halfway. If he ever overcame his resentment of her, he would be a valuable ally.

He bowed stiffly, a formality only. "Thank you for seeing me," he said. "What I have to say is important."

"Say it then."

She did not offer him a seat or anything to drink. He was all business and would have refused both. When he was with her, he was mostly anxious to be gone again.

"I think you should resign your office," he said.

She stared at him, speechless in the face of such audacity.

"I don't say this to attack you," he continued. "Or because I don't respect what you have done. I say it because I think it will help the order if you do as I suggest. You are a smart woman. You understand the situation well enough. There are too many at Paranor who do not think you should lead them.

There are too many here who cannot forget your past. Or forgive you of it. I admit I am one of them. Such prejudice hamstrings your efforts at accomplishing almost anything you undertake. If you were no longer leader, the prejudice would be removed. Another might do better."

She nodded slowly. "I don't think you intend putting yourself forward as Ard Rhys, Traunt Rowan. Who, then?"

He took a deep breath. "Whomever you name," he said finally.

It took him some effort to concede her this, and she wondered at its source. He was close with those vipers Shadea a'Ru and Iridia Eleri, who he knew she would never support, yet he had named neither. Why?

"You were chosen to form this order," he continued, his voice calm and persuasive. "No one could argue that you haven't done what you set out to do in bringing it to life. But perhaps you were not meant to lead it. Perhaps your purpose ended once the Third Council came into being. Another role might work better, one less visible in the larger scheme of things. Have you considered that?"

She had. She had considered every scenario that might break the logjam the Third Council found itself enmeshed in. But she still did not judge any other alternative acceptable under the present circumstances. Things were too unsettled for her to step down, too uncertain for her to let another take her place. To begin with, there wasn't anyone strong enough of whom she approved. The factions already established within the order would tear almost anyone else apart. Anarchy would claim the Third Council and destroy it. She could not allow that.

"I admire and appreciate your honesty and your boldness," she told him. "Not many would have dared to come to me with this suggestion. I don't know that I can do what you ask, but I will consider it."

He nodded, clearly unhappy. "I have never told you what

brought me to Paranor, but I think you need to hear it now. It is no secret that we are not friends. You have probably already guessed that it has something to do with your past. My parents were Federation officials who became victims of your manipulations when you were the Ilse Witch. They were destroyed politically because of you. The reasons no longer matter. The fact remains that they died broken and despised even by their closest friends. Dannon and Cela Scio. They were members of the Coalition Council, at one time. Do you remember them?"

She shook her head.

He shrugged. "It doesn't matter. I took my mother's family name so no one here, especially you, would make the connection. My purpose in coming was to see to it that you did not subvert the Druid Council in the same way you had subverted other political bodies—to make sure that you really were Ard Rhys and not still Ilse Witch. I was willing to let go of the past if you had changed. I thought that might be enough. But it isn't. You are still linked to your past in the minds of too many, both inside and outside Paranor's walls. You are rendered ineffective by acts you committed before you became Ard Rhys. That won't change; it can never change. I have stayed on as a Druid only because I believe you must be made to leave."

The heat of anger rose in her face, a faint blush she could not prevent. "Your opinion does not necessarily represent that of the majority. Nor is it necessarily right."

"Resign your office," he repeated. His expression was suddenly hard and fixed. "Do so now, tonight. Announce it to all. Time does not allow for extended deliberation on the matter."

She stared at him in surprise. He was practically ordering her to leave. "Time allows for more deliberation than you seem willing to afford me. I said I would consider your demand, Traunt Rowan. That will have to be enough."

He shook his head. "It isn't nearly enough. I should have come to you long before this. Pay attention to me, Ard Rhys. Events have a way of piling up and stealing away our choices."

"Do they do so here? What are you trying to say? Why is this so urgent? Tell me."

For a moment, he hesitated as if thinking he might, then simply turned away and went out the door, slamming it behind him with such force that she felt the vibrations in the stone beneath her feet.

"Have you brought it?" Shadea a'Ru demanded as she stepped out of the darkness of the hidden passageway into the light of the room.

Sen Dunsidan regarded her with bemusement. "Good evening to you, too."

She took her time closing the wall panel behind her, watched it slide smoothly back into place, and let her temper cool. As impatient as she was to get on with things, it would do her no good to argue with Dunsidan at this point.

"My apologies," she said, turning back to him with a smile. "I am more than a little nervous about all this, as you might guess. I am also anxious to get it over with."

He nodded. "Understandable, Shadea. But haste often results in mistakes, and we can't afford to have any here."

She gritted her teeth against what she was tempted to say and let the moment pass. They were never going to have much of a relationship, Sen Dunsidan and she. The one they had was one of convenience and nothing more. As much as she wanted the Ard Rhys out of the way, she was only slightly less anxious to be rid of him. He was a treacherous, self-serving snake, a man who had built his career on the misfortunes and failings of others. She had heard the stories about his despicable uses of children and women, and she believed them all. Once Grianne Ohmsford was eliminated, she would turn her attention to him. But for the moment, they must remain allies, and she would play that game as best she could.

"There won't be any mistakes," she said.

She moved over to the table with the wine carafe and poured herself a glass. His room was rich with tapestries and rugs, with wine and sweets, and with good smells. It contrasted sharply with her spare and unassuming quarters some floors below. She felt no jealousy; finery and comforts were a sign of weakness. They made demands that caused one to lose focus on what really mattered. She would not allow that in herself, but was more than willing to allow it in him. It would make it easier to break him down and destroy him when the time to do so arrived.

"How do you know that the potion you have brought me works as you think? What if you have been betrayed?"

She watched for a reaction. He merely shrugged. "I haven't tested it myself, but I am assured it is lethally effective."

"Assured by whom?" she asked. "Who gave you this 'liquid night,' Prime Minister?" she pressed. "You didn't mix it up yourself. Such a potion requires magic, and you have none. Who do you know who has such magic? Did someone at Paranor assist you? Someone not allied with me? Do you play us against each other?"

His leonine features lifted slightly. "I don't discuss my alliances. What does it matter, anyway? If it doesn't work, what have you lost? Only a little of your time. I will have lost your trust completely. I am the one at risk, Shadea."

He lifted his own wineglass and toasted her. "But it will work. By morning, the Ard Rhys will be a memory and all the talk will be of you, the new Ard Rhys. I know something of how this works, Shadea. I know because it happened to me when I coveted the position of Prime Minister. The order will be frightened and confused. It will be looking for direction and for someone to supply it. No one else has the backing you possess. The matter will be settled quickly. I salute you, Ard Rhys to be."

She ignored his patronizing, wondering how she could find out who had given him the potion. She would find out, she had decided. But short of torturing him on the spot, she would not find out immediately. She would have to bide her time, something at which she had gotten quite good.

"Let's not get ahead of ourselves, Prime Minister." She finished the wine and set down her glass. "What will you do when the news comes? Stay or go?"

"I will depart immediately, the expected reaction for a head of state when someone as important as the Ard Rhys disappears. It will give you a chance to consolidate your power before we have our meeting to arrange an alliance. Perhaps by then you will have discovered evidence of Free-born participation in the matter, and I will be able to use that discovery as a lever for pressing the war."

"Something you intend to do by any means possible." She made it a statement of fact.

He smiled. "The fortunes of war are about to change for the Free-born and their allies, Shadea. With your support, the change will come about much more quickly."

She nodded. The room, with its rich smells and opulent feel, was beginning to wear on her. As was this fool. "We have our understanding, Prime Minister. No need to discuss it again. No need to talk further at all, this night. Do you have it?"

He rose and walked to the bookcase at the far side of the room, moved several of the books aside, and extracted a small glass bottle with its stopper set firmly in place. The contents of the bottle were as black as a moonless night. Nothing of the room's light reflected from the surface of either the bottle or its contents.

"Liquid night," he declared, and handed her the bottle.

She took it gingerly and studied it a moment. The liquid

night had an opaque texture to it that reminded her of chalk or black earth. It made her feel decidedly uneasy.

She looked back at him. "This is all there is?"

"A little is all that is needed. Nevertheless, use the whole of it. Do it while she sleeps. Do not let even a single drop touch your skin. Then carry the bottle away and destroy it. There will be no trace of what has happened, no sign of anything different. But the Ard Rhys will be gone. As if she had never been."

"You make it sound so easy," Shadea said, giving him a sharp look.

"It will be easy, if you do it right." He stared back at her. "You will be able to do it right, Shadea, won't you?"

"If there is any treachery attached to this gift, Prime Minister," she said carefully, "it will come home to roost on your doorstep."

He reached over for a set of notes he had been writing and began leafing through them. "A word of caution. The Ard Rhys has a brother who possesses the gift, as well. His magic is said to be the equal of hers. You might want to consider what he will do when he discovers that his sister is missing. I understand he went through quite a lot to save her during that airship journey west twenty years back, when he discovered they were related. If not for him, she would still be the Ilse Witch. That makes her an investment he might not be quick to give up on."

"He has little contact with her these days," she replied irritably. "He has little to do with her at all."

He shrugged. "Sometimes a little is all that is necessary where families are concerned. Brothers and sisters are funny that way. You, of all people, should understand that." His smile was smug and indulgent. "It just seems to me that where a potential problem exists, you would be smart to find a solution early."

He studied her momentarily, then lowered his gaze to his notes. "Good night, Shadea. Good luck."

She held her ground a moment longer, thinking how easy it would be to kill him. Then she tucked the bottle into her dark robes, turned away without another word, touched the wall to release the hidden catch, and left him behind.

FIVE

When she was behind the wall panel and out of Sen Dunsidan's room, Shadea a'Ru stood in the darkness of the passageway beyond and breathed deeply to calm herself. Any encounter with the Prime Minister was unsettling, but it was the task that lay ahead that gave her pause now. She touched the hard outline of the bottle inside her robes, to reassure herself that it was safely under her control, then gathered her thoughts. It would have to be done that night, while the Ard Rhys slept. She believed herself safe in her chambers, and she had been until that night. Rock Trolls under the command of Kermadec stood at her doorway day and night, and her own magic warded the chamber against intruders. The passageways that honeycombed the Keep behind its stone walls had been closed off long ago so that, aside from the windows, there was only one way in or out.

But Shadea had found a way to get around all that. The Rock Trolls outside the door were of no use if the attack came from within, which it would. The magic that warded the chamber was of no use if the attack was not something it could protect against, and in this case it wasn't. Finally, although the passageways had been closed off some time back, Shadea had opened a few very recently in expectation of what was planned for that night. She had started with the passageway leading to Sen Dunsidan's quarters, so that they could meet secretly. She had ended with the passageway that led to the chambers of the Ard Rhys. The latter had taken her nearly two weeks because not only was it physically sealed, but it was warded with magic, as well. She had broken down that magic, a painfully slow process, then restored it at its perimeter to give the appearance of still being intact.

She stared into the darkness around her, her eyes adjusting, her thoughts settling. Everything was in place. Everything was as ready as it was ever going to be. Her careful planning and preparation were about to be rewarded.

She allowed herself a fierce, predatory smile and started walking.

Shadea a'Ru had experienced a hard life, but she thought herself the better for having survived its vicissitudes and misfortunes. Surviving had made her strong of body and tough of mind. Without those attributes, she would not be where she was, planning to accomplish something that others could only muse about privately. Terek Molt aside, all the others had enjoyed privileged upbringings with advantages that she had never even come close to enjoying. She didn't resent it or feel cheated because of it; she reveled in it.

She was orphaned by the age of eight, her mother dead in childbirth and her father killed on the Prekkendorran. Shadea and her siblings were separated and sent to live with the families of various relatives, but she ran away at ten and never saw any of them again. She was big for her age and initially awkward, but she was always strong. As she grew, the awkwardness disappeared and her strength increased. She lived in the streets of Dechtera for five years, staying alive by her wits and her daring and the occasional kindness of others.

At fifteen, already close to six feet tall and the physical equal of anyone her age, she began hanging out at the Federation barracks, doing odd jobs for the soldiers. A few thought to test her resistance to their unwanted advances, for she was striking by then, but after they discovered she not only was big and strong but knew how to fight, they left her alone. A few took the time to teach her to use weapons. She was a quick study and naturally gifted. By the time she was twenty, she was already more accomplished than the men she had learned from. At twenty-four, she had served two years on the front lines of the Prekkendorran and gained the respect of everyone who knew about her.

She met the cripple the following year. He was of indeterminate origin, so gnarled and deformed that it was impossible to label his Race. She never learned his name, but names were never important in their relationship. He was a practitioner of the magic arts, primarily a weaver of spells. He was infatuated with her for reasons she never fully understood, and he was willing to trade what he knew for the pleasure of her company. It was an easy bargain for her to make. She stayed with him only one year, time that passed so quickly that in retrospect it always seemed impossible to her that it had really been that long. His health was already failing when they met, and by the end of the year he was dead. But before he died, he taught her what he knew about magic, which was considerable. He was a teacher in search of a student, but he was careful in making his choices. He must have watched her for a time, she decided afterwards, measuring her strengths, determining whether or not she would be worth the effort. Once he had decided that she was and further determined that she was not repelled by his looks, he gave her his full attention for the time that was left him.

He never told her why he decided to spend his last few months teaching her. He must have known he was dying. She thought that maybe it helped him to have a purpose in his life rather than simply waiting for the inevitable. She thought that he took pleasure in watching his own deteriorating skills put to use by someone still young and strong. Perhaps teaching was all he knew to do in his final years, and so he did it. Perhaps he found in her company something that was sustaining and comforting. Perhaps he simply didn't want to die alone. It was hard to tell, but she accepted his gift without questioning it.

Her natural affinity for summoning and employing magic was immediately apparent to both of them. She was able to grasp and employ the subtle art of spell weaving almost from the beginning, her comprehension of the ways in which words and hand movements worked together enabling her to cast simple spells from their first session. The old man was delighted and actually clapped his hands. She progressed rapidly from there, all of it, at first, a mystery that offered such possibilities that she could not help imagining the secrets she would uncover.

After he died, held in her arms as he breathed his last, comforted in the way he deserved to be, she studied alone for several years, closeted away in quarters not far from her Federation soldier friends, whom she still spent time with regularly. But the Federation no longer held any interest for her. It was too regimented, too structured, and she was in need of freedom. She saw that her future lay elsewhere.

Her break with Federation life came about in an unexpected way. She stayed too long and perhaps spoke too freely of leaving. Some took exception, men she knew only casually and didn't much care for. One night, they drugged her and took her out of the city to an abandoned shack on the Rappahalladran's banks. There, they held her prisoner for two days and violated her in unspeakable ways, and when they were finished with her they threw her into a river to drown. Tougher than they suspected, dragging herself to safety through sheer force of will, she survived.

When she had recovered her strength, she went back into the city, hunted them down one by one, and killed them all.

She fled afterwards, because the dead men most certainly had relatives and friends. There had been enough talk that sooner or later some of them would come looking for her. Besides, the incident had soured her on the city and the Federation and her life in general. It was time for her to go somewhere else. She had heard about the Third Druid Council and thought she might find a home there, but she didn't want to ask for admission into the order until she was certain they would not turn her away. So she went west into the Wilderun and the town of Grimpen Ward, the last refuge of fugitives and castoffs of all kinds, thinking to isolate herself and work on her magic skills until she had perfected them. Few came looking for those who hid in Grimpen Ward, where all hid secrets of one sort or another and none wanted the past revealed.

She stayed there until her twenty-eighth birthday, keeping apart from the other denizens, practicing her art with the single-mindedness that defined her personality. She expanded her field of study from potions and spells to the uses of earth power and the elements, particularly the summoning up of shades and dead things that could be made to do her bidding and to offer their insights. Her skills sharpened, but her emotional character deadened proportionately. She had never had trouble killing when it was required; now killing became a means to her magic's ends. Killing was inherent to the unlocking of many of the forms of power she sought to master. Whether of animals or humans, killing was a part of the rituals she embraced. There were other, safer ways in which to proceed, but none so quick or far-reaching in their results. She let herself become seduced. She hastened to her self-destruction.

By the time she met Iridia Eleri, an outcast and a sorceress like herself, she was deep in the throes of dark magic's lure and hungry for a larger taste. Iridia was already half-mad with her own twisted needs, her own secrets, and they formed a friendship based on mutual cravings. Magic could give them everything they desired, they believed; they needed only to master its complexities.

They decided together to go to Paranor and seek admission into the Druid order. They made the journey in a fever, but when they put forth their applications were careful to hide the inner madnesses that drove them. The Ard Rhys was surprisingly easy to fool. She was distracted by the demands of her undertaking as leader of the order, and her primary concern was to find talented individuals willing to serve the Druid cause. Shadea a'Ru and Iridia Eleri seemed to be what she was seeking. What she failed to perceive was that both women dissembled; they were willing to embrace the Druid cause, but only insofar as it was necessary for them to do so and then only for reasons that were peculiarly their own.

After the first three years of service, it was clear to both sorceresses that although Grianne Ohmsford possessed great power, she no longer commanded the authority of the Ilse Witch. She had allowed herself to become weakened by the constraints she had imposed on herself in casting off her past life. She was unwilling to take the risks or make the sacrifices that the witch would have been quick to understand were necessary. Neither Shadea nor Iridia had such compunctions. The order was foundering, and its chances of gaining control over the Races were diminishing daily. Shadea, in particular, was determined to take control of the order and to lead it in the direction she knew it needed to go. Having decided that there was only one way that could happen, she was quick to put aside her oaths of loyalty to the Ard Rhys and to take up the mantle of active dissident.

For five years, Shadea had searched for a way to fufill her ambitions, to topple Grianne Ohmsford and to make herself Ard Rhys. This night, it was finally going to happen.

Her steps quickened as she followed the musty passageway to its secret exit, two floors farther down in a storeroom in which bedding and pallets were kept. Excitement radiated from her smooth, strong face, a palpable hunger that was fierce and alive. She would not falter, she would not fail. If the potion was good, her goal would be achieved and the waiting would end.

If it failed, she hoped only to escape long enough to return to Sen Dunsidan and cut out his heart.

Grianne Ohmsford put aside her notes and writings, her records of past meetings with the Prime Minister, her summaries of efforts undertaken and mostly failed, and prepared herself for bed. Tagwen appeared long enough to brew her a cup of sleeping tea, which she took regularly these days, and to straighten up her room. He fussed about for a time, waiting for her to say something to him, which she finally did. She asked if he had taken Kermadec something to eat, which he had. Trolls took pride in their independence and resourcefulness, and it was not customary for them ever to ask for anything while traveling. It had to be offered voluntarily. This habit was born out of custom and a history of being at war with almost everyone, and it wasn't likely to change anytime soon.

Tagwen also reported that the Trolls guarding her room were in place, something he did every night as a reassurance to her, but to which she paid hardly any attention. She did not feel threatened at Paranor, her prickly relationship with some of the more overtly hostile members of the order notwithstanding. Guards and stone walls, warding spells and watchful eyes were not what would save her in any case, should the need for saving arise. Instincts and premonitions were what protected her, her own resources and not those of others. Years spent as the Ilse Witch had sharpened both to a razor's edge, and she did not think time spent as the Ard Rhys had dulled either.

"Wake me early, Tagwen," she asked him as he prepared to leave.

"I won't need to," he responded. "You will be awake before me. You always are. Good night, mistress."

He went out quietly, closing the door behind him as if it were made of glass. She smiled to herself, wondering what she would do without him. For someone so small and seemingly inconsequential, he was in many respects the most important member of the order.

She wandered over to her tea, sat down, and began to sip the hot mix gingerly. As it cooled, she finished it off, hardly aware of what she was doing, her thoughts on the coming meetings and on the ramifications of what she hoped to accomplish. She let her thoughts stray momentarily to Traunt Rowan and his strangely urgent request, but she quickly moved on to other matters. Resigning her position was out of the question. She thought she would elevate one or two members of the order to positions of greater importance, among them Trefen Morys, who had demonstrated repeatedly that he merited advancement. Gerand Cera was another possibility, but she wasn't sure yet where he stood on the matter of her continuing as Ard Rhys. She toyed with the idea of elevating Traunt Rowan, in spite of his attitude toward her. It might serve to distance him from Shadea a'Ru and Iridia Eleri, something that could only help him. They were the women with the most talent in the order, and neither could be trusted for a moment. Sooner or later, they would have to be dealt with.

Her eyes grew heavy with the drink, and she moved to her bed, slipped off her robe, and climbed beneath the covers. Her last thoughts were of the strange happenings in the ruins of the Skull Kingdom and her determination to discover who had initiated them. A visit to the Hadeshorn and the shades of the Druids might provide insight into the matter, and she had already made the necessary arrangements for the journey. As soon as the meetings with Sen Dunsidan were completed, she would depart with Kermadec, perhaps even telling Tagwen where she was going, just to see the look of disapproval on his face.

She was too tired even to blow out the candles on her writing desk, and so drifted off to sleep with the light of both still flickering brightly in the overlay of the chamber's deep shadows.

Night settled over Paranor, silent and velvet black under a wash of light from moon and stars that spilled from a cloudless sky. Most of the Druids were asleep, only a few who liked working late at night still awake in their rooms and study chambers, keeping to themselves. The Troll watch was in place, not only at the door of the Ard Rhys but at the gates of the Keep, as well. There was no real concern for anyone's safety, no anticipation of the sort of danger that had existed in the time of the Warlock Lord, but the Trolls were careful anyway. Complacency had undone the Druids and their protectors in the past.

Shadea a'Ru stole through the walls of the high tower, following the twists and turns of the secret passageway that led to the sleeping chamber of the Ard Rhys. It was well after midnight, and she knew no better opportunity would offer itself than the one she acted on now. She had swept the musty corridor of magic once again only two days earlier, during the Ard Rhys' absence, and she was quite certain Grianne had not had an opportunity to reset her wardings in the short time since her return. The sorceress moved slowly in the gloom, generating a small finger of magic light to keep from stumbling. She must make no sound in her approach, offer nothing that would alert the sleeping Ard Rhys to her presence. She must maintain the presence of a tiny mouse.

She was sweating freely, her body heat elevated by the closeness of the passageway and her excitement. She was not afraid. She was never afraid. It wasn't that she was reckless or foolish; it was that she understood the nature of risk. Failure in dangerous situations came about because of poor planning or bad luck. The former was something you could control, and if you kept your wits about you, sometimes the latter, as well. She had learned that for people like her, orphans and disadvantaged souls, gains were achieved mostly through risk. That was the nature of her lot in life, and she had long ago accepted it.

The night's activities would measure that acceptance in a way it hadn't been measured before. If she succeeded, she would have a chance at gaining everything she had wanted for so long. If she failed, she would likely be dead.

That was acceptable to Shadea a'Ru. For what was at stake, that was a price worth wagering.

She wondered anew at the source of the liquid night. It bothered her that it had come into the possession of someone who did not himself possess magic. Sen Dunsidan was a high-ranking official in a powerful government, but he lacked the skills and resources to obtain something so powerful on his own. He must have had help, and she didn't like it that help of a magical sort had not come from her. It meant he had another option and might choose to use it down the road, and that could prove dangerous to her. Still, he needed her. Without her, he could not hope to gain control of the Druid order, and without that, his plans for the Free-born could not succeed.

Ahead, the last stairway led upward to the tower chamber where Grianne Ohmsford slept. Shadea slowed automatically, her movements, her thinking, even her breathing, and calmed herself. Soundlessly, she climbed the stone steps to the landing beyond, then stood just outside the section of wall that opened into forbidden territory. She tested the fabric of warding she had left in place and found it undisturbed. The Ard Rhys had not bothered to see if anyone had tampered with her magic. She still thought herself safe.

A fierce rush of anticipation surged through Shadea as she reached into her robes and extracted the bottle of liquid night. Silence concealed her movements, extending from the place she stood to the chamber beyond and then to the Keep beyond that. Dreams and slumber blanketed the rooms of Paranor, where the occupants lay unmoving and unaware. She listened, satisfied, and set the bottle on the floor in front of her.

She was ready.

Carefully, she constructed a series of spells and incantations, setting them atop one another in the space before the door. One after another, she created them with movements and words. No one saw or heard. No one could. She breathed as if there was not enough air to waste on breathing, creating an intricate pattern of small, cautious inhales and exhales. Her life force became a part of her efforts, aiding and supporting. She kept her concentration fixed on the task at hand, neither wavering nor hesitating, working steadily and diligently at her task.

It took her almost an hour to complete the conjurings. Then she knelt before the wall and opened the skin of magic she had left in place, giving herself clear access to the secret doorway and the chamber beyond. She could hear the sound of her heart pumping her blood through her body. It seemed to her that she could hear the Ard Rhys breathing on the other side of the wall, deep in sleep but capable of waking in an instant.

She prepared to remove the stopper from the bottle of liquid night.

Her hands began to shake.

For just a second she faltered, thinking suddenly that she was daring too much; that she was overreaching herself; that her failure to accomplish what she was attempting to undertake was assured; that the moment she tried to place the liquid inside the bedchamber, the Ard Rhys would wake and discover her treachery; that she would have been smarter simply to feed the Ard Rhys poison and be done with it; that this more sophisticated execution would never work. How could it?

Furious with herself, she crushed her hesitation and doubt as if they were annoying insects buzzing in her ears.

She pulled the stopper from the bottle and poured it into the funnel she had created in the last conjuring of magic, sending both the liquid night and the spells that directed it into the chamber beyond.

There, it was done, she told herself, replacing the stopper once more.

She rocked back on her heels to wait.

Grianne Ohmsford woke just long enough to recognize that something was dreadfully wrong, that an alien magic had bypassed her wardings and entered her room. She threw up her defensive magic instantly, but it was already too late. The room was moving—or she was moving in it—consumed by a blackness that transcended anything she had ever known. She fought to get free of it, but could not make herself move. She tried to cry out, but no sound came forth. She was trapped, immobilized and helpless. The blackness was enveloping her, sweeping her away, bearing her off like a death shroud wound about a corpse on its way to interment, clinging and impenetrable and final.

She felt the shroud slowly begin to tighten.

Shades! she swore silently as she realized what was happening, and then the blackness was in her mouth and nose and ears, was inside her body and her mind. She struggled until her strength was gone and with it her hope, and then she lost consciousness.

Still hidden in the passageway behind the wall of the bedchamber, Shadea a'Ru listened to the faint, sudden sounds of movement on the other side, then to the enveloping silence that followed. She was desperate for a look inside, but didn't dare to open the passageway door for fear of what she would find. She held her breath, listening as the silence lengthened.

Then a finger of blackness wormed its way under the door, the leading edge of a clutch of ragged tendrils. They twisted and groped as if seeking to snare her, as if the Ard Rhys was not enough, and Shadea stepped back quickly, poised to flee. She did not know what it was—some residue of the liquid night, perhaps—but she wasn't about to find out. The fingers stretched a bit farther, crooking toward her, then slowly retreated and disappeared back beneath the door.

Shadea a'Ru was sweating heavily, the tunic beneath her Druid robes drenched. Something had happened in the Ard Rhys' bedchamber, something that was the result of what Shadea had done—of that much, she was certain. But she could not know the particulars right away—not until morning, perhaps. No matter how desperate she was to find them out, she could do nothing but go back the way she had come and wait.

She exhaled heavily, quickly, a fear she had never felt suddenly caressing her in an all-too-familiar fashion. She backed away, still watching the door, retreating cautiously down the steps she had climbed more than an hour earlier, listening, listening.

By the time she reached the landing below and turned into the passageway leading out of the Keep's stone walls, it was all she could do to keep from running.

SIX

In spite of the chill she experienced even coming near the bedchamber, Shadea a'Ru made certain she was among the first to discover that the leader of the Druid order was missing. She was there, waiting to speak to Grianne, when Tagwen appeared with breakfast. Employing her most subservient manner, she requested an audience at the Ard Rhys' convenience. Tagwen gave her his patented nod of agreement, the one that said he would act on her request immediately while at the same time wishing she would disappear into the earth, and entered the chamber. As he went inside, Shadea caught a glimpse of the room and saw nothing out of the ordinary.

Maybe, she thought suddenly, nothing had happened after all. Maybe the liquid night had failed.

But a moment later the Dwarf reappeared, looking confused and not a little concerned. Had the Ard Rhys gone out already? he asked the Troll guard. They said she had not, that she had been in her room all night. When Tagwen hesitated, clearly uncertain about what to do next, Shadea stepped into the breach and took over.

"Where is your mistress?" she demanded of the Trolls. "Why isn't she in her room? Have you let something happen to her?"

Without waiting for the response she knew they couldn't give, she brushed past Tagwen and went in, glancing around quickly. The bed was unmade, the covers rumpled and tossed. Last night's sleeping tea was set to one side, the cup empty. Notes for the meeting with Sen Dunsidan lay stacked neatly on her writing table, ready for use. A surreptitious glance at the wall behind which she had hidden and fed the liquid night into the chamber revealed nothing. There was no trace of the potion and none of Grianne Ohmsford, either. There was no indication at all of what had actually happened.

She spun back to face Tagwen, who had entered behind her, a furious look on his rough face. "Where is she, Tagwen?" she snapped, bringing him up short. "What's wrong?"

"Nothing is wrong!" he replied defensively, moving at once to the writing table to snatch up Grianne's notes. "You can't be in here, Shadea!"

"If nothing is wrong, then where is the Ard Rhys?" she demanded, ignoring his protest. "Why isn't she in her room?"

"I don't know," he admitted, a prickly tone to his words, placing himself squarely in her path. "But I don't see that it is your concern in any case."

"It is the concern of all of us, Tagwen. She doesn't belong to you alone. When did you see her last?"

The Dwarf looked mortified. "Just before midnight. She took her tea and was going to bed." He looked around doubtfully. "She must have gone out."

"Without the Troll watch seeing her?" Shadea looked around as if to make sure the Ard Rhys wasn't somewhere plainly in view, then declared, "We need to make a search at once."

"You can't do that!" he exclaimed, appalled. "You don't know that anything has happened to her! There's no reason for a search!"

"There is every reason," she declared firmly. "But we'll keep it quiet for the moment. You and I are the only ones who need know of this until we make certain nothing is amiss. Or would you prefer we stand around doing nothing?"

Clearly at a loss as to what to do, he made no response to her unspoken accusation. Already she was assuming command of the Keep, and he could do nothing to prevent it. He didn't fully realize yet what was happening; his concern for the Ard Rhys was clouding his judgment. Had he been thinking clearly, he might have wondered at how quick Shadea was to act. She smiled inwardly at his obvious confusion. He would do better to forget the Ard Rhys and worry about himself. But he would come to that particular realization too late.

Under the supervision of the sorceress, the Troll watch conducted a search for the Ard Rhys. It took less than an hour and revealed exactly what Shadea had been hoping for: No trace of Grianne Ohmsford was to be found anywhere. At its conclusion, she demanded to know what Tagwen was going to do.

"You were the last one to see her, Tagwen, and she is your responsibility in any case. That is why you were selected to be her personal assistant."

Tagwen looked crushed. "I don't know what could have happened to her. She wouldn't leave Paranor without telling me. She was preparing for this morning's meeting with the Prime Minister just last night, when I brought her tea and said good night. I don't understand it!"

He was clearly holding himself responsible, even though there was no reason for him to do so save out of loyalty to his mistress. That was what Shadea was counting on. "Well, Tagwen, let's not panic," she soothed. "It isn't time yet for the meeting. She may have slipped away to do some thinking on it. She comes and goes like that now and then, doesn't she? Using her magic so no one can tell what she's about?"

Tagwen nodded doubtfully. "Sometimes."

"Perhaps she has done so here. You wait for her in her chambers and I will look for her myself. I will use my own magic in an effort to trace her movements. Perhaps I can read something of them in the air." She patted his shoulder. "Don't worry, she'll turn up."

With that false reassurance to placate him, she departed the bedchamber and went to the rooms of her confederates. One by one, she advised them that the plan was working. As expected, there was some grumbling from each over her decision to act alone, but their discontent was more than offset by their euphoria. The Ard Rhys was dispatched. Now they must begin to gain control of the Druids and the Keep. Once it became known that the Ard Rhys had disappeared, confusion and indecision would quickly settle over Paranor. A vacuum would open with the loss of Grianne Ohmsford's leadership, and no one would want to be too quick to step into it. Shadea's name must be the first mentioned as the logical choice, in part premised on her early involvement and willingness to take action. It must appear that of all those who might be called upon to take charge, she was the one in the best position to do so.

For that to happen, she must not only have verbal support from her allies, but also have demonstrated her ability to serve. The best way to accomplish that was to offer up a scapegoat to bear responsibility for what had happened to the Ard Rhys. Someone must be made to bear the blame, and she had already decided who that would be. Her confederates were to spread the rumor that the Ard Rhys had been murdered and that the Rock Trolls who guarded her were in some way responsible. There was no proof nor could there be, of course, but in the heat of the moment, many would find reason to believe it was true. A word here and there was all that was required. With enough talk, momentum would build in favor of that explanation, and it would take on the appearance of logic.

A fierce rush of elation surged through Shadea as she left her allies and made her way back through the corridors of the

Keep to the bedchamber of the Ard Rhys. It was happening just as Sen Dunsidan had promised, as she had hoped, as fate had whispered to her time and again. She was meant to lead the order. She was meant to wield its power.

"Shadea a'Ru, Ard Rhys!" she whispered to the walls and shadows marking her passage.

She found herself wondering if Grianne Ohmsford had awakened yet and discovered where she was. Perhaps the hapless Ard Rhys would not get a chance to come awake, but while she still slept would be set upon by the denizens of the place to which she had been dispatched. Perhaps she was already dead.

Shadea wished she could be there to see it for herself.

Tagwen had served the Ard Rhys for almost the whole of her time as leader of the Third Druid Council, and he believed that he knew her as well as anyone alive. Even though he was her close friend and confidant, he understood that she could not tell him everything. No one who commanded the responsibility and power that she did could afford to trust completely in anyone. But he believed that when she wished to talk out her problems, to reveal her concerns to another human being, she thought of him first. So he found it disturbing that she would slip out of her quarters during the night without telling him. The longer he thought about it, the more uncomfortable he grew. Shadea a'Ru, as much as he disliked and distrusted her, might be right to worry. That his mistress wasn't back for her breakfast on a day in which she had such an important meeting was very unlike her.

A practical man, Tagwen understood the implications of her absence. She would not cast the day's meeting aside without good reason. She would never act out of haste or panic; she thought everything through first, considering the ramifications of her choices. If she had left her quarters voluntarily, there would be good reason for it. If she had chosen not to confide in him, there would be good reason for that, as well. But if she did not resurface soon, he had to accept that words like *voluntary* and *choice* had nothing to do with the matter and that something bad had happened to her.

He sat in her chambers for what felt like an endless amount of time, his uneasiness and discomfort growing, his patience slipping. He could hear the sounds of increased activity in the hallways beyond, a clear indication that the Druids were beginning to discover that something was wrong. Shadea had not returned from her search, a search he was not at all confident would succeed in any case, given the Ard Rhys' opinion of her. He walked around the room, looking at everything, trying to make some sense of what had happened. He didn't like the look of the unmade bed, the appearance of which suggested she had departed in a rush.

But no one could get into the room, he told himself in trying to shake off his fear that she had been attacked. The Troll watch was fiercely loyal, and the Ard Rhys had installed warding spells all through the walls to protect herself. If something bad had happened to her, there would be some sign of a struggle. Besides, no enemy could slip into Paranor without being detected. Wouldn't the watch have seen and sounded an alarm?

Unless, of course, the enemy was someone already within the walls. He rubbed his beard furiously as he considered the possibility. There were some who might take action against her, however misguided. Shadea a'Ru was one. But how likely was that, given the risk of failure and discovery? Any Druid who tried such a thing would have to be mad! He shook his head. It didn't bear thinking on too closely. Not yet, at least.

Suddenly it occurred to him that she might have gone to see Kermadec. The Rock Troll was still camped outside the walls of the Keep, waiting to depart to wherever it was that the Ard Rhys had decided to go. Something important was happening in connection with these mysterious comings and goings, the one planned for the next day and the one just finished a day earlier, so it was not so farfetched to wonder if perhaps his mistress was off pursuing that business again.

He was on his feet and moving toward the doorway when Shadea reappeared from the hallway and stepped inside.

"Nothing," she said, shaking her head in frustration. "I searched everywhere in the Keep and on the grounds outside, and there is no trace of her that isn't at least a day old. I don't like it, Tagwen." She looked at him thoughtfully. "How reliable is this Troll Kermadec?"

Tagwen was horrified. "Entirely. He is a trusted friend, has been so forever." He allowed his indignation to show. "Much more so than some others I might name."

"Yet he is responsible for choosing her guard, including the two who stood watch last night and now have no idea where she is." She cocked her head. "He was the last to see her outside these walls, wasn't he? Don't bother to deny it; she was seen. What was that meeting about?"

The Dwarf was furious. "None of your business, Shadea! I don't discuss the affairs of the Ard Rhys without her permission—with you or anyone else! Wait for her return to ask such questions!"

She gave him an indulgent look. "Perhaps I should ask Kermadec in her absence, since you seem unwilling to do so. Why don't you ask him to come up to her chambers to discuss what has happened?"

Tagwen realized two things immediately. First, that Kermadec would never set foot inside the Keep. He had made that plain enough quite some time ago, and he was not about to change his mind for Shadea a'Ru, whom he distrusted anyway. Second, if he were foolish enough to accept the invitation nevertheless, perhaps out of concern for the Ard Rhys, he would not come out again. Shadea a'Ru was looking for someone to blame for the Ard Rhys' disappearance. Tagwen felt that instinctively. Why she felt it was necessary—or her responsibility—was beyond him, but what was happening was clear.

The Rock Trolls had never been a popular choice as protectors of the Druids. Elves had been used traditionally, a practice begun by Galaphile during the First Druid Council. An Elf himself, Galaphile had felt more comfortable relying on his own people in the wake of the destruction of the Old World and a thousand years of barbarism. Elven Hunters had warded the Druids until the fall of Paranor at the hands of the Warlock Lord. When the Third Council was convened, it was thought that Elves would be called upon again. But the Ard Rhys did not trust Kylen Elessedil sufficiently to rely on him to choose her protectors. By the time of his death, she was already committed to Kermadec and his Rock Trolls. Perhaps she felt more comfortable with them because her relationship with Kermadec did not owe anything to politics. She liked the independence of the Trolls; they gave their allegiance only when they felt it necessary and did not give it lightly. If they were your allies, you could rely on them.

None of that history would help the situation if Shadea managed to manipulate it, as she obviously intended. The Rock Trolls had responsibility for the safety of the Ard Rhys, and the Ard Rhys had disappeared right under their noses. It wouldn't take much effort for the sorceress to convince the order that the blame should be laid squarely at their feet.

Tagwen glared at Shadea. "Kermadec won't come inside; you know that."

"I do," she agreed. "But if he doesn't, then I will take that as proof of his complicity in whatever has happened and dismiss him along with all of his Trolls. I don't want them guarding the rest of us if they can't do any better job of it than they did with the Ard Rhys." She paused, a finger lifting to rest lightly on one cheek. "Refusing to come into the Keep suggests he is hiding something, Tagwen. If he isn't, he should tell us so—all of us, who depend on him for our safety. Tell him I said he should explain himself, if he can."

"Who gave you the right to tell anyone what to do, Shadea a'Ru?" the Dwarf demanded, standing his ground. "You don't command the Druid order."

She smiled. "Someone has to, in the Ard Rhys' absence. My name has already been put forth. I will serve as best I can, but serve I will. I can do no less." She looked past him at the empty room. "Go on, Tagwen. Do what I tell you."

He started to object again, to say something so terrible it would leave no doubt about how he felt. Then he realized that an unguarded response might be exactly what she was hoping for. Something bad was going on, and he was beginning to believe that Shadea had a part in it.

He held his tongue. Better to keep his head. Better to stay free. Someone needed to tell Kermadec what was happening, to warn him of the danger.

Nodding curtly, he went out the door and down the hallway, his eyes downcast, his face flushed. A part of him wanted to run out of there as fast as he could and not come back. He was suddenly afraid, looking about as he went at the faces of those he passed, seeing suspicion and doubt and in some cases outright anger. As Shadea had said, the word was already out. Schemes were being hatched and alliances formed. If the Ard Rhys did not resurface soon, everything was going to go Shadea's way.

On impulse, he made a short detour to the Rock Troll living quarters in the north courtyard and asked one of the watch commanders to bring a dozen of his men to the north gates on orders of the Ard Rhys. The commander did not argue. Tagwen had carried messages of this sort to him before from time to time; there was nothing unusual about this one.

Once outside the walls of the Keep, Tagwen went to the

edge of the forest and called for Kermadec. He knew the Maturen was camped somewhere just beyond the north gates. Waiting, he rubbed his beard and folded his arms across his burly chest, trying to think what he could do to stop Shadea from taking control.

"Bristle Beard!" Kermadec called with a laugh. His guttural tongue was rough-edged and resonant as he stepped out of the trees and stretched out his hand in greeting. "What's the matter with you? You look as if you swallowed something sour. Could your day be going better, old Dwarf?"

Tagwen clasped hands with the Troll. "It could. But yours isn't looking so good, either." He glanced quickly over his shoulder. "Better listen carefully to me, Kermadec. I don't know how much time we've got, but it isn't much."

Quickly, he explained what had happened to the Ard Rhys, then what had brought him down to find Kermadec. The Rock Troll listened silently and without interrupting, then looked up expectantly as his watch commander and a dozen fully armed Trolls appeared through the gates.

"I thought it best that you not be left alone, whatever you decide," Tagwen explained. "I don't like what's happening in there. Shadea is manipulating things in a way that suggests she intends to take control of the order. When the Ard Rhys reappears, this will stop quick enough, but in the meantime I think you are at some risk."

The Maturen nodded. "Shadea a'Ru wouldn't dare this if she didn't have reason to believe it would succeed. That isn't good. I don't know what's become of the Ard Rhys, but she hasn't been down here since she went inside after our return. I don't suppose it will hurt to tell you we were in the ruins of the Skull Kingdom, looking into rumors of strange fires and shadow movements. We saw something of them while we were there, a clear indication of magic at work. The Ard Rhys intended to visit the shades of the Druids at the Hadeshorn to ask their advice on the matter. But I don't think she would have gone there without me. Or at least without letting me know."

"Or me either, though she might not tell me as much as you about what she was doing." Tagwen looked put-upon. "But she wouldn't just leave."

"Something has happened to her, then," Kermadec said, anger reflected in his blunt features. "It may have something to do with what we witnessed in the Knife Edge. Or it may have something to do with what's happening here. I don't trust Shadea or her friends. Or a whole lot of the others, for that matter. Druids in name only, no friends to the Ard Rhys or to the Druid cause."

Tagwen hugged himself. "I don't know what to do, Kermadec," he admitted.

The Rock Troll walked over to the watch commander and spoke quietly with him for a moment. The watch commander listened, nodded, and disappeared with his men back inside the walls. Kermadec returned to Tagwen.

"I'm pulling all the Trolls out of the Keep and down to the gates. We will stand watch there for another few days. If the Ard Rhys returns, things can go back to where they were. If she doesn't and we're dismissed, we'll go. As long as we hold the gates, we can keep ourselves safe. Shadea can order us out, but she can't do much more than that."

"Don't be too sure of that. She has command of powerful magic, Kermadec. Even your Trolls will be at risk." The Dwarf paused. "You won't go inside, will you? Promise me you won't."

Kermadec grunted. "Oh, come now, Tagwen. You know what would happen if I did. Shadea and her bunch would have me in irons quicker than you could blink. It would suit them perfectly to announce that I was responsible for the disappearance of the Ard Rhys. Neither truth nor common sense would prove much of an obstacle to the expediency of having me locked up until things could be sorted out. Besides, the matter is likely already decided. I'm to be cast as the villain, even if no proof is ever offered. Wiser heads would prevail in different circumstances, but not here. I told the Ard Rhys she would be better off dismissing the whole lot of them and starting over. But she wouldn't listen. She never does." He shook his head. "I can't help thinking that her stubbornness has something to do with what's happened to her."

"I wouldn't argue the point," Tagwen said. He was wishing he had been more insistent about her precautions while inside the walls. He was wishing he had stayed in her bedchamber last night to keep watch.

"I think I might go back into the ruins of Skull Mountain and take another look around," Kermadec announced. His blunt features tightened, eyes shifting away from the Dwarf. "I might see something more, might find something. I don't think I can sit around here doing nothing. My men don't need me; they know what to do."

"You don't want to go into the Skull Kingdom alone," Tagwen said, shaking his head for emphasis. "It's too dangerous up there. You've said so yourself, many times."

The Maturen nodded. "Then I won't go alone. I'll take someone with me, someone who's a match for spirits and dark magic. But what about you, Bristle Beard? You can't go back inside, either. Shadea will have you in irons, as well, as soon as she thinks of it. Or worse. You're in some danger, too."

Tagwen stared at him. He hadn't considered the possibility of anything happening to himself. But he remembered the looks cast his way by some of the Druids he had passed. Anyone capable of making the Ard Rhys disappear wouldn't have much trouble doing the same with him. It might be convenient if he did, given the fact that he was likely to raise a considerable fuss if they tried to name a new Ard Rhys.

Which, he supposed, was exactly what Shadea a'Ru was trying to do right that minute. He was dismayed at the prospect. He could do nothing to prevent it.

"I'll go with you," he said, not much liking the idea of visiting the Skull Kingdom but liking less the idea of staying on alone at Paranor.

Kermadec shook his head. "I have a better idea. The Ard Rhys has a brother living at a way station called Patch Run on the Rainbow Lake. The family operates an airship service that hires out to fly expeditions into remote regions of the Four Lands. He and his Rover wife are airship pilots."

"I know," Tagwen interrupted. "The Ard Rhys told me about them. His name is Bek."

"The point is, the brother has the use of magic, too. He and his sister are pretty close, even though they don't see all that much of each other these days. Someone ought to tell him what's happened. He might be able to use his magic to find her."

Tagwen nodded doubtfully. "It's worth a try, I guess. Even if she shows up in the meantime, maybe he can talk some sense into her about what's happening at Paranor. We don't seem to be able to."

The big Troll reached down and placed his hands on the Dwarf's sturdy shoulders. "Don't be gloomy, old friend. The Ard Rhys has a lot of experience at staying alive."

Tagwen nodded, wondering if that was what matters had come to, that his mistress was fighting for her life.

"Let's find her," the Maturen said quietly. "Let's bring her safely home."

Shadea had dismissed the Trolls standing guard at the door of the Ard Rhys' bedchamber and was conducting a thorough search of the rooms, just in case anything incriminating or useful was lying about, when Iridia Eleri appeared. The Elven sorceress's cold, perfect features radiated triumph, and she gave her coconspirator a satisfied nod.

"We have approached them all and won them over, or at least the larger part of them," Iridia said. "Most have committed to supporting you as temporary Ard Rhys until this matter can be sorted out. Almost all are suspicious of the Trolls, wondering how they could have kept adequate watch and still let this happen. There is enough confusion and doubt that they are ready to blame anyone at whom a willing finger points." She glanced around. "Have you found anything?"

Shadea shook her head. "Tagwen took her notes when he left to convey my message to Kermadec. I didn't see him do so or I would have stopped him. He may have taken more than that, but it doesn't matter. We have what we want. Neither he nor the Troll will be back inside."

"Don't be too sure." Iridia's strange eyes had a hard look to them, as if her thoughts were of darker things still. "The Trolls have withdrawn from the Keep and massed at the gates, taking up watch. It looks like they are expecting trouble, but intend to hold their place for as long as they can."

Shadea a'Ru nodded slowly, staring back at Iridia, thinking that nothing was easy, not even now. "We'll let them be for the moment. After I've been named Ard Rhys, I'll deal with them myself."

"Kermadec isn't with them. I don't know where he's gone. Tagwen has disappeared, as well. We might want to think about finding them." Iridia stepped close, her voice dropping to a near whisper. "We might want to think about another possible hindrance to our plans. Her brother, the one who lives below the Rainbow Lake—if he finds out what has happened, he might decide to do something about it. He has her magic and strong ties with the Rovers. He could cause a lot of trouble for us."

Sen Dunsidan had said the same thing. For a moment Shadea wondered at the coincidence, then dismissed it as nothing more. It was a logical consideration for all of them, one she might have been too quick to dismiss before.

"Do we know where her brother can be found?"

Iridia nodded. "A way station called Patch Run."

Shadea took her arm and smiled. "Let's send someone to tell him ourselves."

SEVEN

Penderrin Ohmsford came out of his crouch in the forward compartment of the cat-28's starboard pontoon, rocked back on his heels, and surveyed his handiwork. He had just finished resplicing both sets of radian draws off the single mast to stacked sets of parse tubes mounted fore and aft on both pontoons, giving the small sailing vessel almost double the power of anything flying in her class. The stacked tubes were his own design, conceived late one night as he lay thinking about what he might do to make her faster. He was always thinking about ways to improve her, his passion for airships and flying easily a match for that of the other members of his family, and when your uncle was Redden Alt Mer, that was saying something.

He had built the cat two years earlier at the beginning of his apprenticeship with his father. It was the first major project he had undertaken on his own. It was a rite of passage experience that demonstrated he should no longer be considered a boy, although he was still only in his teens. The vessel he chose to construct was a twenty-eight-foot catamaran—thus the cat-28 designation. It was a racing vessel, not a fighting ship, its decking mostly sloped and its gunwales low, its pontoons only slightly curved and lacking rams, and its sleeping compartment set into the decking right below the pilot box and barely large enough to lie down in. Its single mast was riggod with a mainsail and a jib, and all of its spares and gear were stored in holds in the pontoons.

It was a fast ship to begin with, but Penderrin was not the sort to take something as it was and leave it alone. Even with his parents' larger airships, the ones outfitted for long-term expeditions and rough weather, he was always experimenting with ways to make them better. He had been living around airships all his life, and working on them had become second nature. He wished his parents would let him fly more, would give him a chance at the larger ships, especially *Swift Sure*, their favorite, the one they were on now, somewhere out in the Wolfsktaag Mountains. But like all parents, they seemed convinced that it was better to bring him along slowly and to make certain he was old enough before he was allowed to do the things he had learned to do years earlier.

His full name was Penderrin, but everyone called him Pen except for his mother, who insisted on calling him Penderrin because it was the name she had chosen and she liked the sound of it. And his uncle, who called him Little Red, for reasons that had something to do with his mother and their early years together. Pen's long hair was a dusky auburn, a mix between his mother's flaming red tresses and his father's dark ones, so he supposed Little Red was an apt nickname, even if it irritated him to be called something his mother was once called. But he liked his uncle, who his mother had told him to call Big Red, so he was willing to put up with a few things he wouldn't have tolerated otherwise. At least his uncle let him do some of the things his parents wouldn't, including piloting the big airships that flew the Blue Divide. His blue eyes brightened. In another couple of months, he would get a chance to visit Big Red in the coastal town of March Brume and fly with him again. It was something he was looking forward to.

He stood up and surveyed the cat-28 one more time, making sure everything was as it should be. For now, he would have to satisfy himself with flying his single-mast, small to be sure, but quick and sturdy, and best of all, *his*. He would test her out in the morning to make certain the splicings were done properly and the controls for feeding the ambient light down through the radian draws operating as they should. It was tricky business, splitting off draws to channel energy to more than one parse tube, but he had mastered the art sufficiently that he felt confident this latest effort would work.

He glanced at the late afternoon sky, noting that the heavy mist lying over the Rainbow Lake had thickened with the approach of storm clouds out of the north. The sun had disappeared entirely, not even visible as the hazy ball it had been earlier. Nightfall was approaching and the light was failing fast. There would be no sunset this day. If the storm didn't blow through that night, visibility would be down to nothing by morning and he would have to find something to do besides test out his splicing.

"Rat droppings," he muttered. He didn't like waiting for anything.

He finished putting his tools back into their box and jumped down off the cat-28. It was in dry dock, tethered close to the ground and out of the water until he was ready to take her out for her test run. If a storm was coming, he had to make ready for it, although the cat was secure enough and *Steady Right*, the other big expedition airship, was anchored in a sheltered part of the cove. With his parents gone east, he was responsible for taking care of the airships and equipment until they returned, which wasn't likely to happen for at least another two months. It was all familiar territory to him, though. He had looked after things since he was twelve, and he knew what was needed in almost any situation. What he missed when his parents were away was being out there with them. It reminded him that they still thought of him as a boy.

He carried the toolbox into the work shed and shut and

barred the double doors. He was average in size and appearance, neither big nor small, his most striking feature his long auburn hair, which he kept tied back with brightly colored scarves in the Rover fashion. But the commonness of his physical makeup hid an extraordinary determination and an insatiable curiosity. Pen Ohmsford made it a point to find out about things that others simply accepted or ignored and then to learn everything he could and not forget it. Knowledge was power in any world, whether you were fifteen or fifty. The more he knew, the more he could accomplish, and Pen was heavily committed to accomplishing something important.

In his family, you almost had to be—especially if you didn't have the wishsong to fall back on.

He regretted its absence sometimes, but his regret was always momentary. After all, his mother didn't have any magic either; she was beautiful and talented enough that it probably didn't matter. His father rarely used his magic, though he had been born with it and been forced to rely on it extensively before Pen was born.

But his aunt? Well, his aunt, of course, was the Ard Rhys, Grianne Ohmsford, whose use of magic was legendary and who had used it almost every day of her life since the time she had become the Ilse Witch. She was so closely defined by her magic that the two were virtually inseparable.

He knew the stories. All of them. His parents weren't the sort to try to hide secrets about themselves or anyone else in the family, so they talked to him freely about his aunt. He knew what she had been and why. He understood the anger and antipathy her name invoked in many quarters. His uncle Redden would barely give her the time of day, although he had grudgingly admitted once to Pen that if not for her, the remnants of the crew of the *Jerle Shannara*, including himself and Pen's parents, would never have returned alive. His parents were more charitable, if cautious. His father, in particular, clearly loved his sister and thought her misunderstood. But they had chosen different paths in life, and he rarely saw her.

Pen had seen her only twice, most recently when she had come on his birthday to visit the family. Cool and aloof, she had nevertheless taken time to fly with him aboard her airship and talk about his life at Patch Run. She had made a point of asking if he sensed any growth of the wishsong's magic inside his body, but had not seemed disappointed when he told her he didn't. Her own magic was never in evidence. Other people talked about it, but not her. She seemed to regard it as a condition that was best left undiscussed. Pen had respected her wishes, and even now he did not think it was a subject he would talk to her about, ever, unless she brought it up first.

Still, magic's presence marked the history of the Ohmsford family, all the way back to the time of Wil Ohmsford, so it was hard to ignore, whether you had the use of it or not. Pen knew that it tended to skip whole generations of Ohmsfords, so it was not as if he was the first not to possess it. His father said it was entirely possible that it was thinning out in the bloodline with the passage of the years and the increase in the number of generations of Ohmsfords who had inherited it. It might be that it was fading away altogether. His mother said it didn't matter, that there were more important attributes to possess than the use of magic. Pen, she insisted, was the better for not having to deal with its demands and was exactly who he was meant to be.

Lots of talk and reasoning had been given over to the subject, and all of it was meant to make Pen feel better, which mostly he did. He wasn't the sort to worry about what he didn't have.

Except that he didn't have his parents' blessing to go with them on their expeditions yet, and he was getting impatient at being left home in the manner of the family dog.

He walked down to the cove and did a quick check of *Steady Right*, tightening the anchor ropes and cinch lines so that if a blow did materialize, nothing would be lost. He glanced out over the Rainbow Lake when he was finished, its vast expanse stretching away until it disappeared into a haze of clouds and twilight, its colors drained away by the approach of heavy weather. On clear days, those fabled rainbows were always visible, a trick of mist and light. On clear days, he could see through those rainbows all the way to the Runne Mountains. Such days gave him the measure of his freedom. He was allowed the run of the lake, his own private backyard, vast and wonderful, but forbidden to go beyond. His invisible tether stretched to its far shores and not a single inch farther.

He wondered sometimes if he would have been given more freedom if he had been born with the wishsong, but he supposed not. His parents weren't likely to think him any better able to look after himself because he had the use of magic. If anything, they might be even stricter. It was all in the way they saw him. He would be old enough to do the things he couldn't do now when they decided he was old enough and not before.

But then, how old had his father been when he had sailed aboard the *Jerle Shannara*? How old, when he had crossed the Blue Divide to the continent of Parkasia? Not much older than Pen, and his adoptive parents, Coran and Liria Leah, had given him permission to go. Admittedly, the circumstances compelling their agreement had been unusual, but the principle regarding a boy's age and maturity was the same.

Well, that was then and this was now. He knew he couldn't compare the two. Bek Ohmsford had possessed the magic of the wishsong, and without it he probably wouldn't have survived the journey. It made Pen want to know how *that* felt. He would have liked to have the use of the wishsong for maybe a day or two, just to see what it was like. He wondered how it would feel to do the things that his father and aunt could do. Had done. He was curious in spite of himself, a natural reaction to the way things could have been versus the way they were. He just thought it would be interesting to try it out in some way, to put it to some small use. Magic had its attractions, like it or not.

His father talked about it as if possessing it wasn't all that wonderful, as if it was something of a burden. Easy for his father to say. Easy for anyone who had the use of it to say to someone who didn't.

Of course, Pen had his own gift, the one that seemed to have come out of nowhere after he was born, the one that allowed him to connect with living things in a way no one else could. Except for humans—he couldn't do it with them. But with plants and animals, he could. He could always tell what they were feeling or thinking. He could empathize with them. He didn't even have to work at it. He could just pay attention to what was going on around him and know things others couldn't.

He could communicate with them, too. Not speak their language exactly, but read and interpret their sounds and movements and respond in a similar way. He could make them understand the connection they shared, even if he clearly wasn't of their species.

He supposed that could be considered a form of magic, but he wasn't sure he wanted to designate it as such. It wasn't very useful. It was all well and good to know from gulls that a storm front was building in the west or from ground squirrels that a nut source was dwindling or from a beech tree that the soil that fed its roots was losing its nutrients. It could be interesting to tell a deer just by the way you held yourself that you meant no harm. But he hadn't found much point in all that. His parents knew about it, and they told him that it was special and might turn out to be important one day, but he couldn't see how.

His uncle Redden wanted him to read the seas when they went fishing, when they flew out over the Blue Divide. Big Red wanted to know what the gulls and dolphins were seeing that might tell him where to steer. Pen was glad to oblige, but it made him feel a bit like a hunting dog.

He grinned in spite of himself. There was that image again. A dog. The family dog, a hunting dog. Maybe in his next life, that was what he would be. He didn't know if he liked the idea or not, but it was amusing to think about.

The wind was whipping across the lake, snapping the line of pennants attached atop the trees bracketing the cove entrance to measure velocity, a clear indication that a storm was indeed approaching. He was just turning away to go inside when he caught sight of something far out on the water. It was nothing more than a spot, but it had appeared all at once, materializing out of the mist. He stopped where he was and stared at it, trying to decide if it was a boat. It took him several minutes to confirm that it was. Not much of a boat, however. Something like a skiff or a punt, little and prone to capsizing.

Why would anyone be out in a boat like that in such weather?

He waited for the boat to come closer and tried to decide if it was headed for Patch Run. It soon became apparent it was. It skipped and slewed on the roughening waters, a cork adrift, propelled by a single sail and a captain who clearly did not know a whole lot about sailing in good weather, let alone bad. Pen shook his head in a mix of wonder and admiration. Whoever was in that boat wasn't lacking in courage, although good sense might be in short supply.

The little boat—it was a skiff, Pen determined—whipped off the lake and into the cove, its single occupant hunched at the tiller. He was a Dwarf, gray-bearded and sturdy in build, cloaked against the wind and cold, working the lines of the sail as if trying to figure out what to do to get his craft ashore. Pen walked down to the edge of the water by the docks, waited until his visitor was close enough, then threw him a line. The Dwarf grasped it as a drowning man might, and Pen pulled him into the pilings and tied him off.

"Many thanks!" the Dwarf gasped, breathing heavily as he took Pen's hand and hauled himself out of the skiff and onto the dock. "I'm all worn out!"

"I expect so," Pen replied, looking him over critically. "Crossing the lake in this weather couldn't have been easy."

"It didn't start out like this. It was sunny and bright when I set off this morning." The Dwarf straightened his rumpled, drenched clothing and rubbed his hands briskly. "I didn't realize this storm was coming up."

The boy smiled. "If you don't mind my saying so, only a crazy man would sail a ratty old skiff like this one in *any* weather."

"Or a desperate one. Is this Patch Run? Are you an Ohmsford?"

Pen nodded. "I'm Pen. My parents are Bek and Rue. Are you looking for them?"

The Dwarf nodded and stuck out his hand. "Tagwen, personal assistant to your aunt, the Ard Rhys. We've never met, but I know something about you from her. She says you're a smart boy and a first-rate sailor. I could have used you in coming here."

Pen shook the Dwarf's hand. "My aunt sent you?"

"Not exactly. I've come on my own." He glanced past Pen toward the house and outbuildings. "Not to be rude, but I need to talk to your parents right away. I don't have much time to waste. I think I was followed. Can you take me up to them?"

"They're not here," Pen said. "They're off on an expedition in the Wolfsktaag and won't be back for weeks. Is there something I can do to help? How about some hot cider?"

"They're not here?" Tagwen repeated. He seemed dismayed. "Could you find them, if you had to? Could you fly me to where they are? I didn't expect this, I really didn't. I should have thought it through better, but all I knew was to get here as quickly as I could."

He glanced over his shoulder, whether at the lake and the approaching storm Pen couldn't tell. "I don't think I can find my parents while they're in the Wolfsktaag," the boy said. "I've never even been there. Anyway, I can't leave home."

"I've never been there, either," Tagwen allowed, "and I'm a Dwarf. I was born and raised in Culhaven, and other than coming to Paranor to serve the Ard Rhys, I've never really been much of anywhere."

Pen grinned in spite of himself. He liked the strange little man. "How on earth did you find your way here, then? How did you manage to sail that skiff all this way from the north shore? If you get out in the middle of Rainbow Lake on days like this, you can't see anything but mist in all directions."

Tagwen reached into his pocket, fished around, and pulled out a small metal cylinder. "Compass," he advised. "I learned to read it at Paranor while exploring the forest that surrounds the Keep. It was all I had to rely on, coming down through the Dragon's Teeth and the Borderlands. I don't like flying, so I decided to come on horseback. When I got to the lake, I had to find a boat. I bought this one, but I don't think I chose very well. Listen, Pen, I'm sorry to be so insistent about this, but are you sure you can't find your parents?"

He looked so distressed that Pen wanted to say he could, but he knew his parents used the wishsong to hide their presence in dangerous places like the Wolfsktaag, the better to keep themselves and their passengers safe. Even if he knew where to begin to look, he doubted that he could locate them while they were using magic.

"What is this all about, anyway?" he asked, still unsure what the Dwarf wanted. "Why is all this so urgent?"

Tagwen drew a deep breath and exhaled so vehemently that Pen took a step back. "She's disappeared!" the Dwarf exclaimed. "Your aunt, three nights ago. Something happened to her, and I don't think it's something good. It hasn't been safe for her at Paranor for some time; I warned her about this over and over. Then she went into the Skull Kingdom with Kermadec to investigate some disturbance there, and when she came back, there was supposed to be a meeting with the Prime Minister—another snake in the grass—but sometime during the night, she just vanished, and now I don't know what to do!"

Pen stared at him. He didn't know who Kermadec or the Prime Minister were, but he could follow enough of what the Dwarf said to know that his aunt was in trouble. "How could she disappear from her own room?" he asked. "Doesn't she have guards? She told me she did. Rock Trolls, she said. Big ones."

"They're all big." Tagwen sighed. "I don't know how she disappeared; she just did. I thought that maybe your parents could help find her since I've done everything I can think to do. Perhaps your father could use his magic to track her, to discover where she's gone. Or been taken."

Pen thought about it. His father could do that; he had done it before, though only once when Pen was with him, when their family dog disappeared in the Duln. His father probably could track Grianne, although only if she left a trail and hadn't just gone up in a puff of smoke or something. Where the Ard Rhys was concerned, anything was possible.

Tagwen rubbed his beard impatiently. "Is there anything you can do to help me or must I go alone to find them?"

"You can't find them on your own!" Pen exclaimed. "You wouldn't have one chance in a thousand! You barely managed to sail across Rainbow Lake in that skiff!"

Tagwen drew himself up. "The point is, I have to do something besides sit around hoping the Ard Rhys will show up again. Because I don't think she will. I've pretty much reconciled myself to it."

"All right, but maybe there's another way, something else we can do." Pen shrugged. "We just have to think of what it is."

"Well, we'd better think of it pretty fast. I told you I don't have much time. I'm pretty sure I was followed. By Druids, I should point out, who don't want your aunt back, whether or not they're responsible for her disappearance in the first place. I expect they have decided I might be more trouble than I'm worth and would be better off 'disappeared' somewhere, as well."

He paused dramatically. "On the other hand, it is possible that they don't care about me one way or the other, but are coming down here to see about you and your parents. They know about your father's magic, just as I do. You can decide for yourself what use they might choose to make of it, should they find your parents before I do."

Pen was taken aback. He didn't even know those people, Druids with whom his family had not been involved even in the slightest. That was his aunt's world, not theirs. But it seemed that Tagwen believed the two were not as separate as Pen had believed.

He wondered what he should do. His choices were somewhat limited. He could either tell Tagwen that he was unable to help, confined to this way station by direct order of his parents, who had made it quite clear he was forbidden to go anywhere while they were away and made him promise he would remember that—or he could break his word. It might be in a good cause to chance the latter, but he didn't care for the odds of his explaining it to his parents if he was successful in helping the Dwarf find them. That's if nothing else happened on the way to doing so, which was far from certain given the distance he must travel and the dangers he was likely to encounter.

He sighed wearily. "Let me think about this. Come up to the house for a glass of hot cider, and we can talk about it."

But the Dwarf's face had gone white. "I appreciate the offer, Pen, but it comes too late. Have a look."

He pointed out across the lake. An airship was making its way toward them through the drifting curtains of mist—a big, sleek three-master, as black as midnight. Frozen by the vessel's unexpected appearance and the consequences it heralded, Pen stared. All of a sudden, he wished his parents were there.

"Whose is it?" he asked Tagwen.

"It is a Druid ship."

Pen shook his head, watching the vessel's slow, steady approach, feeling knots of doubt begin to twist sharply in his stomach. "Maybe they're just . . ."

He trailed off, unable to finish the thought.

Tagwen stepped close, a smell of dampness and wood smoke emanating from his clothing. "Tell you what. You can wait here and find out what they want if you wish, but I think I will be moving along. Maybe I won't go out the way I came in, however. Do you have a horse you can let me borrow?"

Pen turned to look at him. There was no mistaking the mix of determination and fear he saw in the Dwarf's eyes. Tagwen wasn't taking any chances. He had made up his mind about the ship and its inhabitants, and he did not intend for them to find him. Whatever Pen decided to do, the Dwarf was getting out.

The boy looked back across the lake at the airship, and in

the wake of the uneasiness that its dark and wicked look generated, his indecision faded.

"We don't have any horses," he said, taking a deep breath to steady himself. "How about a small airship and someone to sail her, instead?"

EIGHT

In that single instant, Penderrin Ohmsford's life was changed forever. Given what had happened already at Paranor, it might have been changed in any event, but likely not in the way his decision to go with Tagwen changed it. Later, he would remember thinking at the time that making the decision felt like a shifting of the world, not so much in the noisy manner of an earthquake but in the quiet way of the light deepening at sunset. He would remember thinking, as well, that he could do nothing about it because his family's safety was involved and he couldn't ignore the danger to them just to protect himself.

He took hold of Tagwen's arm and propelled him up from the landing to the dry dock where the cat-28 was tethered, telling the Dwarf to get aboard. There was no time to outfit her in the right way, to gather supplies and equipment of the sort a proper expedition required. He had her packed with spare parts, so that he could fix her if something went wrong out on the lake, but that was about it. He took just a moment to run into the shed for his toolbox, grabbing up a water container and some dried foodstuffs that he kept around to nibble on, then bolted back out the door.

He wondered for just an instant how big a mistake he was making. Then he dismissed the thought completely because he had no time or patience for it. Hesitation in circumstances

like these always led to trouble, and he thought he probably
had trouble enough with things just the way they were.

"Strap that safety line around your waist!" he called up
to Tagwen, tossing the bag of foodstuffs and the water container onto the deck. "Stuff these into one of the holds in the
pontoons!"

He worked his way swiftly from one tethering line to the
next, loosening the knots from the securing pins and tossing
the rope ends back onto the cat's decking. He did not look out
again at the approaching airship, but he felt the weight of its
shadow. He knew he had to get airborne and away before it
got much closer or he would not be able to gain the protective
concealment of the Highland mists and the low-slung clouds
that would hide his escape. With luck, they might not even
see him leaving, but he could not count on that.

When all the lines were unknotted save the one that secured the bow, he paused to look around the compound and
tried to think if he was forgetting anything. A bow and arrows, he thought, and he rushed back into the shed to take a
set from the weapons cupboard, along with a brace of long
knives.

Rushing out again, he climbed aboard the cat-28, finding
Tagwen, arms wrapped protectively about his knees, already
strapped in and hunkered down in the aft hold of the starboard pontoon. It looked so comical that Pen wanted to
laugh, but he resisted the impulse, instead scurrying to raise
the sails to draw down whatever ambient light this gray day
offered. There would be energy stored in the parse tubes, but
the diapson crystals were small and not designed for long-
term storage, so he could not rely on that alone to elude the
larger ship.

He found himself wondering suddenly if its occupants
would even bother coming after him. After all, they couldn't
know who he was or what he was about. They were likely just

to land and walk up to the house in the mistaken belief that
the presence of *Steady Right* indicated that his family was
still in residence. By the time they found out differently, he
would be far away.

But what if Tagwen was wrong? What if the Druids were
actually there to help in some way? Maybe those aboard the
approaching ship were not among his aunt's enemies, but her
friends. They might have come for the same reason Tagwen
had come—to seek help from his father in tracking down the
Ard Rhys. This could all be a big mistake.

He glanced at the Dwarf. Tagwen was staring out at the
lake, his eyes wide. "We're too late, Pen," he whispered.

Pen wheeled around. The big airship was right on top
of them, sliding through the entry to the cove to hover over
the water in front of the docks. It had advanced much more
quickly than Pen would have believed possible, which indicated all too clearly how powerful and fast it really was.
It might even be a match for *Swift Sure*, although he didn't
think the airship existed this side of the Blue Divide that was
that fast.

He saw her name carved into her great, curved rams, bold
and etched in gold. *Galaphile*.

"That's her airship!" Tagwen exclaimed in dismay. "Your
aunt's! They're using her own ship!"

"Get down!" Pen hissed at Tagwen. "Hide!"

The Dwarf ducked below the gunwales of the pontoon, and
Pen threw a canvas over him, concealing him from view. He
had no idea what he was going to do, but whatever it was,
there was no point in taking chances until he found out if the
Dwarf was right about who these visitors were.

There was also no point in pretending that he didn't see
them, so he turned to watch the *Galaphile*'s dark hull settle
heavily into the waters of the cove. The skies over Rainbow
Lake were darkening steadily with thunderheads and rain-

squalls. It was going to be a bad storm when it hit. If he was going to make a run for it, he was going to have to do so soon.

He watched as a long boat was lowered over the starboard pontoon. Half a dozen passengers sat hooded and cloaked within, dark figures in the late afternoon gloom. Several took up oars and began to row, pointing the boat toward the docks. Pen caught a glimpse of their lifted faces as they strained against the oars. Gnomes, swarthy and sharp-featured, yellow eyes glittering and cold.

Something about the Gnomes convinced him instantly that Tagwen was right. He couldn't say exactly why, because he had encountered Gnomes before at Patch Run and on his travels about the lake. He stepped into the pilot box, un-hooded the parse tubes stacked on both sides of the cat, and pushed the controls to the port and starboard thrusters forward just far enough to nudge the diapson crystals awake.

"Whatever happens," he whispered to Tagwen, his head lowered to hide his words, "don't let them know you're there."

"You'd better worry about yourself," came the muffled reply.

The long boat had landed, and its occupants were climbing onto the dock and walking toward the compound, spreading out in all directions right away, a maneuver clearly intended to cut off anyone trying to get around behind them. Pen was terrified by then, standing alone on the deck of the cat-28, the brace of long knives strapped about his waist and the bow and arrows at his feet pathetically inadequate for mounting any kind of a defense. He couldn't begin to fight off men like those. Funny, he thought, how quickly he had given up on the possibility that they might be friendly.

One of them separated from the others and came toward him. This man wasn't a Gnome, and he wasn't wrapped in their mottled green and brown cloaks. This man wore the dark robes of a Druid. He was a Dwarf, and as he pulled back his hood to give himself a better field of vision, Pen immediately thought him twice as dangerous as the Gnomes. He had the stocky, square build of all Dwarves, the blunt, thick hands and the heavy features. But he was tall for a Dwarf, standing well over five feet, and his face looked as if it had been chiseled from rough stone, all ridges and valleys, nothing smooth or soft. His razor-edged eyes found the boy, and Pen could feel them probing him like knives.

But Pen stood his ground. There was nothing else to do except to run, and he knew that would be a big mistake.

"Can I help you?" he called out as the other neared.

The Dwarf came right up to the cat and climbed aboard without being invited, an act that in some quarters was considered piracy. Pen waited, fighting to control his terror, catching sight of the heavy blades the Dwarf wore strapped beneath his robes.

"Going somewhere?" the Dwarf asked him bluntly, glancing around in a perfunctory manner, then back at Pen.

"Home," Pen answered. "I'm done for the day."

He thought he kept his voice from shaking, but if he hadn't, there was nothing he could do to steady it that he wasn't already doing.

"Is this the Ohmsford place?" the Dwarf asked, squaring up before him, much too close for comfort. Behind him, the Gnomes were beginning to poke around in the shed and under the canvas-sheltered stores and equipment. "Bek Ohmsford?"

Pen nodded. "He's away, gone east on an expedition. I don't expect him back for weeks."

The Dwarf studied him wordlessly for a moment, eyes searching his, measuring. Pen waited, his heart frozen in his chest, his breathing stopped. He didn't know what to do. He understood now why Tagwen had been so afraid. The Dwarf's gaze made Pen feel as if wild animals were picking him apart.

"Left you to look after things?" the Dwarf pressed.

Pen nodded again, not bothering with an answer this time.

"He must have some faith in you, boy. You don't look very old." He paused, a lengthy silence. "I'm told Ohmsford has a boy about your age. Penderrin. That wouldn't be you, would it?"

Pen grinned disarmingly. "No, but he's my friend. He's up there at the house, right now."

He pointed, and when the Dwarf turned to look, Pen shoved him so hard the Dwarf lost his balance, tumbled off the deck of the cat, and fell to the ground. Pen didn't think about it; he just did it, an act of desperation. He leapt into the pilot box and shoved the thruster levers all the way forward, unhooding the parse tubes completely. The response from the cat was instantaneous. It lurched as if it had been struck from behind, bucking from the surge of power fed into the crystals, snapping the bowline as if it were string, and careening directly toward the *Galaphile*.

Pen, braced in the pilot box and hanging on to the controls for dear life, had only an instant to respond to the danger. He pulled back on the port thrusters, swinging the cat left to sweep past the foremast of the Druid airship, coming so close that he might have reached out to touch her. Shouts and cries followed after him, then a volley of arrows and sling stones. The whang and snap of them caused him to crouch deep in the box, gasps escaping him in little rushes as arrows embedded themselves in the wood frame of his momentary shelter. The cat shot out over the waters of the cove and surged through an opening in the conifers to Rainbow Lake and the approaching storm.

What had he done?

There was no time to consider the matter and little time for much of anything else. He caught a glimpse of Tagwen flinging off the canvas covering and peering back at the flurry of activity onshore, where the Dwarf and the Gnomes were rushing for the long boat. Pen's heart was pounding so hard he could hear it inside his ears. It would take them only minutes to reach the *Galaphile*, and then they would be coming after him. As big and fast as the Druid airship was, they would quickly run him to earth.

If they caught him now . . .

He didn't bother finishing the thought. There was no time for thinking about anything but flying the cat. He gave her all the power the diapson crystals could deliver, bringing her up to a little over two hundred feet, then turning her east down the lakeshore toward the distant Highlands and the heavy mists that draped those rugged hills. Concealment could be found there, a way to lose pursuit, his best hope for finding a way to escape.

"Do you know who that was?" Tagwen gasped from his shelter, peeking frantic-eyed over the gunwales. "That was Terek Molt! He would have cut you to ribbons! Still might, Penderrin Ohmsford! Can this ship fly any faster?"

Pen didn't bother with an answer. The Highlands were still some distance away, and a quick glance over his shoulder revealed the dark rams of the *Galaphile* nosing into view out of the cove, already in pursuit. Those Gnomes were sailors; they knew what they were doing. He had hoped that they were land creatures filling in, but he should have known better. Druids wouldn't bother using anyone who wasn't good at what was needed.

"If Terek Molt is behind this, then I was right about the Ard Rhys!" Tagwen shouted, and then disappeared back down into the pontoon hold.

Pen canted the mainsail to take advantage of the storm wind howling across the water. The cat was buffeted and shaken by its force, but propelled forward, as well, riding the back of sharp, hard gusts. Rain was falling steadily, picking up strength as clouds closed about. The storm would help to hide them, but Pen didn't want to be caught out on the lake when it struck. A blow of that magnitude could knock a cat-28 right out of the skies.

He took her down to less than a hundred feet off the surface of the water, hugging the shore as he fought to regain land. They were well beyond the Duln and the mouth of the Rappahalladran, the Highlands already visible on their right, rugged and mist-shrouded under a ceiling of clouds hung so low that the horizon had disappeared.

"Penderrin!" Tagwen shouted in warning.

Pen turned and found the *Galaphile* looming out of the rain and mist, closing the distance between them far too quickly. How much time had passed since they fled from her? It didn't seem like any time at all. Pen glanced ahead, then angled the cat to starboard, heading directly off water and inland, seeking the cover of the Highlands. If he could gain the hills, he would look for a place to set down, somewhere leafy and shadowed where he couldn't be seen from the air. But if one didn't present itself immediately, he would have to keep flying. On balance, his situation seemed hopeless, his chances so poor he couldn't imagine what he had been thinking to try running in the first place. What if Terek Molt had the use of magic to track them, just like his aunt? Druids had all sorts of magic they could call upon.

Pen, on the other hand, had none at all.

Straight into the mists he flew, recklessly disregarding what might be hidden there. Cliffs and rocky outcroppings dotted the coastline, dangerous obstacles for any craft and disastrous for one as small as his. He had flown the hills repeatedly over the years, but not in such poor weather and not under such desperate circumstances. He kept his eyes locked on the movement of the clouds and mist and listened to the sound of the wind as it shifted. White curtains enveloped him, closing everything away. In seconds, he was alone in an impenetrable haze of rain and mist.

The rain increased, and he was soon soaked through. There hadn't been time to grab anything to protect himself against the weather, so he couldn't do much to ease his discomfort. A glance over his shoulder revealed no sign of the *Galaphile*, so he performed a quick compass check and turned east again, changing direction. He was hoping the Druid airship would continue to follow the course he had just abandoned. He thought about taking the cat higher to reduce the odds of colliding with the cliffs, but he couldn't chance it; the higher he rose, the thinner the mists and the greater the risk of discovery. His pursuers were too close.

He dropped his speed and edged ahead, watching cliffs appear and fade to either side through the curtain of rain and mist, angling the cat gingerly between the gaps. The intensity of the storm was increasing, buffeting his craft more heavily now and threatening its stability. He pushed the thrust levers forward again, increasing power to counter the wind. Fat raindrops hammered off the wood decking like pebbles. He had already released the stays and dropped the mainsail to the deck in a heap, otherwise the wind would rip it to shreds. He was so cold by then that he was shivering. Visibility was reduced to almost nothing. If things got any worse, he was going to have to set down.

Time slipped away on ghost steps. Watching and listening, he waited for danger signals to register. He was far enough inland that he was behind the hills that formed the coastal barrier, gaining some measure of protection from the onslaught of the storm. It was rough going even there, but he no longer feared he would be forced down.

He hunched his shoulders and took a deep breath to calm himself. He felt his pulse slow. There was still no sign of the *Galaphile*.

He was beginning to think he had gotten away altogether when abruptly the Druid airship appeared right in front of him, *Galaphile* emerging from the haze like an apparition out of the netherworld, huge and forbidding. Pen gasped in spite of himself, shocked by the suddenness of it, then swung the cat hard to starboard to come in behind and under the bigger ship, hoping against hope that no one aboard her had caught sight of him.

But someone had. The *Galaphile* immediately began to come about, then to drop rapidly, intent on crushing the cat beneath its hull, smashing it in midair, and sending its passengers tumbling into the hills below. The boy countered the maneuver with the only option left to him, slamming all the thrust levers forward at once, expending every bit of power the diapson crystals could muster, in an effort to get clear. The little craft lunged forward, surging through the mist and rain like a frightened bird, throwing Pen back against the pilot box wall.

Down came the *Galaphile*, dropping toward her like a stone. For just an instant—the cat a little too slow, the warship a little too close—Pen was certain they were not going to get clear. The cat's mast snapped as the warship hull caught its tip, and the little ship lurched and dropped beneath the weight of the larger craft. Pieces of mast and rigging collapsed all around Pen, splintering the walls of the pilot box. The boy dropped to his knees and ducked his head as debris rained down on him. The cat shuddered from the blow, but then abruptly broke free with a scraping and splintering of wood. Lifting away as the bigger ship continued to drop, it ran hard and fast under the full power of its crystals until it disappeared into the mist.

Pen rose cautiously from behind the walls of the pilot box. The shattered mast had snapped off midway up; the top half had fallen away completely, and the lower half was bent at a rakish angle across the rim of the box. Pen had to steer with the remnant of the mast practically in his face, but he was so grateful to have escaped that he scarcely noticed. He was breathing hard, and his hands were fastened on the control levers in a death grip.

"What happened?" Tagwen demanded in a strangled gasp.

"Nothing," Pen answered, refusing to look at him. His hands on the levers and his eyes on the mist kept him from shaking too badly. He swallowed hard. "Get down. Stay out of sight."

Night arrived, and the storm began to diminish. The winds died away and the rain slowed to a drizzle. Mist and clouds still masked the horizon in all directions, but the buffeting the cat had experienced earlier was gone. With darkness to help conceal them, Pen felt marginally safer. The *Galaphile* had not reappeared, and he was beginning to think that their last encounter had happened solely by chance. Otherwise, she would have found him again by then. He knew he was grasping at straws, but straws were all he had.

He told Tagwen that he could come up on deck, and after hesitating, the Dwarf did so. Pen gave him the controls to hold and dragged out an all-weather cloak from a storage bin to throw over his soaked clothes. The temperature was dropping quickly, even though the winds had died away and the rains slowed, and he needed to stay warm. He was navigating by compass readings, unable to catch more than a brief glimpse of the land below and nothing of the stars above. At least he was no longer simply running away; he was flying toward something, as well. Having fled Patch Run, his plan was to undertake a search for his parents in the Wolfsktaag Mountains as Tagwen had suggested. It wouldn't be easy, and it might not even be possible, but it was all he could think to do. If he could manage to locate them, Tagwen could explain what had brought him to Patch Run, Pen could relate what had happened since, and they could decide what to do from there. The whole business would be safely out of Pen's hands, which was the only sensible place for it to be.

Riding through the empty, misted night, cold and miserable, he found himself missing his parents in a way he would not have believed possible a day earlier. It made him realize how much of a boy he still was. He didn't like to think of himself that way, but it was hard to pretend he was all grown up when he felt the way he did. All he wanted was to find his father and mother and go home again. No more running away and hiding from terrifying Dwarf Druids and their Gnome strongmen. No more flying blind in a damaged ship through strange lands.

All of which served to remind him of how much trouble he was really in. Sooner or later he was going to have to set down to make repairs to the cat's damaged mast and then take a look around to determine how far east the storm had blown him. All that was left for him to do was to decide how long he would wait before doing so.

In the end, the decision was made for him. He must have expended more power than he thought, or perhaps had less to start with, because sometime around midnight the diapson crystals began to give out. He knew at once what was happening when the ship began to stall, slowing sharply and dipping its bow in fits and starts. Enough power remained to land, and he did so at once. With Tagwen shouting in his ear, demanding to know what was wrong, he put the cat into a slow glide and eased her downward in search of somewhere flat and open to land.

He had no idea where he was but was relieved to find patchy stretches of forest clearings bordering the recognizable expanse of Rainbow Lake only a few miles to the north, and he steered the failing cat in that direction. He took a quick look about, peering through the mist, but saw nothing of their pursuers. Maybe things were going to work out, after all.

A broad, dark stretch of ground opened ahead of him, and he took the cat toward it. He was almost on the ground when he realized it was a marsh. Angling the nose of the cat up sharply, he skipped over the bog and settled down hard at the very edge of a thick stand of trees east. The cat slammed into the ground, skidded wildly for a moment, and then bumped up against a tree trunk and stopped.

"Haven't you had any practice landing this thing!" Tagwen demanded irritably, hauling himself out of the hold into which he had tumbled.

Pen finished hooding the parse tubes and bringing the thrust levers all the way back. "Don't be so grumpy. We're lucky to be down in one piece. Smooth landings are for undamaged ships."

Tagwen huffed, then looked around. "Where are we?"

Pen shook his head, peering over the lip of the pilot box at the broken mast and damaged rigging. "Don't know."

"Well, wherever it is, I don't much care for the look of it."

"The Highlands have rough features, but they're safe enough. At least, that's what my parents say."

The Dwarf climbed back onto the deck and stood staring out at the night. "This doesn't look like the Highlands to me."

Pen glanced up at once. A quick survey of the surrounding countryside confirmed Tagwen's assessment. Instead of hills and valleys, the terrain consisted of low, flat stretches of marshy ground abutting heavy stands of forest that soon turned into a solid wall to the east. Rainbow Lake was still there, glimmering dully in the misty dark, but nothing else seemed quite right.

He looked at the black trunks of the massive trees ahead of them, many of them well over a hundred feet tall. There were no trees like those in the Highlands. A chill ran through him, and it was from more than the damp and the cold. This wasn't Leah. The storm had blown them right through the Highlands and into the country beyond—country so dangerous that his parents had forbidden him to go into it under any circumstances.

He was inside the Black Oaks.

NINE

They could do nothing about their situation that night, so they hunkered down to wait for morning. The cat couldn't fly until there was power for the diapson crystals, and there wouldn't be power for the crystals until there was light from which to draw it. Even then, the problem wasn't solved, because they needed to rig the mainsail and radian draws to absorb the ambient light into the crystals, and they couldn't do that on any kind of permanent basis without a mast. They couldn't replace the mast until it was light enough to see to go into the Black Oaks—a whole other kind of problem—to find a tree suitable for the purpose. Then they had to cut down the tree, haul it back to the airship, shape it, attach the iron clips and stays that would hold it and the rigging in place, and put it up.

Pen, sunk down in a funk that defied his best efforts to dispel it, estimated conservatively that such an operation might take as long as three days. In the meantime, they were grounded in one of the most dangerous places in the entire Southland.

Nor could they do much to ease their physical discomfort. Soaked through and chilled to the bone, they might have welcomed even a little warmth. But a fire was out of the question while the *Galaphile* was hunting them, and Pen could not use the diapson crystals to generate even the smallest amount of heat because all their stored power was exhausted. He had not had time to pack the right provisions for this experience, so the best they could do for shelter was to strip off their wet clothes, crawl into the sleeping space under the pilothouse, and wrap up in spare sails to try to stay warm.

But only one of them could do this at a time because the other needed to stay topside and keep watch. Even Tagwen saw the wisdom in that. The *Galaphile* was of obvious concern, but the creatures that lived in the Black Oaks offered a more immediate threat. Gray wolves ran in packs large enough to challenge even a moor cat. The swamps were filled with snakes and dragon beasts. There were rumors of even larger, more dangerous things, some in the Black Oaks, some out in the Mist Marsh bordering it to the northeast. While they had weapons with which to defend themselves, neither Pen nor Tagwen was particularly anxious to test them out.

Things could be worse, Pen thought darkly as they sat staring at each other and the night, but not by much and not in any way he could immediately identify.

"Is there any food?" Tagwen asked glumly.

They were sitting inside the pilot box, talking about what they would do when morning came. The sky was clearing, the first stars and a hint of moonlight visible now through the broken clouds. Pen knew it was well after midnight, the beginning of a new day.

Wordlessly, he retrieved the pack of dried stores he had snatched up on his way out of the work shed and handed it to the Dwarf. Tagwen rummaged around inside and produced some dried beef and a rather sorry-looking hunk of cheese. He split both and handed half to the boy. Pen accepted his meal wordlessly and began to eat.

What was he doing out in the middle of nowhere, completely disabled? How had he ever let this happen?

"We should get some sleep," he said wearily.

"I'll keep watch," Tagwen offered, working his knife across the cheese rind. "I'm more rested than you are, after that storm."

Pen didn't argue; he was exhausted. "All right." He yawned.

"I don't sleep much anyway," Tagwen continued. "I used to stay awake for hours sometimes while your aunt was sleeping, just sitting there with her. I was always there for her when she was sick. I liked doing that—just sitting there. It made me feel I was doing something to help her, something besides keeping her affairs organized."

"What is she like?" Pen asked suddenly.

The Dwarf looked at him. "You've spent time with her."

"Not very much. Not enough to know her well. She doesn't let you know her well. She keeps you at a distance."

"She does that even to me. I can tell you that she lives with her past more than most. She's haunted by it, Penderrin. She hates who she was and what she did as the Ilse Witch. She would do anything to take it all back and start over. I don't think anyone understands that. The Druids mostly think she hasn't changed all that much, that once you have the kind of magic she does, you don't regret anything. They think she's the same underneath, that she just masks it from them."

"I don't know what she was like before," Pen said. "But I think she is a good person now. She doesn't want to get close, but she wants to help. She tries to be kind. At least, that's how she was with me, and she didn't even know me then. What do you think has happened to her?"

Tagwen shook his head. "Whatever it is, I think it has something to do with Terek Molt and Shadea a'Ru and the rest of their little group of traitors. At first I thought it had something to do with her trip into the Northland a few days before she disappeared, but I don't think that now."

He took a few minutes to explain what he knew about Grianne Ohmsford's journey into the ruins of the Skull Kingdom with the Maturen Kermadec, then segued right into a dissertation about the cliques of Druid troublemakers who had made things so difficult for the Ard Rhys at Paranor. The boy listened attentively, thinking that there was a lot about his aunt that he didn't know, much of it because his parents never discussed it. He was seeing her in an entirely new light now, and his admiration for her was growing.

"I would have walked away from all that a long time ago," he said. "I think Kermadec is right. She should just start over."

Tagwen shrugged. "Well, it's all to do with politics and appearances, Pen. If she were free to act as she chose without consequences, I expect there would be some very surprised Druids when she was finished."

Pen was silent for a moment, contemplating the ramifications of what he had just learned. If someone had acted against his aunt, as powerful as she was, and that same someone was responsible for sending Terek Molt and those gimlet-eyed Gnomes after him, then he was in a world of trouble—much more than he had thought he was. He wondered what was at stake that would cause someone to take such drastic action. If it was Shadea a'Ru, then perhaps the lure of becoming Ard Rhys was enough. But given his aunt's dark history, he thought it more likely that it had something to do with revenge or misguided loyalties or fanatical beliefs. Those who committed atrocities always seemed to do so out of a misconceived sense of righteousness and the greater good.

"Do you think she's dead, Tagwen?" he asked impulsively.

It was a terrible thing to ask the Dwarf, who was beside himself with feelings of guilt and despair already, and Pen regretted asking the question as soon as it was out of his mouth. But boys ask those kinds of questions, and Pen was no exception.

"I don't care to think about it," the Dwarf said quietly.

Pen cringed at the sadness he heard in the other's voice. "It was a stupid question."

Tagwen nodded noncommittally. "Go to sleep, Pen," he said, nudging him with his boot. "There's nothing more to be done this night."

Pen nodded. There didn't seem to be. He wasn't at all certain how much could be done on waking, but at least a new day might grace him with a better attitude. The damp and cold had leeched all the good feelings out of him. The running and hiding had stolen his confidence. They would both come back with the advent of a new day, just as they always did with a little rest and a little time.

He rose and stepped out of the pilot box, ducked down into the sleeping compartment, and rolled himself into a square of sailcloth. He was asleep almost at once.

He dreamed that night, and his dreams were dark and frightening. He was fleeing through a forest, the trunks huge and black, whipping past him in a blur as he ran. He was running as fast as he could, but he knew it wasn't fast enough to escape what was chasing him. It was close behind him, its shadow looming over him, and if he was to look back at it, even for a moment, he would be doomed. He didn't know what was back there, only that it was something terrible. All he could do was run from it and hope that eventually he would find a way to escape.

But his fear overcame his reason, and he turned to look—just a glimpse, nothing more. The moment he did so, he knew he was doomed. A massive airship hovered right above him, dropping slowly, preparing to crush him. The airship had eyes as cold as those of a snake, razor-sharp fangs, and a long, wicked tongue that licked out at him. The ship was alive, but it was what lay inside, what he couldn't see from where he was on the ground, that really terrified him. What waited in the bowels of the airship was what would have him after the ship had crushed him into the earth. He would still be alive, but he would wish he wasn't.

With the airship so close he could feel its wood brush against his hunched back, he threw himself to one side into a deep ravine, and then he was falling, falling . . .

He woke with a start, sitting up so abruptly he bumped his head against the decking of the pilot box. Pain ratcheted through him and tears flooded his eyes. He sat holding his head for a moment, trying to clear his thoughts, to make the nightmare go away. But it lingered, stronger than before, pressing down on him, as if it were still happening in real life.

Consumed by this unreasonable, yet nevertheless unshakable fear, he crawled from the sleeping space onto the deck of the cat, breathing in the night air to clear his head. It was still dark, but the clouds had dissipated and the sky was bright with stars and moon. Sitting with his back against the wall of the pilot box, he glanced at the darkness, listened to the silence, and tried to shake off the effects of the dream.

Then he rose to look forward over the pilot box wall and saw the *Galaphile* flying directly toward him.

He felt his heart stop, and his breath caught in his throat, tightening down into a hard knot of fear. He could not quite believe what he was seeing, even though it was right in front of him and unmistakable. He caught a glimpse of Tagwen asleep inside the pilot box, oblivious to the danger. Pen wanted to reach out and wake him, but he could not make himself move. He just stood there, staring helplessly as the massive bulk of the airship grew larger and larger, bearing down on him like the airship in his dream, preparing to crush the life out of him.

And then abruptly, it changed course.

There was no reason for it. If anyone was on deck searching for them, they would have been seen. The moonlight was too clear and bright for any other result. Yet the *Galaphile* swung sharply to port and away, flying back toward the shoreline of Rainbow Lake, an act so unexpected and improbable that it left Pen open-mouthed.

"Tagwen!" he whispered harshly, groping for the other's shoulder.

The Dwarf awoke with a start, scrambling into a sitting position as he struggled to figure out what was happening. Pen steadied him with his hand, drew his attention, then pointed at the retreating airship. Tagwen stared at it, confusion and shock mirrored on his rough features.

"It was right in front of us," Pen explained, keeping his voice to a whisper. "I had a dream about it, came up on deck, and there it was! Right there! It had us, Tagwen. It couldn't have missed us, sitting out like this in the moonlight, even at night. But it did. All at once, it just turned and flew off."

He knelt next to the Dwarf, taking quick, short breaths, feeling light-headed. "What happened? Why didn't it see us?"

"Perhaps it didn't recognize you," a voice replied from behind them.

For the second time in only minutes, Pen experienced heart failure, jumping with the unexpected sound, almost falling over Tagwen, who was just as startled. Crouched in one corner of the pilot box, man and boy turned to see who had spoken.

An old man stood looking at them, an ancient so bent and gnarled that it seemed impossible he could have managed to climb aboard. He braced himself with a polished black staff that glistened like deep waters in moonlight, and his robes were so white they gleamed like the moon itself. Long gray hair and a heavy beard fell about his chest and shoulders, and his eyes had an oddly childlike twinkle to them, as if the old man had never quite grown up all the way.

Pen, recovering from the shock of finding him there, said, "Why wouldn't they recognize us?"

"Sometimes things don't look quite the way we expect them to," the old man said. "Especially at night, when shadows drape the world and mask the truth."

"We were right out in the open," Pen persisted. He stood up again, deciding there was nothing to be afraid of. He looked at the ancient's strange eyes, finding himself drawn to something reflected in them, something that reminded him of himself, though he couldn't say what. "Did you do something to make them not see us?"

The old man smiled. "Penderrin Ohmsford. I knew your father, years ago. He came looking for something, too. I helped him find what it was. Now, it seems, it is your turn."

"My turn?" Pen stared at him. "How do you know who I am? My father didn't tell you, did he? No, this was before I was born, wasn't it?"

The old man nodded, amused. "Your father was still a boy, just as you are now."

Tagwen struggled to his feet, straightening his rumpled clothes and squaring his stocky body away. "Who are you?" he asked boldly. "What are you doing out here? How do you know so much about Pen and his father?"

"So many questions," the old man said softly. "Life is full of them, and we spend it seeking their answers, first of one, then of another. It is our passion, as thinking creatures, to do so. Do you not know me, Tagwen? You are of the Dwarf people, and the Dwarf people have known me for centuries."

But it was Pen who answered, hesitating only a moment before saying, "I know who you are. The King of the Silver River. My father told me of you—how you came to him when he was traveling with my uncle, Quentin Leah, into the Eastland. You showed him a vision of my aunt, before he knew she was his sister. You gave him a phoenix stone to help protect him on his journey across the Blue Divide."

All who resided in the Four Lands knew the legend of the King of the Silver River, though not all believed it. He was said to be a Faerie creature, as old as the Word itself, come into being at the same time and made part of the world in its infancy. The last of his kind, he was caretaker of wondrous gardens hidden somewhere in the Silver River country, a place where no humans were allowed. He was seen now and then by travelers, always in different forms. Sometimes he would give aid to them when they were lost or in peril. He had done as much for several generations of Ohmsfords, going all the way back to Shea and Flick, in the time of the Druid Allanon. Others in the Four Lands might doubt his existence, but those like Bek, who had encountered him, and Pen, who had heard his father's story, did not.

"Well spoken, Penderrin," the old man said. "You are clearly your father's son. What we must determine now is if your courage is a match for his." He came forward in a sort of half shuffle, stopping at the pilot box steps. "Are you brave enough to undertake a journey to find your missing aunt and bring her safely home again?"

Pen glanced quickly at Tagwen, searching for reassurance and finding only surprise and confusion. It was what he should have expected. No one could answer such a question for him.

"She badly needs you to do this," the King of the Silver River assured him. "She is trapped in a very dangerous place, and she cannot get home again without your help. No one can save her but you, Penderrin. It is an odd set of circumstances that makes this so, but it is the way of things nevertheless."

Tagwen grunted. "This boy is the only one who can help the Ard Rhys? No one else? What about his parents? What about his father, Bek Ohmsford? He has the same magic as his sister, a very powerful magic, to assist him. Surely, he should be the one to make this journey."

The old man leaned more heavily on the black staff and

cocked his head as if seriously considering the question. His gaze was distant and just a little sad.

"Often, it is the least likely among us who is in a position to accomplish the most. It is so here. Bek Ohmsford cannot help his sister this time. Penderrin is just a boy, and it would seem impossible that a boy would be best able to save so powerful a wielder of magic as Grianne Ohmsford, Ard Rhys and Ilse Witch. Certainly those who have sent her to her prison would never think it possible. Perhaps that is why they have overlooked him. In truth, they think it is his parents they need to fear, and so seek them out, just as you do."

"I knew it!" Tagwen exclaimed angrily. "It was Shadea a'Ru and Terek Molt and the rest of them! They've done this to her!"

He was practically beside himself, and Pen felt compelled to put a cautioning hand on his shoulder, but the Dwarf barely seemed aware of him. He stamped his foot furiously. "Vipers! Treacherous snakes! Kermadec was right all along! She should have rid herself of the lot of them long ago and none of this would have happened!"

The King of the Silver River passed his hand in front of the Dwarf's eyes, causing him to sigh heavily and grow calm again. "It isn't as simple as that, Tagwen. In fact, there are others responsible, as well, others who are from different places and pursue different goals. But the most dangerous of those who would see the Ard Rhys destroyed is someone of whom the others are not even aware. That one plays the others as a master does his puppets, pulling the strings that guide their actions. Wheels within wheels, secrets yet unrecognized. The danger is far greater than it appears, and it threatens far more than the life of the Ard Rhys. Yet she is the key to restoring a balance, to making things right again. She must be returned to the Four Lands in order for everything else that is necessary to happen." He looked at Penderrin. "You alone can bring that to pass."

Pen sighed, thinking that only a day ago he was wondering how to best pass the time in Patch Run until his parents returned. He had been anxious for an adventure, eager to be with them in the Wolfsktaag, to be a part of their lives as guides of an expedition. Now he was being recruited to undertake an expedition of his own, one that appeared to be far more dangerous than theirs. How quickly things changed.

"What is it you want me to do?" he asked.

The King of the Silver River climbed the steps to the pilot box, not in a weary shuffle, but in a smooth, effortless glide. One wrinkled hand came to rest on the boy's shoulder. "You must abandon your efforts to find your parents; they cannot help you in this. If it were possible for them to do so, I would have gone to them first. I shall speak with them in any case to warn them of the danger from your enemies. But your parents' time is past, Penderrin; it is your time now. You must go in search of your aunt without them, and you must do so at once."

"Then I shall go with him," Tagwen declared bravely. "Finding the Ard Rhys is my responsibility, too."

The King of the Silver River glanced at him appraisingly, then nodded. "You will make a good and loyal companion, Tagwen," he said. His eyes shifted back to Pen. "Such companions will be needed. Find them where you will, but choose them with caution."

He leaned forward, and his thin, aged voice lowered until it was almost a whisper. "Listen carefully. A potion has been used against the Ard Rhys, a magic of great power. The potion is called liquid night. It has imprisoned your aunt in another place, one that cannot be reached by ordinary means. A talisman to negate its magic is needed. The required talisman is a darkwand. It is a conjuring stick and must be fashioned by hand from the limb of a tree called a tanequil. The tanequil is sentient; it is a living, breathing creature. It will give up a limb only if it is persuaded of the need for doing so. It must act freely. Taking the limb by force will destroy the magic that it bears. Someone must communicate with the tanequil in a language it can comprehend. Someone must explain to it why its limb is so important. Penderrin, you have the gift of magic, the talent with which you were born, to do this."

Pen was speechless. He was being told that his little magic, which he had repeatedly dismissed as being virtually useless, was suddenly his most important possession. He could hardly believe it, but the old man's words bore weight, and he could not bring himself to dismiss them out of hand.

"How will I know what to do?" he asked. Even if he wasn't sure yet whether he would go—and he most certainly wasn't—he had to know what was needed if he did. "How will I know what language to speak to it or how to shape this darkwand from its limb?"

The King of the Silver River smiled. "I cannot tell you that. No one can. But you will know, Penderrin. When it is time, you will know. You will understand what to do, and you will find a way to do it."

"Well, we have to find this tree first," Tagwen interjected, huffing doubtfully. "How do we do that? Is it far away?"

"The tanequil grows in a forest on an island deep in the Charnal Mountains. To reach it, you must pass through gardens that were once the center of an ancient city called Stridegate. Trolls and Urdas inhabit the surrounding forests and foothills. They will know the way to enter and pass through."

Pen shook his head. "I don't know if I can do this." He looked at Tagwen. "I've never even been out of the Borderlands."

"I don't know if you can, either," Tagwen replied. His bearded face was scrunched up like crumpled paper. "But I think you have to try, Pen. What else can you do? You can't abandon her."

He was right, of course, but Pen was beset with doubts. The Charnal Mountains were more dangerous than the Black Oaks, and to try to penetrate them with as little experience as he had and not even a sense of where to go seemed foolish.

The King of the Silver River sighed with what seemed deep regret. "Life offers few certainties, Penderrin. This journey is not one of them. Hear me out, for there is more to know. What I have told you is only a first step. Your journey begins with your search for the tanequil. It begins with your shaping of a darkwand. But it ends in another place altogether. The darkwand must be taken to Paranor and the chamber of the Ard Rhys. There, the talisman's magic will give you passage through the curtain of liquid night to where the Ard Rhys has been imprisoned. Only you, Penderrin, and you alone. No other may go with you. Not even Tagwen. When you find your aunt, the darkwand will give you passage back again—you, because you bear the wand, and your aunt, because the magic of the wand negates that of the liquid night."

He paused. "But remember, no other may pass. The magic's thread is slender and fragile, and it cannot be rewoven or lengthened to accommodate others. Passage over allows passage back, but there can be no deviations. There can be no exceptions."

Pen was not at all sure why the other was making such a point of this, but he thought it was in reference to something very specific, something that the old man did not want to reveal in greater detail. That was in keeping with what he knew to be true about the ways of the ancients, the Faerie creatures who were the first people. They spoke in riddles and always held something back. It was in their nature, very much as it was in the nature of the Druids, and that would never change.

What should he do?

He looked into the eyes of the old man, then at Tagwen's

rough face, and then off into the night, where possibilities were still shaping themselves and dreams still held sway. He had never been put in a position where so much depended on a decision and the decision must be made so quickly.

Then, almost without thinking about it, he put aside his objections and concerns as secondary to his aunt's needs. He stood staring down at the wooden deck of the pilot box for a moment, measuring the depth of his commitment. It all came down to the same thing, he supposed. If their positions were reversed, would his aunt do for him what he was being asked to do for her? Even without knowing her any better than he did, he was certain of the answer.

"All right," he said softly, "I'll go."

He looked up again. The King of the Silver River nodded. "And you will come back again, Penderrin. I see it in your eyes, just as I saw it more than twenty years ago in your father's."

Pen took a deep breath, thinking that what was mirrored in his eyes was probably more on the order of bewilderment. So much had happened so quickly, and he was not sure yet that he understood it all or even that he ever would. He wished he had more confidence in himself, but he supposed you got that only by testing yourself against your doubts.

"Where has my aunt been imprisoned?" he asked the old man suddenly. "Where do I have to go to find her?"

The King of the Silver River went very still then, so still that at first it seemed as if he had been turned to stone and could not speak. He took a long time to consider the boy's question, his ancient face a mask of conflicting emotions. The silence deepened and turned brittle with suspense.

The longer Pen waited for a response, the more certain he became that he would wish he hadn't asked.

He was not mistaken.

When the King of the Silver River had gone, Penderrin slept, exhausted by the day's ordeal. He woke again to sunshine and blue sky, to soft breezes blowing off the Rainbow Lake, and to birdsong and crickets. Tagwen was already hard at work, clearing away the debris from their landing. Pen joined the Dwarf in his efforts, neither of them saying much as they labored. They cut away the mast, then found a suitable tree from which to fashion a new one. It took them most of the day to shape it, then set it in place. By the time it was firmly attached to the cat, the sun had gone west and the shadows were lengthening.

They ate dinner on the deck of the airship, a patched-together meal of foodstuffs left aboard from an earlier outing, fresh water and foraged greens. Fish would have helped, but they would have had to eat it raw since neither was willing to risk a fire. They had not seen the *Galaphile* since the previous night, and they believed themselves safe from it there in the lands of the King of the Silver River, but there was no point in taking chances.

Dinner was almost finished before Pen spoke about the previous night. By then, he had spent the better part of the day thinking it through, repeating the words of the King of the Silver River in his mind, trying to make them seem real.

"Did it all happen the way I think it did, Tagwen?" he asked finally, almost afraid of what he was going to hear. "I didn't imagine it?"

"Not unless I imagined it, too," the Dwarf replied.

"Then I agreed to go find my aunt?"

"And me with you."

Pen shook his head helplessly. "What have I done? I'm not up to this. I don't even know where to make a start."

Tagwen laughed softly. "I've been giving it some thought, since I saw how dazed you were last night. One of us needed to keep a clear head. You may have the means to secure this darkwand, but I have the means to look out for us. I think I know what we need to do first."

"You do?" Pen didn't bother to hide his surprise. "What?"

The Dwarf grinned and pointed toward the setting sun. "We go west, Penderrin, to the Elven village of Emberen."

TEN

She awoke to the sound of weasel voices, raspy and sly, the words indistinguishable one from the other. The voices giggled and snickered, little taunts intended to disparage her, to make her feel vulnerable and weak. She listened to them from within layers of cotton that wrapped about her like a chrysalis. The voices hissed with laughter. She was a nameless corpse, they whispered, an empty shell from which the life had been leeched away, a body consigned to the earth's dark breast for burial.

She fought against a sudden stab of panic. She was Grianne Ohmsford, she told herself in an act of reassurance. She was alive and well. She was only dreaming. She was asleep in her bed, and she remembered . . .

She drew a sharp, frightened breath, and her certainties were gone as quickly as the voices, disappeared like smoke. *Something had happened.*

Still wrapped in cotton that filled her head and mouth, that bound up her thoughts and clogged her reason, she tried to move her arms and legs. She could do so, but only with great effort. She was terribly weak and her body was responding as if she had slept not for one night but for a hundred. She brought one hand to her breast and found she was still wearing her nightclothes, but no blankets covered her. The air smelled stale and dead, and she could not feel even the smallest trace of a breeze. Yet where she slept within the towers of

Paranor, there was always a breeze and the air smelled of the trees, fresh and green.

Where was she?

The softness of her sleeping pad and comforter were gone. She felt hard ground beneath her bare arms; she smelled the earth. Her panic returned, threatening to overwhelm her, but she forced it down. She had no patience for it and no intention of giving it power over her. She was not harmed; she was still whole. Deep breaths, one after the other, calmed and steadied her.

She opened her eyes, peeling back the layers of deep sleep into which she had sunk, squinting into hazy gray light. It was night still. She was staring at a darkened sky that domed overhead in a vast leaden canopy. Yet something was wrong. The sky was cloudless, but empty of moon and stars. Nor was the sun in evidence. The world was cast in the sullen tones of a storm's approach, shrouded in layers of silence, in hushed tones of expectation.

It must be twilight, she decided. She had slept longer than she thought. The sun was down, the moon not yet up, and the stars not yet out—that would explain the strange sky.

The weasel voices were gone, a figment of her imagination. She listened for them and heard nothing, either in her mind or in the real world. But there was no birdsong either, or buzzing of insects, or rustle of wind in the trees, or ripple of water in a stream, or any sound at all save the pounding of her heart.

It took her a while, but she finally forced herself to move, rolling to her side and then into a sitting position, wrapping her arms about her drawn-up knees to keep herself in place. Slowly, her vision sharpened from a watery haze to clarity, and the spinning that had begun when she levered herself upright faded.

She looked around. She sat in a ragged, blasted landscape, surrounded by trees that were wintry and thick with withered leaves. The trees had the look of blight about them, sickened so that they could no longer thrive. Because she was sitting on a high piece of ground overlooking several valleys and, farther out, a river, she could see that the forest extended for miles in all directions, bleak and unchanging. Farther out still, at the edges of her vision, mountains loomed stark and barren against the skyline.

Paranor was nowhere in evidence. Nor was there any sign of anything else man-made—no buildings, no bridges, no traffic on the river, not even a road. No people. No life. Seemingly, she was alone in this empty, alien world.

And yet . . .

She took a second look around, a more careful look, seeing her surroundings with a fresh eye and, to her surprise, recognizing what she saw. At first, she couldn't believe it. She was still struggling with the idea that somehow she had been transported in her sleep—drug induced, she was certain—to a strange and terrible place, all for reasons that were not yet apparent. Disoriented and confused, she had misread what was now patently clear. The land she was looking at, although now turned lifeless and empty, was the land she had gone to sleep in last night.

She was still in Callahorn, in the Four Lands.

Yet it was not the Callahorn she knew and, from what she could see of it, only a ruined shell of the Four Lands.

She sat staring off into the distance, her gaze shifting from feature to feature to make certain. She took note of the Dragon's Teeth, their jagged outline unmistakable, as familiar to her by then as her own face. And there, a glimpse of the Mermidon, south and west where the mountains broke apart. The plateau on which she sat was where the Druid's Keep had stood. North, south, east, and west, the geography was just as it had been for thousands of years.

But blasted and leeched of life, a corpse of the sort she had thought herself to be on waking.

And where was Paranor?

She could reach only one conclusion. Either she had awakened in the aftermath of the Great Wars or gone into a future in which a similar catastrophe had occurred. But that was impossible.

She checked herself carefully to make certain she was all in one piece, and having done so, managed to get to her feet. Her dizziness and the sluggish feel of waking from a deep sleep had worn off, and her strength was beginning to return. She gave it a few more minutes, still puzzling through her situation, still trying to make sense of it. She couldn't, of course. There was no way to do so without knowing both where she was and how she had gotten there.

She realized she was hungry, and she started to look for food. In her world, the one she had left behind that looked like this one but apparently wasn't, there would have been berry bushes in a clearing near a stream not far from where she stood. While Ard Rhys, she had gone there from time to time to pick the fruit, a private, secret indulgence about which only Tagwen knew.

But it was unlikely that such sweet fruit grew anywhere in this world. Her hunger would have to wait.

She started to walk through the trees, looking for water. As she walked, she listened futilely for the sounds of other life. What sort of world was she in where there were no birds? Were there any people, any creatures at all? Was it possible that she was the only living thing there? The forest was empty and dead, smelling of its own decay. The gray light was unchanging and oppressive, and the sky remained empty of sun, moon, or stars. Even of clouds. The dark, ruined world felt incomplete, as if it were only a faintly cast shadow of the real world.

She found a stream finally, but the water looked so foul she decided against drinking it. She sat down again, her back against a blighted oak, and looked off into the shadowed trees, into the distance, reasoning out what had happened. Clearly, she hadn't come on her own; someone had caused her to be transported. She could safely assume it had not been done for her benefit. Most likely, given the number of enemies she had made, it had been done to get her out of the way. Further, it had been done using magic, because there was no other explanation for how something so difficult could have been accomplished. Yet no one she knew possessed such magic. Not even she could transport people to other places.

So perhaps it had been accomplished by someone who was not of her world, but of another.

But what world would that be? Surely not *this* one.

She gave up thinking about it finally, deciding that she should walk to the edge of the bluff for a better look around. Something else must exist in the place, another creature, another life form. If she could find it, whatever it was, she might be able to determine where she was. If she could do that, she would have a better idea of how to get back to where she belonged.

The walk took her only a short time, though it left her winded and fatigued. She wasn't herself yet, and she would have to be careful how she expended her energy until she was. Thin and diaphanous, her nightclothes billowed about her as she walked. They were warm enough for the moment, but totally inadequate for the task at hand. They would deteriorate quickly. Yet where would she find anything to replace them?

When she stood again upon the heights, close to the bluff edge and still in the shadow of the lifeless trees, she began a slow scan of the countryside, searching for movement that would identify life.

She was in the middle of this search, completely absorbed in her efforts, when the Dracha appeared. Her concentration was so intense that at first she didn't even know it was there. But in its eagerness to reach her, it stepped upon some twigs and gave itself away. Even so, it was on her so quickly that she barely had time to react. At the last possible moment, she threw herself to one side as it lunged for her, leathery wings spread wide, jaws snapping. She managed to avoid the jaws, but one wing caught her a glancing blow and sent her spinning. The breath left her lungs as she slammed into a tree trunk, and the air before her eyes danced with dark spots.

A Dracha, she thought in disbelief. *It can't be. It's not possible. They don't exist anymore.*

But there it was nevertheless, wheeling about to come at her again. It was big for a Dracha, fully twenty feet long from nose to tail and wing tip to wing tip, sinuous body heavily muscled and covered with glistening scales, back ridged with spines and razor-edged plates, legs crooked and claw-tipped.

Knowing she was dead if she didn't act quickly, she righted herself against the tree trunk and screamed the magic of the wishsong at the beast. Her voice was hoarse and raw from her long sleep, the magic badly managed and scattershot at best, but it was enough. It caught up the Dracha and threw it away as if it were made of straw. The creature hissed and shrieked, enraged at what was being done to it. She saw the fury mirrored in its lidded yellow eyes. She saw it in the twist and snap of its scaly body as it tumbled away into the trees.

Then her voice gave out; she was still too weak to sustain the magic for more than a few seconds. She staggered to her feet, watching as the damaged beast hauled itself upright, dazed and battered, but still dangerous. It turned toward her, eyes glistening from the shadow of its horned brow, the sound of its breathing heavy and thick with anger. Long neck extended, it flicked its tongue out from between rows of dagger-sharp teeth. It stared at her balefully for a long moment, weighing its options. She held her ground, staring back. If she tried to run, it would be on her in seconds. All she could do was to run her bluff and hope it worked.

For a moment, she was certain it wouldn't. The Dracha was

too furious even to think of backing away. It would come for her because that was its nature. It was a dragon and dragons were relentless. It would not back away until one of them was dead.

But then it surprised her. Perhaps it decided she wasn't worth the trouble after all, that she was too dangerous, that there was easier prey. It spat venom, came toward her a few steps in menacing fashion, then turned away almost disdainfully and disappeared into the trees.

She took a deep breath to steady herself. A Dracha. There hadn't been Drachas in the world in thousands of years, not since the time of Faerie. There were dragons still, though only a few, hidden in the mountains, in deep caves and bottomless crevices, in places far beyond the reach of men. But no Drachas—no small flying dragons of that sort.

She took a long moment to consider what encountering one meant. Her thinking shifted. There were no dragons in the aftermath of the Great Wars. There were barely any humans. Was she somewhere farther back in time, before the age of humans, when only Faerie creatures existed? That would explain the presence of the Dracha and the absence of Paranor. It would explain why the geography of the world about her looked so familiar, yet was devoid of buildings like Paranor. There would have been no buildings and no people in the first age, when the world was still new, populated by Faerie creatures that required no shelter save that provided by nature.

But had the age of Faerie been so bleak? She hadn't thought so from her readings. She had not imagined it possible. That world was newly made and fresh. This world was dying.

A rustle in the branches overhead drew her attention. The sound was so slight that she almost missed it. But her encounter with the Dracha had put her on guard, and so she glanced up and caught sight of the creature. She stepped back automatically, tensing in expectation of a second attack, but what she found instead of another Dracha was some sort of monkey. It skittered through the trees on spindly limbs, flashes of its hairy, gnarled form appearing through breaks in the ragged boughs. Having been seen, it was trying frantically to escape.

Impulsively, she yelled at it. She didn't pause to think about what she was doing, merely acted on an instinctive need to stop whatever it was from getting away. She was successful. Startled by the sound of her voice, the creature lost its grip and fell, tumbling end over end through the limbs to land with an audible grunt not a dozen yards from where she stood.

It lay dazed and twitching as she walked over to it, and she glanced about as she approached in case it had friends in hiding. But no others appeared, and this one seemed barely able to draw breath after its long fall. It lay on its side, panting heavily, face upturned to the sky. She changed her mind about it as she got closer; it wasn't a monkey, after all. It was hard to say what it was. What it most resembled was a Spider Gnome, but it wasn't that, either. Whatever it was, it was easily the ugliest creature she had ever seen. It was barely four feet tall. Its body was all out of proportion, with bony protrusions and elongated limbs. Coarse black hair sprouted in thick patches from the top of its head and from its dark, leathery skin through rents in its worn pants and tunic.

It recovered and struggled up, still trying to get away from her. She grabbed it by the scruff of the neck and held it fast, holding it away from her as it tried to bite her, using teeth that were considerably sharper than her own. She shook it hard and hissed at it, and it quit trying to bite. It hung limply in her grasp for a moment, then began to chatter wildly. It spoke a language she didn't recognize, but the cadence and tonal repetition suggested it might be a derivation of the tongues with which she was familiar. She shook her head to show she didn't understand. The creature just kept talking, faster now, gesturing wildly. She answered, trying various Gnome dialects. It paused to listen, then shook its own head in reply and began to chatter again. It was so animated that it was bobbing up and down as it spoke, giving it the look of a disjointed puppet, its limbs manipulated by hidden strings.

She set it down and released it, pointing at it in warning to keep it from trying to flee again. It frowned at her and folded its arms over its chest, managing to look defiant and frightened at the same time. She tried a handful of Dwarf and Troll dialects, but it didn't seem to understand those, either. Each time, it would stop and listen to her words, then start chattering away in its own language, as if through insistence and repetition she could be made to understand.

Finally, it plopped down in the grass, arms folded over its chest, eyes turned away, mouth set in a disapproving line. She saw the knife at its waist for the first time, an odd-shaped narrow blade that curved and was serrated at the tip. She saw a small pouch attached to a belt, both decorated with beads sewn into the leather. The pockets cut into the sides of its worn pants were sculpted with thread. Whatever species it was, it was advanced beyond the Spider Gnome level. By the same token, it wasn't a member of any race she could put a name to.

She gave up on the Dwarf and Troll dialects and was about to give up on the creature, as well, thinking that it was hopeless, that she should leave it and move on, go hunt for something else. Then she decided, rather impulsively, to try speaking to it in the Elven language, even though the creature looked nothing like an Elf. But the Elves were the oldest species in the world and their language had been around the longest. The response was immediate. The creature shifted to a variation of what she was speaking at once, and she could understand him clearly.

"Stupid woman!" it snapped, the words strange-sounding in the odd dialect, but comprehensible. "Yelling at me like that. Look what you did to me! Look how far I fell! I could have broken every bone in my body!"

He rubbed his arms as if for emphasis, daring her to contradict him. She narrowed her gaze at him. "You should watch what you say to me. If I don't like what I hear, I might break every bone anyway."

He grimaced. "I could hurt you, if I wanted. You ought to be afraid of me." His odd face scrunched up, and his tongue licked out like a cat's, revealing the razor-sharp teeth. "Who are you? Are you a witch?"

She shook her head. "No, I am Ard Rhys of Paranor. I am a Druid. Where am I?"

He stared blankly at her. "What's wrong with you? Why don't you know where you are? Are you lost?" He didn't wait for an answer. "Tell me what you did to that Dracha. Magic, wasn't it? I've never seen anything like that. If you aren't a witch, you must be a sorceress or a Straken. Are you a Straken?"

There was another name she hadn't encountered outside of the Druid Histories. Strakens were powerful magic wielders out of the world of Faerie, gone for thousands of years. Like the Dracha.

"Is this the Faerie world?" she asked, beginning to think it must be.

The spindly creature stared at her, head cocked. "This is the land of the Jarka Ruus. You're inside the Dragon Line, above Pashanon. You must know that! Where is it you come from?"

"Paranor. Callahorn. The Four Lands."

She paused with each name, searching his eyes for recognition and finding none. But the words *Jarka Ruus* meant something to her. She had heard them before, though she couldn't remember where. "What are you?" she asked him "What Race do you belong to? Are you a Troll?"

"Ulk Bog," he announced proudly. He smiled, showing all

his considerable teeth. "But I don't have a home at present because I'm traveling. This country is too dangerous. Dragons everywhere, all sorts, and they like to eat my kind. Of course, I try to eat their eggs, so I guess it's fair they should try to eat me. But they're much bigger than I am, for the most part, so I have to be careful. Anyway, I don't want to stay here anymore. Where are you going?"

She didn't have the faintest idea, of course, since she didn't even know where she was. She wasn't at all sure she was going anywhere until she figured out what had happened to her. Nevertheless, she pointed west, if only to satisfy him, at the same time trying to figure out how to extract some useful information.

"Ah, Huka Flats. Good choice. Soft earth for burrows and tender rats to eat." He hitched up his belt. "Maybe I should go with you, since you don't seem to know the way. I know it. I've been everywhere."

Ulk Bogs had disappeared with the world of Faerie, as well, she was thinking. Everything suggested she had gone back in time to the beginning of things, back before Men were created. The idea was so ridiculous that she kept searching for a better answer, but nothing else suggested itself.

"Are there lots of dragons here in the Dragon Line?" she pressed. "Big ones, as well as the Drachas?"

"You *are* a stranger, aren't you?" he said. He was growing bolder again, more confident. He puffed out his narrow chest. "Of course there are big ones. Wyverns and Frost Dragons. Fire Drakes, too, though not so many of those. Some live right down here in the forests, like the Drachas. You have to watch out for them all the time. That's how I happened to be up in that—"

He stopped himself quickly, looking away into the trees. "Well, how I was, uh . . . how I was . . ."

"That Dracha I encountered was hunting you, wasn't it?" she guessed. She leaned close. "Don't lie to me, little rodent."

The Ulk Bog sneered at her. "It wasn't my fault it found you instead of me. I didn't do anything to make it come after you. I was just trying to hide in the trees, because Drachas don't climb and they can't fly close in where there are branches that might get in the way of their wings, so I . . ."

She held out her hand beseechingly and stopped him mid-sentence. She doubted he was telling the truth, but then again she wasn't sure he would recognize the truth if it bit him on the nose. There wasn't much about Ulk Bogs in the Druid Histories, but if they were all like this one, they were pretty good at shifting blame.

"Never mind," she told him. "It doesn't matter."

She cast about for help from any quarter, but there was none to be found. She was alone and stuck with this fast-talking creature unless she set him free, which she wasn't ready to do quite yet. She still might learn something from him if she gave herself a chance. Even by just letting him rattle on, she might stumble over something that would help.

"Tell me your name," she said.

He drew himself up. "Weka Dart. What's yours?"

"Grianne." She abandoned the Ard Rhys designation because it clearly meant nothing to him. "Tell me more about the Dragon Line. Have there ever been any buildings up here on this bluff? A castle, perhaps?"

He laughed. "Dragons don't need buildings! They rule this territory of the Jarka Ruus. Everything else stays away. If you want buildings, you need to go down onto the plains where the Straken live. Your kind."

My kind. She remembered suddenly that they were speaking in the Elven tongue—an ancient dialect, but Elven nevertheless, a Faerie language. The Elves were the original people, the only true Faerie Race to survive the Great Wars. There had been Elves forever in the world. If this was the past, even if she was all the way back to the time of the Word, there would be Elves.

"Tell me, Weka Dart," she said. "Are there Elves close by? Where do the Elves live?"

The look he gave her was filled with disdain. "Are you stupid? There are no Elves here! Elves are forbidden! We cast them out, back when we made this world! *Jarka Ruus ba'enthal corpa u'pahs!*"

She had no idea what he was saying, but she got the message anyway. "But there must be Elves. You are speaking in the Elven tongue."

He became enraged. "I speak Ulk Bog, *my* tongue, *my* language, and it does not sound anything at all like Elfish! I will hurt you if you say that again, whether you are Straken or not! No one can call an Ulk Bog an Elf! We are the free peoples, the world of the *ca'rel orren pu'u*! Jarka Ruus!"

For a moment she was afraid he was going to attack her; his face was twisted in fury, and his breathing had turned quick and dangerous. She could not imagine why he was reacting that way. If he knew about the Elves, this must be the Old World, and the Elves had always been a part of it, not separate from it, not until after the war when the bad Faerie creatures had been exiled to—

She went still, realization flooding through her, so dark it threatened to bury her in an avalanche of horror. No, she must be mistaken, she thought. But she remembered now the origin of the words *Jarka Ruus*. She had never heard them spoken; she had read them. They were words from the Druid Histories—Elven words, whether Weka Dart liked it or not. They meant *banished peoples*, and they had been used first in a time before the Four Lands existed, long ago in the beginning, when the war fought between good and evil Faerie creatures reached its climax.

But she had to be certain. "Ulk Bog," she said to him. "You say there are dragons. Are there giants, as well? Are there demon-spawn and goblins? Are there warlocks and witches and ogres?"

He nodded at once. "Of course."

She took a deep breath. "Are there Furies?"

He grinned at her with unsettling purpose. "Everywhere."

She was frozen by that single word. *Everywhere.* Furies. No Elves, only monsters that preyed on each other and those more helpless. The Ellcrys had shut them all away thousands of years ago in a place that no human had ever gone into.

Until now.

She exhaled slowly. She was inside the Forbidding.

ELEVEN

"What's wrong with you?" Weka Dart asked, leaning forward for a closer look, his ferret face wrinkling with something that could have been either suspicion or distaste. "Are you going to be sick? You look as if you might be thinking about it."

She barely heard him. She was stunned to the point of being unable to speak. *Inside the Forbidding!* The words roared in her ears like the howl of a high wind, blotting out every other sound and leaving her wrapped in confusion and disbelief. It was such an impossible idea that she could not bring herself to quit looking for a way to dismiss it. No one had ever been inside the Forbidding. There was no way to get inside, for that matter. The barrier was made strong enough to keep the demons and their kind inside, but it had a similar effect on those without. There was no congress between them, not even the smallest contact.

Once, five hundred years ago, the barrier had ruptured with the failing of the Ellcrys. Grianne's ancestor Wil Ohmsford had been instrumental in helping an Elven girl named Amberle, the Chosen of the tree, find the Bloodfire to create a new Ellcrys and restore the barrier. But other than that one time, there was no instance in recorded history of demons or humans crossing over from one realm into the other. There was simply no way for it to happen.

Yet happen it had, because she was inside the Forbidding,

and she could argue against it all she wanted, but it was so. If there were Furies here, there could be no mistaking it. Weka Dart was an Ulk Bog, and all the Ulk Bogs of ancient times, of Faerie, had been sent into the Forbidding along with the other creatures who were indiscriminately predatory. The things that lived inside the Forbidding were savage and raw, unable to function in a climate of civilized behavior, unable to overcome their instincts for killing. She understood the darkness that drove such creatures, for as the Ilse Witch it had driven her, as well. When the darkness took hold, becoming the hard edge of emotions best kept buried and unexamined, there was no act a creature could not justify.

"Do you want some water? I can run for some, not far. I don't like the way you look. Did that Dracha bite you? Are you poisoned?"

Weka Dart was pressed so close to her now that his sharp features were only inches from her own. She saw the warts and blemishes on his dark skin, where the hair failed to cover them. She saw the sharpness of his teeth and heard the hissing of his breath. It was like looking closely at a weasel.

"Back away from me," she said, and he did so instantly, cowering slightly at the harsh sound of her voice. "There's nothing wrong with me, Ulk Bog. I was thinking."

Thinking of how desperate her circumstances had become. No situation she could imagine was worse. Being inside the Forbidding was a death sentence. She did not know who had found the means to place her there or how she would ever get out again, but she was the Ard Rhys, even there, and she held herself together with an iron will forged in countless struggles she had survived and her enemies had not.

She took another deep breath and looked around to reassure herself that the geography of the land about her was what she remembered it to be. It hadn't changed. The Dragon's Teeth formed a barrier on three sides, allowing small glimpses of grasslands and rivers beyond, all of it familiar, while north the Streleheim stretched away in bleak, misty emptiness.

She tried to reason it through. If she was inside the Forbidding, then the Forbidding was not another place entirely; it was the same place on a different plane of existence, an alternate world and history, one that had progressed little since the time of Faerie. Her world had seen an entire civilization rise and fall in a holocaust of power gone mad. This one had failed to progress beyond the time of its creation out of Elven magic, thousands of years ago. One had seen Races created out of myth, out of a time when they were real, made new again by the changes wrought in the survivors of the Great Wars. The other had seen its denizens frozen in time, until the myth was reality born of nightmare.

No wonder Weka Dart and probably most of those who lived here spoke a variation of the Elven tongue she knew from her studies. Once, all creatures had spoken the same tongue, born of the Word's magic, given life and a chance at unity that they had tossed away.

"Have you always been the banished people?" she asked Weka Dart. "Do you keep histories of this? Does anyone?"

"Strakens and warlocks keep our histories, but they do not agree on what it is," the Ulk Bog responded. He rubbed his sharp chin and sneered. "They like to change it to suit their own purposes. Liars and cheats, all! But those like myself who are not burdened with magic know the truth. The history is the history! It is not just what anyone says! Jarka Ruus have been here a thousand, thousand years, since they chose to be rid of the Elves and their kind, to come here and be free!"

A reasonable interpretation, she thought, for creatures that did not want to see themselves as exiled, but as self-determinative. The irony was that they still referred to themselves as Jarka Ruus—the banished people. Perhaps it was in the nature of all people that they should reinvent themselves to keep their pride and dignity intact. Monsters and demon-kind had the same need for self-respect as humans.

She stopped herself in midthought, aware that she had missed something. "Are there others here like me?" she asked, thinking that since she had been sent here out of her own world, perhaps others had, as well.

"Strakens? Of course!"

"No, not Strakens. Humans."

He stared at her. "What are humans?"

"People who look like me. Smooth-skinned." She tried to figure out what else she could say. "Anyone who looks like me."

He looked uneasy. "Like you? Some, not many. Strakens and warlocks and witches can look like anything with their magic." He rubbed his hands together nervously and looked about. "Can we go? That Dracha probably has friends. It might have gone to fetch them. Drachas are smart, and even a Straken as powerful as you can't stand against a pack of them."

She stared him down. He knew something that he wasn't telling her, something important. She could see it in the shift of his eyes and hear it in his voice. But she decided to let it go for the moment. He was right about not lingering. It was too dangerous to stay anywhere for long inside a place like the Forbidding. Everything here was hunter or prey in its turn, and she could not afford to be seen as the latter.

She cast about again, trying to decide on a direction. She would have to choose one, whether it would take her any-where useful or not. She had to get moving, away from this haven for dragons. Geographically, this world was the same as her own. She could use that, if she could just think how. Something about the similarity between the two should sug-gest a solution, a place to go, a way to survive.

She would have liked to use her magic, but she couldn't think of a way in which that would be helpful. The wishsong could do many things, but it didn't allow for opening doors between worlds. Besides, she was pretty sure that if she used it for that purpose, the amount of magic required would almost certainly attract unwanted attention.

Then, abruptly, she had her answer. She should have seen it at once. If the Forbidding was a mirror of her own world, it would have an equivalent to the Hadeshorn and perhaps a gateway to the Druids. If she could raise their shades here, as she would have been able to do there, she might be able to discover what she should do. As a working idea, it had promise. Besides, since it was the only idea she had, it was worth a try.

She looked at Weka Dart. "I'm going east, below the Dragon's . . . below the mountains."

The Ulk Bog furrowed his brow and said something unintelligible, clearly unhappy.

"You don't have to come with me. I can go alone."

She hoped he would agree with her, thinking that he would be of little help in any case. But Weka Dart, still not looking at her, still frowning, shook his head. "You may need me to help you find your way, being a stranger. The land is unsafe for strangers. It doesn't get any better where you want to go. Safer west, but I suppose you have your reasons for not going there right away. Maybe later."

He looked up suddenly, eyes narrowed. "But you don't want to go east. You want to go south through the mountains. I know you call them something else, but here they are called the Dragon Line. We should go below them before we go east. Too dangerous to try to go back the way I have come."

He was so eager to have her do what he wanted that she was immediately suspicious.

"We can take one of the passes," he continued quickly. "That will put us in Pashanon. There are cities and villages. Fortresses, too. Do you know someone there? Another Straken, perhaps?"

Clearly he was hiding something, but she had already

made up her mind to go the way he was suggesting, and she decided to let it drop for now.

"Listen to me, Weka Dart," she said quietly, kneeling so that she could look him in the eye. She held him frozen in place with the force of her gaze, a prisoner to her eyes. "You are not to call me a Straken again. Is that understood?"

He nodded hurriedly, mouth twisting, gimlet eyes bright and eager. "You are in disguise?" he guessed.

She nodded. "I want my identity kept secret. If you travel with me, you must agree. You must call me Grianne."

He laughed, a rather scary sound, all rough edges and rasps. "I will do exactly as you wish, so long as you do not knock me out of any more trees!"

She straightened. Maybe this would work out, after all. Maybe she would find a way out of here. "Let's be off," she said.

Without waiting for his response, she started away.

They walked all day—or more accurately, she walked while he scurried, a sort of crablike motion that employed all four limbs and carried him from one side to the other in a wide-ranging and aimless pattern. She was astonished by his energy, which was boundless, and by his seeming unawareness of the fact that he was covering twice as much ground as was necessary for no reason. She decided, after watching him scramble about for several hours, that it must be genetic to Ulk Bogs. She knew very little about the species, having only touched on the subject in her reading of the Druid Histories, and so had little to go on. Nevertheless, in this case observation seemed enough.

The country they traveled through was both familiar and strange to her, its geographical features similar to those of her own world, but not the same. The differences were often small, ones she could not specifically identify but only sense. It was not surprising to her that the world of the Forbidding, impacted by an alternate history, would not reflect everything exactly. In her world, the topography had been altered by the destructive effects of the Great Wars. The basic landmarks were identifiably the same—the mountains, passes, bluffs, rivers, and lakes—but certain features were changed. The landscape gave her the impression that she was revisiting a familiar place, yet seeing everything in an entirely new light.

They did not encounter any other dragons. They saw huge birds flying overhead, ones that were neither Rocs nor Shrikes, and Weka Dart told her they were Harpies. She could not make out their women's faces, but could picture them in her mind— narrow and severe, sharp and cunning. Harpies were mythical in her world, thought to be nothing more than the creation of ancient storytellers. But they were among the creatures banished in the time of the creation of the Forbidding, and so only the stories remained. To see one here, real and dangerously close, made her think about all the other dangerous things that were here, as well, creatures that would hunt her for food or sport or for no reason at all. It was an unpleasant prospect.

It had the effect, however, of distracting her. Since her awakening and realization of what had happened to her, she had given little thought to the problems she had left behind; they were distant and just then beyond her control. In a sense, it was liberating. The Druid Council, fractured by its contentious members and constant scheming, was a world away, and would have to get on without her as best it could. She hadn't been able to say that in almost twenty years, and there was a certain relief in being able to do so now.

The weather inside the Forbidding never changed, earth and sky rendered gray and colorless by an absence of sunlight and a heavy, unbroken ceiling of clouds that in the distance flashed with lightning and rumbled with thunder. Sunset was little more than a deepening of the gray they had traveled through all day. Vegetation everywhere had a blighted and wintry look to it, as if sickened by the soil in which it grew. Nothing of the world suggested that living things were welcome or encouraged. Everything whispered of death.

By day's end, they had reached the southern mouth of one of the passes leading out of the mountains and were looking down from the foothills into the plains that Weka Dart called Pashanon, which in her world would be Callahorn. Burnt, stunted grasses grew in clumps over miles of hardpan earth and barren hills that stretched away from countless miles through a scattering of high, windswept plateaus.

"We need a safe place to sleep," the Ulk Bog declared in his odd, phlegmy voice, casting about for what he wanted. "Ah, there!"

He pointed to a huge chestnut set back from the bluff at the edge of a stand of trees that marched upward into the foothills like soldiers.

"We have to sleep in a tree?" she asked him doubtfully.

He gave her a wicked grin. "Try sleeping on the ground, Straken, and see what friends you make during the night."

She was not happy that he was still calling her *Straken* after she had warned him, but she supposed there was no help for it. He addressed her as he saw her, and nothing she said was likely to change that.

"Is it safer in the trees?" she asked.

"Mostly. We are less visible in the trees and the worst of the things that hunt at night don't climb. Except for vine serpents." He grinned, his teeth flashing like daggers. "But there are not so many of those this high up." He started away into the trees. "Wait here."

He was gone for some time, but when he returned, he was carrying an odd assortment of roots and berries, which he deposited at her feet triumphantly. He clearly thought that this was what she would want to eat, and she decided not to disappoint him. She thanked him, cleaned the food as best she could, and ate it, grateful for the nourishment. Afterwards, he directed her to a small stream. The water seemed clean enough to drink, and so she did.

She was aware of the light failing around her, of the darkness settling in, heavy and enfolding. The silence of the day was deepening, as well, as if what little noise she had been able to discern on her travels had gone into hiding. The look and feel of the land around her was changing from gloom to murk, the kind of darkness she understood, the kind in which predators flourished. But the darkness here had a different feel to it. Partly, it was the absence of moon and stars. Yet the smell and taste of the night air were different, too, fetid and rotting, and it carried on its breath the scents of carrion and blood. She felt a tightening in her stomach, a response of her magic to unseen dangers.

"Better get up into that tree now," Weka Dart urged, looking skittish and uneasy as he led her back from the stream, his side-to-side movements becoming quick feints.

She was aware that he hadn't eaten anything of what he had brought her, and she asked him about it. His response was a grunt of indifference. They climbed the chestnut and settled themselves in a broad cradle formed by a conjoining of branches. Any sort of rest seemed out of the question, she thought, feeling the roughness of the bark digging into her back. She glanced down at her nightgown and found it tattered and falling away. Another day of this, and she would be naked. She had to find some clothes.

"Tomorrow," he told her, on being asked what she should do. "Villages and camps ahead. Clothes can be found. But you're a Straken—can't you make clothes with magic?"

She told him no. He seemed confused by this. The hair on the nape of his neck bristled. "Magic can do anything! I've seen it myself! Are you trying to trick me?"

"Magic cannot do everything. I should know." She gave him a sharp look. "Anyway, why would I want to trick you? What reason would I have for doing so?"

His face tightened. "Everyone knows Strakens have their own reasons for doing things. They like tricking other creatures. They like to see them squirm." He was squirming himself, the fingers of his hands twisting into knots. "You'd better not try to trick me!"

She laughed in spite of herself. "You seem awfully concerned about being tricked. Why would that be, I wonder? A guilty conscience, perhaps?"

His eyes were furious. "I have a right to look out for myself! Strakens are not to be trusted!"

"I am not a Straken, Weka Dart," she said again. "I've told you that already. Pay attention to me this time. Look at me. I am not a Straken. I am an Ard Rhys. Say it."

He did so, rather reluctantly. He seemed determined that whether she admitted it or not, she was a Straken and not to be trusted, which made it odd that he had chosen to ally himself with her. Or rather, she corrected, choose her as a traveling companion. Clearly, if he felt as he did about Strakens, he would not travel with her if he could avoid it. It made her wonder what he was after.

"I should cover our tracks before the big things start to hunt," he announced suddenly, and disappeared down the trunk of the tree before she could stop him.

He was gone a long time, and when he returned he was gnawing on something he held in one hand. It was hard to tell what it might have been, but it looked as if it was the remains of a ferret or rat. All that was left were the hindquarters. There was blood on the Ulk Bog's mouth and face, and a wicked glint in his eyes. "Tasty," he said.

"You look happy enough," she observed, meeting his challenging stare. She had seen much worse than this, if he thought to shock her.

"Fresh meat," he declared. "Nothing already dead. I'm no scavenger."

He consumed what was left with relish, teeth tearing the

raw meat into bite-size shreds that he quickly gulped down. Finished, he wiped his mouth with the back of his hand, licked his fingers, and belched. "Time for sleep," he announced.

He stretched himself out on one of the limbs, looking as if sleep would come easily. "Where are your people, Weka Dart?" she asked him, too uncomfortable herself even to think of sleeping.

"Back where I came from. Still living in their burrows. They are a shortsighted, unimaginative bunch. Not like me. That's why I left. I decided there was more for me in life than burrows and roots. But not if I remained with them."

What a liar, she thought. Even the way he spoke the words gave him away. He must think she would believe anything. It made her angry. "Where is it you intend to go?" she pressed, keeping her anger carefully hidden.

He smacked his lips. "Oh, that's for me to know. I have plans for myself. I may tell you when I get to know you better."

"Won't you be missed?" She had put up with this Ulk Bog's deceptions long enough and had decided to do something about it. He was relaxed and unsuspecting. It was a good time to teach him a lesson. She began to hum softly, bringing up the magic of the wishsong and layering it about him. "Parents? Brothers and sisters?"

He shrugged, yawned. "No family. No friends, either, for that matter. Not ones I care about leaving behind. Ulk Bogs are a stupid lot, most of them. Can't see beyond their ground roots and mushrooms."

"Roots can be tender and mushrooms sweet," she ventured, the magic beginning to insinuate itself into his thinking. "You were quick enough to bring them to me. Why don't you eat them?"

He laughed foolishly, the magic taking hold. He had no defense against it. A Druid would have brushed her efforts aside effortlessly, but Weka Dart didn't even know what she was doing to him. "I could tell you were the sort that ate roots and berries. Not me. I need meat, fresh meat. Keeps me strong. Makes me dangerous!"

She had a strong hold over him now, so she began to press harder. "Not eating roots was what got you in trouble in the first place, wasn't it?" she asked, guessing at the truth, reading it in his poor attempt at lying. "What sort of fresh meat did you eat? It must have been something that was forbidden to Ulk Bogs."

"More foolishness!" he snapped defensively. "What difference did it make? They weren't even ours! They were tender, and I only ate a few! There were plenty more where those came from! But you would have thought I had eaten my own children!"

"Instead of someone else's?"

"Another tribe's offspring, useless to everyone! Weren't even missed for a long time!"

"But when they were missed? . . ."

"All my fault, not even a chance at an explanation!"

"So they drove you out."

"I left before they could. It was clear what they intended for me, and I saw no reason to endure it. Stupid burrow people! Rodents! They are food for bigger things themselves, little more than rats to dragons and ogres and such! If you don't want to be prey, you have to be predator! I told them this, I told them! What good did it do? What reward did I get? A promise of punishment if I stayed and no more babies to eat. Impossible! I had a taste for them by then. I couldn't give them up just because the others didn't feel the same way I did!"

He stopped suddenly and stared at her, wild-eyed. "Why did I tell you that? I didn't want to tell you that! Not any of it! But I did! How did that happen? What did you do to me?"

"I helped you come to terms with the truth, little man," she said softly. "I don't like liars and deceivers. I was one myself, and I know them for what they are. You were perfectly willing for me to believe that you are traveling about to see the world. But the truth is that you are running away, perhaps from other Ulk Bogs searching for you because you ate their babies. You want me to protect you, but you don't want to tell me why. All this talk about my tricking you has got to do mostly with you tricking me."

"You used magic on me! You are a Straken, just as I said!"

"I am not a Straken . . ."

But Weka Dart was having none of it. He was so incensed he didn't even try to listen to the rest of what she was going to say, leaping to his feet, hissing and spitting like a scorched cat, and baring his teeth at her as if to attack. Then down the tree trunk he skittered, still raging at her, leaping away with a final epithet and disappearing into the dark.

She waited for him to return, unable to believe that he wouldn't. Staying with her seemed too important for him to allow his pride to stand in the way. But after a while, when he failed to reappear, she gave up listening for him, deciding that she was better off without him in any case. Anything that would eat its own kind, whatever the reason, was not suitable company. If he stayed, she would have to watch him every minute, always wondering when he might turn on her. Let him go off on his own and be done with it.

But in the ensuing silence, she became aware again of how different she felt inside the Forbidding. For as much as that world resembled the one she had come from, it was not the same. Where before she had always been comfortable in the darkness, here she was uneasy. The night had a decidedly different feel. Smells, tastes, and sounds were just strange enough to bother her, to make her think that she must watch her every step. She was convinced she could make her way to that world's version of the Hadeshorn, if it existed, and attempt a summoning of the shades of the Druids. But was she ready for the things she might meet along the way? It was one thing to face down a Dracha, but another altogether to stand against a pack of Furies. She was powerful in her world, but how powerful was she in the Forbidding?

She stared out into the blackness, not at all certain she wanted to find out the answer.

TWELVE

"Concentrate," he said, his disembodied voice coming from just over her left shoulder, soft and reassuring. "Remember what you are trying to do. Slow and steady. Keep the air moving at the same speed all the time. Breathe through your mind as well as your lungs."

She thought that an odd, but accurate way of expressing what was needed, and she did her best to comply. Using her skills, she exhaled and then blew the air in a steady, concentrated stream across the clearing to the leaf that hung suspended midair twenty yards away. She watched the leaf hover like a bug, vibrating slightly in response to the gentle currents, reacting to the fingers of magic she was using to control it. A small skill, in the larger scheme of things, but one that took her farther than she had gone before. She was getting better at using the magic, at perfecting the Druidic talents he sought to teach her, but she was still not as good as either of them wanted her to be.

"Now, lift gently," Ahren Elessedil instructed, still keeping out of her line of sight, not wishing to distract her any more than was necessary. He understood the delicacy of what she was doing. He preferred that she learn the sophisticated maneuvers first. The ones that relied on power and weight would come later and more easily.

Khyber Elessedil moved the leaf higher, taking it up another two feet until it was well out of reach of anyone standing under it. It was harder keeping it aloft, the wind currents stronger at the increased height, the force of gravity working with more insistence. She felt impatient with the exercise, as she did with so many, but she was determined to succeed. It was not easy for the daughter and sister of Elven Kings to persevere, knowing it would be much easier simply to accept the path her father, and now her brother, had laid out for her. But though she was born into the royal family, she had never felt a part of court life, and she did not think that was likely to change.

A bird flew by, bright orange and black-tipped at its wings and beak. Distracted by its beauty, she lost her concentration, and the leaf fluttered to the earth and lay still.

Her uncle came up beside her and placed his hand on her shoulder. "He was beautiful, wasn't he? Such a brilliant orange."

She nodded, angry and disappointed with herself. "I'll never learn anything if I keep letting myself be distracted by beautiful birds!"

"You'll never find any joy in life if you don't." He came around and stood facing her. "Don't be so hard on yourself. This takes time. It takes practice. I didn't learn it all at once either."

Warmed by his reassurances, she smiled in spite of herself. They were remarkably alike in personality, both possessed of quiet determination and strong emotions. Their dark features and hair gave them a similar appearance as well, and of late Khyber was as tall as her uncle, having grown the past year, edging toward womanhood, toward the marriageable age her brother welcomed and she loathed. Fine for him to want to marry her off so that she would be out of his hair, but that didn't make it right for her. She loved her brother, but he was nothing like her. In fact, aside from her mother, the member of the family she was closest to was standing right in front of her.

No one wanted to hear that, of course, since her uncle was not welcome in Arborlon. He had become, over the course of the years, the member of the family that the others were ashamed to acknowledge. They would have locked him away if he had been foolish enough to try to make a life with them, but Ahren Elessedil had decided to go another way a long time ago.

He patted her shoulder and glanced at the sky through the heavy canopy of tree limbs. "Midday. Why don't we have something to eat before we continue? It is easier to concentrate when your stomach isn't rumbling."

Which hers was, she realized with embarrassment. Sometimes she could barely tolerate herself, a vessel for shortcomings and ungovernable urges that betrayed her at every turn.

She followed him back through the woods to the village, her strides matching his, thinking that food would be good and his company over a glass of ale even better. She loved talking with her uncle—just talking with him. He was so interesting; he had done so many things in his life. He was not yet forty, and he was recognized everywhere as a Druid of immense importance and power. The Ard Rhys herself considered him indispensable, and she had visited him many times over the years, although Khyber had never been fortunate enough to be present when she did. Ahren Elessedil had sailed on the *Jerle Shannara* with the Ard Rhys, her brother Bek, and a handful of others whose names were now legendary. He had been one of the fortunate ones to survive. If not for him, the Ard Rhys might have failed in her efforts to restore the Druid Council at Paranor. It was his support of Grianne Ohmsford that had cost Ahren his place at court, that had earned him rebuke and exile from first his brother and now his brother's son. He had deserved neither, in her

opinion, but she was alone in her support and was herself increasingly isolated by the male members of the Elessedil
house.

Well, it hardly mattered in her uncle's case, given the use
to which he had put his life. He had gone to Paranor with
the first of the new Druids and studied the Druidic arts with
the Ard Rhys. He was not blessed with natural talent, his sole
use of magic previously confined to the Elfstones he had retrieved on his long-ago voyage. But he was a quick study and
had an affinity for tapping into earth magic, which was at the
heart of all Druid studies. He learned quickly, becoming
strong enough to take his talent back into the Westland fifteen
years ago, to the village of Emberen, where he had devoted
his life to caring for the land and its people. He was good at
what he did, and all had benefited greatly, no matter what the
others in her family thought.

The problem, of course, was that none of them could get
past what they perceived as Ahren's betrayal of his father,
who had died at the hands of assassins dispatched by the Ard
Rhys, when she was still the Ilse Witch. They could not forgive Ahren for tricking his elder brother, who became King
afterwards, into sending Elves to serve as Druids under the
woman who had killed their father. That he would be a part of
such subterfuge, knowing as he did the truth of things, proved
to be incendiary, once it was discovered. An order of exile
was issued immediately, and all were forbidden even to speak
his name. By then, he was already gone, of course, studying
with the Ard Rhys and those he had brought to serve her, the
first of many who would come to Paranor. Even the fact that
the Ard Rhys had been transformed so utterly by the power of
the Sword of Shannara made no difference to the Elessedils.
Nothing would satisfy them, short of seeing her dead and
gone. That would change when enough time had passed and
enough new Kings had ascended the Elessedil throne, but
change of that sort was very slow.

"How much longer will you be able to stay with me?" Ahren asked her suddenly.

She laughed. "Anxious for me to be gone, now that you've seen how inept I am?"

"You have put your finger on it," he agreed. "Nevertheless, I am concerned about your brother's response to your increasingly frequent visits."

Kellen hated her visits to Emberen, but even as King he could not do much to prevent them. She had told him as much, suggesting that he had enough to worry about with the war on the Prekkendorran. He had inherited the war after their father was killed, and Kellen had made it his life's mission to see it concluded with a Free-born victory—something that at present looked none too likely. Between governing the Elves and waging his pet war, Kellen had little time for her. She knew he hated his uncle, but he ignored Ahren because it was easier than taking more direct action. Of course, Kellen didn't yet realize the nature of her visits. If he discovered what she was up to—or, more to the point, *when* he discovered it—he would put a stop to things in a heartbeat. But by then, she hoped, she would be a student at Paranor and beyond his reach. She hadn't told her uncle yet, but she thought he must suspect as much. She was not in line for the throne, since her brother had produced male heirs and the line of succession ran down the male side of the family ladder until it stopped and females were all that were left. So it shouldn't matter to the rest of her family what she did so long as she stayed out of the way.

For the moment, she was willing to accept that compromise, having little interest in Arborlon and family in any event, though there were times when her resolve was sorely tested.

"My brother is off visiting the Prekkendorran," she said, brushing Ahren's concerns aside. "He gives little thought to me. For the most part, he doesn't even know where I am. He doesn't know now, as a matter of fact."

Ahren looked at her. "Does anyone?"

"Mother."

He nodded. "Your passion for the Druidic arts, for elemental magic's secrets, can't sit well with her. She sees you married and producing grandchildren."

Khyber grunted. "She sees poorly these days. But then I don't do much to enlighten her. She would only worry, and Kellen gives her reason enough for that. Besides, she has grandchildren—my brother's sons, good, stout, warrior lads, all three. They fill her grandmotherly needs nicely."

They walked into the village and down the single road that formed its center, to Ahren's small cottage at the far end. He had built it himself and continued to work on it from time to time, telling her he found working with his hands relaxing. He kept a project in the works at all times, the better perhaps to get through the demands of his service to the Westland. At present, he was installing a new roof, a shingle-shake overlay that required hand-splitting new shingles to replace the old. It was taxing and time-consuming, which she supposed was just what he wanted.

They sat at a small outdoor table in the sunlight and ate cheese, apples, and bread washed down with cold ale from his earth cellar. Food and drink always tasted better in Emberen than at home. It had to do with the company, but also with the life of the village. In Emberen she was just Khyber to everyone she knew, not Princess or Highness or some other deferential term. Nothing was expected of her save common courtesy and decent manners. She was just like everyone else, or as much so as was possible in a world of inequities.

Her command of the Druid magic set her apart, of course, just as it did Ahren. Well, not as much so as Ahren, who was more highly skilled in its use. But the point was that the villagers regarded the use of elemental magic as a trade, a craft of great value and some mystery but, ultimately, of much good. Her uncle had never done anything to persuade them otherwise, and she intended to follow in his steps. She knew the history of magic in the Four Lands, both within and without the family. All too often, magic had caused great harm, sometimes unintentionally. In many places, it was still mistrusted and feared. But with the formation of the new Druid Council, the Ard Rhys had mandated that magic's use embody caution and healing in order for it to be sanctioned. In spite of her checkered past—or perhaps because of it— she had dedicated the Druid order to that end. Khyber had witnessed the results of that commitment in the nature of the service undertaken by Druids like her uncle, who had left Paranor and gone out into the Four Lands to work with its people. The effect of their efforts was apparent. Slowly, but surely, the use of elemental magic was being accepted everywhere.

She would undertake such a mission, as well, one day soon. She would study at Paranor and then go out into the Four Lands to apply her skills. She was determined to make something of her life beyond what the others in her family had envisioned. It was her life, after all, not theirs. She would live it the way she chose.

"I want to work with the stones again this afternoon," she announced, thinking suddenly of something else entirely and feeling a sudden heat rise to her face.

One of their lessons was in the cracking open of rocks by touch and thought applied in precise combination, a technique in which envisioning a result leads to its happening. A Druid could manage it, just as easily as tearing paper between fingers. She hadn't found the skill for it herself, but she was determined it would be hers.

"We can do that," he agreed. "So long as you swear to me

that you are not violating any promises or arousing any concerns by being here."

"Nothing out of the ordinary. I have another week before my brother returns and looks to find everything the way he left it. I will be back by then."

But not before you show me what you know about what I carry, she thought to herself. *My secret, for now, but I will reveal it to you before I leave and you will teach me to make use of it.*

Her heart pounded at the prospect. She was uncertain how her request would be received—uncertain, for that matter, of his reaction to what she had done. She had taken an enormous chance, but she had learned a long time ago that if you didn't take chances now and then in a royal family, nothing ever was permitted you that you really wanted. Mostly, her family wanted to keep her safe and compliant, and she had never wanted to be either of those.

It was surprising to her that after all these years, any of them really thought she would ever be docile. When she was little, she was her brother's worst nightmare. Kellen was older and stronger, but she was always the more daring. She learned everything first and learned it quicker. She was the better rider, her bond with horses instinctual and passionate. She was better with weapons, able to battle him to a draw when he was a head taller and she barely strong enough to wield the practice blades. When he was intent on his studies of court practices and statesmanship, she was off wandering the forests and river country that surrounded her home. At eight, she ran away and got as far as the Sarandanon before a family of wheat farmers recognized her and brought her back. At twelve, she had already flown in an airship all the way to Callahorn, stowed away in the hold until she was discovered.

And all that didn't even touch on the times she had disguised herself as an Elven Hunter to go off on dangerous forays into country so wild that if her father had been alive, she would have been locked in her rooms for a month when she was brought back.

But he wasn't alive, by then; he was dead, killed on the Prekkendorran. Her brother was King, and he was still intimidated by her. He gave her a lecture that would have scorched paint in a rainstorm before turning his mind to less troublesome concerns, but a lecture was nothing to her.

She brushed back her thick, unruly hair. Sometimes she thought she should just cut it all off and be done with it, but her mother would have reacted to that much the same way she would have reacted if Khyber had announced she was going to marry a Troll. There was no point in antagonizing her mother, who was her sole source of support and confidence.

She finished off her cheese and bread, watching her uncle surreptitiously. It was hard to know what he was thinking. His expression never really changed, the result of his Druid discipline, which taught that emotions must be contained if magic was to be successfully wielded. She wanted to tell him what she had done when he was in a good mood. But how could she know? She grimaced. She recognized what she was doing. She was procrastinating. She should just tell him. Right here. Right now.

Nevertheless, she did not. She finished her glass of ale, rose, and began to clear the table of plates and glasses. It was one of the small services she could perform on her visits, and she liked doing something for her uncle that no one else would. He lived alone, and some said he did so because he preferred it that way. He had been in love a long time ago with a seer on the *Jerle Shannara*, though he had never said as much when speaking of her. He had been only a boy himself in those days, younger even than she was now, and much more sheltered. The seer had been killed on the voyage, and

Khyber was fairly sure he had never gotten over it. She had done something important for him, something that had helped him grow into the man he was, although once again he never said exactly what that something was.

Since then, there had been only one other woman—a sorceress, who had loved him desperately. Khyber had seen them together, and it was frightening how determined the other woman was that Ahren Elessedil should be hers. But he had decided otherwise and never spoke of her now. Apparently, she was as exiled from his life as he was from Arborlon's.

"Have you ever thought about returning to Paranor?" she asked impulsively, pausing on her way into the house with the dishes.

He looked at her. "Now and then. But I think I belong here, in the Westland. Paranor is a place for study and Druid politics. Neither is for me. What are you really asking, Khyber?"

She made a face. "Nothing. I just wondered if you ever missed the company of other Druids, the ones who still remain at Paranor."

"You mean her," he said, his smile sad and ironic. He was too quick, she thought. He could read her mind. "No," he said. "That's done."

"I just think it would help if you had someone living here with you. Someone to help you. So you wouldn't be lonely."

It sounded stupid, even to her. He laughed. "Well, it wouldn't be her, in any case. She isn't the kind to help others when she has herself to worry about. Why are you so eager to see me partnered? I don't see you looking around for someone to marry."

She stalked into the house without replying, thinking that her good intentions were wasted on her uncle. He was right about her, of course, but that was beside the point. She was too young to marry, and he would soon be too old and too set in his ways. In fact, he already was, she decided. There was no room in his life for anything but his work. She didn't know why she thought that it might be otherwise. He would live alone until he died, and she might as well accept it. She would just have to do the best she could for him on her visits and hope he got by the rest of the time.

She had just returned for the rest of the dishes when she heard a shout from the other end of the village, and Elves came running out of their houses and workshops, looking skyward.

"An airship," Ahren said, getting to his feet at once.

No airships ever came to Emberen. It was too small and too isolated. There was only one road, and much of the year it was sodden and rutted and virtually impassable by wagon or cart. Khyber always came on horseback, knowing that she could be assured of getting in and out again that way. Flying vessels in that part of the world were rare. Some of the Elves who lived in the village had never even seen one.

She followed Ahren down the road and through the village toward the sound of the shouting, joining the flow of the crowd and trying to make out the ship through the heavy canopy of limbs. She had no idea where it might find a place to land in woods as heavy as those surrounding Emberen, but she supposed there must be a large enough clearing somewhere nearby. Ahren was striding ahead, gray Druid robes whipping about his ankles, and she thought from the purposeful nature of his walk that he was concerned that whoever had taken the trouble to fly an airship to Emberen might not have their best interests at heart. A rush of excitement flooded through her at the prospect of whom it might be. Maybe the routine of her studies was about to take an unexpected, but rather more interesting turn.

The crowd reached the end of the road and turned down a pathway that led into the trees. Overhead, she caught a glimpse of movement. The airship appeared momentarily and was gone again, circling the trees. It wasn't very big—a skiff at best.

She broke into a narrow clearing just as the airship started down, a slow looping motion that brought it in line with a narrow opening in the forest canopy. She could see it clearly by then, a small skiff of the sort favored by Southlanders who did their flying across the inland lakes. Even though it was coming down at a precipitous decline, she didn't think that its power had failed. Nevertheless, given the tightness of the space, the pilot was taking a dangerous risk. Whoever was flying had better be pretty good or the airship would end up in pieces in the trees.

"They're landing!" someone belatedly cried out in surprise.

As the pilot continued to maneuver toward the slot, the Elves scattered back into the trees, pointing and shouting. Khyber stood her ground, not wanting to miss the details of the landing. She had flown on airships, but never seen one landed in a space so small. She wanted to see how it was done. She wanted to see if the pilot could do it.

She got more than she bargained for. It appeared the craft would touch down before it reached her, but at the last minute it lurched drunkenly, skipped across the forest floor, and came right at her. If Ahren hadn't yanked her out of the way and thrown her down, she might have been struck by the pieces of metal that broke loose and flew wildly in all directions. The little skiff slammed into the ground, tore open huge ruts with its pontoons, and came to a halt not twenty feet from where she crouched.

Ahren released his grip on her arm and stood her back up. "You need to pay better attention, Khyber," he said quietly.

She rubbed her arm and shrugged carelessly. "Sorry, Uncle Ahren. I just wanted to watch."

The Elves began to filter out of the trees for a look at the airship's occupants, one of whom, a boy who was younger than she was, stood on the skiff's deck, surveying the damage and shaking his head. She stared. Was he the one who had been flying the skiff? This boy? Then a second head popped up from one of the storage holds in the starboard pontoon, a Dwarf who looked as if he didn't know whether to strangle the boy or embrace him.

"Is that Tagwen?" Ahren whispered in disbelief. "Shades, I think it is. What is he doing here?"

With Khyber right beside him, he hurried forward to find out.

THIRTEEN

Penderrin Ohmsford hauled himself out of the pilot box, brushed off his rumpled clothes, and surveyed the little skiff with no small sense of satisfaction. Another vessel would have broken apart on impact, coming in as fast and as hard as she had. That they were down safely at all was a miracle, but he had survived tougher landings and had never really been in doubt about the outcome.

Tagwen did not share that reaction. The Dwarf was incensed as he climbed out of the storage bin into which he had fallen, and pointed a shaking finger at the boy.

"What's the matter with you? Are you trying to kill us? I thought you said you could fly this thing! Didn't you tell me you could? Why your aunt thinks you are so good at flying escapes me! I could have done a better job myself!"

His beard was matted with leaves and twigs and dirt clots, and a rather large leaf stuck out of his hair like a feather, but he failed to notice, the full weight of his attention given over to Pen.

Pen shrugged. "We're down and we're safe, and we're walking away," he pointed out. "I think that ought to be good enough."

"Well, it isn't good enough!" Tagwen snapped.

"Well, why not?"

"Because we should be dead! This time we were lucky!

What about next time? What about the time after that? I'm supposed to be able to depend on you! I said I would come with you in search of the Ard Rhys, but I didn't say I would commit suicide!"

"I don't see why you're so angry!" Pen snapped, made angry himself by the other's irascible behavior.

"Tagwen, is that you? As I live and breathe, it is! Well met!"

The shout came from one side, drawing their attention and putting an end to their arguing. The speaker was an Elf about the same age as Pen's father, but with a more careworn face and with an even slighter build. A girl walked beside him, darker complected and more intense. Her eyes were riveted on Pen, and he had the feeling that she was making up her mind about him before she even knew who he was. Then she smiled when she saw him looking back at her, a disarming, warm grin that made him regret his hasty conclusion.

"Tagwen!" the speaker exclaimed again, reaching up to take the Dwarf's hand. "What are you doing out here? And on an airship?"

"Desperate times require desperate acts," Tagwen advised philosophically. He extended his own hand, and they shook. "I must say, flying with this boy is as desperate as I care to get." He paused, glancing over at Pen ruefully. "Although I will admit, in all fairness, that he has saved my life several times on our journey."

He reached out a hand and guided Pen to the forefront. "Penderrin Ohmsford, this is Ahren Elessedil. You might have heard your father speak of him."

"Ah, young Pen!" the Elf greeted enthusiastically, shaking his hand, as well. "I haven't seen you since you were too tiny to walk. You probably don't remember me."

"My father does indeed speak of you all the time," Pen agreed. "My mother, as well."

"They were good friends to me on our voyage west, Pen. If not for your father's help, I would not have returned." He gestured toward the girl. "This is my niece, Khyber, my brother's daughter. She visits from Arborlon."

"Hello again, Khyber." Tagwen nodded to her. "You have grown up."

"Not all that far," she replied, her eyes staying on Pen. "That was a spectacular landing," she said. "I didn't think you were going to make it down."

Tagwen went crimson again, the disapproving frown returning to his bluff features, so Pen jumped down from the decking with a mumbled thanks and quickly added, "Tagwen's right. I was lucky."

"I think it was more than that," she said. "How long have you been flying airships?"

"Enough about airships!" the Dwarf huffed, noticing for the first time the debris in his beard and brushing it clean with furious strokes. "We have other things to talk about." He lowered his voice. "Prince Ahren, can we go somewhere more private?"

Elves were gathered all around by then, come out of the trees to take a closer look at the airship and its occupants. Children were already scurrying around the pontoons and under the decking, making small excited noises amid squeals of delight. A few of the braver ones were even trying to climb aboard while their parents pulled them back.

"My cottage is just up the road, Tagwen," Ahren Elessedil said. "We can clean you up and give you something to eat and drink. Khyber makes the best mango black tea in the Westland, a secret she won't share even with me." He gave the girl a wink. "Leave the skiff. She'll be all right where she is. She's an object of curiosity, but the villagers won't harm her."

"I don't care whether they harm her or not!" Tagwen groused. "I've had more than enough of her for one day, thanks very much!"

They walked back through the village, Ahren Elessedil leading with Tagwen at his side, Pen following with Khyber. No one said very much, respecting the Dwarf's wishes that they wait until they were in private to talk. Pen was thinking that even though Tagwen had insisted the Elven Prince-turned-Druid could help them in their search for the Ard Rhys, Ahren didn't look up to it. If anything, he looked too soft and frail for the physical demands of such an endeavor. A strong wind might blow him away, the boy thought. But looks were misleading. Ahren Elessedil had survived the voyage of the *Jerle Shannara* when more than twenty others had not, and he wasn't a Druid then. Tagwen had warned Pen not to judge Ahren too quickly, that what was visible on the surface was not necessarily representative of the man inside. Pen hoped he was right.

"Your father is Bek Ohmsford?" Khyber Elessedil asked him.

He nodded. "Do you know the story from your uncle?"

"All of it. It is the most famous story of this generation. My family doesn't much care for it because they hold your aunt responsible for my grandfather's assassination and Uncle Ahren responsible for helping her escape them and found the new Druid order at Paranor. My brother is the worst. I don't agree with any of them. That's why I'm here. I am training with my uncle to be a Druid. In secret."

"Your family doesn't know?"

She shook her head. "They think I come here only to visit, so they leave me alone. They don't know the truth."

He stepped a little closer, lowering his voice. "My parents don't know where I am. They think I am still back in Patch Run."

"What will they do when they find out you're not?"

He smiled. "Track me down. They can do it, too. But they won't find out for a while. They're off in the Anar on an expedition, guiding customers hunting and fishing. They won't get back for weeks. So they won't know."

She smiled back. "Looks like we have something in common."

They reached Ahren's cottage, where the Druid provided Pen and Tagwen with fresh clothes, a bucket of water, and cloths with which to wash up. The pair did so, and returned to find that Khyber had prepared the promised black tea and set out some cheese and bread, as well. Since neither had eaten since early morning, when they had set out from somewhere below the Mermidon, they devoured the food hungrily and drank down the entire pot of tea.

When they were finished, Tagwen rocked back in his seat, glanced across the table at Ahren to be certain he was listening, and said, "I'll tell you why we've come now, but it might not be something you want to share with Khyber." He gave her a pointed look. "No offense is meant, young lady, but the truth is you might be better off not knowing what we have to say. There is some danger involved."

The girl looked at her uncle, who shrugged. "I am not much good at keeping secrets from Khyber," he said, smiling. "In any case, she would have it out of me before the sun was down. If you don't mind, I'll let her stay to hear your story."

Tagwen nodded. "She can quit listening when she decides she doesn't want to hear any more. I'll leave it at that."

Leaning forward, arms resting on the tabletop, bearded face scrunched up so that he looked as if he was about to undertake the most difficult task of his life, he began his story. He related the events surrounding the disappearance of the Ard Rhys, the dismissal of Kermadec and his Rock Trolls, his own decision to seek help from Grianne's brother, his arrival at Patch Run and meeting with Pen, and their subsequent flight from Terek Molt and the crew of the Druid airship *Galaphile*. He ended with the unexpected appearance of the King of the Silver River, come out of nowhere to save them from Terek Molt and to tell them of what they must do.

The longer Tagwen's story went on, the more ridiculous it sounded to Pen and the more foolish he felt for coming even that far. What the King of the Silver River expected him to do—even if you accepted that it really was the King of the Silver River and not some malevolent shade—was patently impossible. For a boy with no practical magic to go alone into the Forbidding was so arrogant and pigheaded that no right-thinking person would even consider it. Pen didn't have to know the particulars of what lay behind the Faerie magic that closed away the creatures of the Forbidding to know that he had virtually no chance of surviving a journey inside. He might be able to find and secure the darkwand from the tanequil—though that was debatable, as well—but he saw no way he could reasonably expect to rescue the Ard Rhys once he had done so.

By the time Tagwen had concluded, Pen could not bring himself to look at Ahren Elessedil. He imagined himself in the other's shoes, thinking that he would dismiss this whole business in a heartbeat. The Dwarf had been so certain Ahren would help them, but looking at it now, Pen couldn't see any reason why.

He glanced over at the Druid in spite of himself and found the other staring back.

"This is a terrible responsibility you have been given, Penderrin," Ahren Elessedil said quietly. "I am surprised you found the courage to accept it."

Pen stared. It was not what he had expected the Druid to say. "I was just thinking that it might have been a good idea to think it through a little more."

"Are you worried that you acted in haste? Or that you might have been tricked in some way because it all sounds so incredible?" The Elf nodded. "I remember feeling that way more than once during my time on the *Jerle Shannara*. I don't think you can avoid such feelings. Maybe second-guessing what you choose to do in difficult situations is necessary if you are to find peace of mind. Blind acceptance of what you believe to be the dictates of fate and circumstance is dangerous."

"Do you think it really was the King of the Silver River?" Pen asked impulsively.

The Druid pursed his lips. "Your father met him years ago, on his way to Arborlon. He told me of the meeting later; he described it. Not so much how the King of the Silver River looked—that wouldn't matter anyway because he can change his appearance. He described how it happened and how it made him feel. Your experience sounds as if it was the same. Yes, Pen, I think it was him."

He glanced at Khyber, who was staring at Pen with rapt attention. "Khyber believes it was, don't you, Khyber?"

She nodded at once. "I believe it all. But what are we going to do about it, Uncle Ahren? Sorry, what are *you* going to do about it?" she corrected herself.

"I told the boy to come here," Tagwen confessed, straightening. "It's my fault we have involved you in this. But I know how you feel about the Ard Rhys, and I couldn't think of anyone else to turn to. I don't think we can do this on our own. We managed to get this far on grit and luck." He grimaced. "I can't imagine how we will get all the way into the Charnals alone."

"But we can if we have to," Pen added quickly.

Tagwen shot him a withering glance. "You have more confidence in what we can accomplish than I do, Penderrin."

Ahren Elessedil smiled ruefully. "Confidence isn't to be discouraged, Tagwen. Nor overrated, Penderrin. Remember— we seek a balance in all things."

"But you will help them, won't you?" Khyber pressed eagerly.

"Of course, I will help. The Ard Rhys has been both mentor

and friend to me; I would never abandon her or those who feel about her as I do." He paused, looking again at Tagwen. "But much of what you have told me is troublesome. I think there is still a great deal about this business that we don't know. Shadea a'Ru, Terek Molt, and those others are dangerous, but they lack sufficient power to imprison the Ard Rhys within the Forbidding. It took the magic of an entire Elven nation to create the Forbidding in the first place. Nothing passes through the barrier except when the Ellcrys fails. She doesn't do so now, so far as I know."

He glanced at Khyber for confirmation. "She was well when I departed Arborlon a week ago," she said.

"She wouldn't have declined so precipitously without our hearing about it," Ahren continued. "No, some other force is at work here—something hidden from us. We may not find out what it is until we reach the Ard Rhys, but we must be wary of it."

He paused. "A more immediate problem is that those who have worked against the Ard Rhys will be searching for Pen. They will not stop simply because he has escaped them once. Perhaps they realize that he has the potential to help her. Perhaps they are simply looking to tie up loose ends. The King of the Silver River helped you escape once, Pen, but he will not be able to help you a second time. You are beyond his reach now."

"They were searching for my father when they came to Patch Run," Pen pointed out. "Maybe they will forget about me and go after him."

The Druid shook his head. "They will keep looking. Eventually, they will find you. So we must act quickly. Do you have any idea at all where in the Charnals the tanequil can be found?"

Pen shook his head. "Only what the King of the Silver River told us—that it grows on an island beyond the ruins of a city called Stridegate and that Urdas and Trolls might help us find the way. Nothing more than that."

"I can use earth magic to try to seek it out through lines of power and air currents," the Druid mused, looking off into the woods, as if he might find the answer in the trees. "But that approach is uncertain. We need something more definite."

"What you need," Khyber declared suddenly, "are the Elf-stones, the seeking stones."

Pen knew the stories of the Elfstones, which had been given by the Druid Allanon to Shea Ohmsford to aid him in his search for the Sword of Shannara and then had been held for many years by other members of the Ohmsford family. They had been returned to the Elven people during the reign of Wren Elessedil, an Ohmsford cousin, and remained there until they disappeared with Kael Elessedil fifty years earlier. Ahren Elessedil had recovered them on the voyage of the *Jerle Shannara* and given them to his brother in exchange for help in forming the Third Druid Council.

Ahren frowned. "What do you know of the Elfstones, Khyber?"

"Enough, from listening to my father and brother. They spoke of them often, before my father's death, usually when they thought I couldn't hear. They believed the Stones could be used as a weapon against the Federation."

The Druid thought about it a moment. "Well, I won't deny that the Elfstones would help us. But I don't have possession of them or any reasonable hope of persuading your brother to lend them to me. We will have to find another way."

"Maybe not." Khyber reached in her tunic and produced a small pouch. With a determined, almost defiant look, she held it out. "I took them from their hiding place because I wanted you to teach me how to use them. I was going to tell you later, when I found the right way to do so, because I knew you would be angry with me. But I guess I can't wait any longer, so here they are. If you want to be angry, go ahead."

She thrust them at her startled uncle, who immediately said, "Khyber, you have gone too far."

Her lips compressed defiantly. "My brother refuses even to look at them since our father died. They serve no purpose being locked away. Besides, I have as much right to use them as any other member of the family. The Elfstones belong to all the Elves. The Elessedils are caretakers and nothing more. Someone has to learn to use them. Why not me?"

"Because you are not King of the Elves and do not have his permission!" Ahren snapped, balancing the pouch in his palm as if weighing the option of throwing it into the trees. "What will happen when Kellen finds out what you have done? You won't be making any more trips to Emberen!"

Khyber shrugged. "He won't find out. I replaced the Elfstones with pebbles. As I said, he never even looks at them. In any case, that's not what's important. What's important is the Ard Rhys. Uncle Ahren, we can use the Elfstones! We can find the tanequil with their magic! You know we can! Don't you want to help Pen and Tagwen?"

Ahren Elessedil flushed angrily, his composure beginning to slip. "Don't twist my words, Khyber. I know what matters. I also know a great deal more about the use of the Elfstones than you do. They are a dangerous magic. Using them has consequences you know nothing about. Ask Penderrin about his family history. Why in the world did you think I would agree to this? What makes you think you should be the one who knows how to use them?"

"Because no one else dares!" she snapped. "No one but me! If I am to be a Druid, I should know how magic works in all its forms. You teach me earth magic, and that can have consequences, as well. Aren't I careful with the earth magic? Don't you think I would be careful with the Elfstones, too? Don't you trust me? Anyway, things have changed. I have given you the Stones so that you can help Pen and Tagwen. Are you going to do so or not?"

She glared at him, and Pen found himself holding his breath in astonishment. He would never have dared to talk to the Druid that way. Whatever bond she shared with her uncle, it was much stronger than he had imagined. She wasn't afraid of him at all—not intimidated in the least. He risked a quick glance at Tagwen, who seemed equally surprised.

"If you use the Elfstones, you can discover if what the King of the Silver River told Pen is true," she continued insistently. "You can see whether or not there is even a tanequil to be found. Then we can at least know whether there is a chance of helping the Ard Rhys by looking for it."

It was hard to argue with logic like that, and Ahren Elessedil didn't even try. He gave his niece a final look of reproof, then opened the pouch and poured the contents into his hands. The Elfstones glimmered a deep blue in the midday sun, their facets mirroring the world about them in prismatic colors. There were three of them, perfectly formed, flawless, and beautiful. Pen remembered the legends. One Elfstone each for the heart, mind, and body, together forming a whole that responded to the strength of the user. Only those born of Elven blood could use them, and only if they were freely given or claimed by the user. Once, they had belonged to the Ohmsfords, and it was Wil Ohmsford's inadvisable but necessary use of them to help the Elven girl Amberle that had altered his body and passed on to his scions the magic that was dying out with Pen.

"I will use the Stones, Khyber," Ahren Elessedil said, "because you are right in believing that only by using them can we be certain that the tanequil is real. If the Elfstones reveal it to us, then we know the journey to reach it should be made. But understand something else. I spoke of consequences. By using the Stones, I risk revealing our intentions to Shadea a'Ru and her allies. The Elfstones are a powerful magic, and its release will be detected. When that happens, those we seek to escape will come looking."

"They will come anyway, Uncle Ahren," Khyber pointed out defensively. "You just said so."

Ahren nodded. "But now they will come sooner. By nightfall, in all probability. We will no longer have time to think about what we are going to do. The decision will have been made. We will have to leave Emberen—Penderrin, Tagwen, and myself in search of the tanequil, and you back to Arborlon."

Khyber Elessedil shook her head at once. "I'm going with you. I have no other choice. Uncle Ahren, please, let me finish before you say anything! You are going to take the Elfstones with you because you know you will need them again. Since I can't return home without them, I will have to go, as well. But there is another reason, an even better one. If something happens to you, neither Pen nor Tagwen can use the Stones because they aren't Elves. That leaves me, if you teach me how. I know it isn't what you want. I know you don't like the idea. But you know it's necessary. Finding and rescuing the Ard Rhys is what matters."

She paused. "I want this, Uncle Ahren. I want to help. I want to do something besides sit around in Arborlon and wait for my family to marry me off. I want my life to matter. Please. Let me come."

He studied her for a moment, then turned to Tagwen. "Is there any other Druid at Paranor that we can trust to come with us?"

Tagwen frowned and pulled absently at his beard. "If you're asking me if there is anyone I can be sure of, the answer is no. I trust some more than others, but at this point I don't know how deep the conspiracy goes. You know how things are as well as I do." He squared his shoulders. "I think we ought to take her with us. She's older than this boy and she's able. We might need her. I don't like to think about it, but something could happen to any of us. The rest have to be able to carry on."

Ahren Elessedil shook his head in dismay. "I regret agreeing to let you listen to this conversation in the first place, Khyber. This isn't something you should be involved in."

"It isn't something any of us should be involved in," she replied. "But we all are, aren't we? Let me come."

He took a long time making up his mind, and Pen was certain that he was going to say no. Pen's parents would have said no to him, had they been in a position to do so. Parents didn't want their children taking the sort of risks involved here. Parents wanted their children safe at home. He didn't think it was any different with uncles and nieces.

"All right," Ahren said finally, surprising them all. "You can come with us—mostly because I can't think of what else to do with you. Sending you home will just get you in worse trouble, and whatever trouble comes of this ought to be mine. But you must agree to do as I say, Khyber. Whatever I tell you to do on this journey, you do it. No arguments, no excuses. I know you; I know how you think. Give me your word."

She nodded eagerly. "You have it."

Ahren sighed, tightened his fingers about the Elfstones, rose from the table, and stretched out his arm. His eyes closed in concentration, but his face remained calm. "Stand back from me," he said softly. "Watch carefully what the magic shows. Remember it well."

Not certain what to expect, they backed away from him, eyes riveted on his outstretched hand. Slowly his fingers opened to the light. His concentration deepened. The seconds crawled past.

Then abruptly, light exploded from the crystals in a deep cerulean starburst, brightened until the sun itself disappeared behind the enveloping blue, then shot away into the distance in a blinding flare. It arced away through the trees and beyond, through mountains and hills and the curve of the earth itself. Some of what they saw was recognizable—the Dragon's

Teeth and the Charnals, the Mermidon and the Chard Rush, even the sweep of the Streleheim and the dismal emptiness of the Malg. Forests came and went, one a shelter for gardens that eclipsed in beauty and complexity anything they had ever seen, a profusion of flowers and silvery waterfalls painted against a shimmering backdrop of green.

When the light finally came to rest, somewhere so far away that the distance could barely be calculated, it was illuminating a strange tree. The tree was huge, larger than the black oaks of Callahorn, broad-limbed and wide-leafed. Its bark was smooth, a mottled black and gray. Its leaves were deepest green with an orange border. The tree was bathed in dappled sunlight and surrounded by a dense forest of more familiar trees—oaks, elms, hickories, maples, and the like. Beyond the trees, nothing was visible. The tree seemed incredibly old, even in the wash of the Elfstones' light, and Pen felt certain as he looked upon it that it was as old as Faerie. He could feel its intelligence, even in what was no more than a vision. He could sense its life force, slow and rhythmic as a quiet heartbeat.

The blue light held steady for a moment, then flared once and was gone, leaving the watchers staring at nothing, half-blind and stunned by the suddenness and intensity of the experience. They blinked at each other in the ensuing silence, the image of the tree and it surroundings still vivid in their minds.

Ahren Elessedil closed his fingers about the Elfstones. "Now we know," he said.

"Or think we do," Tagwen grumbled.

Pen swallowed against a sudden tightness in his throat. He was dizzy at what seeing the tree had made him feel, deep inside where instincts governed thought. "No, Tagwen, that was it," he said softly. "I could *feel* it. That was the tanequil."

Ahren Elessedil nodded. "We are settled on what we must

do." He dumped the Elfstones back into their pouch and tucked the pouch into his tunic. "Time slips away, and it doesn't favor us by doing so. Let's move quickly."

FOURTEEN

Midday at Paranor was dark and forbidding, the skies gone black with storm clouds and the air as still as death. There had been no sunlight all day, only a hazy glow at sunrise before the enveloping clouds screened even that away. Birds had long since gone to roost in sheltering havens, and the winds had died away to nothing. The world was hushed and waiting in expectation of thunder and lightning and fury.

Shadea a'Ru glanced through the open window of her chambers, her face a mirror of the weather. She should have felt triumph and satisfaction, a reward for her successes. She had dispatched Grianne Ohmsford into the Forbidding and taken her place. The Druid Council, albeit with some reluctance and after considerable debate, had named her Ard Rhys. Her cohorts controlled all the major positions on the council, and Sen Dunsidan, as Prime Minister of the Federation, had officially recognized her as head of the order. The Rock Trolls under Kermadec had been dismissed and sent home in disgrace, blamed for the disappearance of the Ard Rhys and, in more than a few corners, suspected as the cause for it, as well. Everything had worked out perfectly, exactly as she had hoped and planned.

Except for that boy.

She ran her fingers distractedly through her chopped-off blond hair, letting the short ends slip through her fingers like the loose threads of her perfect plan. It was all because of

Terek Molt, who was the most reliable of her coconspirators and the one Druid she thought she could depend upon. To let that boy—that slip of a boy—make a fool of him like that was unforgivable. It was bad enough that none of them had thought to lock up Tagwen, who they should have known would not sit idly by and do nothing after his beloved Ard Rhys disappeared, but to lose the boy, as well, was too much. She should have taken care of the matter herself, but it was impossible for her to do everything.

She stalked to the door and stood staring at it a moment, thinking to go out again to calm herself. She had walked the corridors earlier, an intimidating presence to the Druids she now commanded. They would obey her because she was Ard Rhys, but also because they were afraid of her. No one would challenge her openly while she had the backing of Molt and the others and the Ard Rhys was gone, though some would plot behind her back, just as they had plotted against Grianne Ohmsford. She could do nothing about them until they tried to act, but she could let them know she was watching and waiting to catch them out.

She walked back to the window and looked out again. The first sharp gusts of wind were rippling the tree limbs, signaling the approach of the rainstorm. She had half a mind to put all of them out into it, every last Druid—to make them hike to the Kennon Pass and back again as an exercise in deprivation and humility. Some of them might not come back, and it wouldn't make her unhappy if they didn't.

Her thoughts returned to Tagwen and the boy. They might have escaped her for the moment, she thought, but sooner or later she would find them again. The parents, as well. She had Druids and airships looking for all of them and had put out the word to all corners of the Four Lands. She had kept it simple. The ones she sought were members of Grianne Ohmsford's family and they were in danger. Help could be given them at Paranor, where their Druid protectors would keep them safe. Anyone seeing them was to send word. As incentive, she had offered a substantial reward. Most would ignore the offer, but the greedy among them would look around. Someone would see the boy and his Dwarf companion and report them. And when they were found, she would deal with them herself.

She was contemplating the satisfaction that enterprise would give her, when a sharp knock sounded, and without bothering to wait for her to respond, Terek Molt barged in.

"What do you think you are doing?" she snapped at him. "Rooms have doors for a reason, Molt!"

"We've found them," he rumbled in his deep, subterranean voice, ignoring her. "West, across the Mermidon."

She started. "Tagwen and the boy?"

"Only moments ago, someone used Elfstone magic. It was visible on the scrye waters in the cold chamber. Iridia was there to see it. There is no mistaking what it is."

The cold chamber was where the Druids read the lines of power that crisscrossed the Four Lands. The scrye waters were the table of liquid on which all uses of magic revealed themselves as ripples that indicated the extent of the power expended. Grianne Ohmsford herself had implemented it at Paranor more than a dozen years ago, a tool she had employed as the Ilse Witch.

"Elfstones?" she asked. She did not yet understand the connection.

"Of course, Shadea," he said, smiling with such satisfaction that she wanted to tear his face off. "They've escaped us and gone for help from the one Druid who might actually give it."

"The Elven Prince!" she hissed. "But he doesn't have the use of the Elfstones. His brother keeps them."

"Not so well protected that he couldn't get to them if he chose. He would do so to save the Ard Rhys. No, it has to be him. The readings come from that part of the Westland where he keeps his home. Tagwen would know to go there and take the boy with him."

"I am surprised they chanced using the Stones. Ahren Elessedil must know we will be watching for any use of magic."

"But how else can he find the Ard Rhys?" Molt pointed out. "He has no choice but to use the Stones."

She nodded slowly, thinking it through. "True enough. He can't know what we've done to her, even if he suspects we're responsible, unless he uses the Stones." She hesitated. "Wait. Did you say that Iridia was the one who discovered this use?"

Terek Molt's laugh was low and rough. "I thought of that, too. I asked her if she was certain. She insisted there was no mistake. It was Elfstone magic. I told her she had better be sure, since you would question it. She is waiting to speak with you in the cold chamber." He paused, a faint smile twisting his mouth at the corners. "She wants to be the one to go after him."

"I would expect nothing less. Such a fool."

She walked to the window and stared out at the darkening skies. She could not leave the matter to Iridia, but then Terek Molt had not proved particularly adept at settling things, either. She should do this herself, yet she did not think it wise to leave Paranor just yet. She was too newly settled in as Ard Rhys. Someone else must make certain that Tagwen and the boy, and now Ahren Elessedil, as well, did not succeed in their efforts.

"Perhaps we should let this matter lie," Terek Molt said quietly. "After all, even if they know what we have done with the Ard Rhys, there is nothing they can do to help her."

"Is that so?" she asked without bothering to look at him. "Are you so certain?"

"Certain enough."

"You assume too much. Besides, they can cause us a great

deal of trouble, even if they cannot reach her. I don't want to chance it. Better that we remove them from the picture."

"That could cause us more trouble still. Others will know what we have done. Killing a boy and an old man is one thing. Killing a Druid is something else again. That's what you intend, isn't it?"

"I intend to do whatever is necessary to make certain our efforts do not fail. I expect you to do likewise." She turned back to him. "Ready the *Galaphile*, but do not tell Iridia. I don't trust her in this matter, not where Ahren Elessedil is concerned. She may think she can blind herself to her feelings, but I don't care to chance it. Better that she remain here. I will tell her after you are gone. Given the look of the weather, you won't leave today. If the storm passes by nightfall, leave then."

He turned for the door.

"Stay a moment," she said. "I have more to say to you. Heed me well. Are you listening, Terek?"

The Dwarf turned back slowly, brow darkening in anticipation of what he knew was coming. "Speak your mind, woman."

"First," she said, walking over to stand directly in front of him, "don't come into this room again until you are invited. Not for any reason."

She waited for his response. He grunted and shrugged.

"Second, don't fail me again. I would not be pleased if you did."

He laughed. "I am less concerned about pleasing you than pleasing myself, so spare me your threats. The matter of finding and dispatching the boy and the old man has become personal. I don't like to be tricked. They used magic of some sort or I would have had them. I intend to see that accounts between us are settled."

She held his fierce gaze a moment, then nodded. "Fair

enough. But that may not prove to be so easy now that you must contend with Ahren Elessedil, as well. Dispatching him may prove troublesome, even for you. So I am sending someone to help."

The Dwarf glowered at her. "Who? If not Iridia . . ."

"Another Druid would only muck up the waters. You don't need another Druid to get this business settled." She paused. "I'm going to send Aphasia Wye."

Terek Molt turned his head aside, though barely, and spit very deliberately on her carpet. "No."

"This isn't open to debate."

"I won't put that monster on any ship I command. Get someone else, if you think you can."

"I don't want anyone else. If I wanted someone else, I wouldn't be talking with you! Where is your backbone? Are you afraid? Think how it will look if you stay behind after failing so badly the first time. Some will see it as a weakness, and you can't afford that." She drew her robes about her in a dismissive fashion. "Be smart about this, Druid. You are the best of the lot and you know it. I depend on you. Don't make me question my faith in you."

"You've never had faith in anyone but yourself, Shadea."

"Think what you want. What matters is that you understand that Aphasia Wye is coming with you. Stop worrying. He won't dare to cross you."

The Dwarf snorted derisively. "Aphasia Wye will cross anyone if opportunity allows for it. He's a monster, Shadea. There isn't anything that creature won't do—or anyone he won't do it to. Shades, we don't even know what he really is!"

She laughed. "He's the most efficient assassin I have ever seen! What more do you want him to be? I don't care what sex or race or breed he is! I don't care how loathsome you find him! You're not partnering with him! You're putting him to work! Stop whining!"

Terek Molt was seething, his chiseled face turned red, the muscles of his forearms knotted. He was as dangerous at that moment as she had ever seen him, and if she was foolish enough to give him an opening, he would kill her before she could blink. But she faced him down, keeping his eyes locked on hers and making him see that no matter how dangerous he was, she was more dangerous still.

"Don't even think it, Dwarf," she hissed softly. "Remember who I am."

He glared at her a moment longer, then looked away, furious still, but no longer threatening. "Someday you will go too far with me, Shadea." His voice was eerily calm. "Be careful of that day."

"Perhaps," she replied, reaching past him to open the door. "But until then, you will listen to me when I tell you what to do. Go ready the airship. When the storm passes, you will sail at once."

His big hands tightened into fists as he considered saying something more. Then, without doing so, he turned his back on her and walked away.

She waited until he was well away and her frustration with his recalcitrance had faded before she departed for the cold chamber to find Iridia Eleri. The sorceress would not be happy with what Shadea intended to tell her. Unfortunately, disappointing Iridia was unavoidable, because the sorceress was only as reliable as her control over her feelings about Ahren Elessedil, which meant she was not reliable at all. Iridia had set her mind on the matter long ago, and Shadea was not going to be able to change it, even if she tried.

Love was like that.

Denial only sharpened its edges.

Shadea entered the cold chamber and found Iridia standing at the broad stone basin set in its center, bending close as she read the movement of its contents. The scrye waters were shallow and deep green, shielded from the elements by the walls of the tower and the sides of the basin. Disturbances came solely from magic channeled through the earth's lines of power. Just then they manifested themselves as concentric ripples fanning out from a point just west of center. Iridia's slender hands moved in time to the ripples, as if to trace their liquid ridges back to her doomed love. Her perfect features radiated her intensity, a mix of light and dark, pale skin and black hair. Her Elven features were drawn taut by her concentration, emphasizing what could be both passionate and cruel about her. Shadea stood in the doorway and watched her for a long time, observing. Iridia, captive to her memories and her dreams, didn't even know Shadea was there. It was possible that the madness Iridia had always seemed so close to embracing was finally coming to her.

"Iridia!" she called sharply.

The sorceress turned at once. "Have you heard?"

Shadea walked over to her. "Terek told me of it. Is there no chance that you are mistaken?"

The delicate features hardened. "What do you take me for? I don't make mistakes of that sort. It was Elfstone magic, which means it could be him. I want to make certain of it, Shadea. You will have to send someone in any case. It should be me."

Shadea shook her head. "It should be anyone but you. What will you do if you find him and he looks at you and you cannot act? Don't tell me it cannot happen because I know better. I was there, Iridia, when you lost him. You were inconsolable for weeks. He was the one you wanted—the one you will always want."

"I don't deny that!" she snapped. "But that part of my life is over. I am committed to our efforts here. If he stands in our way, if he acts to help *her*, then I want him dead! I have the right to watch him die. I ask nothing more than that. If he is to be killed, I want to be there to see it. I want my face to be the last face he sees in this life!"

Shadea sighed. "You only think you want that. What you want is for him to take you back again, to tell you that he loves you still, despite what has happened. If he were to do so, you would abandon your cause and us in a heartbeat. No, wait, Iridia—don't lie to yourself. You would, and you know it. Why wouldn't you? I don't condemn it. I would do the same in your place."

"You would do nothing of the sort," the other woman sneered. "You have never loved anyone but yourself. Don't pretend to understand me. I know love compels me, but it compels me in ways other than those you seem so quick to attribute. Love doesn't compel me to embrace him; it compels me to see him suffer!"

"Yes, but not at your hands." Shadea moved away, gazing out the tower window at the enfolding darkness and roiling storm clouds. Outside, the wind began to howl and the rain to fall in heavy curtains that lashed the stone walls.

"Better at my hands, where we can be certain of the result, than at the hands of Terek Molt, who has already failed us once!"

"Better at another's hands entirely. I am sending Aphasia Wye to make certain the job is done right."

She glimpsed Iridia's face out of the corner of her eye, and the look confirmed what she had already decided about the other's feelings for Ahren Elessedil.

"Iridia," she said softly, turning back. "Distance yourself from this matter. Leave it to others to determine what is needed. You have suffered enough at the hands of the Elven Prince. He has betrayed you already and would do so again. His loyalty is to her, not to you. That will never change. To place yourself in a position where you must test your resolve is foolish and dangerous. It asks too much of you."

The sorceress stiffened, her lips tightening to a thin, hard line, her perfect features cast in iron. "And you think too little of me. I am not a fool, Shadea. I am your equal and in some ways your better. I have experiences you do not; don't be so quick to dismiss me as a lovesick child."

"I would never do that."

"You not only would, you do!" Iridia's glare would have melted iron. "If Ahren Elessedil has used the Elfstones to try to help that woman, I want him dead as much as you do. But I want to see it happen. I want to watch him die!"

"Do you?" Shadea a'Ru paused. "I would have thought you'd had enough of that sort of thing. How many more of those you profess not to love, but secretly do, must you watch die before you are satisfied?"

Iridia's face went white. "What are you talking about?" There was an unmistakable warning in her words.

Shadea ignored it, her gaze cold and empty. "The baby, Iridia. You remember the baby, don't you? You didn't love her, either."

For a long moment Iridia neither moved nor spoke, but simply stared at Shadea, the look on her face one of mixed incredulity and rage. Then both drained away with frightening swiftness, leaving her features calm and dispassionate. "Do what you want," she said.

She turned and walked away without looking at Shadea. As she went through the door, she said softly, "I hate you. I'll see you dead, too."

As Iridia disappeared down the tower stairs, Shadea glanced after her, thinking for just a moment that she should go after her, then deciding otherwise. She knew the sorceress. Iridia was quick to anger, but she would think the situation through and realize she was being foolish. It was better to let her be for now.

She looked down at the scrye waters in the basin. The ripples had disappeared; the surface had gone completely still.

Ahren Elessedil would be made to vanish just as swiftly.

*   *   *

One last task remained to her, the one she dreaded most. She had no more love for Aphasia Wye than did Terek Molt, but she found him useful in carrying out assignments that others would either refuse or mishandle. She had already seen enough of the latter in the hunting down of Grianne Ohmsford's family, and the task would get no easier with Ahren Elessedil added to the mix. Terek Molt might protest her decision, but it was a matter of common sense and expediency. One Druid of her inner circle was all she cared to spare for the venture, and one was probably not enough.

As she passed through the towers and hallways of the Keep, by sleeping rooms and meditation chambers, the resting and the restless, her mind focused on the task ahead. She wanted the business over, but not before she had accomplished what was necessary. She had given the matter considerable thought since Terek Molt's return. It was a mistake—her mistake, unfortunately—to have thought of the Patch Run Ohmsfords as ordinary people. The boy and his parents might not be Druids, but that did not render them commonplace. The magic that was in their blood, and their long history of surviving against impossible odds, made them dangerous. It would require a special effort to overcome both, one that she would not underestimate again.

It would help that she had the services of Aphasia Wye. But something more was needed.

She descended the winding stairways of the Keep into its depths, into the cellars and dungeons that lay far underground in the bedrock, dark places where the Druids seldom ventured. Her destination was known only to her, now that Grianne Ohmsford was gone, a place she had discovered some years ago while shadowing the Ard Rhys in an effort to discover her secrets. She had been good at shadowing even then, having developed the skill in her early years when the uses of magic were first revealing themselves to her. It was dangerous to challenge Grianne Ohmsford's instincts, but she managed it with the aid of a fine-grained, odorless dust that rendered the other's tracks visible in a wash of prismatic light. Layering the dust in the dark places she knew the other sometimes went, she would wait for her return before sneaking back down to read the trail. She had gotten lucky once or twice, but never again as lucky as with what she now sought to retrieve.

She entered the deep center of the Keep, the heart of the fortress, down where the earth's heat lifted out of its churning magma to warm the rooms above. She found it interesting that the Druids would build their home atop a volcanic fissure that might erupt and destroy them one day. But the Druids lived in harmony with the earth's elements and found strength in what was raw and new. She understood and appreciated that. A proximity to the sharp edge that divided life and death was compelling for her, as well.

The passageways narrowed and darkened further. So far down, there was no need for space or light. She thought that some of the corridors had not been walked in a thousand years, that some of the cells and rooms they fed into had not seen life in thousands more. But she sought nothing of life that day, only of death. She moved in silence, listening for sounds of the spirit creature that lived in the pit beneath the Keep and warded Paranor and its magic. It slept now and would slumber until awakened. So long as the Druids kept occupancy and life, it would lie dormant. She knew the stories of its protective efforts. The stories were legend. They did not frighten her, however. Rather, they intrigued her. One day, she would come down to take a closer look at it. Spirits were something she understood.

She pondered for a moment the circumstances that had led her to that moment. She had no regrets about how she had achieved her position, but she would have preferred that it be otherwise. She wasn't evil, just practical. She was the right choice to be Ard Rhys, the better person for the title, but that did not mean she was happy with the way she had obtained it. Climbing over the backs of others to get what you wanted was suited more to politicians and to royalty than to students of magic. She would have preferred to face Grianne Ohmsford in combat, but a decision based on the outcome of trial by magic would not have been accepted by the others—neither her allies nor her enemies. Druids, for all their examination and study, were conservative by nature. History had taught them that independence and disobedience led to disaster, so they preferred that matters progress in an orderly fashion.

That couldn't happen here. Not with the Ilse Witch as Ard Rhys and the fate of the order hanging in the balance. Shadea had understood that from the beginning. Unlike the others, she had chosen to act.

She reached a heavy iron door at the end of a corridor and stopped. Placing her fingers on a set of symbols cut into the metal, she closed her eyes and pressed in deliberate sequence. It had taken her a while to unlock the puzzle, but in the end she had done so. Tumblers clicked and a bolt slid back. The door opened.

Inside, the room was round and dark save for a single, flameless lamp set in a raised stanchion at the chamber's center. Heavy stone blocks encircled a mosaic floor in which runes had been carved in intricate patterns that suggested story panels. There was only the one door leading in and no windows. There were no openings in either the walls or floor. The ceiling domed away in shadowed darkness.

A tomb for the dead and their possessions, Shadea thought. A space where things were placed with a strong expectation that one day they would be forgotten.

She walked to the stanchion, stood with the heel of her right boot pressed against one edge of its square base and fitted into an invisible depression beneath, then walked straight ahead until she reached the wall. Placing the palms of both hands flat against the stone at waist height, she worked the tips of her fingers around until she found the hidden depressions in the stone, then pushed.

A heavy panel swung open on hidden hinges, revealing a deep, ink-black chamber.

Her smile said everything about her expectations for what waited within.

She entered without the use of fresh light, relying on the faint glow of the lamp behind her. Her eyes adjusted quickly, and she saw what she had come for. She walked over to a low pedestal set against one wall, opened the iron box sitting on top of it, and took out the velvet pouch that rested within. She handled it carefully, the way she might a deadly snake, taking care not to grip it too strongly but to balance it in the palms of her hands. Even more carefully still, she reached inside to extract what was hidden there.

Slowly, gingerly, she drew out the Stiehl.

It was the most deadly weapon in the world, a blade forged in the time of Faerie in the furnaces of the Grint Trolls. Infused with lethal strains of arcane fire magic, it could penetrate anything, no matter how thick or strong. Nothing could stand against it. It had been in the hands of the assassin Pe Ell in the time of the Shadowen and Walker Boh, and he had used it to kill the daughter of the King of the Silver River. The Druid had recovered it afterwards and hidden it here. No one had known where it was since. No one, but Grianne Ohmsford and now Shadea.

She held it by its handle, feeling the markings that signified its name where they were carved into the bone plates. The blade gleamed silver bright, its surface smooth and flawless. It had survived thousands of years without a mark. Grianne had kept it concealed for the same reasons as Walker Boh—it was too dangerous to reveal. It was an assassin's weapon, a killer's tool.

It belonged, Shadea told herself, in a killer's hands, in an assassin's sheath. It belonged in the hands of a master. She would see that it found its way there. She would see that it was put to the use for which it was intended. The lives it snuffed would be well spent.

She sighed. She wasn't being evil, she told herself for a second time that afternoon. She was just being practical.

She put the Stiehl away, closed the chamber anew, and climbed out of Paranor's dark cellars to the light above.

FIFTEEN

With the decision made to go in search of the tanequil, Ahren Elessedil arranged for horses to transport the party on the first leg of their journey, and within an hour they were mounted and riding out of Emberen. Seemingly unconcerned about its contents, the Druid didn't even bother to close up his cottage, leaving everything pretty much the way it was. Pen had the feeling that the Druid wasn't much attached to possessions and, in the tradition of Druids who did service in the field, thought them mostly superfluous. The boy didn't pretend to understand this, having worked hard for everything he had, but he supposed that his own attachments were mostly the result of habit and not because he valued his belongings all that much. Still, he had to fight a strong urge to go back and lock up.

They rode south along the main roadway, stopping frequently to say good-bye to the villagers, Ahren making a point of telling everyone he spoke to that they would be gone for several weeks. Pen thought it odd that he would make the information public and was further confused when they departed in the wrong direction and a dozen miles outside the village turned not east toward the Charnals, but west.

When he finally gathered up courage enough to ask what they were doing, Ahren Elessedil smiled. "Confusing the enemy, I hope. If they come to Emberen, which I expect they will, the villagers will tell them we left heading south. If they track us that way, they will find that we have turned west. But they will lose our trail when we reach the Rill Song because we will leave the horses there and catch a barge downriver to the Innisbore and the inland port of Syioned. At Syioned, we will find an airship to take us where we really want to go."

"An airship?" Pen asked.

"An airship offers speed on a direct line and doesn't leave tracks. If I'd had one at my disposal in Emberen, we would have taken it from there. But horses will have to do for now." He laughed. "You should see your face, young Pen!"

They rode all that day and most of the next through the Westland forests before reaching the Rill Song and a way station that offered the use of barge transport downriver. The weather stayed warm and bright, the storm that was lashing Paranor and the Druid's Keep having passed north a day earlier. They rode steadily, stopping only to eat and sleep, and in that time Pen managed to find discomfort in ways he hadn't dreamed possible. Horses were not a regular part of his life, so riding for such long stretches left him aching from neck to ankles. Having done little riding himself, Tagwen didn't fare much better. Both Elves seemed untroubled by the effort, but on the first evening Khyber took time to give the Dwarf and the boy a liniment she carried in her pack to ease their pain.

Leaving the horses behind at the way station, they boarded the barge late in the afternoon of the second day and set out anew. The Rill Song was deep and wide at that time of the year, and they had no trouble making headway on its turgid waters. When darkness set in, they navigated by moonlight so bright it might have been the middle of the day. Ahren could have tied up on the riverbank and let them all sleep, but he seemed anxious to continue on while light permitted and so they did. Pen was just as happy. He did not care to chance another run-in with Terek Molt.

The following day, they passed below Arborlon, its treetop spires just visible over the lip of the Carolan. The storied

Elfitch, the heavily fortified ramp that gave access to traffic coming in from the west, rose like a coiled snake from the eastern bank of the river to the bluff. Elves worked their way through the switchbacks and gates, a steady stream of commerce coming from and going to the Sarandanon. Pen found himself thinking about the battle fought between the Elves and their allies and the demons from the Forbidding almost five hundred years earlier. He stared at the Elfitch as they sailed past, trying to imagine the strength of its iron being tested against the frenzy of the demons. Thousands had died in that struggle. The legendary Border Legion had been decimated. The Elves had lost one out of every three able men. Their King, Eventine Elessedil, had been killed.

Pen wondered if another battle of the same sort was waiting down the road—if in spite of what Khyber said, the Ellcrys was failing again and the demons had found another doorway out of their prison.

They passed other boats on the river, and now and again they saw airships sailing overhead, a mix of warships on their way to the Prekkendorran and freighters on their way to less angry places. The weather stayed sunny and warm. There was no sign of the *Galaphile*. There was no sign of trouble of any sort. Pen began to think that maybe things weren't so bad.

Three days later, they reached the Innisbore, a body of water so vast that even if sun had broken through the clouds long enough to burn away the mists that lay in ragged strips across her choppy surface, the far shores would still have been out of view. It was late in the day when they maneuvered their barge into the landing area just beyond the mouth of the river, arranged for its docking and transport back upriver, and began the two-mile walk up the lake's eastern bank to the city of Syioned. Thunderheads were forming up again to the west, another storm beginning to build in that midseason time of storms. That they were commonplace at this time of the year didn't make them any less inconvenient, Pen thought. If one struck while they were grounded, they would not be able to fly out until it passed. That could take up to several days. Impulsively, Pen asked Ahren if they might be able to leave yet that day, but the Druid told him they didn't even have a ship arranged as yet and probably wouldn't before week's end.

Pen settled into a funk that matched the approaching weather. He didn't like delays, especially where flying was concerned. He was already itching to get back in the air. That was his life at Patch Run, and although he understood he had left that life behind, he couldn't pretend he didn't want it back. Traveling by horse and barge and on foot was all well and good, but flying was what he craved. The sooner he got back in the air, the better he would feel about himself.

But just then, patience was needed. Deep twilight had settled in by the time they reached the outskirts of the city, and his stomach was rumbling. They found an inn on a side street not far off the road leading in that served food and offered rooms. It was sufficiently far off the beaten track that Ahren Elessedil felt comfortable with staying there for the night. They ate at a table in the back of the common room, and by the time they were finished, Pen's eyes were heavy with sleep.

He didn't remember going up to his room afterwards. He didn't remember stripping off his clothes and tumbling into the bed. All he remembered, thinking back on it, was the sound of the rain beating on the shingled roof as the storm arrived.

"It doesn't look like it's ever going to stop," Pen observed glumly, staring out the window of the inn.

The rain fell in sheets as it had been doing all night, flooding the roadways and turning low-lying stretches of waterfront into small inlets. The glass of the window he looked through was sufficiently obscured that he couldn't see more than a dozen yards. Not much of anyone was moving about outside. Nothing was flying. Pen was not happy.

Khyber studied the gaming board in front of her, nodding absently at his comment. "Give it time, Pen. Storms out here are worse than they are inland. But they pass." She moved a piece to confront one of his. "If you're worried about pursuit, just remember that if we can't fly, neither can they."

"I don't like being grounded like this," he growled. "I feel trapped." He took her piece with one of his own. He thought about Ahren Elessedil and Tagwen. "How long have they been gone now?"

She shrugged, eyes on the board. The Druid and the Dwarf had gone out early that morning in search of passage. With no one flying, the airship Captains would be gathered at their favorite inns and ale houses, passing the time while they waited to get back in the air. A few among them might be looking for business, and out of those there had to be at least one that the Druid would consider hiring. In their situation, discretion was as important as speed, and he wasn't going to sign on with anyone with whom he didn't feel comfortable. He wanted one of the Rovers, accomplished mercenaries who knew how to keep their mouths shut. Syioned was a regular stop for transport from the coast and continuing farther inland to the landlocked cities. Rover Captains made the run all the time, and more than a few of them would be here now.

Pen and Khyber had been told to stay at the inn, out of sight and trouble. The Druid was worried that someone would notice them and remember later, when those who hunted them found their way to the port. The less they were seen, the better. Especially Pen, with his distinctive long red hair. The inn was crowded, but those gathered were clustered in private groups and engaged in their own conversations. Not much attention was being paid to anyone else.

"When did you start flying airships?" Khyber asked. She looked up at him. "You must have been doing it a long time."

He nodded. "Since I can remember. My mother always flew and my father, as well, after he met her. They took me with them everywhere after I was born, even when I was a baby. I remember learning to steer when I was barely old enough to stand on an upended crate and look over the pilot box railing."

"I wanted to fly," she said, "but my father, when he was alive, and after he died, my brother, insisted that someone always go with me. In a big warship with lots of the Home Guard for protection, I might add. Even after I began traveling out on my own, old enough to know how to take care of myself, I wasn't allowed to go by airship."

He shrugged. "You haven't missed that much."

She laughed. "What a terrible liar you are, Penderrin! You can't possibly believe that! You're the one who can't wait to get back up in the skies! Admit it!"

"Okay, I admit it." He was laughing, too. "But you can make up for what you've missed. I could show you."

He moved another piece, and she responded. She was good at the game, but not nearly as good as he was. He had an innate sense of what she was going to do even before she did. She studied the board intently, aware that she was being backed into a corner.

"Have you thought about the fact that your father and my uncle Ahren were about the same age we are now when they sailed on the *Jerle Shannara*?" she said.

"More than once."

"Do your parents ever talk about what it was like?"

"Once in a while; a lot of their friends died on that voyage, and I don't think they like to remember it." He looked at her. "How about your uncle? Does he ever say anything?"

She shook her head, her brow creasing. "He doesn't like to talk about it, either. Because of the seer, I think. He was in love with her, though he won't say so now. It's too painful for him." She cocked her head. "Are you afraid of what we're doing, Pen?"

He leaned back, thinking about it. Was he afraid? What did he feel? He hadn't really stopped to think about it. Or maybe hadn't allowed himself, afraid of what he might discover.

"No," he answered, then immediately grimaced. "All right, yes, but only in a general sort of way. I don't know enough to be afraid of anything specific yet. Except for that Druid, that Dwarf. He was pretty scary. I'm afraid of him."

She brushed back strands of dark hair that had fallen forward over her face as she bent to the board. "I'm not afraid. I know some magic, so I can protect us if I have to. Uncle Ahren knows a lot of magic, though he doesn't show it. I think he's probably a match for anyone. We'll be all right."

"Glad you think so."

"Don't you have some of your father's magic? He had the magic of the wishsong, like your aunt Grianne, didn't he?"

Pen nodded. "True. But he didn't pass it on to me. I think the bloodline has grown thin after all these years. He's probably the last. Just as well, he'd tell you. He doesn't trust it. He uses it now and then, but not much. He's just as happy I don't have any."

"It might help if you did."

Pen paused, considering whether or not he should tell her about the talent he did have. "Maybe."

"You could protect yourself a little better. From those renegade Druids and their magic. From what you might come upon inside the Forbidding. Don't you think so?"

He didn't reply. They went back to the game, moving pieces until only eight remained on the board. Pen knew by then that he would win, but he let the game continue anyway. Playing it helped pass the time.

"Do you remember what Tagwen said about the tanequil giving me the darkwand if I could find it?" he asked her finally. He leaned forward over the board as if concentrating, deliberately lowering his voice. "It's because I do have magic."

She leaned in to meet him, their foreheads almost touching. Her Elven features sharpened with surprise. "What sort of magic? The wishsong? But you said not."

"No. Something else. Something different." He fiddled with one of the pieces, then took his hand away. "I can sense what living things are thinking, what they are going to do and why. Not people. Birds and animals and plants. When they make sounds, noises or cries or whatever, I can understand what they are saying. Sometimes, I can make the sounds back, answer them."

She cocked one eyebrow. "That seems to me like it could be pretty important. I don't know how exactly, but I think it could be. Have you told Uncle Ahren?"

He shook his head. "Not yet."

"Well, you should. He ought to know, Pen. He's a Druid. He might know something about it that you don't, maybe a way you can use it that will help us." She paused, studying his face. "Are you afraid to tell him? You can trust him, you know."

"I know." His eyes locked on hers. "I just don't talk about it much. I never have."

They went back to playing, the sound of the rain beating against the window increasing in intensity. All around them, voices and laughter fought to hold their ground. The flames of the lamps on the walls and the candles on the tables fluttered like tiny flags as the wind slipped through cracks and crevices in the wood boarding and gusted through the open door every time someone entered or left.

"I'll tell him when he comes back," Pen said finally. He moved his assault piece to confront her control. "Stand down. You lose, Khyber."

They played another game and were in the middle of a third when the door opened to admit a drenched Ahren Elessedil and Tagwen. Shedding water from their all-weather cloaks like ducks come ashore, they hurried over to the boy and girl.

"Get your things together," Ahren told them quietly, bending down so that rainwater dripped on the tabletop. "We've found a ship."

They gathered up their gear, strapped their packs over their shoulders, and departed the inn for the ship that the Druid had engaged. Better that they settle in at once so they could be ready to leave when the storm abated, the Druid advised. They had to walk from the side street on which the inn was situated back to the main roadway and down to the docks, then along the waterfront to where the ship was tied up at the pier. As they slogged through the downpour, Ahren Elessedil provided the details.

"The ship is the *Skatelow*. Appropriate name for its uses, I'd guess. Low and sleek in her hull, raked mast, lots of rigging on the decks. She can't carry much in the way of passengers or freight with all the sail she stores, but she can probably outrun almost anything flying."

"Made for our uses," Tagwen grunted, his words nearly drowned out by a sudden gust of wind.

"Not much in the way of comforts, but adequate for our needs," the Druid continued. "Her Captain is a Rover named Gar Hatch. I don't know anything about him other than what I've learned from talking with him and what a few on the waterfront tell me. He's got a reputation for being willing to try anything, and they all say he can go places no one else would even think of trying. If I read him correctly, he's done a lot of what we're after—carrying passengers who want to keep it quiet. He's charming, but there's some snake in him, as well, so watch what you say. He knows we want to go east to the Lazareen, but that's all I've given him to work with. What he cares about most is the money he will get, and I've satisfied him on that count."

"The Lazareen?" Khyber asked.

"An inland lake at the foot of the Charnals, the first step of our journey. That's all the Rover knows of our plans just yet."

They walked on for a while, not speaking, heads bent against the wind and rain. Pen was not only wet, he was cold. He had been out in the weather a lot aboard airships and knew how to dress for it, but in his haste to leave the inn this afternoon, he hadn't given much thought to his personal comfort. He was regretting that oversight now.

"Penderrin."

Ahren Elessedil had dropped back to walk beside him, letting Khyber and Tagwen go on ahead. Pen hitched up his pack and moved closer so that he could hear. The rain obscured the Druid's face and ran off his shoulders in sheets.

"I took the liberty of telling Captain Hatch that you had extensive airship experience," he said. "I'm afraid I put you on the spot rather deliberately." The hood shifted, and Pen caught a glimpse of his Elven features, somber and intense. "I don't trust this fellow entirely; he's a mercenary, and mercenaries always look out for themselves first. But he was the best I could do, and I didn't want to delay our departure. The longer we wait, the better the chance that those hunting us will get wind of where we are."

Pen nodded. "I understand."

The Druid leaned closer. "The reason I told Hatch about your experience is so that he knows at least one of us can determine if he's doing what he's supposed to. I don't want him telling us one thing and doing something else. I don't want him thinking he can put one over on us. I don't say that would happen, but I want to guard against it. I don't know that much about airships; I never did. Your father was the pilot and your mother the navigator when it was needed. I was always just a passenger. That's never changed. Khyber and Tagwen know even less than I do. In fact, I think it's something of a miracle that Tagwen managed to reach you on his own."

"I thought that, too, after he told me what he'd done." Pen blinked away the rain that swept into his eyes.

"Stay alert on our journey, Pen," Ahren said. "Don't make it obvious, but keep an eye on what's happening with the navigation of the ship. If anything looks wrong, tell me. I'll deal with it. Can you do that?"

"I can do it."

"Gar Hatch doesn't know who we are, but that doesn't mean he won't find out. If he does, he might be tempted to make use of that information. The Druids are already looking for you. They've put it about that because of what happened to your aunt, you might be in danger, as well, and should be protected. If you're seen, word is to be sent to them immediately."

He hunched his shoulders against the wind. "I gave him only first names, thinking it safe enough at the time, but now I wish I hadn't given him even that. News of the Druid search didn't reach Syioned until this morning, but now that it has, Hatch may hear of it. He isn't a stupid man. Be very careful, Pen."

He moved away again into the rain, his cloaked form dark and shadowy in the gloom. Pen stared after him, slowing.

Be very careful. Easily said, he thought; not so easily done.

Aware suddenly that he was falling behind, he hurried to catch up with the others.

Sixteen

The storm raged on through the rest of the day and all that night, but by daybreak it had begun to diminish. By the time the general population of Syioned was stirring awake, the *Skatelow* had cast off her moorings and was under way.

Pen and his companions had been huddled belowdecks since boarding, trying their best to sleep through the storm's fury, and they had not had more than a rain-drenched glimpse of their vessel. Now, with the skies clearing and the sun a bright wash in the east, they came on deck to look around.

Their transport was a sloop, a new design for airships, although a very old one for sailing ships. Ahren Elessedil had described it accurately. It was low and flat and clearly built for speed. A single mast and spars were rigged to fly a mainsail, foresail, and flying jib. In his travels, Pen hadn't seen much of the latter, another sailing ship feature that had been converted for airship usage. A broad, billowing sail that traditionally captured the wind off the bow and gave the vessel extra thrust, the jib was used by airships to absorb a wider swath of ambient light that could be converted to energy by the diapson crystals that powered the ship. The *Skatelow* lacked the pontoons that serviced most of the older airships of the catamaran design, relying instead on its pilot's sailing skills and the flatness of its hull to keep it steady in the air.

Pen liked the *Skatelow* right away. It had been modified from its original design considerably to eliminate anything that might slow its flight. Except for the mast and rigging, everything else was tucked away belowdecks or in storage bins. Even the pilot box was recessed into the hull to cut back on drag. Everything was sleek and smooth, the ship a great swift bird that could hunt or run as needed. It was powered by eight diapson crystals, the most in use for a ship of only seventy-odd feet. Anything more and the thrust might have torn her apart. Even with eight, the Captain had to know what he was doing.

Gar Hatch did, and he let Pen know it right from the first. Pen had been abovedecks less than five minutes when the Captain of the *Skatelow* hailed him over.

"Penderrin!" he called out from the pilot box. "Stand to, lad! Give an old sailor an ear to bend!"

Obediently, Pen walked down the deck to the box and climbed in beside Gar Hatch. The Rover was a big man, heavy and square through his midsection with huge arms and legs—a tree trunk of a man. Bushy hair sprouted from his face and head, even from his sizeable ears, giving him the appearance of a great woolly bear. When he spoke he had a tendency to rear back, his stomach thrust out and his chin tucked so far into his beard that his mouth disappeared entirely. What remained visible were his sharp, hawkish eyes, bright and dangerous.

"You're a sailor yourself, I'm told," he said, his deep, rough voice rising from somewhere inside his beard. His breath smelled of fish and sea salt. "Been so since you were a small lad, an early old salt. Spent years sailing airships big and small about Rainbow Lake and the rivers that feed her. Good for you!"

"My parents are the real sailors," Pen said. "I learned what I know from them. They take customers on expeditions into the Eastland." He stopped himself quickly. Remembering Ahren Elessedil's admonishment, he was aware that he had already said more than he should have. "I just fly with them once in a while and look after the ships in dock," he finished carefully.

Gar Hatch didn't seem to notice. "Grew up that way myself," he said. "Learned what I know from my father and uncles, sailors all. On the coast, off the Blue Divide, whichever way the wind blew. We flew the big ships mostly, but I had my own skiff when I was your age. Got one of those yourself, your uncle tells me."

My uncle? "Yes, that's right," Pen answered quickly. "A cat-28. I built it myself."

"Did you now? Good for you, Penderrin!" The Rover laughed, his belly shaking with the effort. "Best way to learn about airships is to build one. Haven't got the skills for that myself, but I've helped those who do. I learned keel from mast quick enough that way, so when I flew I understood if the lady didn't like the way she was being treated."

Pen grinned. "I like this ship. I've never flown one, but I've seen them and I know how they're made. This one is made to fly fast. Have you run out the string on her?"

Hatch roared. "That's the lad! Ask what matters, and no beating around the main mast! Sure, I've had her thrusters all the way open, and let me tell you, Penderrin, she can fly faster than fast! Nothing alive can catch her, save for the big birds off the coast, and they might have to work some to do it. She's a glutton for speed, this one. You're right, though. I gave her all her curves, all her smooth limbs and soft lines. She's my lady, she is."

He paused. "You've never flown a sloop, did you say? Lad, that's unconscionable! Do you want to try now?"

Pen could hardly contain his excitement. "You'd let me?"

"A sailor like yourself, born to the air?" Hatch leaned forward, his fish breath in Pen's face. "Take the helm, Captain Pen."

Despite Ahren Elessedil's warnings about the big man, Pen was desperate to fly the sloop, so he put aside his misgivings. It wouldn't hurt to accept the offer, he told himself. He was just going to test his skills a bit, try out the controls, and see if he could manage the vessel. He had flown other airships of the same sort, some much bigger. *Skatelow* couldn't be that much more difficult.

Gar Hatch backed away, and Pen stepped up to the helm. He glanced down quickly, noting thrusters, lifts, banking levers, and the like, all familiar to him, though located in somewhat different positions than he was used to. The compass was set dead center above the half wheel that managed the keel rudder.

"There you be, young Pen," the Rover Captain declared cheerfully. "A fine and proper set of controls for a fine and proper young sailor. Give her a try, lad."

Pen did so, easing into things slowly, carefully, setting trim before taking the airship a little higher with the lifts. She nosed upward, but he felt the tension in her hull, then a slight shaking. He frowned as he worked to steady her. It wasn't as easy as he had thought. Everything was the same, but the sloop's responses were less certain than he would have liked. He adjusted the thrusters and felt her shake some more. An effort at resetting trim proved unsuccessful. He eased the power back, glancing over at Gar Hatch.

The Rover's sharp eyes were glittering. "Not so easy as it looks, is it?" he asked, and Pen could see he wasn't expecting an argument. "Flying a sloop is not the same as flying a cat-28 or even a warship with pontoons and rams for stability. A sloop needs tender loving care from a master who knows her needs."

He smiled, but even through the heavy growth of beard Pen could see the teeth behind. He realized with a sinking feeling that Hatch had been testing him. Knowing how difficult it would be for someone unfamiliar with the sloop to sail her, he had enticed Pen into trying so that he could judge the boy's skills. The Rover was one step ahead of Ahren Elessedil; he knew that Pen had been asked to check up on him, even without having been present at the conversation. Now he had Pen's measure, and the boy had helped him take it.

Gar Hatch stepped forward and took back the ship's controls, easing Pen out of the way without seeming to do so.

"You keep in mind, Penderrin," he said softly, looking over at the boy as he steadied the vessel anew, "that there's only one Captain on this ship. Do that and we'll get along fine. Now out of the box you go. Back down on the deck with the others. That's a good lad."

Pen left without a word, burning with frustration and shame, so furious with himself that he could have spit. But there was no help for it, and he refused to give Gar Hatch the satisfaction of seeing him react. Fighting to control himself, he stood alone at the starboard rail, his gaze directed resolutely forward even though he could feel the Rover Captain's eyes on his back. He should have paid better attention to Ahren Elessedil's warning. But that was water over the dam. What mattered was how well he remembered the lesson he had just been taught. Well enough, he promised himself. The next time Gar Hatch tried to make a fool of him, things would turn out differently.

It was late in the afternoon of that same day when Cinnaminson came on deck. She climbed up through the hatchway leading from the narrow sleeping quarters below, stepping into the crimson light of the sunset like a shade. Pen was sitting with Khyber at the aft rail, still stewing over the way he had let himself be fooled by Gar Hatch, when he saw her. He did not know where she had come from or what she was doing there. He had thought that besides the four who had booked passage there were only Hatch and two crewmen.

Now this apparition had appeared. He stopped talking in mid-sentence, causing Khyber, who had not been paying close attention, to look up from her writing and follow his gaze.

She was only a girl, no older than Pen, younger than Khyber, her slender form wrapped in something soft gray and green that might have been a long robe and shimmered like the sea. She looked to have woken from a deep sleep, her short, sandy blond hair disheveled and her face tilting toward the light as if to make certain of the time. Pen thought her beautiful, although he would later revise that judgment to striking, and sometime later to captivating. Her features were delicate, but unremarkable and not quite perfect. Still, they intrigued him. What mattered more was the way she moved, not looking at anything while seemingly aware of all. She glided rather than walked, the soft whisper of her gown marking her passage as she came toward them.

It was when she had almost reached them that Pen saw her eyes. They were milky white and empty, staring straight ahead at nothing. She was blind.

Pen did not know who she was. He did not know her name. What he did know was that he would never forget her.

"Are you our passengers?" she asked them, looking off into a space they did not quite occupy.

Pen nodded, then realized she couldn't see him. "Yes, two of them, anyway. I'm Pen and this is Khyber." He had presence of mind enough, though just barely, to remember to use only first names.

"I'm Cinnaminson," she told them. "I'm Gar Hatch's daughter."

She stretched out her hand and waited for them to take it, which they did, one after the other. Her smile was winsome and a bit fragile, Pen thought, hesitant and protective at the same time, which seemed right for her condition. But there was strength to her, too. She was not afraid to come up against what she couldn't see.

"Traveling to the Charnals," she said, making it a statement of fact. "I like that part of the world. I like the feel of the mountain air, the smell and taste of it. Snowmelt and evergreens and ice."

"Do you always come on these trips?" Khyber asked, looking doubtful about the whole business.

"Oh, yes. Ever since I was eight years old. I always go. Papa wouldn't fly anywhere without me." She laughed softly, milky eyes squinting with amusement. "I am an old salt, he tells me, a child of the air and sea."

Khyber arched a questioning eyebrow at Pen. "I am surprised he would allow you aboard at so young an age when you could not see to help yourself. It seems dangerous."

"I see well enough," the girl replied. "Not so much with my eyes as with my other senses. Besides, I know every inch of the *Skatelow*. I am not in any real danger."

She sat down beside them, moving effortlessly to find a place between them, her gray and green robes settling about her like sea foam. "You don't fly, do you, Khyber?"

"No. But Pen does. He was born to airships."

Her gaze shifted, not quite finding him. "Don't tell my father. He doesn't like it when other flyers come aboard. He's very jealous of what's his."

Pen thought, without having any better reason to do so than the way she said it, that she was including herself in that assessment. "Too late," he told her. "He found out from my uncle and already made a point of letting me know how lacking I am in real skills."

Her smile dropped. "I'm sorry, Pen. I would have warned you if I had known. Papa can be very hard."

"Is he hard on you?"

The smile returned, less certain. "I am his most important crew member," she said, not quite answering the question. She hesitated. "He wouldn't want me to tell you this, but I will anyway. I am his navigator."

Pen and Khyber exchanged a quick glance. "How do you manage that?" the Elven girl asked. "I didn't think you could navigate if you couldn't see."

The milky eyes shifted slightly toward the sound of Khyber's voice. "I don't see with my eyes. I see with my other senses." She bit her lip. "I can do things to help Papa that don't require sight." Again, she paused. "You mustn't tell Papa I told you any of this. He wouldn't like it."

"Why wouldn't he like it?" Pen asked.

"Papa worries about outsiders, people other than Rovers. He doesn't trust them."

Nor do we trust him, Pen thought. Not a good situation.

"I still don't understand this navigation business," Khyber pressed, her brow furrowing. "Tell us something more about how you help your father."

"Cinnaminson!"

All three turned in the direction of the voice. Gar Hatch had turned around in the pilot box and caught sight of them. He looked furious. "Come help your Papa, little girl," he ordered brusquely. "You've sailor work to do."

She stood up at once. "Coming, Papa." She glanced down quickly. "Say nothing!" she whispered.

She left without another word, walking straight to the pilot box and climbing in. Pen watched to see what would happen and wasn't sure if he was relieved or disappointed when nothing did. Gar Hatch put his hand on his daughter's shoulder, patted it briefly, and turned back to steering the vessel. Cinnaminson remained standing beside him.

"What do you make of that?" he asked Khyber.

"A bad business that we should stay out of," she answered. She regarded him thoughtfully. "I think we ought to cut your hair. That long red mane is too recognizable. Maybe we should dye it, too."

She put down her writing tools and went off to find her scissors.

* * *

They were told at the evening meal that, after dark, passengers were not allowed topside until morning. It was a rule of long standing aboard the *Skatelow* and the Captain's express order. The reason given was concern for safety; a fall at night from the ship's sleek decking would almost certainly result in death. It was better if everyone but the crew stayed below. Ahren Elessedil assured the Rover that the order would be obeyed, and Pen went to bed with every intention of breaking it.

He woke sometime after midnight and slipped from his bed on cat's paws, brushing absently at his newly shorn hair, grimacing at the roughness of its feel. Hardly anything was left of it; Khyber had done a thorough job. He glanced at Tagwen, who was snoring loudly in the berth above him. Clearly, the Dwarf would not wake. Ahren and Khyber shared a cabin down the hall, so he was less concerned about them. He took several deep breaths to settle himself, then moved to the door. He stood there for a moment, listening, but heard nothing. When he stepped outside, the corridor was empty. Other than the creaking of the rigging and the soft rustle of the mainsail in the almost dead night air, everything was silent.

He went down the corridor and up the stairway, stopping often to listen. Having done that sort of thing any number of times before, he was not particularly worried about getting caught, but he did not care to be embarrassed by Gar Hatch again. So he went slowly and cautiously, and when he reached the head of the stairs and found the hatchway open, he stopped yet again.

Above, not far from where he stood, he heard voices. It took him only seconds to recognize whose they were.

". . . not fair that I never get to talk to anyone. I don't tell them anything about us, Papa. I just like hearing about their lives."

"Their lives don't matter to us, girl," Gar Hatch responded, firmly but not unkindly. "They aren't of our people and you won't see them again after this journey."

"Then what does it matter if I talk to them?"

"It matters in ways you don't understand because you are still a child. You must listen to me. Be pleasant to them. Be helpful when it is needed. But do not go out of your way to speak to them. That is a direct order, sailor."

There was silence after that. Pen remained standing where he was, listening. He wanted to peek outside, but he was afraid that if he did, he would be seen. The moon was three-quarters full and the sky clear. There was too much light to take a chance. He wondered what was going on up there that he wasn't supposed to see. As far as he could tell from what he was hearing, nothing at all.

"I'm going below to sleep for a few hours," Hatch announced suddenly. "You take the helm, Cinnaminson. Keep her on course, no deviations. There's no weather on the horizon, so the sail should be smooth enough. You know what to do. Come get me if there's trouble. Good girl. I'll come back before dawn."

Pen retreated down the steps as swiftly as he could manage, reached his cabin and stepped inside. He stood with his back against the door and listened as Gar Hatch trudged past toward the Captain's quarters. The Rover's footsteps receded, a door opened and closed, and everything was silent again save Tagwen's snoring.

For a moment, Pen determined to go topside again. But he was nervous about it now, afraid that Hatch might come back and catch him. What had he said? *You take the helm, Cinnaminson?* How could she do that if she was blind? Was she up there all alone, steering the airship and charting their course when she couldn't see? That didn't seem possible, and yet . . .

He stood awhile longer, debating what to do. In the end, he

went back to bed. Khyber was right. It was none of his business, and he shouldn't mix in it. Ahren wouldn't like it if he jeopardized their safety through his interference. He couldn't afford to antagonize Hatch while they depended on him.

Perhaps, he thought, he would just ask Cinnaminson the next time he saw her. If she would speak to him, that was.

He went back to bed to think about it some more and was asleep in moments.

SEVENTEEN

They flew north out of the Westland, then turned east across the Streleheim Plains down the corridor that lay between the Dragon's Teeth and the Knife Edge Mountains. It was a shipping lane used by almost everyone traveling west and east above Callahorn, and they passed other airships at regular intervals. The weather remained good, the skies clear and calm, the days warm and dry, the nights deep and cool, and there were no more storms. The *Skatelow* kept a steady pace, but not a fast one, staying low and hugging the forestline above Paranor. She sailed at night as well as during the day, and Gar Hatch put her down only twice in three days for fresh water and brief repairs.

Pen spoke with Cinnaminson every day, several times a day, and there was no indication from her behavior that she was trying to avoid him. In fact, she seemed eager to search him out, although she never did so in a way that suggested she was disobeying her father's wishes. Pen, for his part, tried to make their meetings seem to those who might observe to be about something other than their growing friendship. But he didn't even try to pretend to her that he wasn't interested. He was captivated, and even at his young age he could not mistake what he was feeling for her. He was excited just at the prospect of seeing her, and every day brought new opportunities to do so. He looked forward to those moments with an anticipation that made him ache.

But he never asked her about that first night. The more he thought about doing so, the less comfortable he felt. In the first place, he had been spying on her, and he didn't want her to know that. Nor could he think of a way to broach the subject without seeming to pry. It wasn't his place to ask her what she was doing for her father. At best, it would make her uncomfortable because anything she told him would be a betrayal. He still wanted to know how she could sail an airship despite being blind, but he decided it would have to be her idea to tell him.

He had plenty of time to indulge his newfound attraction for her. Tagwen was often airsick and seldom appeared topside. He was a Dwarf, he pointed out sourly, and he belonged on the ground. Khyber had resumed her Druid studies and spent most of her time with her uncle. Pen would see them sitting across from each other on the decking, heads bent close in conversation, the girl taking notes and making animated gestures that indicated she was trying to understand what he was teaching. Much of the time, they remained in their cabin, freer to engage in open discussion than when the Rovers were present. Khyber, always intense, seemed more so now that they had set out, perhaps appreciating better than Pen did the weight of the task she had agreed to shoulder.

But Pen, too, spent much of his time thinking about why he was there, a passenger aboard an airship bound for the Charnals and country few had ever explored. He no longer questioned whether what he was doing was the right thing. He no longer even questioned the motives of the King of the Silver River in sending him. He just accepted it and concentrated instead on how he was going to get through in one piece. If he allowed himself to think about the larger picture, it was too overwhelming to contemplate. So much was expected of him, and he had no reason to believe those expectations were justified. He found he could manage better if he considered things incrementally. Step one was escaping the *Galaphile* and Terek Molt. He'd done that. Step two was reaching Emberen and enlisting help from Ahren Elessedil. He'd done that, too. Step three was embarking on the journey east.

When he got to step four, however, things became a little less clear. Finding the tanequil was the goal, but he had the feeling that there were a few other steps in between and he would not find out what they were right away. Only time would reveal them, and it would not do to try to plan too far ahead. That he was making the journey on faith in the first place helped him accept that, but it didn't make him any less anxious about the outcome.

Spending time with Cinnaminson relaxed him most. He understood it was an indulgence, one that was difficult to justify given the seriousness of his purpose. But he understood, as well, that something was needed to distract him from his doubts and fears, and turning his thoughts to Cinnaminson helped. He wasn't foolish enough to expect that this infatuation would grow into something more. He knew it would be finished when they reached their destination and disembarked from the airship. But it did no good to think in those terms. Better to allow a little light into a darkened room than to worry about what would happen once it faded.

On the third day, they were sitting in the bow where he was pretending to write and she to listen to what he had written, their backs to the pilot box and Gar Hatch.

"Can you tell me where you are going?" she asked him quietly.

"I can tell you anything, Cinnaminson."

"Not anything. You know you can't do that."

He nodded to himself. She understood some things better than he did. "We go into the Charnals, looking for the ruins of an ancient city. Ahren wants to look for something there."

"But he brings you and Khyber and Tagwen to help him," she said. "An odd company for such an effort."

Her fingers brushed his wrist, a soft swirl that made him itch all the way down to his toes. "I won't lie to you," he said finally. "There's more to this. I'm sworn to secrecy."

"Better that you tell me so than deceive me. I have traveled with enough passengers to know when they keep secrets. My father is paid to keep it so. But I want to know that you will be safe when you leave me. I want to know that I might see you again someday."

His hand closed on hers, and he stared into her milky, empty eyes. She did not see him, but he could feel her watching in other ways. He studied her face, the lines and curves and softness, the way the light fell against her skin. He loved to look at her. He could not have told anyone why, just that he did. "You will see me again," he said quietly.

"Will you come find me?" she asked him.

"I will."

"Even if I am flying somewhere on the *Skatelow*, you will look for me?"

He felt his throat tighten. "I don't think I could do otherwise," he said. "I think I have to."

Then, without thinking about who might be watching, he leaned forward and kissed her on the mouth. She kissed him back without hesitation. It was a thrilling, tantalizing kiss, and he immediately wanted more. But he was playing a dangerous game, and contemplating the way it might end tempered his enthusiasm sufficiently that he kept himself in check.

He broke away, not daring to look back at the pilot box. "Sorry," he said.

"Don't be sorry," she answered at once, leaning into his

shoulder, head lowered so that her hair brushed his bare arm. "I wanted you to do that."

"Your father won't like it."

"My father wasn't looking."

Unable to help himself, he glanced over his shoulder. Gar Hatch was turned away, working on placing lines at the rear of the box. She was right; he hadn't seen anything.

Pen looked back at her. "How did you know that?"

She gave him a smile that reached all the way into his heart. "I just did," she said, and kissed him again.

"I wish you'd stop following Cinnaminson around like an eager puppy," Khyber told him late that same day while they were sitting together at the bow of the *Skatelow*. She brushed back her thick dark hair and stared out at a sky lit purple and rose, her brow furrowed by deep lines of condemnation.

"I like her," he said.

"As anyone can plainly see, including her father. Even Uncle Ahren has noticed, and he usually doesn't bother with such nonsense."

He frowned. "Nonsense?"

"Well, it is. Do you have any idea what you're doing? You're going to get us in a lot of trouble if you aren't careful."

"You don't know everything."

"I know what I see. What everyone sees. I don't think you've thought this through. Or if you have, you've managed to leave out the important parts. You know how her father feels about outsiders. He doesn't want anything to do with us beyond taking our money. Rovers live by a different code of behavior than the rest of us. Everyone knows that. So why do you persist in nosing around after Cinnaminson?"

He looked sharply at her. "Stop it, Khyber."

"Stop what? Stop telling you the truth?"

"You don't have to be so mean about it! Have you forgotten that my mother is a Rover?"

They glared at each other, each silently daring the other to say something more, each refusing to give ground. Pen knew Khyber was right about Cinnaminson, even if he wouldn't admit it. He knew he shouldn't be interested in her, even in a casual way and certainly not in the way he was. But he didn't know what he could do about it. It wasn't as if he had chosen for it to happen. It just had. Now he was stuck with his feelings, and he couldn't cast them aside or bundle them up and stick them in a locker. He was way beyond that, and besides, he wasn't at all sure he wanted to change things anyway.

"We're being careful," he said finally.

She snorted. "How, exactly? Are there things happening between the two of you that I'm not seeing? I certainly hope not, because what I am seeing is already way too much."

He wheeled on her. "Just because your brother wants to marry you off and you don't like the idea doesn't mean the rest of us have to feel the same way about things!"

"Oh, are you thinking of marrying her?"

"That's not what I mean!" He was furious now. "I mean I don't have to be as close-minded as you obviously are! I don't have to be like you!"

"Keep your voice down!" she hissed.

Behind them, Gar Hatch stood in the pilot box. Pen shot him a quick look, but he didn't seem to notice the boy. His eyes were directed forward, toward the horizon.

"You're being unreasonable!" Pen hissed back at her. "We're just friends!"

She started to reply, then stopped herself. Her face softened, her anger faded, and she nodded slowly. "All right, Pen. Let's drop the matter. What right do I have to tell you how to behave, anyway? Ask my family how well behaved I've been. I haven't the right to lecture you."

He sighed wearily, looking out over the bow toward the approaching night. "I know I shouldn't be doing this. I know I should just stay away from her. I know that."

Khyber put her hand on his shoulder and squeezed. "But you can't and you won't and I don't have the right to ask you to do so. I wouldn't want you telling me what to do if our positions were reversed. But I worry, anyway. I don't want you disappearing over the side of the ship one night just because you smiled at this girl once too often. Everything we're doing depends on you. We can't afford to lose you. Just keep that in mind when you're thinking about how pretty she looks."

He exhaled sharply. "You don't have to worry about that. I can't stop thinking about it. That's part of the reason I like being with her. She helps me forget for a little while."

They didn't say anything for a long time as they looked out at the skyline, listened to the cries of the seabirds and the hum of the ship's rigging. The western sky had gone shadowed and gray with the setting of the sun, and the first star had appeared in the north.

"Just be careful," Khyber said finally.

He nodded, but did not answer.

The fourth day of travel dawned gray and sullen with storm clouds layered all across the northwest horizon, roiling and windswept as they bore down on the Streleheim. Pen came on deck at first light to find Gar Hatch and both Rover crewmen hard at work taking down the sails, tightening the rigging, and lashing in place or carrying below everything that might be lost in the blow. Cinnaminson was standing in the pilot box, her face lifted as if to taste the raindrops that had begun to fall.

He thought at first to go to her, then decided against it. There was no reason to do so, and it would call needless attention to his infatuation. Instead, familiar enough with what was needed to be able to help, he went to help the crewmen secure the vessel. They glanced at him doubtfully as he joined them in their work, but said nothing to discourage it. Behind him, Ahren and Khyber appeared, as well, standing in the hatchway, stopped by a wind that had begun to howl through the rigging like a banshee.

"Get below!" Gar Hatch bellowed at them. His gaze shifted to Pen. "Penderrin! Take Cinnaminson down with them, then come back on deck! We need your strong back and skilled hands, lad! This is a heavy blow we're facing down!"

Pen dropped what he was doing and raced at once to the pilot's box, slipping precariously on decking slick with dampness. He heard Cinnaminson shouting at him as he reached her, but her words were lost in the shrieks and howls of the wind. Shouting back that everything would be all right, he took her arm and steered her out of the pilot box and over to the hatchway, bending his head against the sudden gusts that swept into him. Again, she tried to say something, but he couldn't make it out. Ahren was waiting to receive her, and Pen turned back at once to help the beleaguered Rovers.

"Safety lines!" Gar Hatch roared from the pilot box, where he had taken over the controls.

Pen found one coiled about a clasp on the mainmast and snapped the harness in place around his waist. The *Skatelow* was dropping swiftly toward the plains as Gar Hatch sought shelter. The Rover Captain had to set her down or she would be knocked out of the sky. But finding a place that would offer protection from the wind and rain was not so easy when it was impossible to see clearly for more than a dozen yards.

The sails were down by then, so the boy hurried forward to secure the anchor ropes and hatch covers. Rain began to fall in sheets, a deluge that soaked Pen in only seconds. He had not worn his weather cloak on deck, and his pants and tunic offered no protection at all. He ignored the drenching, blinking away the torrent of water that spilled out of his hair and into his eyes, fighting to reach his objective. Still descending toward the plains, a stricken bird in search of a roost, the airship was shaking from the force of the wind.

Pen had almost reached the bow when the other end of his safety harness whipped past him like a snake, shooting out through the railing and over the side. It took him a moment to realize what had happened, that it had somehow come free, and his hesitation cost him his footing as the snap of the line jerked him off his feet. He went down on his back, his hands grasping for something to hold on to as he began to slide toward the open railing, skidding on rain-slick decking, unable to stop himself. He had only a moment to wonder how the line had come loose before he was tumbling over the side.

He would have fallen to his death if he had not caught hold of one of the stanchions, and even so, the effort of stopping himself nearly dislocated his arms. He hung helplessly over the side, legs dangling and arms stretched to the breaking point. For a second, he thought he would not be able to hold on. The airship was lurching and heaving as the wind whipped at it, and it felt as if everything was about to let go.

"Penderrin!" he heard Gar Hatch scream.

He looked across the decking through the rain to where the Rover Captain stood braced in the pilot box with a coiled line gripped in both hands. Catching the boy's eye, he gave the line a heave that sent it flying all the way forward and across the railing, not six feet from where Pen hung suspended. Working the line with both hands, Gar Hatch whipsawed it back and forth across the railing until it fell over Pen's shoulder.

"Grab on!" the big man shouted.

The boy hesitated. There was no reason for his safety line to have come loose unless someone had released the locking pin. The man best in position to do that was the one offering to help him now. If he wanted Pen dead, all he had to do was wait for him to grab the line, then release it. Pen would be over the side and gone. Was that what Gar Hatch intended for him? Was he incensed enough about Cinnaminson to kill Pen?

The airship shuddered violently, and Gar Hatch was thrown to one side in the box. "Hurry, lad!" he cried out.

Pen released his grip on the stanchion, one hand at a time, and transferred his weight to the rope the big man had thrown him. As he hung from it, the line the only thing keeping him from tumbling away, he experienced a terrible certainty that he had made a mistake and was going to pay for it with his life.

Then Gar Hatch began to haul on the rope, and Pen felt himself being lifted back over the side of the vessel and onto the deck. In seconds, he was back aboard and flat on his stomach as he crawled toward the pilot box, his heart still in his throat.

Gar Hatch extended his hand over the side of the box and pulled him in effortlessly, dark eyes glittering. "There, now! Safe again! That was close, Penderrin! What happened to your line? Did you check to see that it was secure at the masthead before buckling in?"

Pen had to admit he had not. "No. I didn't think there was any need."

"Haste is a dangerous enemy aboard an airship," the Rover Captain declared, tucking his chin into his beard. "You want to be careful how you go, especially in weather like this. Good thing I was watching out for you, lad." His eyes narrowed. "Good thing, too, I decided you were worth the trouble of saving. Another man with another daughter might have thought otherwise. You want to remember that." He gave Pen a none-too-gentle shove. "Down you go with the others till this is over. Better think on what I just said while you're there."

Pen made his way out of the pilot box and across the decking to the hatchway, a cold place opening in the pit of his stomach. Behind him, he heard the Rover Captain laugh.

EIGHTEEN

"**S**afety lines don't come loose for no reason at all," Khyber Elessedil whispered, poking him in the chest to emphasize her point. "They don't get put away with one end left unattached, either."

Outside, the wind hammered and the rain beat against the wooden hull of the *Skatelow* as if to collapse it to kindling.

"I thought that, too," Pen answered, shaking his head. The cold feeling wouldn't leave him. It had found a home, deep inside, and even being down in the companionway and out of the weather didn't ease its chill. "But I couldn't argue about it with him, because he was right—I hadn't checked it."

They were huddled together in his tiny cabin, talking in low voices and casting cautious looks at the closed door as they did so. Creaks and groans filled the silences, reminders of the precariousness of their situation. Overhead, they heard the heavy boots of the Rover crewmen as they moved about the decking, making sure the airship didn't break free of her moorings. They had landed only minutes ago in the lee of an oak grove at the edge of Paranor's forests, anchored about five feet off the ground while they rode out the storm. Gar Hatch had come below immediately and taken Cinnaminson to his cabin. Ahren and Tagwen were in the Druid's quarters already by then, the Dwarf sicker than Pen had seen a man in some time.

Khyber frowned. "It doesn't matter what he says anyway.

The point is, we know how he feels. I doubt that he cared all that much whether you went over the side or not. A fall would have been an unfortunate accident, but accidents happen. Carelessness on your part, he'd say, exactly what he warned you against earlier. He doesn't have to answer for your failure to listen. But saving you works even better. It lets him make clear to you how vulnerable you are. He's made his point. Now you know for sure not to come near his daughter anymore."

She paused. "You do know that now, don't you?"

He sighed. "Stop trying to tell me what to do, Khyber."

"Someone has to tell you! You don't seem capable of figuring things out on your own!" She scowled and went silent, and they both looked away, listening to the wind howl across the decking. "I'm just trying to keep you from getting killed, Pen."

"I know."

"What was Cinnaminson trying to tell you when you were bringing her down? Did you find out?"

"Just to be careful, to watch out for myself, that's all."

"She knew. She was trying to warn you." Khyber shook her head. "I wish this trip was over. I wish we were rid of these people."

He nodded, thinking at the same time that he wished he were rid of everyone but Cinnaminson. It didn't seem fair that a simple friendship should put him in so much danger. He still couldn't quite bring himself to believe it, although he had no illusions about what Gar Hatch might be capable of. Khyber was right about what happened topside. He might never know if Hatch intended for him to go over the side, but he knew for certain that he had been warned.

"Well, the trip will be over soon enough," he muttered, suddenly bone weary and heartsick. "Probably nothing else will happen now anyway."

Khyber exhaled sharply. "I wouldn't bet on it."

Although he didn't say so, Pen guessed he wouldn't, either.

The storm passed around midday, the winds dying down and the rain ending, and the *Skatelow* resumed her journey east. By then, she was above the Jannisson Pass, leaving Paranor and Callahorn and sliding north along the foothills fronting the Charnals and the Eastland. The weather turned sultry, and the skies were clouded over and gray for as far as the eye could see. Water birds soared overhead from the mountain lakes and rivers, white flashes against the gloom, their cries eerie and chilling. Far to the east and south, the departing storm clouds formed a dark wall splintered by flashes of lightning.

Except for the still-airsick Tagwen, everyone was back on deck by then, looking out at the distant mountains, catching the first glimpses of their destination. It was another day's journey to the Lazareen, but Pen felt a shift in his thinking anyway. His time with Cinnaminson was growing short, for after the Lazareen there was only another day's flying before they left the airship. He marveled that only yesterday it seemed as if they had all the time in the world, and now it seemed that they had almost none. Part of his attitude was fostered by what had happened earlier, but even that wouldn't have discouraged him entirely, had they had another week to spend together. But he could do nothing to prolong their journey's ending, could change nothing about parting from Cinnaminson.

They flew up the corridor leading off the Streleheim toward the Malg Swamp, a misty flat smudge across the landscape on their left, the terrain in dark counterpoint to the rolling green foothills on their right. Gar Hatch took the airship lower, trying to avoid the heavier mix of clouds and mist that layered the sky with a thick ceiling between swamp and mountains. As they neared the Malg, the water birds disappeared, replaced by swarms of insects that defied winds and airspeed to attack the ship's passengers in angry clouds. Gar Hatch swore loudly and took his vessel up until finally the insects dropped away.

Pen spit dead gnats from his mouth and wiped them from his nostrils and eyes. Cinnaminson appeared next to him, moving over from the pilot box with unerring directional sense, never wavering in her passage, and he was reminded again of how, even blind, she seemed able to see what was going on around her.

He was about to ask her what her father had said to her in his cabin, but before he could do so, he heard something in the cry of a heron that winged past so close it felt as if he could reach out and touch it. He looked at it sharply, hearing in its call a warning he could not mistake. Something had frightened the bird, and that did not happen easily with herons.

He scanned the horizon, then saw the dark swarm of dots soaring out of a deep canyon cut into the rugged foothills.

Birds, he thought at once. Big ones. Rocs or Shrikes.

But they didn't fly like birds. There was no wing movement, and their shapes were all wrong.

They were airships.

"Captain!" he shouted over to Gar Hatch and pointed.

For a long second, the big man just stared at the shapes, then he turned back with a dark look on his face. "Cinnaminson, get below and stay there. Take the other young lady with you. Penderrin, come into the pilot box. I'll need you."

Without bothering to wait for a reply, Gar began shouting at the Rover crewmen, both of whom jumped in response. Within moments, they were hoisting every scrap of sail they could manage, a clear indication that whatever was coming, Gar Hatch intended to run from it.

Cinnaminson was already descending through the hatchway, but Khyber was having none of it. "I'm staying," she declared firmly. "I can help."

"Go below," Ahren Elessedil ordered her at once. "The Captain commands on this ship. If I need you, I'll call. Stay ready. Pen, let's find out what is happening."

Be careful, Khyber mouthed silently to the boy as she disappeared from view.

Together, Pen and the Druid hurried over to the pilot box and climbed inside. Gar Hatch was setting the control levers, readying them for when the sails were all in place. He scowled at Pen and the Druid as if they might be responsible.

"Put on your safety lines," he ordered. "Check both ends of yours, young Penderrin. We've no time for mistakes here."

Pen held his tongue, doing as he was told, buckling himself into his harness and testing the links. Ahren Elessedil did the same.

"Sometimes I wonder if it's worth it, making these runs," Gar Hatch growled. He nodded toward the approaching dots. "Those are flits. Single-passenger airships, bothersome little gnats. Quick and highly maneuverable. Gnome raiders use them, and that's who those boys likely are. They want to bring us down for whatever we've got aboard. They'll do it, too, if they get close enough. I wouldn't worry normally, but that storm took something out of the *Skatelow*. She's faster than they are when she's working right, but she's down in her power about three-quarters and I haven't the time to do the work necessary to bring her back up again until we reach the Lazareen."

"We can't outrun them?" Ahren asked.

Gar Hatch shook his head. "I don't think so. If we get far enough ahead of them, they might lose interest. If they know the ship, they might fall off. If not . . ."

He shrugged. "Still, there's other ways."

He yelled at the crewmen to make certain they were ready,

then shoved the thruster levers all the way forward. The *Skatelow* shuddered with the sudden input of power from the radian draws and shot ahead, lifting skyward at the same time. Hatch worked the controls with swiftness and precision, and Pen could see that he had been down that road before. Even so, the flits were getting closer, growing larger and beginning to take shape. Pen saw the Gnomes who were crouched in their tiny frames, faces wizened and burnt by wind and sun. Gloved hands worked the levers that changed the direction of the single-mast sail, a billowing square that could be partially reefed or let out to change direction and thrust. At present, all sails were wind-filled, catching the light, powering the flits ahead at full speed.

Pen could already see that the *Skatelow* had no chance of outrunning them. The angle of attack and her injuries from the storm didn't allow for it. The flits would be on them in moments.

"Penderrin, lad," Gar Hatch said almost calmly. "Do you think you know enough by now to take the helm and keep her running full out?"

The boy nodded at once. "I think so."

"She's yours, then," the Rover said, stepping aside. "You look like you might have fought a battle or two in your time," he said to Ahren. "How are you with rail slings?"

They went out of the pilot box, safety harnesses trailing after them, and worked their way across the deck to either side of the mainmast. A Rover crewman joined each of them, and in teams they began to set up the rail slings, pulling the catapults out of storage bins and setting the pivot ends into slots cut into the deck. Pen had never seen a rail sling before, but he understood their function right away. Built like heavy crossbows, they sat on swivels that could be pointed in any direction over the railings. A hand winch cranked back a sling in which sat a missile the size of a fist. When the sling was released, the missile hurtled out into the void, hopefully striking something in the process.

Hitting a moving target with one of those weapons while flying in an airship was virtually impossible, unless the target was huge, in which case no damage was likely to occur. But used against a swarm of targets, like the flits, a rail sling might have some success. Miss one flit and you still had a chance at half a dozen more.

The rail slings were barely in place and loaded when the first of the flits reached them. The flits by themselves were useless as weapons, too small and fragile to ram a larger vessel or to shear off a mast. The Gnomes' intent was to sever the radian draws or rigging or to shred the ambient-light sheaths. They did this by using poles with razor-sharp blades bound about the business end.

In seconds, the flits were everywhere, coming at the *Skatelow* from every direction. Pen kept the airship steady and straight, knowing that this offered Gar Hatch and Ahren Elessedil their best chance at bringing down their attackers. The rail slings were firing by then, and a few of the tiny ships went down, sails holed or masts shattered, plummeting earthward like stricken birds. One either miscalculated or failed for some other reason and crashed into the *Skatelow*'s hull, shattering on impact. Another became tangled in the bigger ship's rigging and crashed to the deck, where its pilot was seized by one of the Rovers and thrown overboard.

But the flits were inflicting damage on the *Skatelow*, as well. Several of her rigging lines had already been severed, and one radian draw was frayed almost to the breaking point. The mainsail had a dozen rents in the canvas, and the flit that had become tangled in the rigging had brought down several spars. The *Skatelow* was still flying, but Pen felt the unevenness of her effort.

When the frayed draw finally snapped, he switched off power to the crystal it fed and transferred what remained to the others. But the airship was shaking and bucking and no longer responded smoothly.

"Hold her steady!" Gar Hatch bellowed angrily.

Another flit whipped past Pen, the pole and blade sweeping down at his head, and he barely managed to duck away from it. Sensing the ship was in trouble and its crew unable to do any more to help her or themselves, the raiders were growing bolder. One good strike on one more essential component, and the vessel would not be able to stay in the air. She would fail quickly, and then she would be theirs.

They were deep into Northland country by that time, flying close to the Malg, and mist had closed about them in a heavy curtain that reduced their vision to almost nothing. The flit attacks seemed to materialize from nowhere as they winged out of the haze and then disappeared back into it again. How the Gnome pilots could find their way under such conditions was beyond Pen. He was struggling to see anything.

"Take her up!" Hatch shouted at him.

He did so, lifting her nose into the soup just as a Gnome raider came right across the bow. The flit simply disintegrated, but pieces of it ricocheted everywhere, severing lines forward and starboard and cutting loose the flying jib. The *Skatelow* slewed sideways in response, and Pen could no longer make her do anything. Gar Hatch abandoned his rail sling and clawed his way back across the deck to regain the controls.

In the midst of that chaos, with the *Skatelow* beginning to fall and the flits attacking like hornets, Ahren Elessedil stepped away from his rail sling, stood at the center of the airship's deck, and raised his arms skyward, his robes billowing like dark sails. For a moment he stood without moving, a statue at rest, eyes closed, head lifted. His face was calm and relaxed, as if he had found peace within himself and left the madness behind.

Then his hands began to weave like snakes and his voice to chant, the sound low and guttural and unrecognizable as his.

Gar Hatch had hauled himself into the pilot box and taken over the controls from Pen with an angry grunt. His hands were flying over the levers and wheels, but when he looked up long enough to catch sight of Ahren Elessedil, he froze. "What in the name of sea salt and common sense is the man doing?" he demanded.

The boy shook his head. He knew. "Saving us," he answered.

Behind them, Khyber had come out on deck, grasping the hatchway frame to hold herself steady, and was shouting at her uncle in disbelief.

Gnome raiders, bladed poles lowered to skewer him, were darting at the Druid from all directions. But try as they might, they could not get close enough to do so. Mist obscured their vision and gusts of wind knocked them aside, the mix roiling faster and faster, taking on the shape of a massive funnel. Heads began to turn in response. Aboard the *Skatelow*, the Rovers were shouting. Astride the flits, there wasn't the time or energy to spare for it. The mist and wind had become a deadly whirlpool surrounding the airships and then closing on them.

Ahren Elessedil's arms were stretched above his head, as if he sought to grasp something that was just out of reach. The funnel cloud of mist and wind continued to tighten. It caught the outermost flits and engulfed them. One minute they were there, fighting to stay aloft, and the next they were gone. The rest tried to flee, banking their tiny ships in all directions, seeking a means of escape. Some came right at the *Skatelow* and Ahren Elessedil, but they could not get close enough to strike at either. One by one, they were plucked from the sky by the funnel. One by one, they disappeared until all were gone.

The Druid lowered his arms, the mist dissipated, the winds died, and the whirlwind vanished, as well. Not a flit remained in the sky. Everything was the way it had been before the attack, the air hazy and gray but calm. The *Skatelow* sailed on, wounded but able to continue. In the distance, a sliver of sunlight broke through the clouds.

Ahren Elessedil walked back over to the pilot box and beckoned to Pen. "Let's help clear the decks and put away the rail slings," he said. He glanced at Gar Hatch. "Odd weather we're having, isn't it? No one would ever believe such strange things could happen. A man would be crazy even to suggest it."

Pen smiled inwardly. The Druid knew something about giving warnings, as well. Which was a good thing, he supposed, since now everyone aboard knew what he was.

NINETEEN

Late in the morning of the following day, they arrived at Anatcherae, the inland port on the Lazareen that serviced all traffic passing north along the corridor formed by the Charnal Mountains to the east and the Knife Edge Mountains to the west. They reached their destination more quickly than anticipated because tailwinds filled and sunshine fed the sails and because Gar Hatch had been able to complete repairs to the damaged radian draw before nightfall of the previous day. It was a smooth flight the entire way after their escape from the flits, with no further trouble arising to impede their passage.

Anatcherae was an old city built by a mix of Trolls and Bordermen following the Second War of the Races, when Southlanders were mostly keeping to themselves below Callahorn but trade was flourishing everywhere else. A sprawling, ramshackle outpost in its early days, it grew quickly, the principal port servicing trappers and traders coming out of the Anar, Callahorn, and everywhere the Troll nations made their homes. It had become a major city, though still with the look and feel of a frontier town, its buildings spread out along the southwest shore of the lake, timber and shingle structures that were torn down and replaced as the need arose and without much thought to permanency. Even though the greater part of the populace lived in the city, most did not intend to make

Anatcherae their final stop along life's road and so did not build for the long term.

The *Skatelow* set down at the waterfront docks, where warehouses and barns loomed like low, squat beasts bent down for a drink at the Lazareen's dark waters, their mouths open to receive what the lake would deliver. Airships crowded the waterfront, most of them large freighters and warships. Traffic leaving the docks passed down roads flanked by ale houses, pleasure dens, and inns of various descriptions. Shops and homes lay farther inland, away from the bustle and din of the docks, back from the raw edge of seaport life.

Standing on deck while the harbormaster towed the *Skatelow* to her assigned slip, Pen took a moment to glance over his shoulder in the other direction, back across the lake. The Lazareen was legendary. A broad, slate-gray body of water that seldom changed color in any weather, it was believed to run several thousand feet deep. Rumor had it that in some places it reached all the way to the netherworld and thereby provided the souls of the dead a doorway to the domain of the living. Mountains framed its rugged banks to the east and south, walls of stone that kept those souls contained. Dozens of rivers had their origins in snowmelt glaciers thousands of feet higher up, the confluence of their waters tumbling through canyons and defiles to feed the lake. Cold winds blew down out of snowy heights to mix with the warmer air of the flats and create a swirling mist that clung to the shorelines like gray moss. Pen did not like the Lazareen, he decided. It had the look and feel of the Mist Marsh, a place the boy was all too familiar with and wished never to visit again.

The *Skatelow* eased up against the dock, and the Rovers set about securing her. When Gar Hatch came over to speak with Ahren, Pen listened in.

"I'll be needing several days to make repairs before we continue on," the Rover Captain advised in a gruff voice, hitching up his pants to emphasize that work lay ahead.

"Maybe more. Once that's done, we'll continue on to where you need to go, and then I'll be dropping you off and saying good-bye."

"I don't think we discussed being dropped, Captain," the Druid said, frowning. "I think the agreement was that you would wait until we came out again from our search."

"That was then, this is now. The agreement is changed." Gar Hatch spit over the side. "Others need a little business done, as well, and rely on me to conduct it for them. I require my ship to do so. I can't make a living while she sits idle. You don't pay enough for that. Give me a time and a place, and I'll come back for you. My Captain's word on it."

"There isn't any way of knowing when we'll be finished. We can increase your purse, if it's a matter of money."

The Rover shook his head. "Sorry, mate. This isn't about money."

Ahren Elessedil smiled. "You are a Rover, Gar Hatch. It's always about money."

The big man laughed and glanced over at Pen. "You listening close, young Penderrin? Here's a man who knows the way of the world. He's right, too. Everything is about money, one way or the other." He looked back at the Druid. "Still, I can't let myself be tied down for so long. You might not even come back from wherever it is you're going. I've seen already the sort of business you do, and it isn't reassuring to puzzle on. So I'm dropping you and that's the end of it."

The Druid nodded. "I could find other passage and cancel our agreement here and now, Captain Hatch. I would be justified."

"You could try," the big man amended. "But you won't find anyone else to take you where you want to go that knows the ways of that country like I do. You won't find anyone who can sail the mists and the night like I can. Maybe most important of all, you won't find anyone who can keep his mouth shut about who you are and what you're doing. You might want to bear that in mind."

"But can I trust you? I find I have serious doubts."

Gar Hatch smiled and inclined his head. "Put aside your doubts, sir. My word is good."

The irony of that statement probably did not escape the Druid, but he let it pass. "Three days, Captain. That's as long as I'll give you to do your business here. We leave on the fourth. We'll find lodgings ashore and check back with you. I won't press for you to wait on us, if you've decided against it. But there will be no further changes to our agreement, and I expect a close watch on the tongues of your people. Don't disappoint me."

He went down the hatchway to his cabin to bring up Tagwen. Khyber was already on the dock, looking around eagerly.

Pen sensed Gar Hatch staring at him and met his stare, refusing to look away when it lingered too long. The big man laughed. "You've been a revelation for me, Penderrin. A treasure and a find."

"Can I say good-bye to Cinnaminson?" Pen asked.

He hadn't seen her since the attack of the flits. Gar Hatch had kept her shut away in his cabin, not even allowing her to come on deck at night, advising his passengers that she was ill. Pen had thought several times to sneak down and see for himself, but each time he thought to try, Gar Hatch was somewhere close, watching.

It was his last chance until they reboarded in three days' time, and anything could happen between now and then. Hatch could promise what he wished, but that didn't mean it was likely to happen.

The Rover Captain smiled. "Better you don't, lad. What she's got might be catching. Wouldn't do to have you come down with a fever while you're resting in port. Your uncle is mad enough at me already. You'll see her when you come back aboard."

I'll never see her again, Pen thought. But he could do nothing about it short of forcing a confrontation, and he was aware how much trouble that would cause.

He turned away without a word, shouldered his pack, and started down the ladder. He was halfway to the pier when he heard his name called.

"Pen, wait!"

Cinnaminson appeared at the railing, blind eyes staring downward without finding him. He started back up the ladder and stopped when he was close enough to see Gar Hatch glaring at him in the background.

"I'm feeling better now, Pen," she said, giving him a small wave and a smaller smile. "I just wanted to say good-bye." Then she whispered so softly that only he could hear, "Come back tonight."

She turned away quickly and went to her father, who took her by the arm and steered her below again, not bothering with even a glance at Pen. The boy stood watching until they were out of sight, then went down the ladder with his heart in his throat.

With Ahren Elessedil leading, the four companions walked down through the center of the city, mingling with the crowds as they searched for a likely place to secure lodging for the days ahead. Pen could barely make himself concentrate on the task at hand, his mind still on Cinnaminson and her whispered words. *Come back tonight.* He was intoxicated by them, made light-headed at the prospect of what they meant, chilled by the prospect of the danger at which they hinted. He wasn't afraid, though. He was fearless when it came to her. He understood that by even considering a secret return, he was risking not only his own safety but also the success of his undertaking. Yet he couldn't help himself. He had to go to her.

It took them the better part of an hour to find what Ahren was looking for, a small, prosperous inn just off one of the main roadways, one that was better kept than those closer to the docks, one frequented by other travelers than sailors. It was called Fisherman's Lie. It sat on a corner that opened onto a small plaza and was wrapped by a veranda that fronted both streets. Broad double doors opened into the common room, where travelers sat to visit and drink glasses of ale. Tables and benches and a long serving bar took up most of the available space. Flowers grew in boxes under the windowsills, and baskets hung from the veranda and eaves, splashes of color to brighten the clapboard facade.

Ahren left the other three on the porch while he went inside to take rooms. The less they were all seen together, the less likely it was that anyone would make the connection to the four the Druids were hunting. Since Khyber had cut Pen's hair short and bound his head in a scarf, none of them was particularly noticeable. But there was no point in taking chances. Those tempted by the money the Druids offered would be looking hard.

The Elf emerged in moments with the rooms secured. They went into the dining room after that and sat at a table in the back while waiting for their food. Sipping at glasses of cold ale, they talked about their situation.

"Hatch knows who I am," Ahren said quietly, eyes scanning the mostly empty room as he spoke. "Or at least he knows *what* I am. He might not know my name yet, but there is a good chance he will find out. Or if not him, then one of the crewmen. All of them will be asking around, talking with other Rovers."

"Maybe not," Pen offered hopefully. "You might have scared him out of it."

Ahren smiled. "Not likely. Not that man. If he finds out who we are, he will look for a way to turn it to his advantage. It's his nature. So we have to be very careful until we set sail again. That's why I didn't tell him where he could find us. He mustn't know. If he betrays us, our enemies will still have to search us out. That won't be easy in a city of this size."

"We should just leave him right here and now and be done with it!" Tagwen snapped. He scowled into his glass. "Take him up on his offer. That way we can stop worrying about him."

"But not about getting to where we have to go," Ahren replied. "I don't trust him, either, but he is right when he says we will have trouble finding anyone else to fly us into the Charnals. Even by looking, we risk giving ourselves away. Say what you want about Hatch, he knows how to sail. His reputation is one of getting in and out of tight places. We need that. I think we have to stick with him."

"One of us could watch the *Skatelow* and see who comes and goes," Khyber suggested.

Her uncle shook his head. "That's too risky and too time-consuming. Besides, any one of them could give us away. We can't watch them all. Better to keep our heads down and wait this out. I will speak with Hatch each day to see how matters stand. If he lies to me, I will know. The rest of you will remain here, inside, out of sight. No one leaves the inn without permission until it is time to sail. Agreed?"

All of them nodded, but Pen knew it was an agreement he was going to break.

He waited until it was dark and Tagwen was asleep before slipping out of his bed. He crossed the room in his bare feet, boots in hand, and went through the door without a sound. Instead of leaving by the inn's front entrance, he went out the back, taking the rear stairs to the street. Cloaked and hooded, he went quickly toward the waterfront. The night air was clear and sharp, turned cold after sunset, and the sky was bright with stars. It was close to midnight, but the streets were still bustling with activity, the denizens of the ale houses and pleasure dens just beginning their night's fun. Many were sailors, come from all over, a mix of travelers passing through. None of them looked at him. None spoke.

He was taking a chance, risking everything. He was neither happy nor sad about it, felt neither guilt nor satisfaction. Such things didn't matter to a boy who thought he was in love. What mattered was that Cinnaminson was waiting, and the thought of her drove every other consideration from his mind. His excitement gave him courage and determination. It gave him a sense of invulnerability. Whatever happened, he was a match for it. His certainty was so complete that he never stopped to question whether his bravado might be playing him false. On that night, there was no place in his heart for rational thinking.

He reached the waterfront and began working his way down the docks. New ships had arrived, some of them bigger than anything he had ever seen. He looked closely for the *Gala-phile* as he went, but did not see her. Nor did he see Terek Molt or any other Druids. Loading and unloading went on about him, unceasing, unending, and all seemed as it should.

When he reached the *Skatelow*, he moved into the shadows across from her, staying well back from the light. There was no sign of life aboard. Even the storm lamps were extinguished. The boarding ladder was pulled up, signaling that visitors were unwelcome. On the piers to either side, similarly darkened ships lay at rest, sleeping birds awaiting the dawn.

Pen eased along the wall of the warehouse that fronted the slip, then moved just to the edge of the light that pooled down from the lamps hung over the entrance doors. He stood there, undecided, searching the contours of the *Skatelow* for signs of life.

Then he saw her. She appeared all at once, beckoning to him, knowing somehow that he was there. He took a chance, his throat tightening with anticipation. He stepped into the light, crossed the dock to the mooring slip, and stopped just below where she stood.

"Cinnaminson," he said.

Her blind gaze shifted and her hair shimmered in the moonlight. "Wait," she whispered. She moved at once to the ladder and dropped it over the side. "Come up. They're all in town at the ale houses and won't be back before dawn. We're alone."

He did as she said, climbing the ladder and hauling himself aboard. He stood on the decking in front of her, and she reached to take his hands. "I knew you would come," she said.

"I couldn't stay away."

She released his hands and pulled the ladder back aboard. "Sit with me over here, out of the light. If they come, they need me to lower the ladder to let them aboard. By then, you can be over the side."

She led him to the far side of the pilot box, where the shadows were deepest, and they sat down with their shoulders touching and their backs to the low wall. Her milky eyes turned to find him. "Let's not tell each other any lies tonight," she whispered. "Let's tell each other only truths."

He nodded. "All right. Who goes first?"

"I do. It was my idea." She leaned close. "Papa knows who you are, Penderrin Ohmsford. He knew Ahren Elessedil was a Druid after what happened during the flit attack, and he found out the rest from asking around the docks. He didn't give you away, or let on that you were passengers on the *Skatelow*, but he knows."

Her smooth features were tight with trepidation and uncertainty, her chin lifted as if to take a blow. Pen touched her cheek. "Ahren told us this might happen. It isn't unexpected. But he had to reveal himself if he was to save us."

"Papa knows this, and he doesn't forget such favors. I don't think he intends you harm. But I don't always understand how he thinks, either." She took his hands again. "Will you tell me where you are staying? So that if I discover you are in danger, I can warn you?"

He hesitated. It was the one thing he had been ordered not to reveal, no matter what. He had promised to keep it a secret. And now Cinnaminson was asking him to violate his trust. It was a terrible moment, and his decision was made impulsively.

"We are lodged at Fisherman's Lie, about half a mile into the city." He squeezed her fingers. "But how will you find us, even if you need to? You'll have to ask for help, and that's too dangerous."

She smiled. "Let me tell you another truth, Penderrin. I can find you anytime I want, because even though I am blind, I can see with my mind. I have always been able to do so. It is the way I was born—with a different kind of sight. I travel with Papa because I can see better than he can in darkness and in mist and fog, bad weather, storms of all sorts. I can navigate by seeing with my mind what is hidden to his eyes. That's why he can go into places others cannot—across the Lazareen, into the Slags, places cloaked by weather and gloom. It's like a picture that appears behind my eyes of everything around me. It doesn't work so well in daylight, although I can see well enough to find my way about. But at night, it is clear and sharp. Papa didn't know I could do this, at first. When Mama died, he began taking me to sea rather than leaving me with her relatives. He never liked them or they him. Having me travel with him was less trouble than finding someone he trusted to raise me at home. I was still very young. I thought I was being given a chance to prove I was worth keeping. I wanted him to love me so that he wouldn't give me up. So I showed him how I could read the sky when no one else could. He understood my gift, and he began using me to navigate. I let him do so because it made me feel secure. I was useful, and so I believed he would keep me."

She paused. "Papa doesn't want anyone to know this. Only the two men who serve as crew know, and they are his cousins. Both are sworn to secrecy. He is protective of me; I am his daughter and helpmeet. But I am also his good-luck charm. Sometimes, he isn't clear on the difference. I think he loves me, but he doesn't know what loving someone really means."

She reached out and cupped his face in her hands. "There. I've given you a gift—a truth no one else has ever heard."

He took her hands in his own and squeezed them gently. "You've kept this to yourself a long time. Why are you telling someone now, after so long? Why disobey your father's wishes like that? I wouldn't have minded if you had kept it secret."

She freed her hands, and her fingers brushed at her hair and face like tiny wings. "I am tired of not being able to talk about it with anyone. Not talking about it is like pretending I am someone other than who I really am. I have been looking for someone to tell this to. I chose you because I think we are the same. We are both keeping secrets."

"I guess that's so," he said. He sat back against the pilot box wall. "Now it's my turn to tell you a secret. I hardly know where to begin, I have so many. You know who I am, but you don't know what I am doing here."

"I can guess," she said. "The Ard Rhys is your aunt. You are here because of her. But the Druids say you are in danger. They say that what happened to her might happen to you if you are not found and brought to them. Is that true?"

He shook his head. "I'm in danger, but mostly from them. Some of them are responsible for what's happened to her. If they find me, I might end up the same way. I escaped them when they came looking for me in Patch Run. So now I'm running away."

"Are you looking for your parents?"

"I'm looking for my aunt. It's complicated." He paused. "We promised to tell each other truths tonight, so let me tell you one. You have a kind of magic that no one else has. So do I. Like you, I was born with it. It is probably a part of the magic my father inherited, something that's been passed down through the Ohmsford bloodline for generations. Only, mine is different."

He exhaled softly, searching for a way to explain. "I can tell what plants and animals are feeling and sometimes thinking. They don't talk to me exactly, but they communicate anyway. They tell me things with their sounds and movements. For instance, I know if they're afraid or angry and what causes them to be so."

"Your gift is not so different from my own," she said. "You can see things that are hidden from other people and you can see them without using your eyes. We are alike, aren't we?"

He leaned forward. "Except that I am free and you are not. Why is that, Cinnaminson? Could you leave your father if you wanted? Could you go somewhere else and have a different life?"

It was such an impulsive question that he surprised himself by asking it. Worse, he had nothing beyond encouragement to offer if she answered yes. What could he do to help her in his present circumstances? He couldn't take her with him, not where he was going. He couldn't offer to aid her while Ahren was so determined not to aggravate Gar Hatch.

She laughed softly. "Such a bold question, Penderrin. What should I do? Leave my Papa and run away with you? A blind girl and a fugitive boy?"

"I guess it sounds silly," he admitted. "I shouldn't have asked."

"Why not?" she pressed, surprising him. "Do you care for me?"

"You don't have to ask that."

"Then you must care *about* me, too. So it seems right to want an answer. I like it that you do. Yes, I want a different life. I have looked for it. But you are the first to whom I have talked about it. You are the first to ask."

He stared at her face, at her smooth features, at the smile that curved her lips, at her strange blank eyes. What he felt for her in that instant transcended love. He might say that he loved her, but he didn't know all that much about love, so saying it wouldn't mean anything. It was only a word to him; he was still only a boy. But this other feeling, the one that was more than love, encompassed whole worlds. It whispered of connection and sharing, of confidences and truths like the ones they had told each other tonight. It promised small moments that would never be forgotten and larger ones that could change lives.

What could he give her that would tell her this? He struggled to find an answer, lost in a sea of confusing emotions. Her hands were holding his again, her fingers making small circles against his skin. She wasn't saying anything. She was waiting for him to speak first.

"If you were to decide you wanted to leave your father, I would help you," he said finally. "If you wanted to come away with me, I would let you. I don't know how that could happen. I only know that I would find a way."

She lowered her head just enough that the shadows grazed her face and hid her expression. "Would you come for me wherever I was, Pen? It is a bold thing to ask, but I am asking it anyway. Would you come for me?"

"Wherever you are, whenever you have need," he whispered.

She smiled, her face lifting back into the light. "That is all I need to know." She sat back and turned her face to the starlit sky. "Enough of making promises and telling truths. Let's just sit together for a little while and listen to the night."

They did so, side by side, not saying anything, their hands in their laps, their shoulders and hips touching. The sounds of the waterfront rolled over them in small bursts and slow meanderings, brief intrusions from a place that seemed far away. The night turned colder, and Pen wrapped them both in his cloak, putting his arm around her to lend his warmth, feeling her small form melt against him.

After a time, she leaned over and kissed him on the cheek. "You must leave now. It grows late. They will return. Go back to your room and sleep." She kissed him again. "Come again tomorrow, if you can. I will be waiting."

He rose and walked with her to the ladder, scanning the dock for signs of approaching Rovers. The docks were empty now. She lowered the ladder for him, and he climbed down. He stood looking up at her as she pulled it away again, then he turned and went down the waterfront.

Cinnaminson.

Nothing in his life, he knew, would ever be the same again.

TWENTY

Grianne Ohmsford woke to a morning so dismal and gray that it might have drifted out of the marshy depths of the Malg Swamp, an apparition come in search of the unfortunate Jarka Ruus. It felt alive and hungry. It had a shape and feel. The air it breathed smelled of fetid water and brushed at the skin with greasy, insistent fingers. The clouds that formed its hair were so low in the sky as to be indistinguishable from the misty beard that curled about its ragged face. Everything about it whispered of hidden danger and lost souls. In its presence, heartbeats quickened with the uneasy and certain knowledge that death, when it appeared, would be quick and unexpected.

The Ard Rhys was cramped from sleeping in the cradle of tree limbs, her body aching and stiff. She had slept, though she did not pretend to understand how, and she had kept her perch and not fallen as she had feared she would. Climbing down through brume that would have discouraged even the most intrepid seabird, she caught sight of the tracks that crisscrossed the earth directly below, and decided she had been lucky to have survived the night with no more than her sore muscles. Weka Dart had been right to warn her against trying to make her bed on the ground.

She glanced around, scanning the mist and gloom for some sign of the devious little Ulk Bog, thinking he might have come back during the night, even as mad at her as he had been when he left. After all, he had gone to a lot of trouble to persuade her to allow him to accompany her, and she found it hard to believe that he would toss it all away because of a perceived slight. He didn't seem the type who would allow insults to get in the way of ambitions. She still wasn't sure what he was after, only that he was after something. But there was no sign of him, so she accepted that he had gone his own way after all.

Just as well, she told herself.

Except that she didn't know the country, and that put her at a disadvantage. She knew in general how she should go, given that the Forbidding mirrored the Four Lands. She could estimate the location of the Hadeshorn from what she knew of its location in her own world. But the mist was confusing, and her sense of direction skewed by the different land formations. Worse, she would have to risk encountering the monsters that inhabited the Forbidding, without knowing who and what they were. At least Weka Dart had knowledge of the things she needed to avoid.

But there was no help for it. Nor help for her lack of food and water. She would have to forage for both as she traveled, hoping that she would recognize the former when she saw it. Water should be less of a problem, although just then she didn't want to assume anything.

She stretched her aching limbs and looked down at herself. Ragged and dirty, she was a mess. Her clothes were almost in shreds, her pale skin showing through the gaps in ways that didn't please her. She wrapped her tattered nightdress closer and told herself she would have to find something else to wear soon or she would be naked as well as starving and lost. She couldn't travel much farther without boots, either. Her feet were already scraped and bleeding, and she hadn't even gotten to the rocky climb to the Hadeshorn.

When I find out who did this to me . . .

She was about to set out when there was movement in the

trees to one side and Weka Dart, bristle-haired and spindly-limbed, emerged carrying a cloth-wrapped package in both arms. He caught sight of her and stopped, his sharp teeth showing as he smiled broadly.

"Ah, Grianne of the trees. Sleep well, did you? You don't look so bad for having spent the night aboveground. See all the tracks?" He gestured. "Now you understand what I was telling you."

She stared at him without answering, undecided if she was happy about having him back.

His cunning features scrunched with disappointment. "Don't look at me like that! You should be pleased to see me. How far would you get without me? You don't know anything about this part of the world, anyone can tell that. You need me to guide you."

"I thought you were finished with me," she said.

He shrugged. "I changed my mind. I decided to forgive you. After all, you have a right to know about me, so you did what Strakens do and used your magic to find out. It isn't any different than what any creature of habit would do. Here, I brought you some clothes."

He came forward and dumped the bundle at her feet. She bent down and picked through it, finding leather boots, a loose-fitting cotton shirt, pants, a belt and knife, and the great cloak in which he had wrapped them. All were in good condition and close enough in size to fit her comfortably. She had no idea where he had found them and didn't think she should ask.

"Put them on," he urged.

"Turn your back," she replied.

It was silly, given that an Ulk Bog would not be interested about her that way, but she wanted to assert her authority before he got the wrong idea about who was in charge. If he was going to accompany her on the rest of her journey, as it appeared he was determined to do, she had better set him straight on the nature of their relationship immediately.

She removed the nightdress and put on the clothes, watching him fidget as he stared off into the trees. "I want to know why you insist on coming with me," she told him. "And don't tell me it's because you want to help a stranger find her way."

He threw up his hands. "Can't anyone do a good turn for you without being questioned about it?"

"In your case, no. You don't seem the type to do good turns unless there is something in it for you. So let's be honest about it. What is it that you want from me? Maybe it isn't anything I'll mind giving up, if it means you can get me to where I want to go." She finished buttoning the tunic. "You can turn around now."

He did so, looking sour-faced and ill-used. "I thought Strakens could tell what normal people are thinking. Why don't you just use your magic to find out what I want?"

She didn't bother with an answer, waiting patiently on him. He pouted. "You already know the reason. You just weren't paying attention when I told you. Too self-absorbed, I suspect."

"Tell me again."

He pouted harder. "I got in some trouble with my tribe. I had to flee for my life. They might still be chasing me. Alone, I'm not much good against a lot of the things that are Jarka Ruus. I know how to find my way and mostly how to avoid them, though. So I thought we could help each other." He folded his arms defiantly. "There, are you satisfied, Grianne of the curious mind and endless questions?"

He was being insolent, but she let it go. "I am. For now. But in the future, you will tell me the truth about your motives and your plans, little rodent, or I will feed you to the bigger things you seek to avoid. I don't like surprises. I want to know what you are thinking about. No secret plans, or our bargain is off."

"Then you agree that we should travel together?" he asked.

He was positively gleeful. "That you will watch out for me?" He caught himself. "Well, that we will watch out for each other?"

"Let's just start walking," she said, and turned away.

They walked all that day, traveling east below the Dragon Line and across the grasslands and foothills of the Pashanon. The weather stayed gray and misty, the sun never more than a faint brightness high above them, the world they journeyed through composed of brume and shadows. The air was damp and chilly, a discomforting presence that made Grianne grateful for the clothes and boots that Weka Dart had brought her. The grasslands and hills were coated with moisture that never quite evaporated, yet the land remained barren and life-less. The absence of small birds and little animals was un-nerving, and even the insects tended to be of the buzzing, biting variety. Grasses grew thick and hardy, sawtooth and ra-zorblade spears that were a washed-out green and mottled gray. Trees were stunted and gnarled below the Dragon Line, and many were little more than skeletons. The waters of the ponds and streams were stagnant and algae-laced. Every-where they traveled and everywhere she looked, the world seemed to be sick and dying.

Yet the Jarka Ruus had existed for thousands of years. She tried to imagine a lifetime in such a world and failed. It fright-ened her to think of being trapped there for long. If she had not believed that she would find a way out, she would have been devastated. But she never wavered in her certainty that she would. Those who had sent her there had made a mistake in letting her live. They might think themselves rid of her, but she would prove them wrong.

Her thoughts drifted frequently to the cause of her predica-ment. It was impossible for her to know exactly who had transported her, but she could make an educated guess or two. What baffled her was why they hadn't simply killed her and been done with it. It was what she would have done to them when she was the Ilse Witch. Leaving a dangerous enemy alive to come looking for you later, no matter how difficult the task, was always risky. So why had they let her live? It would have been no more difficult for them to kill her than to send her into the Forbidding. It made her think something else was happening, a reason for her enemies to keep her alive and imprisoned. It also made her ponder anew the source of the power it had taken to put her here. It was more than even the most powerful of the Druids possessed. It was beyond anything that existed in her world.

It was a power, she was beginning to think, that might have come from the Forbidding itself.

Her ruminations kept her occupied for much of her journey. Weka Dart continued to skitter about, dodging sideways and occasionally climbing up and down trees and rock formations, but always moving. He did not talk much, for which she was grateful; absorbed, apparently, in keeping an eye out for the things they should avoid.

There were a great number of those, and they encountered many of them on their way. Ogres and giants stomped through the grasslands, mindless behemoths, dim-sighted and single-minded, with great shoulders hunched and massive arms dragging. Harpies flew overhead, winged shrews that screamed and spit venom at each other and anything below. A scattering of dragons came and went, smaller for the most part and different from the Drachas. Various forms of Faerie creatures were glimpsed, as well, particularly kobolds, which seemed to live in large numbers in that region.

Once, they saw a village of Gormies, far in the distance, a mud and grass huddle of shelters cut like caves into a hillside. Walls fronted the village and spikes jutted out of the earth in pointed warning. The Gormies themselves, ferret-eyed and wiry, crept about their enclosure like shades.

"What would frighten an entire village of those little terrors?" she asked Weka Dart.

He laughed and growled deep in his throat. "Wait and see."

She did so, and a few hours later she had her answer. They had just crested a small rise, catching sight of a valley that stretched away to the east when Weka Dart wheeled around suddenly, hissing, *"Down, down!"* She dropped at once, flattening herself against the earth, pressing into tufts of the spiky grass that grew everywhere, her breathing turned sharp and quick. The Ulk Bog, stretched out beside her, wormed forward just far enough that he could see something that was still hidden from her.

"Watch," he whispered over his shoulder.

She did so, peering into the valley, waiting. The minutes passed and nothing happened. Then an ogre of monstrous size lumbered into view, hunched over and shouldering a massive club. It was young, Grianne guessed, coarse hair black along its spine and across its shoulders, and its thick skin leathery and smooth. It was shaking its head from side to side and brushing at the air as if to ward off gnats or flies. But she saw neither.

"What is it doing?" she whispered.

Weka Dart's eyes were bright. "Listen."

She did, and then she heard it, too—a high-pitched, keening sound that seemed to come from everywhere at once. It was clearly bothering the ogre, who was grunting with annoyance, lifting its head every so often in a futile effort to search out the source. The sound intensified steadily, turning to a wail that cut right to the bone, raw and harsh and filled with pain.

Finally, the ogre stopped walking altogether, turning this way and that, blunt features twisted into an ugly knot. Grianne flattened herself further. The ogre was looking for something on which to vent its irritation, and she had no desire to provide it with a target. Weka Dart lay motionless, as well, but she saw the knowing smile at the corners of his mouth. There was anticipation in that smile, and she did not care for the look of it.

Suddenly, small, four-legged creatures began to appear, coming out of the grasses and from behind the rocks, a handful at first and then dozens. Their sharp-featured cat faces and sleek, sinuous shapes were unmistakable; she recognized them at once, even though she had never seen one before. Furies. She had read about them in the Druid Histories. Only once since their imprisonment had they broken through the Forbidding, doing battle with Allanon and nearly killing him. They were creatures of madness and mindless destruction, the worst of the many bad things imprisoned in this world. They attacked in swarms and were drawn to their victims by a hunger for blood. In the world of the Jarka Ruus, everything avoided them.

They closed now on the ogre, coming at it from all directions, so many that she could no longer count them. The ogre waited on them, its small, piggish eyes already anticipating the damage it would inflict on the creatures. Perhaps because it was young, it did not realize the danger it was in.

When they attacked, leaping blindly at the ogre, it smashed them like flies, wielding club and fists with equal effect. The Furies were smaller and their bodies unprotected, and those it found could not save themselves. But there were too many for the ogre to stop, and soon they had broken through its defenses, biting and tearing at its massive body with teeth and claws. Bits of flesh and patches of hair came away, and in moments the ogre was slashed and bleeding from head to foot. It fought on, killing Furies as long as it could, struggling to stay upright.

But in the end, they pulled it down, severing ligaments and tendons, shredding muscle and flesh, draining its blood and its strength until it was helpless. Bellowing in rage and despair, it disappeared beneath their relentless onslaught, blanketed in a squirming, heaving mass of furry bodies, borne to the earth until its life was gone.

Grianne, who had witnessed many terrible and violent deaths in her own world, nevertheless cringed at this one. The ogre meant nothing to her, and yet she was horrified by what had happened to it. She wanted to look away when the ogre was reduced to its final shudders and gasps, but she could not. It took a tap on her arm from Weka Dart to recall her to her senses.

"This way," the Ulk Bog whispered, "while they are busy."

They crawled through the grasses along the top of the rise and then down the reverse slope until they were out of sight. Once concealed from view, they stood and began walking, neither speaking, concentrating on the sounds that came from the other side of the hill.

When they were far enough away that they could no longer be heard, even by cat ears, Weka Dart turned to her. "Better they find it than us," he said with a wicked smile.

She nodded in agreement. But she did not feel good about it.

They slept that night in the trees again, and Grianne did not offer any objections. She understood how vulnerable they were to the creatures that roamed the Pashanon under cover of darkness. Many she had not even seen, but a single viewing of the Furies was enough to persuade her. The trees offered little enough protection, she guessed, but she would take what she could find.

In her dreams that night, she saw the ogre die again, the scene replaying itself in various forms. Sometimes she was simply a spectator, a passive viewer to the death scene. At other times, she was the victim, feeling the teeth and claws of the cat things tear into her, flailing and helpless beneath their attack, thrashing awake in a cold sweat. At other times still, she was a participant, one of the Furies, assisting in the destruction of another hapless creature, driven by bloodlust and hatred, by feelings she thought she had left behind when she had ceased to be the Ilse Witch.

She woke tired and out of sorts, but she kept it to herself as they continued their travels east, walking the grasslands through another dismal and oppressive day. They followed the banks of what would have been the Mermidon in her world. She didn't bother to ask Weka Dart for its name, content to be left alone while he sidled back and forth about her at his own pace. It rained on that day, and even with the great cloak to protect her, she was soon drenched. They saw little of the land's denizens and no sign of the Furies, and for that she was grateful.

On the afternoon of the third day, they reached a break in the Dragon Line that she recognized as the mouth of the pass leading to the Hadeshorn and the Valley of Shale. A twisting, dark defile, it wound upward into the cliffs and disappeared into the mists.

"Do you know this place?" she asked Weka Dart. Rain dripped off her hood and into her face, and she brushed it out of her eyes. "Have you been here before?"

He shook his head. "Never." He glanced up into the dark mass of rocks. "It doesn't look like a place anyone would want to go."

"It is where I am going," she said. "You needn't. Do you want to wait for me here?"

He shook his head quickly. "I'd better stay with you. In case you need me."

They began to climb, working their way through the rubble-strewn foothills until they had reached the base of the mountains. There, the terrain turned steeper and more treacherous. There were no signs of passage, no marks on the rocks or wearing down of the earth. The pathway she knew to be there in her own world was not there in the Forbidding, and she was forced to blaze it on her own. Perhaps no one had ever come that way before. Weka Dart trailed her with less enthusiasm than he had displayed on the flats, grumbling and muttering the entire way. She ignored him. It had been his choice to come. She was no happier than he was to have to break the trail.

It was not long before they heard the wailing. The sound was unmistakable, a low moaning that might have been just the wind or something alive and in pain. It rose and fell in steady cadence, trailing off entirely at times, only to return seconds later. She tried to ignore it but found it impossible to do so. Changes in pitch and tone set her teeth on edge. The sound raked the rocks of the pass, tunneled deep into its crevices, and slithered down its gaps. Weka Dart hissed in dismay and frustration and covered his ears with his hands. When she looked back at him, his teeth were bared.

The shadows appeared soon after that, sliding out of splits in the walls and from behind rocks. They were not cast as shadows should be, but moved independently of the light, separating themselves from solid objects in ways that should not have been possible. They flowed across the pass, crooked black stains that tracked her progress like predators. When they touched her, their blackness trailed across her skin with icy fingers.

She knew instinctively what was happening. She was being told to turn back. She could feel the warning in the touch of the shadows and hear it in the sound of the wailing. But she ignored it, as she knew she must, and continued on.

By nightfall, they reached a break in the rocks that opened through a thick curtain of gloom and mist to a hole in the sky. Grianne Ohmsford stared in surprise, then realized that the sky was ink black and empty of stars or moon. There was simply nothing there. She walked forward, unable to believe she was seeing correctly.

Beyond the break in the rocks, where the mist and gloom fell away, she found herself standing on a rise that looked out over the Valley of Shale.

It was as she remembered it and yet not. The sharp-edged ebony stones were the same, strewn across the empty slopes like shards of polished glass. But a wall of mist enclosed the valley, a wall so deep and so high that she could see nothing save the black hole of the sky above. The mountains had vanished. The world had disappeared.

All that remained was the Hadeshorn, pooled at the bottom of the valley, its still waters shimmering dully in the deep gloom. Its flat, mirrored surface gave off a faintly greenish light that reflected from the pieces of stone. Mist rose off its surface like steam, but no warmth was to be found in those waters. Even from where she stood, Grianne could feel that the lake was as cold as winter and as lethal as death. Nothing lived there that hadn't crossed over into the netherworld long ago.

Weka Dart scuttled up behind her and peered about. "This place is evil. Why are we here?"

"Because answers to my questions are to be found in the waters of that lake," she replied.

"Well, ask your questions quickly then, and let's be gone!"

The wailing began anew, low and insistent, seeping from the stones and filtering through the air. The shadows reappeared, taking form this time, some familiar, some not, swirling about them like phantoms come to haunt. There were no voices, no faces, no human presence, and yet it seemed as if life might be embodied in the shadows and in the wailing, bereft of substance and soul, trapped in the ether. The sounds and the shadows responded to each other, speeding and slowing, rising and falling, a symbiosis that reflected a terrible dependence.

"Straken, do what you must, but do it quickly!" Weka Dart urged, and there was fear in his voice.

She nodded without looking at him. There was no reason to wait, nothing to be gained by deliberation. She could not know what waited for her when she summoned the spirits of the dead. It might be different here than in the Four Lands. It might be lethal.

It might be her only hope.

Resolved, she started down.

TWENTY-ONE

She felt the presence of the dead almost immediately. They had assumed the forms of the shadows that flitted about her and taken on the voices that wailed from the rocks. They were a part of the air she breathed. As she descended the slopes, she found them all about her, pressing close, trying to recapture something of the corporeal existence they had left behind in crossing over into the netherworld. Shades felt that absence, she knew. Even dead, they remembered the substance of life.

This phenomenon would not have happened in her own world, where shades were confined to the depths of the Hadeshorn and no trespass into the world of the living was allowed. But in the Forbidding, more latitude seemed to be given to the dead, and though not yet summoned from the afterlife, they were already loose in the valley.

She sensed another aberration, as well. The shades that visited her were not friendly. At best, they were hostile toward all living things, but she sensed a specific antipathy toward herself. She could not determine the reason for that right away. They did not know her personally or possess a specific grudge that would explain their attitude, and yet there was no mistaking it. She felt it prodding at her, small barbs that did not sting so much as scratch. There was disdain and frustration in those scratches; there was outright dislike.

Something about her was angering these shades, and although she sought to discover a reason for it, she could not. Shades were difficult to read, their emotions not connected to the physical and therefore not easily understood.

She considered using her magic to push them away, to give herself space in which to breathe. But within the Forbidding, her magic could have unforeseen consequences, and she did not want to risk losing a chance to speak with the shades of the Druids. Her purpose in coming there was to summon them, and she could not afford to be distracted from that effort. The lesser shades were annoying but manageable.

Even so, her journey to the floor of the valley seemed endless. The shades rubbed on her nerves like sandpaper. Their whispers and icy touches left her unsettled and anxious. She felt something of her old self rise in response, an urge to crush them like dried leaves, a desire to scatter them beneath her boot heels. It was what she would have done once upon a time and not given it a second thought. But she was no longer the Ilse Witch, and nothing would ever make her be so again.

She glanced back at Weka Dart. He sat cross-legged on the rise, hands over his ears, face knotted in determination. He was hanging on, but it was taking everything he had to do so.

By the time she reached the edge of the lake, the shadows were draped all about her, frozen scraps of silk burning with death's chill. The wailing was so pervasive that she could hear nothing else, not even the crunching of her boots on the loose stone. The shades had crowded in from every side, gathering strength in numbers until they had enveloped her. She was being suffocated, punished for ignoring their warning. If she failed to rid herself of them quickly, she would be overwhelmed.

She stared momentarily at the calm waters of the lake, at

its columns of steam, fingers of mist risen straight from the netherworld. She knew better than to touch those waters. In her own world, they were deadly to living things, although Druids could survive them. Here, even Druids might be at risk.

Gathering her wits and focusing her determination, she raised her arms and began the weaving motion that would call forth the Druid dead. When the waters of the lake began to stir in response, she added the words that were needed. Slowly, the waters began to churn, the steam columns to geyser, and the lake itself to groan like a sleeping giant come awake. The shades already present fell away, taking with them their wailing and their icy touches, leaving dead space and silence in their wake.

Once rid of her most bothersome distraction, Grianne brought the full force of her power to bear. Using her skills and her experience, she bore down on this other world's Hadeshorn, manipulating it as she would its twin in the Four Lands, summoning the shades that would serve her cause, beckoning them from the depths to the surface, drawing them with her call. The lake surged and heaved with sudden convulsions, and its greenish waters turned dark and menacing. Waterspouts erupted with booming coughs, angry and violent. The lake hissed and spit like a venomous snake.

Her throat tightened and her mouth went dry. Something was wrong. There was resentment in the lake's response. There was resistance. That was not the way it was supposed to be. When the gateway to the netherworld was opened properly, there should be a lowering of barriers that invited a joining. The shades sought for it; it was their one chance to touch even briefly on what they had lost. The lake that gave them that chance had no reason to complain. But it was doing so here. It was more than disgruntled; it was enraged.

Had it been so long since a summoning had occurred in

that world that the lake failed to recognize it for what it was?
Was it possible there had never been a summoning before?

She gave herself only a moment to consider all that before
refocusing on the task at hand. She had come too far to turn
back and would not have done so if she could have. She had
made her decision and she would be the equal of whatever
happened. It was not bravado or foolhardiness that drove her;
it was the certainty that it was her one and only chance to find
a way out of this prison.

It took everything she had to maintain her concentration.
Her instincts were screaming at her to back away, to cease
her efforts. The air was filled with sounds and sensations that
grated on her resolve and wore at her courage. The Hadeshorn
was roiling by then, a volcanic pit threatening to explode with
every new gesture she made, with every new word she spoke.
Her magic, she saw, was anathema there, stirring the currents
that led to the netherworld in the manner of fire on parchment, incendiary and destructive.

Still she continued, implacable and unyielding, as hard as
the stone upon which she stood.

Then the shades began to rise in looping spirals, their trans-
parent forms linked by the trailing iridescence that poured
out of their trapped souls. Like shooting stars, they soared
from the waters and lifted into the air, bright flashes against
the night's firmament. They writhed and wailed piteously,
giving vent to the travesty of their imprisonment, their out-
rage a mirror of her own. They spun like sparks showered
from a fire grown too hot, released in an explosion of heat.
But from where she stood on the shore, she felt only a deep,
abiding cold that permeated the air and left her exposed skin
freezing.

*Where was Walker? Where was Allanon? Where was the
help she so badly needed?*

She bore down, ignoring the cold air and damp spray, the

terrible wailing and the debilitating infusion of fear and doubt. She hardened herself as she had been taught to do in darker times, cloaking herself in her magic and her determination, fighting to keep her hold over the lake and its inhabitants. She had opened the door to the world of the dead to seek answers to her questions, and she would not close it again until she found what she had come for.

Her search ended when her strength was almost gone. A Druid shade surged out of the roiling waters like a leviathan, huge and threatening, scattering lesser shades as if they were krill on which it might feed. Dark robes billowed out, the edges frayed and torn, the opening of its hood a black hole that had no bottom. The lake's greenish light filtered through rents in its empty form, carving intricate patterns that threw strange shadows everywhere.

Grianne Ohmsford stepped backwards in shock.

It's too big! Too massive!

The shade wheeled toward her soundlessly, drawing all the light into itself, extinguishing the smaller shades around it. Within the hood, red eyes flared to life and burned with unmistakable rage. She felt it watching her, measuring her. It advanced as it did so, coming on like a juggernaut that meant to crush her. As powerful as she was, as skilled at magic's uses, she was dwarfed by this presence. She could not decide who it was. Not Walker, she knew. She had spoken with his shade enough times to know how it felt when he appeared. Allanon, perhaps. Yes, Allanon, darkest of them all.

But this dark?

She waited as the shade skimmed across the lake's boiling surface to reach her, growing steadily in size. It gave her no hint of whom it was nor spoke even a single word. It simply advanced, enigmatic and intimidating, testing her resolve to stand fast. She could not look away from it. She was transfixed.

When it was close enough that it had blotted out the entirety of the sky behind it, it stopped, hovering above the Hadeshorn, its dark form riddled and tattered. Grianne brought her arms down now, lowering them slowly, carefully, keeping her eyes fixed on the crimson orbs that burned out of the impenetrable gap in the shade's hood.

—Do you know me, Straken—

Its voice was as empty and cold as the death that had stolen away its life. Her stomach lurched in sudden recognition. Sweat beaded her forehead, though the rest of her was as cold as that voice. She knew who it was. She knew it instinctively. It wasn't Allanon. Or Bremen. Or even Galaphile. Not here, inside the Forbidding. She had forgotten the importance of where she was. She was in a place where only creatures *exiled* from the world of Faerie belonged. She was in a place where only those who felt at home with such creatures would come.

Even from the world of the dead.

What sort of shade would such creatures draw? Only one, she realized belatedly.

The shade of the rebel Druid Brona.

It was the Warlock Lord.

After Grianne Ohmsford had been stolen away as a child and begun her training as the Ilse Witch, fear was the first emotion she had learned to control. It wasn't easy at first. Her family had been killed and she was hunted still. She had no friends save her rescuer, the Morgawr, and he was as dark as anything she had ever imagined. He was impatient and demanding, as well, and when she did not perform as he required, he made certain she realized the consequences of failure. It took her years to get past her fears, to harden herself sufficiently that in the end she was afraid of nothing, not even him.

But she was afraid now. The fear returned in paralyzing

waves that stole away her strength and rooted her in place. It was the Warlock Lord she had summoned, the most powerful and dangerous creature that had ever lived. What could she hope to do with him?

The huge apparition rolled toward her once more, easing across the turgid waters.

—Speak my name—

She could not. She could do nothing but stare. She had summoned the Druids' worst enemy, their most implacable foe, to ask for help that she couldn't possibly hope to receive. It was the worst mistake she had ever made, and she had made many. She had not imagined that anyone but Walker would appear, just as he always did when she came to the Hadeshorn. But it was not the Hadeshorn of her world, but of the Forbidding, and it made perfect sense that in the world of the Jarka Ruus, of the banished people, of the despised and the hated, Brona's would be the shade that would respond to any summons.

She sensed his impatience; he would not wait much longer for her response. If she failed to give it, he would depart, returning to the netherworld and stealing away her last hope. Refusing to speak with him was pointless. He would already know who she was and what she was doing there. He would know what she was seeking.

"No one speaks your name," she said.

—You will. You will dare anything, Ilse Witch. Haven't you always

She cringed inwardly but kept her face expressionless. "You are Brona," she said. "You are the Warlock Lord."

—I am as you name me, Straken. The name causes you to be afraid. It causes you to question what you have done. As it should. Tell me. Why do you summon me—

She mustered her courage, telling herself that he was dead, only a shade, and incapable of harming her physically. Alive, he would have been a very real threat. Dead, he was a threat only if she allowed him to be. If she kept him at bay and controlled her emotions, she was safe enough. She told herself that, but she was not entirely sure. It was not the Four Lands, after all. She was in another world, and the rules might be different.

"I am lost, and I want to go home again."

–You carry your home inside you, dark and tattered as the robes I wear. You bear it in your heart, a sorry, empty vessel. Ask me something better–

Behind him, the lake rumbled in discontent, and a scattering of lesser shades reappeared at the edges of the Warlock Lord's dark form, hovering cautiously.

"Who sent me here?" she asked him.

He made a sound that could have been laughter or something more terrible. Beneath his ragged form, the waters hissed and steamed.

–Not those you suspect, foolish girl–

"Not other Druids? They didn't send me?"

–They are pawns–

Pawns? It made her pause. "Who then?"

The dark form shifted anew, blowing spray and cold into her face, sending shivers down her spine.

–Ask me something more interesting–

Frustrated, she took a moment to think. Shades were notorious for giving vague or incomplete answers to the living. The trick was in determining from those answers what was real and what was false. It would be doubly hard here.

"Why are you even speaking with me?" she asked impulsively. "I am Ard Rhys of the Druids, your enemies in life."

–You are not what you see yourself to be. You are a changeling who dissembles and pretends. You hide whom you really are inside. Others fail to see it, but I know the truth. I speak to you because you are not like them. You are like me–

Although it made her cold inside, she dismissed the comparison out of hand; she understood well enough its source. He was not the first to see her that way nor would he be the last. "How do I get home again? How do I find my way back?"

—You cannot. Someone must find you—

Her heart sank, but she forged ahead anyway. "No one will ever find me here. No one can even get to me."

—You are already found. Someone already comes—

"Here? For me?" She felt her heart jump. "Who does this?"

—A boy—

That stopped her in her tracks. "What boy?"

—He is your way back. When he comes for you, you must be ready to go with him—

A boy. She took a deep breath, her throat tightening with the effort. A boy. There was more to this, there had to be, but she knew he wouldn't tell her what it was. He would make her wait, because that was the nature of the game he played. Besides, the future was uncertain, even for a shade. He could not tell her if the boy would succeed or fail. He could tell her only that the boy was coming. He would let her imagine the rest. She must go another way.

She pulled her cloak closer about her, aware suddenly of how cold she was. It was his presence, the nearness of his evil. Even in death, it was there, in the spray off the lake, in the currents of the air, in the darkness pressing down on her. Death, come alive in the form of his shade, gave power to what he was.

—Ask me something more—

His restlessness had returned, and she was in danger of losing him. But she didn't know where to go next. "Where will I find this boy?"

—At the doorway through which you entered. You waste my

time. Ask me something that matters. Is it possible that you are as stupid as you are pathetic—

She stiffened. He was taunting her and it was working. "Tell me why I am still alive. What reason was there for imprisoning rather than killing me?"

She was certain that he laughed, the sound so raw it made her cringe with embarrassment and rage. The lake's waters spit in response to the sound, and the greenish light that radiated from beneath pulsed with energy.

—To serve the needs of the one who brought you here—

"What needs are those?"

—You ask the wrong question. Ask the right one—

Her mind worked furiously, thinking it through. "Why am I inside the Forbidding?" she asked finally.

Again, the laughter, but cool and soft this time, barely a whisper on the wind.

—That is better, little Straken. You are inside the Forbidding so that the one who brought you here could get out—

She caught her breath. Get out? Someone had gotten out? An exchange, she thought. Of course. The power that had imprisoned her belonged to the thing that sought to escape, not to someone from her own world. Something powerful had wanted out, something clever enough to manipulate those it needed in the Four Lands, and it had found a way through her.

The shade's voice cut through her thoughts, commanding her attention.

—Heed me. You understand some, but not all. Here is the truth you must embrace, if you are to survive long enough to learn the rest. You cannot cast off your true self. You gain power through acceptance of your destiny. Bury your emotions with your foolish ambitions for the Druid Council. Become who you were meant to be, Ilse Witch. Your magic can make you powerful, even here. Your skills can give you domination. Use both. Wield them as weapons and destroy any that challenge you. If not, you will be destroyed, in turn—

"I am not the Ilse Witch," she replied.

—Nor am I, then, the Warlock Lord. I have watched you grow. You were powerful once. You disdained that power for foolish reasons. Had you stayed strong, you would not have been sent here like this. But you have grown weak. Death's cold hand is on you. Your time grows short—

The shade threw out one hand, and a wind howled across the lake, whipping at its robes and sending Grianne to her knees. The lesser shades scattered once more, disappearing into the darkness, lost. The lake boiled anew, spitting and rumbling, a cauldron of discontent, and the Warlock Lord began to retreat back toward its center, burning eyes still fixed on her. She tried to stand again, but the wind beat her down, and it was all she could do to meet that terrible gaze from her kneeling position. So much hatred in those featureless orbs— not for her alone, but for everything that lived. Even in death and from the netherworld, it sought release.

"I am Ard Rhys!" she screamed at it in frustration.

The shade did not respond. It reached the center of the lake and sank from sight, its black form vanishing with the quickness of a shadow exposed to light, gone in an instant, leaving only the lake and the sound of the wailing. Waterspouts exploded into the night, and Grianne backed away on her knees, buffeted by the relentless force of the wind. As she backed away, she fell, tearing her clothing and scraping her knees on the rocks. Shadows fell across her, cast by things she couldn't see. She lowered her head, closed her eyes, and pulled her hood tight against her ears.

I am Ard Rhys!

Then abruptly, everything went still. The wind died, the wailing faded, and the lake quieted once more. She kept her head lowered a moment, then lifted it cautiously. The valley was empty of movement and sound, of anything but a flicker of greenish light that emanated from the depths of the lake and reflected off the crushed stone.

Overhead, the sky was still black and empty of stars. All about the valley's rim, the wall of mist pressed close.

She rose, battered of body and emotions, drained of strength and spirit, and walked away.

TWENTY-TWO

Penderrin Ohmsford had thought he would sneak off to see Cinnaminson again the following night and perhaps the night after that, as well, if the *Skatelow* was still in port. His initial assignation had infused him with such joy and excitement that he could hardly wait for the next one to take place. He knew it was wrong to give so much attention to Cinnaminson when he should be thinking about finding his missing aunt. But the latter was far away, the former all too close. He couldn't seem to help himself; in a struggle of emotions, his sense of responsibility finished a distant second to his passion. All that mattered was that he be with Cinnaminson.

Having thought of little else all that day, he managed to slip away again the next night, only to find that her father and the other two Rovers were still aboard. He stood dockside in the shadows, watching them smoke on deck and listening to their voices. He waited a long time for them to leave, but when it became clear they had no intention of doing so, he gave up and returned to the inn.

The second night was even more frustrating. A new storm moved in, more ferocious than the one they had encountered several days earlier, drenching Anatcherae and halting all traffic for the next twenty-four hours. The rain was so bad that even on the ground visibility was reduced to almost nothing. Pen knew no one would be venturing out in weather like this, including the Rovers aboard the *Skatelow*. There was no point in even thinking about meeting with Cinnaminson.

So he was forced to make do with daydreams, which could not replace the real thing but which at least gave him an outlet for his frustrations. Sitting around at the Fisherman's Lie for hours at a time, sometimes with Khyber, sometimes with Ahren and Tagwen, but mostly alone, he passed the time thinking of ways he could separate her from her father, bring her with him when he returned home, and build a life for the two of them. It was such fantasy that even he knew it didn't bear looking at too closely. He was just a boy and she only a girl, and neither of them had any experience at falling in love. But Pen didn't care. He knew how he felt, and that was enough.

Khyber kept him company much of the time, but she spent hours alone in her room working on her Druid disciplines and exercises, practicing movements and words, and tending to her studies. Ahren worked with her each day, but he was gone much of the time, scouting for news of their pursuers and checking on Gar Hatch's progress with the *Skatelow*. Tagwen surfaced now and again, but mostly he kept to his room. He was less sociable than he had been when it had just been the two of them, and Pen thought it was due in part to his discomfort with life outside of Paranor. Tagwen was used to carrying out his duties for the Ard Rhys in the claustrophobic company of the Druids, and his time at the inn was too unstructured. What he did when he was alone was a mystery, although Pen caught him writing in a notebook on two occasions, and the Dwarf confessed to keeping a diary of their progress to help pass the time. That made as much sense to Pen as what he was doing, moping around about Cinnaminson, so he left the Dwarf alone.

Khyber, on the other hand, chided both of them mercilessly. More driven and disciplined than either, she found their lack of purpose irritating, and took every opportunity to suggest that they ought to do better with their time. Tagwen was incensed, but Pen just ignored her. He was beginning to see her as the big sister he didn't have but had often imagined. She was pushy and insistent, and she thought everyone should see things the way she did. Having talked with her about her life, Pen understood her motivation. She had been forced to fight for everything she had, a young Elven Princess whose life had been charted out for her by her family without any consideration at all for what she wanted. It had only become worse for her after her father's death and her brother's ascension to the throne. Just to come visit with Ahren had required a great deal of fortitude and determination. He could not imagine what would happen to her when her brother found out she was with them.

In any case, by the third day everyone was growing impatient. Pen and his companions were still stuck inside at the inn, and Gar Hatch had given Ahren no indication as to when they were going to set sail again. The rains had subsided, but a rise in the temperature had caused a deep fog bank to settle over the Lazareen and the surrounding lakeshore, the port of Anatcherae included. Visibility continued to hamper travel, and the dockside was quiet.

By midafternoon, with their lunch finished and the prospect of another day in port looming ever closer, Ahren announced that he was going down to the waterfront to tell Hatch that whether he liked it or not they would set sail at dawn. The Rover's reputation was that he could sail in any weather and under any conditions. It was time to prove it. The Druid was clearly displeased, his patience with Gar Hatch exhausted. Pen exchanged a knowing look with Khyber when Ahren told them to pack and be ready to leave when he returned. The boy did not think that Hatch would be given a chance to offer any more excuses. He wished, however, that he had been able to tell Ahren Elessedil what Cinnaminson had told him—that her father knew who they were, knew of their purpose, and might be making plans of his own. He could not say anything, however, without giving away the fact that he had disobeyed the Druid. He rationalized his decision to keep quiet by telling himself that Ahren already suspected Hatch of knowing the truth, which was almost the same as knowing it for a fact, so that the Druid was prepared for it anyway.

Still, it unsettled him to be keeping secrets from his friends. It wasn't that he didn't trust the Druid and his niece and the Dwarf; he did. It was just that once he didn't tell them, later, he didn't know how, and it became easier not to do so at all. It wasn't as if he *couldn't* tell them, when it became necessary. If it ever did. Maybe it never would.

So he kept what he knew about Gar Hatch to himself as Ahren Elessedil went out the door. He plopped down in a wooden chair by the window, alone for the moment, and stared out into the mist. He allowed himself to think briefly of Cinnaminson, then turned his attention for the first time in several days to the more important matter of reaching the tanequil. He was beginning to wonder not so much if he could do so, which he firmly believed he could, but if he could do so in time. His aunt was trapped inside the Forbidding, and he knew enough about what was locked away there to realize that even an Ard Rhys might have trouble staying alive. He knew she was powerful, that her magic had made her one of the most feared humans in the Four Lands. He knew, as well, that she was a survivor, that her entire life had been spent finding ways to stay alive when others either wished her dead or were actively looking for ways to make it happen. She would not be killed easily, even by the monsters that dwelled within the Forbidding.

But she was alone and friendless there and that would put her at a decided disadvantage. Sooner or later, that disadvantage would begin to tell. How many days had she been trapped in there already? At least two weeks, and that was just the beginning of the time that it would take for him to reach her.

Under the best of conditions, he thought, he would need another week or two to find the tanequil. Then he had to persuade it to fashion the darkwand. Then he had to return to
Paranor, get inside the Keep, and use the wand to cross over
into the Forbidding.

How much time would all that require? Two months?
More? Just listing the steps necessary for the rescue demonstrated how impossible the task was. She would be dead before he could reach her. Perhaps she was already dead.

He stopped himself angrily. What was he thinking? The
King of the Silver River would not bother sending him if he
had no chance of success; there would be no point in making
the journey. No, his aunt was alive and she would stay alive
until he reached her. She would die only if he talked himself
out of going on.

If he persuaded himself he should quit.

As he was trying to do now.

He took a deep breath and leaned back in his chair. He
would not think like that again, he promised himself. He
would do what he knew he should and continue on, right up
until the moment that it became impossible for him to do so.
That was what was expected of him; it was what he expected
of himself.

Then Khyber appeared, sat down without a word, pulled
out her folding game board, and cocked an inquisitive eyebrow at him. He smiled in spite of himself.

"I'll give it a try," he said.

Several hours passed and Ahren Elessedil did not return.
As dusk approached and the shadows lengthened, rain began
to fall once more, a steady, obstinate drizzle that dampened
the mist but did nothing to dispel it. Pen went into the common room with Khyber and Tagwen to eat. Mindful of the
need to stay anonymous, they took a table in a back corner,
well away from the door and the stream of traffic entering and

leaving. The Druids were still hunting them, the word still abroad that money would be paid for anyone who brought Pen to their attention. Perhaps they should have worried more about Gar Hatch's mercenary tendencies, since Rovers were always on the lookout for an easy opportunity to increase their fortunes. But Ahren had not seemed concerned, and Khyber had insisted that because the Druid was paying Hatch a great deal more than the Rover could get by turning them in, it made better sense for Hatch to stay loyal to them.

"I don't like it that he's been gone so long," Tagwen growled softly, giving Khyber a hard look. "You don't think something might have happened to him, do you?"

She shook her head. "I think if it had, we would have heard. Word would have spread by now."

"Then where is he?"

Pen took a long pull on his mug of ale. "He might have decided we'd get out of here quicker if he stayed around to supervise Hatch in making the necessary preparations. I don't think he believes the Captain has done all that well on his own."

Tagwen grunted, took a piece of bread from his plate and shoved it into his mouth in one monstrous bite. "Mmmff ummfatt wff."

The boy cocked his head. "I didn't quite catch that." Khyber was shaking her head in disgust.

The Dwarf swallowed. "I said, maybe one of us should go and see."

"That would be you," Khyber snapped irritably, "since Pen and I are forbidden to go outside the walls of this grim little lie-down. Do you want to leave now?"

They went back to eating in silence, turning their attention to steaming plates of fresh fish that the server had brought over from the kitchen. Tagwen rubbed his hands together enthusiastically, any plans for going down to the waterfront put aside for the moment. While eating, they finished off the ale pitcher, and an impatient Khyber rose and walked to the serving bar to get another.

She was waiting for a refill when the doors to the inn banged open and Terek Molt walked into the room, trailed by half a dozen of his Gnome Hunters.

Heads turned to watch them enter, and conversations died. Pen put down his fork and knife and glanced quickly at Tagwen. The Dwarf hadn't seen their enemy yet, but now he caught the look on the boy's face and turned. "Oh, no," he whispered.

They were trapped. The Gnome Hunters were already spreading out, moving through the crowded room like wraiths. Two remained stationed at the only door leading to the street. Pen thought of fleeing through the kitchen, but he didn't know if it led outside or not. His mind raced, seeking a way of escape. Maybe Molt didn't know they were there. He didn't seem to. He was standing in the middle of the room, black cloak shedding water on the wooden floor, hard eyes scanning the room. It was dark back here. He might not see them.

Cows might fly, too.

When the Druid's gaze finally settled on him, Pen went cold all the way down to his feet. There was no mistaking what he saw in that gaze. He wondered how the Druid had found them, how he had come to Anatcherae when they had been so careful to leave no trail. He glanced quickly at the serving bar and saw Khyber preparing to return to the table. She didn't know who Molt was, having never seen him; she didn't realize the danger they were in. He had to warn her, but there was no way for him to do so without giving her away.

It was too late anyway. Terek Molt stalked over to their table and stopped when he was still a few feet away. "You've led me a chase," he said softly. "But it's ended now. Get to your feet and come with me. Don't cause any trouble or it will be the worse for you. I don't much care what it takes to bring you back to Paranor."

Tagwen shook his head stubbornly. "We're not coming with you. Not this boy and not me. We don't want your protection."

The Druid's smile was quick and hard. "I'm not offering protection, Tagwen. I'm offering you a chance to stay alive, nothing more. Don't mistake what this is about. Where is Ahren Elessedil?"

Neither Pen nor Tagwen answered. If Terek Molt didn't know, that meant the Elf was still free. That, in turn, meant there was a chance.

"Get to your feet," the Druid said a second time.

"We know what you've done with the Ard Rhys," Tagwen declared, raising his voice so that those around could hear him clearly. "We know what you'll do with us, too. We're not coming."

There was a muttering in the room, and Terek Molt's hard eyes grew angry. "Enough of this, little men. Get up and walk out of here or I'll drag you out."

A Troll roughly the size of a barn pushed away from the serving bar and took a step forward. His blunt features tightened, one hand resting on a huge mace hanging from his belt. "Leave the boy and the old man alone," he ordered.

Terek Molt turned slowly to face him, away from the still-open doors to the inn, his concentration divided between the Troll and his quarry, so he didn't see Ahren Elessedil step out of the night. "Stay out of this," Molt said to the Troll.

At that point, Khyber pushed away from the bar. Carrying the pitcher of ale in both hands, she crossed the room directly toward the table at which Pen and Tagwen were sitting. Terek Molt glanced sharply at her, but she averted her eyes, as if not daring to look at him, and he started to turn back. "Get up," he said to Pen and Tagwen.

Khyber, from less than six feet away, threw the pitcher of ale all over him.

The room exploded with shouts, its occupants leaping to

their feet in a whirl of sudden movement. Chairs and tables were overturned, and glassware went crashing to the floor. The Troll had his mace free and was swinging it at Terek Molt, who rolled out of the way just in time. But when he came to his feet to strike back, Ahren's Druid magic threw him across the room and against the wall, where he lay in a crumpled heap, screaming in fury. Gnome Hunters came at Khyber, but her hands were already lifted and weaving, and the Gnomes stumbled all over themselves in their efforts to stay upright.

"This way!" she shouted at Pen and Tagwen, and broke for the kitchen.

The boy and the Dwarf didn't stop to ask if she knew what she was doing; they just went after her. The room was in chaos by then, its occupants surging up against one another in their efforts to get clear, most of them trying to reach the front door. The Gnome Hunters, still fighting to regain their equilibrium after Khyber's attack, were bowled over in the rush. A moment later, the lights went out, and the room was engulfed in blackness. Pen and Tagwen were in the kitchen by then, with Khyber just ahead, flinging open the back door that led to the street. Without a backward glance, they plunged into the rain and fog and darkness.

The streets were crowded, and it was difficult to move ahead at a brisk walk, let alone a run. Pen struggled to keep Khyber in sight, Tagwen pushing up against him from behind, both of them jostling and shoving to break free of the knots of people hindering their flight. Ahren Elessedil had disappeared, but Pen thought he must be somewhere close. Behind them, Fisherman's Lie was still in an uproar, shouts turning to cries of pain and anger, the windows breaking out, the entire place in blackness. Pen realized they had left everything behind in their escape, but knew there was no help for it. What mattered was getting away. What counted for something was staying alive.

A burly dockworker shouldered Pen aside effortlessly. As the boy staggered, he felt something rip through his cloak, scoring his left arm. He heard the dockworker gasp and felt him clutch at his arm. As he tried to wrench free, he saw a dagger protruding from the man's chest, the blade buried to the hilt. The man fell heavily into the boy, his dead eyes open and staring.

Pen looked around in shock and caught sight of something big scurrying along the peaks of the roofs, something cloaked and hooded and shadowy. Terek Molt, he thought at once, then realized that there hadn't been time for the Druid to get out of the inn and come after them. The figure on the roof was much larger than Molt in any case, and it didn't move like him. It moved like some huge insect.

It was coming down, toward the dead man and Pen.

"Penderrin!" Khyber called back to him.

He turned at the sound of her voice and began to run anew. Behind him, he heard gasps as the crowd realized what had happened to the dockworker. He didn't glance back to see if they were looking at him. He wasn't about to stop anyway. He wasn't going to do anything but keep running.

They angled down a maze of narrow side streets, grunting and shoving their way clear of passersby, until they finally reached the waterfront. Pen's arm was throbbing, and he glanced down in the light of the dockside lamps and saw blood soaking through his sleeve. The dagger had cut him from shoulder to elbow, the blade so sharp that even the heavy cloak had failed to blunt it.

Who had attacked him? He knew he had been the target, not that dockworker. If the worker hadn't shoved him aside at just the right moment, Pen would be the one lying in the street back there.

Glancing over his shoulder, he saw the shadowy figure giving chase, working its way swiftly along the warehouse roofs, scuttling along in the manner of a spider, arms and legs cocked out from its low-slung body.

It was coming too fast for him to outrun it.

"Khyber!" he shouted in sudden fear.

The girl wheeled back, saw the figure, as well, and thrust out both arms in a warding gesture. The magic caught the figure in midleap and sent it spinning out of sight.

"What was that?" she shouted at him.

He didn't reply. He had no idea what it was. He just knew he didn't want to see it again. Maybe he wouldn't. Maybe the fall had killed it. Or injured it badly enough that it couldn't keep after them.

As they began to run again, he glanced back worriedly. He was right to do so. His pursuer was atop the roofs once more, leaping and bounding from one building to the next, coming fast.

"Khyber!" He grabbed her arm and pointed.

She turned a second time, saw the figure, lifted her arms to summon the magic, and immediately it disappeared. They stood looking for it, but it was as if the night and rain and mist had swallowed it whole. That hadn't happened, of course; it was still out there, coming for him. Only it was on the ground, lost in the shadows.

The hairs on the back of Pen's neck pricked up. He backed toward the water, away from the buildings.

"Run!" Khyber hissed at him.

He did so, Tagwen beside him, their boots pounding on the wooden planks of the docks, the rain and mist a thick curtain all about them. Pen glanced toward the warehouses as he fled, searching for his pursuer. There was no one to be seen. But it was there, still chasing him. He could feel it. If it got close enough, it would use that dagger again. Or another like it. It would send its blade hurtling out of the darkness, and he would be dead before he knew what had happened. His lungs burned and his legs ached from running, but he didn't slow.

He had never been so scared. It was one thing to stand up to an enemy in the light, face-to-face. It was another to be stalked by something he couldn't even see.

They reached the *Skatelow* and clambered aboard in a rush. Not until they were crouched down behind the pilot box did Pen quit feeling as if a fresh blade was already winging its way out of the gloom toward his unprotected back. Scanning the lamplit shadows of the docks, he found no sign of his mysterious hunter. But he was scared enough that he was going to stay right where he was, with his back to the open water.

"What *was* that?" Khyber asked him for the second time, her breathing quick and labored.

Pen scanned the darkness, searching. "I don't know. I don't even know where it came from. Did you see what it did?"

"Killed that man," she whispered.

"But it meant to kill *you*, didn't it?" Tagwen's rough face pressed forward so that their eyes met.

"I think it did," Pen answered, watching the mist shift along the dock front and down the side streets like a serpent. Shadows moved everywhere he looked. "I think it's still out there."

Ahren Elessedil, already on board, was speaking heatedly with Gar Hatch. Ahren's clothes were disheveled and rain-soaked and his face flushed. He glanced over at the three hiding behind the pilot box wall, a hint of uncertainty in his blue eyes, then turned back to the Rover Captain, ordering him to cast off their mooring lines. But Hatch refused to do so, folding his arms across his chest and planting his feet. They weren't ready, he said. They hadn't finished their repairs.

"They've found you, haven't they?" he sneered. "The Druids? You think I don't know who you are or what you are about? I want no part of this. You can't pay me enough to take you farther. Get off my ship!"

His Rover crewmen moved closer, ready to act on his behalf. From somewhere farther down the docks, shouts arose.

The other pursuit—Pen had forgotten about Terek Molt and his Gnome Hunters.

"There!" Tagwen hissed suddenly, pointing left. "Something moved by that building!"

They peered into the gloom. Pen's heart was hammering in his chest, blood pounding in his ears. He was cold and hot at the same time, so afraid that he was holding his breath.

Then a huge shadow burst into view, leaping from the dockside onto the deck of the airship in a single bound, an impossible distance. It landed in a skid, its crooked limbs scrambling to find purchase on the smooth, damp wooden planking. Ahren Elessedil and Gar Hatch, startled, turned to look at it, both of them frozen in surprise. Pen caught the sudden flash of a blade, wicked and bright, but he couldn't make himself move, either. It was Khyber who leapt up, screaming in challenge. Hands outstretched, she summoned elemental magic in the form of a wind that picked up the dark form while it was still trying to regain its balance and threw it back over the side of the vessel into the cold lake waters.

Pen and Tagwen rushed to the side of the airship and peered down. The dark figure was gone.

On the dockside, the shouts were coming closer. Torchlight flickered through the mist. "Cast off," Ahren Elessedil snapped at Gar Hatch, "or I'll put you and your crew over the side and do it myself!"

The Rover Captain hesitated for just an instant, as if perhaps he would test this threat, then wheeled about, ordering his men to release the lines. The ropes fell away, and the airship began to drift from the dock. Pen continued to scan the waters into which the dark thing had fallen, not convinced it had given up, not persuaded it wasn't going to come at him again.

"Safety lines!" Gar Hatch snapped.

The *Skatelow* began to rise and the lake to drop away. Pen exhaled sharply. Still nothing. He glanced at Tagwen. The

Dwarf's rugged features reflected his fear. His eyes shifted to find the boy's and he shook his head.

"Safety lines!" Hatch repeated angrily. "Young Pen! If you can spare the time, would you bring Cinnaminson into the pilot box before you secure yourself?"

Pen waved his response. He took a final look over the side before heading for the hatchway. The lake had disappeared beneath a sea of shifting mist.

Then they were flying into the night, a solitary island in the deepening gloom, leaving Anatcherae and its horrors behind.

TWENTY-THREE

Darkness had fallen, stealing away the last of the daylight. Heavy fog closed on the airship, enfolding it in a swirling gray haze. There was no difference now between up or down or even sideways to those who sailed aboard the *Skatelow*. Everything looked the same. The day had been dreary to begin with, washed of color and empty of sunshine, but the night was worse. The clouds were so thickly massed overhead that there was not even the smallest hint of stars or moon. Below, the waters of the Lazareen had vanished as if drained from an unplugged basin. The lights of Anatcherae had vanished minutes after their departure. The world had disappeared.

Pen brought Cinnaminson to her father. She squeezed Pen's hand as he led her along the corridor from her cabin and up the stairway to the deck, but neither of them spoke. There was too much to say and no time to say it. In the pilot box, she moved obediently to her father's side, saying as she did so, "I'm here, Papa." Pen was dismissed, told to go below, and he moved away. But he lingered at the hatchway with Khyber and Ahren, staring out into the impenetrable fog, into the depthless night. If Cinnaminson wasn't able to navigate blind, he was thinking, they were in trouble. There wasn't even the smallest landmark on which they could fix, no sky to read, no point of reference to track. There was nothing out there at all.

"She's her father's compass, isn't she?" Ahren asked him quietly. "His eyes in the darkness?"

He nodded, looking at the Druid in surprise. "How did you know?"

"It was nosed about at the docks in Syioned. Some say she's his good-luck charm. Some say she can see in darkness, even though she's blind in daylight. None of them have it right. I saw the way she moved the first few days we were aboard. She can sense the position of things in her mind, their location, their look and feel."

"She said she sees the stars in her mind, even in mist and rain like this. That's how she navigates."

"A gift," Ahren Elessedil murmured. "But her father thinks it belongs to him because she is his child."

Pen nodded. "He thinks *she* belongs to him."

They could hear her speaking softly to her father, giving him instructions, a heading to take, a course to follow. His hands moved smoothly over the controls in response, turning the airship slightly to starboard, bringing up her bow as he did so, easing ahead through the gloom. In a less stressful situation, he might have noticed them watching and immediately ordered them below so that they would not discover his secret. He might have refused to proceed at all. But that night he was so preoccupied that he didn't even know they were there.

The mist thickened the farther away from land they flew, swirling like witch's brew around the airship, alive with strange shadows and unexpected movement. There was no wind, and yet the haze roiled as if there were. Pen felt uneasy at the phenomenon, not understanding how it could occur. He glanced again at Ahren Elessedil, but the Druid was staring straight ahead, his concentration focused on something else.

He was listening.

Pen listened, as well, but he could hear nothing beyond the creaking of the ship's rigging. He looked to Khyber, but she shook her head to indicate that she didn't hear anything, either.

Then Pen froze. There was something after all. At first, he wasn't sure what it was. It sounded a little like breathing, deep and low, like a sleeping man exhaling, only not that, either. He furrowed his brow in concentration, trying to place it. It must be the wind, he thought. The wind, sweeping over the hull or through the rigging or along the decks. But he knew it wasn't.

The sound grew louder, crept closer, as if a sleeping giant had woken and was coming over for a look. Pen glanced quickly at Ahren, but the Druid's gaze was intense and fixed, directed outward into the mist, searching.

"Uncle?" Khyber whispered, and there was an unmistakable hint of fear in her voice.

He nodded without looking at her. "It is the lake," he said. "It is alive."

Pen had no idea what that meant, but he didn't like the sound of it. Lakes weren't alive in the sense that they could breathe, so why did it sound as if this one was? He tried to pick up a rhythm to the sound, but it was unsteady and sporadic, harsh and labored. The ship sailed into the teeth of it, sliding smoothly through the fog, down the giant's throat and into its belly. Pen could see it in his mind. He tried to change the picture to something less threatening, but could not.

Then abruptly, ethereal forms appeared, incomplete and hazy, riding the windless mist. They brought the sound with them, carried it in their shadowy, insubstantial bodies, bits and pieces echoing all about them as they moved. Pen shrank back as several approached, sliding over the railing and across the airship's rain-slick deck. Cinnaminson gasped and her father swore angrily, swatting ineffectually at the wraith forms.

"The dead come to visit us," Ahren Elessedil said quietly. "This is the Lazareen, the prison of the dead who have not found their way to the netherworld and still wander the Four Lands."

"What do they want?" Khyber whispered.

Ahren shook his head. "I don't know."

The shades were all around the *Skatelow*, sweeping through her rigging like birds. The breathing grew louder, filling their ears, a windstorm of trouble building to something terrible. Slowly, steadily, vibrations began to shake the airship, causing the rigging to hum and the spars to rattle. Pen felt them all the way down to his bones. Seconds later, its pitch shifted to a frightening howl, a wail that engulfed them in an avalanche of sound. Pen went to his knees, racked with pain. The wail tightened like a vise around his head, crushing his ineffectual defenses. In the pilot box, in a futile effort to keep the sound at bay, Cinnaminson doubled over, her hands clapped over her ears. Gar Hatch was howling in fury, fighting to remain in control of the airship but losing the battle.

"Do something!" Khyber screamed at everyone and no one in particular, her eyes squeezed shut, her face twisted.

Like the legendary Sirens, the shades were driving the humans aboard the *Skatelow* mad. Their voices would paralyze the sailors, strip them of their sanity, and leave them catatonic. Already, Pen could feel himself losing control, his efforts at protecting his hearing and his mind failing. If he had the wishsong, he thought, he might have a way to fight back. But he had no defense against this, no magic to combat it. Nor did any of them, except perhaps . . .

He glanced quickly at Ahren Elessedil. The Druid was standing rigid and white-faced against the onslaught, hands weaving, lips moving, calling on his magic to save them. It was a terrible choice he was making, Pen knew. Using magic would give them away to the *Galaphile* in an instant. It would lead Terek Molt and his Gnome Hunters right to them. But what other choice did they have? The boy dropped to his knees, fighting to keep from screaming, the wailing so frenzied and wild that the deck planking was vibrating.

Then abruptly, everything went perfectly still, and they were enfolded in a silence so deep and vast that it felt as if they were packed in cotton wadding and buried in the ground. Around them, the mist continued to swirl and the shades to fly, but the wailing was no longer heard.

Pen got to his feet hesitantly, watching as the others did the same.

"We're safe, but we've given ourselves away," Ahren said quietly. He looked drained of strength, his face drawn and worn.

"Maybe they didn't come after us," Khyber offered.

Her uncle did not respond. Instead, he moved away from them, crossing the deck to the pilot box. After a moment's hesitation, Pen and Khyber followed. Gar Hatch turned at their approach, his hard face twisting with anger. "This is your doing, Druid!" he snapped. "Get below and stay there!"

"Cinnaminson," Ahren Elessedil said to the girl, ignoring her father. She swung toward the sound of his voice, her pale face damp with mist, her blind eyes wide. "We have to hide. Can you find a place for us to do so?"

"Don't answer him!" Gar Hatch roared. He swung down out of the pilot box and advanced on the Druid. "Let her be! She's blind, in case you hadn't noticed! How do you expect her to help?"

Ahren Elessedil's hand lifted in a warding gesture. "Don't come any closer, Captain," he said. Gar Hatch stopped, shaking with rage. "Let's not pretend we both don't know what she can and can't do. She's your eyes in this muck. She can see better than either of us. If she can't, then send her below and steer this ship yourself! Because a Druid warship tracks us, and if you don't find a way off this lake, and find it quickly, it will be on top of us!"

Gar Hatch came forward another step, his fists knotted. "I

should never have brought you aboard! I should never have agreed to help you! I do, and look what it costs me! You take my daughter, you take my ship, and you will probably cost me my life!"

Ahren stood his ground. "Don't be stupid. I take nothing from you but your services, and I paid for those. Among them, like it or not, is your daughter's talent. Now give her your permission to find a place for us to hide before it is too late!"

Hatch started to say something, then his eyes widened in shock as the huge, ironclad rams of the *Galaphile* surged out of the fog bank.

"Cinnaminson!" he shouted, leaping into the pilot box and seizing the controls.

He dropped the nose of the *Skatelow* so hard and so fast that Pen and his companions slid forward into the side of the pilot box, grabbing onto railings and ropes and anything else that would catch them. The airship plummeted, then leveled out and shot forward into the haze, all in seconds. As quick as that, they were alone again, the *Galaphile* vanished back into the fog.

"Which way?" Gar Hatch demanded of his daughter.

Her voice steady, Cinnaminson centered herself on the console, both hands gripping the railing, and began to give her father instructions, calling out headings. Pen, Khyber, and Ahren Elessedil righted themselves and snapped their safety harnesses in place, keeping close to the pilot box to watch what was happening. Gar Hatch ignored them, speaking only to his daughter, listening to her replies and making the necessary adjustments in the setting of the *Skatelow*'s course.

Pen looked over his shoulder, then skyward, searching the mist for the *Galaphile*. She was nowhere to be seen. But she was close at hand. He sensed her, massive and deadly, an implacable hunter in search of her prey. He felt her bulk pressing down through the haze, looking to crush him over the Lazareen the way she would have crushed him over the Rainbow Lake almost three weeks ago.

He was aware suddenly that the shades had vanished, gone back into the shroud of mist and gloom they had swum through moments earlier, sunk down into the waters of the Lazareen.

"Why didn't the dead go after Terek Molt?" he asked Ahren suddenly. "Why didn't they attack the *Galaphile*, too?"

The Druid glanced over. "Because Molt protects his vessel with Druid magic, something he can afford to do and we cannot." He paused, hands knuckle-white about the pilot box railing, droplets of water beaded on his narrow Elven features. "Besides, Penderrin, he may have summoned the dead in the first place. He has that power."

"Shades," the boy whispered, and the word was like a prayer.

They sailed ahead in silence, an island once more in the mist and fog, a rabbit in flight from a fox. All eyes searched the gloom for the *Galaphile*, while Cinnaminson called out course headings and Gar Hatch made the airship respond. The wind picked up again, set loose as they reached the Lazareen's center, and the haze began to dissipate. Below, the lake waters were choppy and dark, the sound of their waves clear in the fog's silence.

Ahren Elessedil leaned over the pilot box railing. "Where do we sail?" he asked Gar Hatch.

"The Slags," the big man answered dully. "There's plenty of places to hide in there, places we will never be found. We just need to clear the lake."

Pen touched the Druid's arm and looked at him questioningly.

"Wetlands," the Druid said. "Miles and miles of them, stretching all along the northeastern shoreline. Swamp and flood plain, cypress and cedar. A tangle of old growth and grasses blanketed with mist and filled with quicksand that can swallow whole ships. Dangerous, even if you know what you're doing." He nodded toward Hatch. "He's made the right choice."

She has, Pen corrected silently. For it was Cinnaminson who set their course, through whose mind's eye they sought their way and in whose hands they placed their trust.

The mist continued to thin, the sky above opening to a scattering of stars, the lake below silver-tipped and shimmering. Their cover would be gone in a few minutes, and Pen saw no sign of the shore. The mist still hung in thick curtains in the distance, so he assumed the shore was there. But it was a long way off, and the wind was in their face, slowing their passage.

Then, all at once, clouds blew in, and rain began to fall, sweeping across the decking in a cold, black wash, and quickly they were soaked through. It poured for a time, thunder booming in the distance, and then just as suddenly it stopped again. At the same moment, the wind died to nothing.

"Twenty degrees starboard," Cinnaminson told her father. "We'll find better speed on that heading. Oh," she gasped suddenly, "behind us, Papa!"

They all swung about in response and found the *Galaphile* emerging from the remnants of the fog bank, sails furled and lashed, the warship flying on the power of her diapson crystals. She was moving fast, surging through the night, bearing down on them like a tidal wave.

Gar Hatch threw the thruster levers all the way forward and yelled to his Rover crewmen to drop the mainsail. Pen saw the reason for it at once; the mainsail was a drag on the ship in that windless air and would be of less help if the wind resumed from the east. The *Skatelow* was better off flying on stored power, as well, though she could not begin to match the speed of the *Galaphile*. Still, she was the smaller, lighter craft and, if she was lucky, might be able to outmaneuver her pursuer.

The chase was under way in earnest; the fog that had offered concealment only moments earlier all but vanished. Pen did not care for what he saw as he watched the *Galaphile* draw closer. As fast as she was coming, the *Skatelow* could not outrun her. The Lazareen stretched away in all directions, vast and unchanging, and there was no sign of the shoreline they so desperately needed to reach. Clever maneuvers would get them only so far. Cinnaminson was still calling out tacks and headings, and Gar Hatch worked the controls frantically in response, trying to catch a bit of stray wind here, to skip off a sudden gust of air there. But neither could do anything to change their situation. The *Galaphile* continued to close steadily.

Then a fresh rainsquall washed over them, and Ahren Elessedil, seeing his chance, stepped away from the railing, arms raised skyward, and called on his magic to change the squall's direction, sending it whipping toward the Druid warship. It caught the *Galaphile* head-on, but by then it had changed into sleet so thick and heavy that it enveloped the bigger ship and swallowed it whole. Clinging to the *Galaphile* in a white swirling mass, it coated the decking and masts with ice, turning the airship to a bone-bleached corpse.

Now the *Skatelow* began to pull away. Burdened by the weight of the ice, the *Galaphile* was foundering. Pen saw flashes of red fire sweeping her masts and spars, Druid magic attempting to burn away the frigid coating. The fire had an eerie look to it, flaring from within the storm cloud like dragon eyes, like embers in a forge.

Ahead, the fog bank drew nearer.

Ahren collapsed next to Pen and Khyber, his lean face drawn and pale, his eyes haunted. He was close to exhaustion. "Find us a place to hide, Cinnaminson," he breathed softly. "Find it quickly."

Pressed against the pilot box wall, rain-soaked and cold, Pen peered in at the girl. She stood rigid and unmoving at the forward railing, her face lifted. She was speaking so low that

Pen could not make out the words, but Gar Hatch was listening intently, bent close to her, his burly form hunched down within his cloak. He had dropped the *Skatelow* so close to the Lazareen that she was almost skimming the surface. Pen heard the chop of the lake waters, steady and rough. The wind was back, whipping about them from first one direction and then the other, sweeping down out of the Charnals, cold and bleak.

Then they were sliding into the mist again, its gray shroud wrapping about and closing them away. Everything disappeared, vanished in an instant.

"Starboard five degrees, Papa," Cinnaminson called out sharply. "Altitude, quickly!"

Blinded by the murky haze, Pen could only hear tree branches scrape the underside of the hull as the *Skatelow* nosed upward again—a shrieking, a rending of wood, then silence once more. The airship leveled off. Pen was gripping the pilot box railing so hard his hands hurt. Khyber was crouched right beside him, her eyes tightly closed, her breathing quick and hurried.

"There, Papa!" Cinnaminson cried out suddenly. "Ahead of us, an inlet! Bring her down quickly!"

The *Skatelow* dipped abruptly, and Pen experienced a momentary sensation of falling, then the airship steadied and settled. Again there was contact, but softer, a rustling of damp grasses and reeds rather than a scraping of tree limbs. He smelled the fetid wetland waters and the stink of swamp gas rising to meet them; he heard a quick scattering of wings.

Then the *Skatelow* settled with a small splash and a lurch, sliding through water and mist and darkness, and everything went still.

"I was so frightened," she whispered to him, her blind gaze settling on his face, her head held just so, as if she were seeing him with her milky eyes instead of her mind.

"You didn't look frightened," he whispered back. He squeezed her hands. "You looked calmer than any of us."

"I don't know how I looked. I only know how I felt. I kept thinking that all it would take was one mistake for us to be caught. Especially when that warship appeared and was chasing us."

Pen glanced skyward, finding only mist and gloom, no sign of the *Galaphile* or anything else. Around them, the waters of the wetlands lapped softly against the hull of the *Skatelow*. Even though he couldn't see them, he heard the rustle of the limbs from the big trees that Cinnaminson told him were all about them. For anyone to find the *Skatelow* there, they would have to land right on top of it. From above, even if the air were clear instead of like soup, they were invisible. Their concealment was perfect and complete.

Two hours had passed since their landing, and in that time the others had gone to sleep, save for the Rover who kept watch from the bow. Pen stood with Cinnaminson in the pilot box, looking out into the haze, barely able to see the man who stood only twenty yards away. Before that night, the boy would not have been allowed on deck at all. But maybe the rules were no longer so important to Gar Hatch since he and Ahren Elessedil knew each other's secrets and neither was fooling the other about how things stood. Pen didn't think the Rover Captain's opinion of him had changed; he didn't think Hatch wanted him around his daughter. But maybe he had decided to put up with it for the time being, since their time together was growing short. Whatever the case, Pen would take what he could get.

"What are you thinking?" she asked him, brushing damp strands of her sandy blond hair away from her face.

"That your father is generous to allow us to be on deck alone like this. Perhaps he thinks better of me now."

"Now that he knows who you are and who's hunting you? Oh, yes. I expect he would like to be best friends. I expect he wants to invite you home to live with him." She gave him a smirk.

Pen sighed. "I deserved that."

She leaned close. "Listen to me, Penderrin." She put her lips right up against his ear, her words a whisper. "He may have given you away in Anatcherae. I don't know that he did, but he may have. He is a good man, but he panics when he's frightened. I've seen it before. He loses his perspective. He misplaces his common sense."

"If he betrayed us to Terek Molt . . ."

"He did so because he was afraid," she finished for him. "If he is backed into a corner, he will not always do the sensible thing. That might have happened here. I wasn't with him on the waterfront, and I didn't see who he talked to. That Druid might have found him and forced him to talk. You know they can. They can tell if you are lying. My father might have given you up to save his family and his ship."

"And for the money they are offering."

She backed away a few inches so that he could see her face again. "What matters now is that if he has done it once, he might try to do it again. Even out here. I don't want that to happen. I want you to stay safe."

He closed his eyes. "And I want you to come with me," he whispered, still feeling the softness of her mouth against his face. "I want you to come now, not later. Tell me you will, Cinnaminson. I don't want to leave you behind."

She lowered her head and let it rest on his shoulder. "Do you love me, Penderrin?"

"Yes," he said. He hadn't used the word before, even to himself, even in the silence of his mind. *Love.* He hadn't allowed himself to define what he was feeling. But as much as it was possible for him to do so, still young and inexperienced, he was willing to try. "I do love you," he said.

She burrowed her face in his neck. "I wanted to hear you say it. I wanted you to speak the words."

"You have to come with me," he insisted again. "I won't leave you behind."

She shook her head. "We're children, Pen."

"No," he said. "Not anymore."

He could sense her weighing her response. A dark certainty swept through him, and he closed his eyes against what he knew was coming. He was such a fool. He was asking her to leave her father, the man who had raised and cared for her, the strongest presence in her life. Why would she do that? Worse, he was asking her to accompany him to a place where no one in their right mind would go. She didn't know that, but he did. He knew how dangerous it was going to be.

"I'm sorry, Cinnaminson," he said quickly. "I don't know what I was thinking. I don't have the right to ask you to come with me. I was being selfish. You have to stay with your father for now. What we decided before was right—that when it was time, I would come for you. But this isn't the time. This is too sudden."

She lifted her head from his shoulder and faced him, her expression filled with wonder. In the dim light and with the mist damp and glistening against her skin, she looked so young. How old was she? He hadn't even thought to ask.

"You told me in Anatcherae that you would come for me and take me with you whenever I was ready to go," she said. "Is that still true. Do you love me enough to do that?"

"Yes," he said.

"Then I want you to take me with you when we get to where we are going. I want you to take me now."

He stared at her in disbelief. "Now? But I thought—"

"It's time, Pen. My father will understand. I will make him understand. I have served him long enough. I don't want to be his navigator anymore. I want a different life. I have been looking for that life for a long time. I think I have found it. I want to be with you."

She reached out and touched his face, tracing its ridges and planes. "You said you love me. I love you, too."

She hugged him then, long and hard. He closed his eyes, feeling her warmth seep through him. He loved her desperately, and he did not think for a moment that his age or his inexperience had blinded him to what that meant. He had no idea how he could protect her when he could barely manage to protect himself, but he would find a way.

"It will be all right," he whispered to her.

But he knew that he spoke the words mostly to reassure himself.

TWENTY-FOUR

At daybreak, Pen and his companions got a better look at the Slags, and it wasn't encouraging. The wetlands had the look of a monstrous jungle, an impenetrable tangle of trees, vines, reeds, and swamp grasses, all rising out of a mix of algae-skinned waterways that stretched away as far as the eye could see. The eye couldn't see all that far, of course, since the mist of the previous night did not dissipate with the sun's rising, but continued to layer the Slags in a heavy, gray blanket. Swirling in and out of the undergrowth like a living thing, snaking its way through the twisted, dark limbs of the trees and across the spiky carpet of grasses, it formed a wall that promised that any form of travel that didn't involve flying would be slow and dangerous.

Ahren Elessedil took one good look at the morass surrounding the *Skatelow*, glanced up at a ceiling of clouds and mist hung so low that it scraped the airship's mast tip, and shook his head. No one would find them in this, he was thinking. But they might never find their way out again, either.

"Here's how we go," Gar Hatch said, seeing the look on his face. It was warmer in the Slags, and the Rover was barechested and shiny with the mist's dampness. His muscles rippled as he climbed out of the pilot box and stood facing the Elf. "It isn't as bad as it looks, first off. Bad enough, though, that it warrants caution if we stay on the water, and that's what we'll mostly do. We'll drop the mast, lighten our load as best

307

we can, and work our way east through the channels, except where flying is the only way through. It's slow, but it's sure. That big warship won't ever find us down here."

Pen wasn't so sure, but Gar Hatch was Captain and no one was going to second-guess him. So they all pitched in to help take down the mainmast, laying it out along the decking, folding up the sails and spars and tucking them away, and tossing overboard the extra supplies they could afford to let go. It took most of the morning to accomplish this, and they worked as silently as they could manage; sounds carry long distances in places like the Slags.

But they saw no sign of the *Galaphile*, and by midday they were sailing along the connecting waterways and across the flooded lowlands, easing through tight channels bracketed by gnarled trunks and beneath bowers of limbs and vines inter-twined so thickly that they formed dark tunnels. Three times they were forced to take to the air, lifting off gently, opening the parse tubes just enough to skate the treetops to the next open space, then landing and continuing on. It was slow go-ing, as Hatch had promised, but they made steady time, and the journey progressed without incident.

It might have been otherwise, had the Rover Captain not been familiar with the waters. Twice he brought the airship to a standstill in waters that ran deeper than most, and in the dis-tance Pen watched massive shapes slide just beneath the sur-face, stirring ripples that spread outward in great concentric circles. Once, something huge surfaced just behind a screen of trees and brush, thrashing with such force that several of the trees toppled and the waters churned and rocked with the force of its movement. Yet nothing came close to the airship, for Hatch seemed to know when to stop and wait and when to go on.

By nightfall, they were deep in the wetlands, though much farther east than when they had started out, and there was still no sign of their pursuit. When asked of their progress, Hatch replied that they were a little more than halfway through. By the next night, if their luck continued to hold, they would reach the far side.

That couldn't happen any too soon for Pen. He was already sick of the Slags, of the smell and taste of the air, of the grayness of the light, unfriendly and wearing, of the sickness he felt lurking in the fetid waters, waiting to infect whoever was unfortunate enough to breathe it in. This was no place for people of any persuasion. Even on an airship, Pen felt vulnerable.

But perhaps his anticipation of what was going to happen when it was time to leave the *Skatelow* was working on him, as well. Taking Cinnaminson from her father was not going to be pleasant. He did not for a moment doubt that he could do it, did not once question that he could do whatever was necessary. But thinking about it made him uneasy. Gar Hatch was a dangerous man, and Pen did not underestimate him. He thought that Cinnaminson's fears about what might have happened in Anatcherae were well founded. Gar Hatch probably did betray them to Terek Molt. He probably thought they would never live to reach the *Skatelow* to finish this voyage and that was why he was so distressed when Ahren Elessedil reappeared and ordered him to set sail. It wasn't unfinished repairs or stocking of supplies that had upset him; it was the fact that he had been forced to go at all.

What would he do when he found out that his daughter, his most valuable asset in his business, was leaving him to go with Pen? He would do something. The boy was certain of it.

On the other hand, Pen hadn't done much to help matters along from his end, either. He hadn't said a word to his three companions about what he and Cinnaminson had agreed upon. He didn't know how. Certainly, Tagwen and Khyber would never support him. The Dwarf would do nothing that would jeopardize their efforts to reach the Ard Rhys, and the

Elven girl already thought his involvement with Cinnaminson was a big mistake. Only Ahren Elessedil was likely to demonstrate any compassion, any willingness to grant his request. But he didn't know how best to approach the Druid. So he had delayed all day, thinking each time he considered speaking that he would do so later.

Well, later was here. It was nightfall, dinner behind them by now, and the next day was all the time he had left. He couldn't wait much longer; he couldn't chance being turned down with no further opportunity to press his demand.

But before he could act on his thinking, Gar Hatch wandered over in the twilight and said, "I'd like to speak with you a moment, young Penderrin. Alone."

He took the boy up into the pilot box, separating him from the others. Pen forced himself to stay calm, to not glance over at Ahren and Khyber, to resist the urge to check how close they were if he needed rescuing. He knew what was coming. He had not thought Cinnaminson would be so quick to tell her father, but then there was no reason why she should wait. He wished fleetingly, however, that she had told him she had done so.

Standing before Pen, the misty light so bad by now that the boy could barely make out his features, Gar Hatch shook his bearded head slowly.

"My girl tells me she's leaving the ship," he said softly. "Leaving with you. Is this so?"

Pen had given no thought at all to what he would say when this moment happened, and now he was speechless. He forced himself to look into the other's hard eyes. "It is."

"She says you love her. True?"

"Yes. I do."

The big man regarded him silently for a moment, as if deciding whether to toss him overboard. "You're sure about this, are you, Penderrin? You're awfully young and you don't know my girl very well yet. It might be better to wait on this."

Pen took a deep breath. "I think we know each other well enough. I know we're young, but we aren't children. We're ready."

Another long moment of silence followed. The big man studied him carefully, and Pen felt the weight of his gaze. He wanted to say something more, but he couldn't think of anything that would make it any easier. So he kept still.

"Well," the other said finally, "it seems you've made up your minds, the two of you. I don't think I can stop you without causing hard feelings, and I'm not one for doing that. I think it's a mistake, Penderrin, but if you have decided to try it, then I won't stand in your way. You seem a good lad. I know Cinnaminson has grown weary of life on the *Skatelow*. She wants more for herself, a different way of life. She's entitled. Do you think you can take care of her as well as I have?"

Pen nodded. "I will do my best. I think we will take care of each other."

Hatch grunted. "Easier said than done, lad. If you fail her, I'll come looking for you. You know that, don't you?"

"I won't fail her."

"I don't care who your family is or what sort of magic they can call on to use against poor men like myself," he continued, ignoring Pen. "I'll come looking for you, and you can be sure I will find you."

Pen didn't care for the threat, but he supposed it was the Rover Captain's way of venting his disappointment at what was happening. Besides, he didn't think there would ever be cause for the big man to act on it.

"I understand," he replied.

"Best that you do. I won't say I'm the least bit happy about this. I'm not. I won't say I think it will work out for you. I don't. But I will give you your chance with her, Penderrin, and hold you to your word. I just hope I won't ever have cause to regret doing so."

"You won't."

"Go on, then." The big man gestured toward Ahren and Khyber, who stood talking at the port railing. "Go back to your friends. We have a full day of sailing tomorrow, and you want to be rested for it."

Pen left the pilot box in a state of some confusion. He had not expected Gar Hatch to be so accommodating, and it bothered him. He hadn't lodged more than a mild protest, hadn't tried to talk Pen out of it, hadn't even gone to Ahren Elessedil to voice his disapproval. Perhaps Cinnaminson had persuaded him not to do any of those things, but that didn't seem likely to Pen. Maybe, he thought suddenly, Hatch was waiting for the Druid to put an end to their plans. Maybe he knew how unreceptive Pen's companions would be and was waiting for them to put a stop to things.

But that didn't feel right, either. Gar Hatch wasn't the sort to count on someone else to solve his problems. That kind of behavior wasn't a part of the Rover ethic, and certainly not in keeping with the big man's personality.

Pen looked around for Cinnaminson, but didn't see her. She would be up on deck later, perhaps, but since they were not flying that night, she might be asleep. Pen glanced at Ahren and Khyber. He should tell the Druid now what was happening, give him some time to think about it before he responded. But just as he started over, Tagwen appeared from belowdecks to join them, grumbling about sleeping in tight, airless spaces that rocked and swayed. The boy took a moment longer to consider what he should do and decided to wait. First thing in the morning, he would speak with Ahren Elessedil. That would be soon enough. He would be persuasive, he told himself. The Druid would agree.

Feeling a little tired and oddly out of sorts, he took Gar Hatch's advice and went down to his cabin to sleep.

He awoke to shouting, to what was obviously an alarm. Bounding up instantly, still half-asleep, he tried to orient himself. Across the way, Tagwen was looking similarly disoriented, staring blankly into space from his hammock, eyes bleary and unfocused. The shouting died into harsh whispers that were audible nevertheless, even from belowdecks. Boots thudded across the planking from one railing to the other, then stopped. Silence descended, deep and unexpected. Pen could not decide what was happening and worried that by the time he did, it would be too late to matter. With a hushed plea to Tagwen to follow as quickly as he could, he pulled on his boots and went out the cabin door.

The corridor was empty as he hurried down its short length to the ladder leading up and climbed swiftly toward the light, straining to hear something more. When he pushed open the hatch, he found the dawn had arrived with a deep, heavy fog that crawled through the trees and over the decks of the *Skatelow*. At first he didn't see anyone, then found Gar Hatch, the two Rover crewmen, Ahren Elessedil and Khyber standing at the bow, peering everywhere at once, and he hurried over to join them.

"One of the crewmen caught a glimpse of the *Galaphile* just moments ago, right overhead, flying north," the Druid whispered. "He called out a warning, which might have given us away. We're waiting to see if she comes back around."

They stood in a knot, scanning the misty gray, watching for movement. Long minutes passed, and nothing appeared.

"There's a channel just ahead that tunnels through these trees," Gar Hatch said quietly. "It goes on for several miles through heavy foliage. Once we get in there, we can't be seen from the sky. It's our best chance to lose them."

They pulled up the fore and aft anchors and set out. Breakfast was forgotten. All that mattered was getting the ship under cover. Everyone but Cinnaminson was on deck now. Pen thought to go look for her, but decided it would be wrong to leave in the midst of the crisis. He might be needed; Hatch might require help piloting the craft. He stayed close, watching as the Rover Captain took the *Skatelow* through a series of connecting lakes spiked with grasses and studded with dead tree trunks, easing her carefully along, all the while with one eye on the brume-thickened sky. The Rover crewmen moved forward, taking readings with weighted lines, hand-signaling warnings when shallows or submerged logs appeared in front of them. No one said a word.

The channel appeared without warning, a black hole through an interwoven network of limbs and gnarled trunks. It had the look of a giant's hungry maw as they sailed into it, and the temperature dropped immediately once they were inside. Pen shivered. Overhead, he caught small glimpses of sky, but mostly the dark canopy of limbs was all that was visible. The channel was wide enough to allow passage, though the *Skatelow* wouldn't have been able to get through if her mast had been up. As it was, the Rover crewmen had to use poles to push her away from the tangle of tree roots that grew on either side and keep her centered in the deeper water. It was too dark for Pen to see exactly what they were doing, but he was certain they could not have done it without Hatch. He seemed to know what was needed at every turn, and kept them moving ahead smoothly.

Still Cinnaminson didn't appear. Pen glanced over his shoulder repeatedly, but there was no sign of her. He began to worry anew.

Ahead, the tunnel opened back into the light.

Gar Hatch called him into the pilot box. "Take the helm, young Penderrin. I need to be at the bow for this."

Pen did as he was told. Hatch went forward to stand with his men, the three of them using poles to ease the *Skatelow* along the channel, pointing her toward the opening. Now and again, he would signal the boy to swing the rudder to starboard or port.

They were almost through when there was a scraping

sound and a violent lurch. Pen was thrown backwards into the railing, and for an instant he thought that whatever had happened, he had done something wrong. But as he stood up and hurried forward, he realized he hadn't done anything he hadn't been told to do.

Gar Hatch was peering over the side of the airship into the murky waters, shaking his head. "That one's new," he muttered to no one in particular, then pointed out the massive log that the airship had run up on. He glanced up at the canopy of trees. "Too tight a fit to try to fly her. We'll have to float her off and pull her through by hand."

Hatch went back up into the pilot box, advising Pen that he would take the controls. There was no admonition in his voice, so Pen didn't argue. Together with Tagwen, Ahren Elessedil, and the two crewmen, Pen climbed down onto the tangled knot of tree roots and moved forward of the airship's bow. Using ropes lashed about iron cleats, they began to pull the *Skatelow* ahead, easing her over the fallen trunk. Eventually the airship gained just enough lift from Gar Hatch's skilled handling to break free of the log and begin crawling along the swamp's green surface once more.

It was backbreaking work. Bugs of all sorts swarmed about their faces, clouding their vision, and the root tangle on which they were forced to stand was slick with moss and damp with mist and offered uncertain footing. All of them went down at one point or another, skidding and sliding into the swamp water, fighting to keep from going under. But, slowly, they maneuvered the *Skatelow* down the last few yards of the channel, easing her toward the open bay, where the light brightened and the brume thinned.

"Move back!" Gar Hatch shouted abruptly. "Release the ropes!"

Pen, Tagwen, and Ahren Elessedil did as they were ordered and watched the airship sail by, the hull momentarily blocking from view the Rover crewmen who were working across the way. When Pen glanced over again in the wake of the ship's passing, the crewmen were gone.

It took the boy a second to realize what was happening.

"Ahren!" he shouted in warning. "We've been tricked!"

He was too late. The *Skatelow* began to pick up speed, moving into the center of the bay. Then Khyber Elessedil came flying over the side and landed in the murky waters with a huge splash. The faces of the crewmen appeared, and they waved tauntingly at the men on shore. Tagwen was shouting at Ahren Elessedil to do something, but the Druid only stood there, shaking his head, grim-faced and angry. There was nothing he could do, Pen realized, without using magic that would alert the *Galaphile*.

Slowly, the *Skatelow* began to lift away, to rise into the mist, to disappear. In seconds, she was gone.

At the center of the lake, Khyber Elessedil pounded at the water in frustration.

TWENTY-FIVE

No one said anything for a few moments, Pen, Tagwen, and Ahren Elessedil standing together at the edge of the bay like statues, staring with a mix of disbelief and frustration at the point where the *Skatelow* had disappeared into the mist.

"I knew we couldn't trust that man," Tagwen muttered finally.

At the center of the bay, Khyber Elessedil had given up pounding the water and was swimming toward them. Her strokes cleaved the greenish waters smoothly and easily.

"You can't trust Rovers," Tagwen went on bitterly. "Not any of them. Don't know why we thought we could trust Hatch."

"We didn't trust him," Ahren Elessedil pointed out. "We just didn't watch him closely enough. We let him outsmart us."

This is my fault, Pen thought. I caused this. Gar Hatch didn't abandon them because of anything the others had done or even because of the *Galaphile* and the Druids. He had abandoned them so that Pen couldn't take Cinnaminson away from him. That was why he had been so accommodating. That was why he didn't argue the matter more strongly. He didn't care what either Pen or his daughter intended. He was going to put a stop to it in any case.

Khyber reached the edge of the bay and stood up with some difficulty, water cascading off her drenched clothes. Anger radiated from her like heat from a forge as she stalked ashore to join them. "Why did he do that?" she snapped furiously. "What was the point of abandoning us now when we were so close to leaving him anyway?"

"It's because of me," Pen said at once, and they all turned to look at him. "I'm responsible."

He revealed to them what he and Cinnaminson had decided, how she had told her father, and what her father had obviously decided to do about it. He apologized over and over for not confiding in them and admitted that, by deciding to take the girl off the airship, he was thinking of himself and not of them or even of what they had come to do. He was embarrassed and disappointed, and it was all he could do to get through it without breaking down.

Khyber glared at him when he was finished. "You are an idiot, Penderrin Ohmsford."

Pen bit back his angry reply, thinking that he had better just take whatever they had to say to him and be done with it.

"That doesn't help us, Khyber," her uncle said softly. "Pen loves this girl and he was trying to help her. I don't think we can fault him for his good intentions. He might have handled it better, but at the time he did the best he could. It's easy to second-guess him now."

"You might want to ask yourself what Hatch will do to her now that he knows what she intended and no outsiders are about to interfere," Tagwen said to Pen.

Pen had already thought of that, and he didn't like the conclusion he had reached. Gar Hatch would not be happy with his daughter and would not trust her again anytime soon. He would make a virtual prisoner of her, and once again, it was his fault.

Khyber stalked away. She stopped a short distance off and stood looking out at the bay with her hands on her hips, then wheeled back suddenly. "Sorry I snapped at you, Pen. Gar Hatch is a sneak and a coward to do this. But the matter isn't finished. We'll see him again, somewhere down the road.

He'll be the one who goes over the side of that airship the next time, I promise you!"

"Meanwhile, what are we supposed to do?" Tagwen asked, looking from one face to the next. "How do we get out of here?"

Ahren Elessedil glanced around thoughtfully, then shrugged. "We walk."

"Walk!" Tagwen was aghast. "We can't walk out of here! You've seen this morass, this pit of vipers and swamp rats! If something doesn't eat us, we'll be sucked down in the quicksand! Besides, it will take us days, and that's only if we don't get lost, which we will!"

The Druid nodded. "The alternative is to use magic. I could summon a Roc to carry us out. But if I do that, I will give us away to Terek Molt. He will reach us long before any help does."

Tagwen scrunched up his face and folded his arms across his chest. "I'm just saying I don't think we can walk out of here, no matter how determined we are."

"There might be another way," Pen interjected quickly. "One that's a little quicker and safer."

Ahren Elessedil turned to him, surprise mirrored in his blue eyes. "All right, Pen, let's hear what it is."

"I hope it's a better idea than his last one," Tagwen grumbled before Pen could speak, and set his jaw firmly as he prepared to pass judgment.

He showed them how to build the raft, using heavier logs for the hull, slender limbs for the cradle, and reeds for binding. It needed to be only big enough to support the four of them, so a platform measuring ten feet by ten feet was adequate. The materials were easy enough to find, even in the Slags, though not so easy to shape, mostly because they lacked the requisite tools and had to make do with long knives. On more than one occasion Pen had built similar rafts before and knew something about how to construct them so that they wouldn't fall apart midjourney. Working in pairs, they gathered the logs and limbs for the platform and carried them to a flat piece of earth on which they could lay them out and lash them together.

They worked through the morning, and by midday they were finished. The raft was crude, but it was strong enough to support them and light enough to allow for portage. Most important, it floated. They had no supplies, nothing but the clothes they wore and the weapons they carried, so after crafting poles to push their vessel through the swamp, they set out.

It was slow going, even with the raft to carry them, the swamp a morass of weed-choked bays and logjammed channels that they were forced to backtrack through and portage around repeatedly. Even so, they made much better progress than they would have afoot. For just the second time since they had set out, Pen was able to make practical use of his magic, to intuit from the sounds and movements of the plants, birds, and animals around them the dangers that lay waiting. Calling out directions to the other three as they worked the poles, he concentrated on keeping them clear of submerged debris that might have damaged their craft and well away from the more dangerous creatures that lived in the Slags—some of them huge and aggressive. By staying close to the shoreline and out of the deeper water, they were able to avoid any confrontations, and Pen was able to tell himself that he was making at least partial amends for his part in contributing to the fix they were in.

By nightfall, they were exhausted and still deep in the Slags. Pen's pocket compass had kept them on the right heading, of that much he was certain, but how much actual progress they had made was debatable. Since none of them knew exactly where they were, it was impossible to judge how far they still had to go. Nothing about the wetland had changed, the mist was thick and unbroken, the waterways extended off in all directions, and the undergrowth was identical to what they had left behind six hours earlier.

There was nothing to eat or drink, so after agreeing to split the watch into four shifts they went to sleep, hungry and thirsty and frustrated.

During the night, it rained. Pen, who was on watch at the time, used his cloak to catch enough drinking water that they were able to satisfy at least one need. After the rain stopped and the water was consumed, Khyber and Tagwen went back to sleep, but Ahren Elessedil chose to sit up with the boy.

"Are you worried about Cinnaminson?" Ahren asked when they were settled down together at the edge of the raft, their backs to the sleepers, their cloaks wrapped about them. It was surprisingly cold at night in the Slags.

The boy stared out into the dark without answering. Then he sighed. "I can't do anything to help her. I can help us, but not her. She's smart and she's capable, but her father is too much for her. He sees her as a valuable possession, something he almost lost. I don't know what he will do."

The Druid folded himself deeper into his robes. "I don't think he will do anything. I think he believes he made an example of us, so she won't cross him again. He doesn't think we will get out of here alive, Pen. Or if we do, that we will escape the *Galaphile*."

Pen pulled his knees up to his chest and lowered his chin between them. "Maybe he's right."

"Oh?"

"It's just that we're not getting anywhere." The boy tightened his hands into fists and lowered his voice to a whisper. "We aren't any closer to helping Aunt Grianne than we were when we started out. How long can she stay alive inside the Forbidding? How much time does she have?"

Ahren Elessedil shook his head. "A lot more than anyone else I can think of. She's a survivor, Pen. She can endure more hardships than most. It doesn't matter where she is or what she is up against, she will find a way to stay alive. Don't lose heart. Remember who she is."

The boy shook his head. "What if she has to go back to being who she *was*? What if that's the only way she can survive? I listened to my parents talk about what she was like, when they thought I wasn't listening. She shouldn't have to be made to do those kinds of things again."

The Druid gave him a thin smile. "I don't think that's what has you worried."

The boy frowned. "What do you mean?"

"I don't think you are worried about whether we will reach the Ard Rhys in time to be of help. I think you are worried about whether you will be able to do what is needed when the time comes. I think you are worried about failing."

Pen was instantly furious, but he kept his tongue in check as he looked out again into the mist and gloom, thinking it through, weighing the Druid's words. Slowly, he felt his anger soften.

"You're right," he admitted finally. "I don't think I can save her. I don't see how I can manage it. I'm not strong or talented enough. I don't have magic like my father. I'm nothing special. I'm just ordinary." He looked at the Druid. "What am I going to do if that isn't enough?"

Ahren Elessedil pursed his lips. "I was your age when I sailed on the *Jerle Shannara*. Just a boy. My brother sent me because he was secretly hoping I wouldn't come back. Ostensibly, I was sent to regain possession of the Elfstones, but mostly I was sent with the expectation that I would be killed. But I wasn't, and when I found the Elfstones, I was able to use them. I didn't think such a thing was possible. I ran from my first battle, so frightened I barely knew what I was doing. I hid until someone found me, someone who was able to tell me what I am telling you—that you will do your best and your best might surprise you."

"But you just said you had the Elfstones to rely on. I don't."

"But you do have magic. Don't underrate it. You don't know how important it might turn out to be. But that isn't what will make the difference when it matters. It is the strength of your heart. It is your determination."

He leaned forward. "Remember this, Penderrin. You are the one who was chosen to save the Ard Rhys. That was not a mistake. The King of the Silver River sees the future better than anyone, better even than the shades of the Druids. He would not have come to you if you were not the right person to undertake this quest."

Pen searched Ahren's eyes uncertainly. "I wish I could believe that."

"I wished the same thing twenty years ago. But you have to take it on faith. You have to believe that it will happen. You have to make it come true. No one can do it for you."

Pen nodded. Words of wisdom, well meant, but he didn't find them helpful. All he could think about was how ill equipped he was to rescue anyone from a place like the Forbidding.

"I still think it would have been better to send you," he said quietly. "I still don't understand why the King of the Silver River decided on me."

"Because he knows more about you than you know yourself," the Druid answered. He rose and stretched. "The watch is mine now. Go to sleep. You need to rest, to be ready to help us again tomorrow. We aren't out of danger yet. We are depending on you."

Pen moved away without comment, sliding to one side, joining Khyber and Tagwen at the other end of the raft, where both were sleeping fitfully. He lay down and pulled his cloak closer, resting his head in the crook of his arm. He didn't sleep right away, but stared out into the misty gloom, the swirling of the haze hypnotic and suggestive of other things. His thoughts drifted to the events that had brought him to that place and time and then to Ahren Elessedil's encouraging words. That he should believe so strongly in Pen was surprising, especially after how badly the boy had handled the matter of Cinnaminson and Gar Hatch. But Pen could tell when someone was lying to him, and he did not sense falsehood in the other's words. The Druid saw him as the rescuer he had been charged with being. Pen would find a way, he believed, even if the boy did not yet know what that way was.

Pen breathed deeply, feeling a calmness settle through him. Weariness played a part in that, but there was peace, as well.

If my father was here, he would have spoken those same words to me, he thought.

There was comfort in knowing that. He closed his eyes and slept.

They woke to a dawn shrouded in mist and gloom, their bodies aching with the cold and damp. Once again, there was nothing to eat or drink, so they put their hunger and thirst aside and set out. As they poled through the murky waters, stands of swamp grass clutched at them with anxious tendrils. Everywhere, shadows stretched across the water and through the trees, snakes they didn't want to wake. No one spoke. Chilled by the swamp's gray emptiness, they retreated inside themselves. Their determination kept them going. Somewhere up ahead was an end to the morass, and there was only one way to reach it.

At midday they were confronted by a huge stretch of open water surrounded by vine-draped trees and clogged by heavy swamp grass. Islands dotted the lake, grassy hummocks littered with rotting logs. Overhead, mist swirled like thick soup in a kettle, sunlight weakened by its oily mix, a hazy wash that spilled gossamer-pale through the heavy branches of the trees.

They stopped poling and stared out across the marshy, ragged expanse. The islands jutted from the water like reptile eyes. Pen looked at Ahren Elessedil and shook his head. He didn't like the feel of the lake and did not care to try to cross it. Ripples at its center hinted at the presence of things best avoided.

"Follow the lakeshore," the Druid said, glancing at the sky. "Stay under the cover of the trees. Watch the surface of the water for movement."

They chose to veer left, where the shallows were not as densely clogged with grasses and deadwood. Poling along some twenty feet offshore, Pen kept one eye on the broad expanse of the lake, scanning for ripples. He knew the others were depending on his instincts to keep them safe. Out on the open water, trailers of mist skimmed the viscous surface. A sudden squall came and went like a ghost. The air felt heavy and thick, and condensation dripped from the trees in a slow, steady rhythm. Within the shadowy interior of the woods surrounding the lake, the silence was deep and oppressive.

At the lake's center, something huge lifted in a shadowy parting of waters and was gone again, silent as smoke. Pen glanced at Khyber, who was poling next to him on the raft. He saw the fierce concentration in her eyes waver.

They had gone some distance when the shoreline receded into a deep bay overhung with vines that dipped all the way to the water's dark surface. Cautiously, they maneuvered under the canopy, sliding through the still waters with barely a whisper of movement, eyes searching. The hairs on the back of Pen's neck prickled in warning. Something felt wrong. Then he realized what it was. He wasn't hearing anything from the life around him, not a sound, not a single movement, nothing.

A vine brushed against his face, sliding away almost reluctantly, leaving a glistening trail of slime on his skin. He wiped the sticky stuff from his face, grimacing, and glanced upward. A huge mass of similar vines was writhing and twisting directly overhead. Not quite sure what he was looking at, he stared in disbelief, then in fear.

"Ahren," he whispered.

Too late. The vines dropped down like snakes to encircle them, a cascade of long arms and supple fingers, tentacles of all sizes and shapes, attacking with such ferocity and purpose that they had no time even to think of reaching for their weapons. His arms pinned to his sides, Pen was swept off the raft and into the air. Tagwen flew past him, similarly wrapped about. The boy looked up and saw so many of the vines entwined in the forest canopy that it felt as if he were being drawn into a basket of snakes.

Then he saw something else, something much worse. Within the masses of tentacles were mouths, huge beaked maws that clacked and snapped and pulsed with life. Like squids, he thought, waiting to feed. It had taken only seconds for the vines to immobilize him, only seconds more for them to lift him toward the waiting mouths, all of it so quick he barely had time to comprehend what was happening. Now he fought like a wild man, kicking and screaming, determined to break free. But the vines held him securely, and slowly, inexorably, they drew him in.

Then spears of fire thrust into the beaks and tentacles from below, their flames a brilliant azure, burning through the shadows and gloom. The vines shuddered violently, shaking Pen with such force that he lost all sense of which way was up. An instant later, they released him altogether, dropping him stunned and disoriented into the swamp. He struck with an impact that jarred his bones and knocked the breath from his body, and he was underwater almost instantly, fighting to right himself, to reach air again.

He broke the surface with a gasp, thrashing against a clutch of weeds, seeing scythes of blue fire slash through the canopy in broad sweeps, smelling wood and plants burn, hearing the hiss and crackle of their destruction, tasting

smoke and ash on the air. Overhead, the canopy was alive
with twisting vines, some of them aflame, others batting
wildly at burning neighbors. He saw Ahren Elessedil standing on the raft, both hands thrust skyward, his elemental
magic the source of the fire, summoned from the ether and released from his fingers in jagged darts.

"Pen!" someone yelled.

Khyber had surfaced next to the raft and was hanging on
one end, trying to balance the uneven platform so that her uncle could defend them. The swamp waters had turned choppy
and rough, and it was all the Druid could do to keep from being tossed overboard. Pen swam to their aid, seizing the end
of the raft opposite the Elven girl, the vines whipping all
about him.

An instant later, Tagwen dropped out of the canopy, his
bearded face a mask of confusion and terror as he plunged
into the murky waters and then surfaced next to Pen.

"Push us out into the bay!" Ahren Elessedil shouted, dropping to one knee as his tiny platform tilted precariously.

Kicking strongly, Pen and Khyber propelled the raft
toward open water, fighting to get clear of the deadly trap.
Tagwen hung on tenaciously, and Ahren continued to send
shards of fire into the clutching vines, which were still trying
to get at him but were unable to break past his defenses.
Smoke billowed and roiled in heavy clouds, mingling with
swamp mist to form an impenetrable curtain. From somewhere distant, the frightened cries of water birds rose.

When at last they were far enough from the vines to pause
in their efforts, Pen and Khyber crawled onto the raft beside
Ahren Elessedil, pulled Tagwen up after them, and collapsed,
gasping for breath. For several long seconds, no one said anything, their eyes fixed on the smoky mass of tree vines now
some distance off.

"We were lucky," Pen said finally.

"Don't be stupid!" Khyber snapped in reply. "Look what we've done! We've given ourselves away!"

Pen stared at her, recognition setting in. She was right. He had forgotten what Ahren Elessedil had said about how using magic would reveal their presence to those who hunted them. Ahren had saved them, but he had betrayed them, as well. Terek Molt would know exactly where they were. The *Galaphile* would track them to the bay.

"What can we do?" he asked in dismay.

Khyber turned to her uncle. "How much time do we have, Uncle Ahren?"

The Druid shook his head. "Not much. They will come for us quickly." He climbed to his knees and looked around. Everything was clouded with smoke. "If they are close, we won't even have time to get off this bay."

"We can hide!" Pen suggested hurriedly, glancing skyward for movement, for any sign of their pursuers. "Perhaps on one of the islands. We can sink the raft . . ."

Ahren shook his head. "No, Penderrin. We need to go ashore and find a place to make a stand. We need space in which to move and solid ground on which to do it." He handed the boy one of the two remaining poles. "Try to get us ashore, Pen. Choose a direction. Do the best you can, but do it quickly."

With Ahren working on the opposite side, Pen began poling toward shore once more, farther down from where the vines still thrashed and burned, farther along in the direction they had been heading. They made good time, borne on the crest of a tide stirred by their battle with the vines, a tide that swept them east. But Pen sensed that however swiftly they moved, it wasn't going to be swift enough.

This is all my fault, he kept thinking. *Again.*

The haze continued thick and unbroken, layering the surface of the water in a roiling blanket that stank of burning wood and leaves. Slowly, the bay went quiet again, the waters turning slate black and oily once more, a dark reflection of the shadows creeping in from the shoreline. Pen poled furiously, thinking that if they could just reach a safe place to land, they might lose themselves in the trees. It would not be easy to find them in this jungle, this swamp, this morass, not even for Terek Molt. All they needed to do was gain the shore.

They did so, finally. They beached on a mud bank fronting a thick stand of cypress, tangled all about with vines and banked with heavy grasses. They pulled their raft ashore, hauled it back into the trees, and set out walking. The silence of the Slags closed about them, deep and pervasive, an intrusive and brooding companion. Pen could hear the sound of his breathing. He could feel the pumping of his heart.

Still there was no sign of their pursuers.

We're going to escape them after all, he thought in sudden relief.

They walked for several hours, well past midday and deep into the afternoon. The shoreline snaked in and out of the trees, and they stayed at its edge, keeping a sharp eye out for more of the deadly vines and any sign of movement on the bay waters. They did not talk, their efforts concentrated on putting one foot in front of the other, Ahren Elessedil setting a pace that even Pen, who was accustomed to long treks, found difficult to match.

It was late in the afternoon, the shadows of twilight beginning to lengthen out of the west, when they found the eastern end of the lake. It swung south in a broad curve, the ground lifting to a wall of old growth through which dozens of waterways opened. Pen searched the gloom ahead without finding anything reassuring, then took a moment to read his compass, affirming what Ahren, with his Druidic senses, had already determined. They were on course, but not yet clear of the swamp.

Then sudden brightness flared behind them, dispersing the mist and brightening the gloom as if dawn had broken. They wheeled back as one, shielding their eyes. It looked as if the swamp were boiling from a volcanic eruption, its waters churning, steaming with an intense heat. The dark prow of an airship nosed through the fading haze like a great lumbering bear, slowly settling toward the waters of the bay, black nose sniffing the air. Pen fought to keep from shaking with the chill that swept through him.

The *Galaphile* had found them.

TWENTY-SIX

The huge curved horns of the *Galaphile*'s bow swung slowly about to point like a compass needle toward the four who stood frozen on the muddy shoreline. There was no mistaking that she had found what she was searching for. Through the fading screen of mist and twilight's deepening shadows, the vessel settled onto the reed-choked surface of the bay, not fifty yards away, and slowly began to advance. Her sails were furled and her masts and spars as bare and black as charred bones. She had the stark, blasted look of a specter.

"What do we do?" Khyber hissed.

"We can run," Pen answered at once, already poised to do so. "There's still time to gain the trees, get deep into the woods, split up if we have to . . ."

He trailed off hopelessly. It was pointless to talk about running away. Ahren had already said that it was too late to hide, so running would not help, either. The *Galaphile* had already found them once; even if they ran, it would have no trouble doing so again. Terek Molt would track them down like rabbits. They were going to have to make a stand, even without an airship in which to maneuver or weapons with which to fight. Ahren Elessedil's Druid magic and whatever resources the rest of them could muster were going to have to be enough.

What other choice do we have? Pen thought in despair.

The *Galaphile* had come to a stop at the edge of the shoreline, advanced as close to the mud bank as her draft would allow. Atop her decks, dark figures moved, taking up positions along the railing. Gnome Hunters. Pen saw the glittering surfaces of their blades. Perhaps the Gnome Hunters simply meant to kill them, having no need to do otherwise.

"Do you see how she shimmers?" Ahren Elessedil asked them suddenly. His voice was eerily calm. "The ship, about her hull and rigging? Do you see?"

Pen looked with the others. At first, he couldn't make it out, but then slowly his eyes adjusted to the heavy twilight and he saw a sort of glow that pulsed all about the warship, an aura of glistening dampness.

"What is it?" Khyber whispered, brushing back her mop of dark hair, twisting loose strands of it in her fingers.

"Magic," her uncle answered softly. "Terek Molt is sheathing the *Galaphile* in magic to protect her from an attack. He is wary of what we did to him last time, of another storm, of the elements I can summon to disrupt his efforts."

The Druid exhaled slowly. "He has made a mistake. He has given us a chance."

A rope ladder was lowered over the side of the airship, one end dropping through a railing gap and into the water. A solitary figure began to descend. Even from a distance and through the heavy gloom, there was no doubt about who it was.

Pen glanced up again at the cloaked figures lining the *Galaphile*'s railing. All their weapons were pointed at himself and his companions.

"Khyber," Ahren Elessedil called softly.

When she looked over, he passed her something, a quick exchange that was barely noticeable. Pen caught a glimpse of the small pouch as her hand opened just far enough to permit her to see that it was the Elfstones she had been given. Her quick intake of breath was audible.

"Listen carefully," her uncle said without looking at her, his eyes fixed on Terek Molt, who was almost to the water now. "When I tell you, use the Elfstones against the *Galaphile*. Do as you have been taught. Open your mind, summon their power, and direct it at the airship."

Khyber was already shaking her head, her Elven features taut with dismay. "It won't work, Uncle Ahren! The magic is only good against other magic—magic that threatens the holder of the stones! You taught me that yourself! The *Galaphile* is an airship, wood and iron only!"

"She is," the Druid agreed. "But thanks to Terek Molt, the magic that sheathes her is not. It is his magic, Druid magic. Trust me, Khyber. It is our only chance. I am skilled, but Terek Molt was trained as a warrior Druid and is more powerful than I am. Do as I say. Watch for my signal. Do not reveal that you have the Elfstones before then. Do nothing to demonstrate that you are a danger to him. If you do, if you give yourself away too early, even to help me, we are finished."

Pen glanced at Khyber. The Elven girl's eyes glittered with fear. "I've never even tried to use the Elfstones," she said. "I don't know what it takes to summon the magic. What if I can't do so now?"

Ahren Elessedil smiled. "You can and you will, Khyber. You have the training and the resolve. Do not doubt yourself. Be brave. Trust the magic and your instincts. That will be enough."

Terek Molt stepped down off the ladder and into the shallow water, turning to face them. His black robes billowed out behind him as he approached, his blocky form squared toward Ahren Elessedil. He radiated confidence and disdain, the set of his dark form signaling his intent in a way that was unmistakable.

"Move to one side, Khyber," Ahren said quietly, his voice taking on an edge. "Remember what I said. Watch for my signal. Pen, Tagwen, back out of the way."

The boy and the Dwarf retreated at once, happy to put as much distance as possible between themselves and Terek Molt. The warrior Druid's chiseled face glanced in their direction, a slight lifting of his chin the only indication that he noticed them at all. But even that small movement was enough to let Pen see the rage that was reflected in the flat, cold eyes.

When he was twenty feet from the Elf, he stopped. "Give up the boy. He belongs to us now. You can keep the old man and the girl as compensation for your trouble. Take them and go."

Ahren Elessedil shook his head. "I don't think I care to take you up on your offer. I think we will all stay together."

Terek Molt nodded. "Then you will all come with me. Either way, it makes no difference."

"Ultimatums are the last resort of desperate men."

"Don't play games with me, outcast."

"What has happened to you, Terek Molt, that you would betray the Ard Rhys and the order this way? You were a good man once."

The Dwarf's face darkened. "I am a better man than you, Ahren Elessedil. I am no cat's paw, underling fool in league with a monster. I am no tool at the beck and call of a witch!"

"Are you not?"

"I'll say this once. I got tired of the Ard Rhys—of her disruptive presence and her self-centered ways. I got tired of watching her fail time and again at the simplest of tasks. She was never right for the position. She should never have assumed it. Others are better suited to lead the Druid Council to the places it needs to go. Others, who do not share her history."

"A full council vote might have been a better way to go. At least that approach would have lent a semblance of respectability to your efforts and not painted all of you as betrayers and cowards. Perhaps enough others on the Druid Council might have agreed with you that all this would not have been necessary." The Elven Prince paused. "Perhaps it still might be so, were someone of character to pursue it."

He made it sound so reasonable, as if treachery could be undone and made right, as if the conversation was between two old friends who were discussing a thorny issue that each hoped to resolve. "Is it too late to bring her back?" he asked the other.

The Dwarf's face darkened. "Why bring her back when she is safely out of the way? What does it matter to you, in any case? You have been gone from the council and her life for years. You are an outcast from your own people. Is that why you think so highly of her—because she is like you?"

"I think better of Grianne Ohmsford than I do of Shadea a'Ru," the Elf replied.

"You can tell her so yourself, once we are returned to Paranor." Terek Molt came forward another step, black cloak billowing. One hand lifted and a gloved finger pointed. "Enough talk. I have chased you for as long as I care to; I am weary of the aggravation. You might have gotten away from me if those Rovers hadn't stranded you in this swamp and then betrayed you to us. Does that surprise you? We caught up with them early yesterday, trying to slip past us in their pathetic little vessel. That Captain was quick enough to tell us everything once he saw how things stood. So we knew where you were, and it was just a matter of waiting for you to show yourselves. Using magic was a mistake. It led us right to you."

Ahren nodded. "Unavoidable. What have you done with the *Skatelow* and her crew?"

The Dwarf spit to one side. "Rover vermin. I sent them on their way, back to where they came from. I had no need of them once they gave you up. They'll be halfway home by now and better off than those who so foolishly sought to use their services." He looked past the other now to Pen. "I am done talking. Bring the boy. No more arguments. No further delays."

Ahren Elessedil's hands had been tucked within his cloak. Now he brought them out again, balled into fists and bright with his magic's blue glow. Terek Molt stiffened, but did not give ground. "Do not be a fool," he said quietly.

"I don't think Pen should go with you," Ahren Elessedil said. "I think you intend him harm, whether you admit to it or not. Druids are meant to protect, and protect him I shall. You have forgotten your teachings, Terek Molt. If you take one step nearer, I shall help you remember them."

The Dwarf shook his head slowly. His gloved hands flared with magic of his own. "You are no match for me, Elessedil. If you test me, you will be found wanting. You will be destroyed. Step aside. Give the boy to me and be done with this."

They faced each other across the short stretch of mud and shallow water, two identically cloaked forms born of the same order but gone on separate paths. Elf and Dwarf, faces hard as stone, eyes locked as if bound together by iron threads, poised in a manner that suggested there would be no backing down and no quarter given. Pen found himself tensed and ready, as well, but he did not know what he would do when doing something became necessary. He could not think of anything that would help, any difference he could make. Yet he knew he would try.

"Your ship," Ahren Elessedil said suddenly to Terek Molt, and nodded in the direction of the *Galaphile*.

The Dwarf turned to look, did so without thinking, and in that instant Ahren attacked, raising both hands and dispatching the elemental magic that he commanded in a burst of Druid fire. But it was not the other man he targeted; it was the warship, his elemental magic striking the vessel with such force that it was rocked from bow to stern. The infuriated Dwarf struck back instantly, his own fire hammering into the

Druid. Ahren Elessedil had just enough time to throw up a shield before the other's magic knocked him completely off his feet and sent him sprawling in the mud.

It was a terrible blow, yet Ahren Elessedil was up again immediately, fighting off the warrior Druid's second thrust, steadying his defenses. Now arrows and darts cast down by the Gnome Hunters who were gathered at the railing of the *Galaphile* began to rain on the beleaguered Elf. Pen and Tagwen threw themselves out of the way as a few stray missiles nearly skewered them, then began crawling toward the protective shelter of the trees. Khyber screamed in rage, bringing up her own small Druid-enhanced magic to protect herself, and crouched down close by Ahren, poised to strike but still waiting on her uncle's command.

Ahren Elessedil was fighting for his life, down on his knees with his hands extended and his palms facing out, as if in a futile effort to ward off what was happening. His protective shield was eroding under the onslaught of Terek Molt's attack, melting like ice under searing heat. Yet once again, he chose to strike not at the Dwarf, but at the warship, diverting precious power from his defenses. Pen could not understand what the Elf was thinking. Ahren already knew that the ship was protected, that it was a waste of time and effort to try to damage her. Why was he persisting in this method of attack?

Yet suddenly, improbably, the *Galaphile* began to shudder, massive hull and ram-shaped pontoons rocking as if caught in a storm instead of resting in shallow water. Something of what Ahren was doing was making a difference, after all. Terek Molt seemed to sense it, as well, and redoubled his efforts. Druid fire exploded out of his fingers and into the Elf, staggering him, crumpling his shield. Pen heard Ahren call out to Khyber, the signal for which she had been waiting, and immediately she had the Elfstones in hand, arms outthrust. Brilliant blue light built about her fist, widening in a sphere that caused the boy to shield his eyes.

Then the magic exploded from her clenched fingers in a massive rush that swept over the *Galaphile* like a tidal wave. For a single instant the Druid warship was lit like a star, blazing with light, and then it burst into flames. It didn't catch fire in just one place or even a dozen. It caught fire everywhere at once, transformed into a giant torch. With a monstrous whoosh it detonated in a fireball that rose hundreds of feet into the misty swamp sky, carrying with it the Gnome Hunters, bearing away a twisting, writhing Terek Molt, as well, the latter sucked into the vortex. A roar erupted from the conflagration, burning with such fury that it scorched Pen and Tagwen a hundred yards away, sweeping through the whole of the Slags.

In seconds, the *Galaphile* and all who had sailed her were gone.

Pen looked up from where he lay flattened against the mud and scorched grasses. Smoke rising from his blackened form, Ahren Elessedil lay sprawled on his back at the shoreline. Khyber knelt in shock some yards away, her arms lowered, the power of the Elfstones gone dormant once more. Her head drooped, as if she had taken a blow, and the boy could see her eyes blinking rapidly. She was shaking all over.

He forced himself to his feet. "Tagwen," he called over to the Dwarf, finding him through eyes half-blinded by smoke and ash. Tagwen looked up at him from where he was huddled in a muddied depression, his eyes wide and scared. "Get up. We have to help them."

The boy staggered across the flats, head lowered against the heat of the still-fiery bay. Flames and ash-smeared waters were all that remained of the *Galaphile*. Pen glanced at the charred mix, baffled and awed by what had taken place, trying unsuccessfully to make sense of it.

He reached Khyber and knelt beside her. He touched her shoulder. "Khyber," he said softly.

She did not look up or stop shaking, so he put his lips to her ear, whispering, "Khyber, it's all right, it's over. Look at me. I need to know you can hear me. You're all right."

"So much power," she whispered suddenly. She stopped shaking then, her body going perfectly still. A long sigh escaped her lips. She lifted her head and looked out across the fiery surface of the wetlands. "I couldn't stop it, Pen. Once it started, I couldn't stop it."

"I know," he said, understanding now something of what had transpired. "It's all over."

He helped her to her feet, and they stumbled together to where Tagwen knelt beside Ahren Elessedil. Pen knew at a glance that the Druid was dying. A handful of arrows and darts had pierced him, and his body was blackened and smoking from the explosion. But his eyes were open and calm, and he watched their approach with a steady gaze.

Khyber gasped as she saw him, then dropped to her knees and began to cry, her hands clasped helplessly in her lap, her head shaking slowly from side to side.

The Druid reached out with one charred hand and touched her wrist. "Terek Molt tied his magic to the *Galaphile*," he whispered, his voice dry and cracked with pain. "To protect her. When I attacked, he strengthened the connection until he was too committed to withdraw it. The Elfstones couldn't tell the difference. To them, the *Galaphile* was a weapon, an extension of Molt. So it consumed them both."

"I could have helped you!"

"No, Khyber." He coughed and blood flecked his burned lips. "He couldn't be allowed to know that you had the Elfstones. Otherwise, he would have destroyed you."

"Instead, he destroyed you!" She was crying so hard that she could barely make herself understood.

The ruined face tilted slightly in response. "I misjudged the extent of my invulnerability. Still, it is a reasonable trade." He swallowed thickly. "The Elfstones are yours now. Use them with caution. Your command of their power . . ." He trailed off, the words catching in this throat. "You've seen the nature of your abilities. Strong. Your heart, mind, body—very powerful. But the Stones are more powerful still. Be wary. They will rule you if you are not careful. There is danger in using them. Remember."

She lifted her tear-streaked face and looked over at Pen. "We have to help him!"

She was almost hysterical. Pen was frightened, unable to think of what to say to her. There was nothing they could do. Surely she could see that. But she looked so wild that he was afraid she might try something anyway, something dangerous.

Ahren Elessedil's hand tightened on her wrist. "No, Khyber," he said. He waited until she looked back at him, until she met his terrible burned gaze. "There is nothing to be done. It is finished for me. I'm sorry."

His eyes shifted slowly to Pen. "Penderrin. Twenty years ago, when I sailed on the *Jerle Shannara* with your father, a young girl gave up her life for me. She did so because she believed I was meant to do something important. I would like to think this is part of what she saved me for. Make something good come out of this. Do what you were sent here to do. Find the Ard Rhys and bring her back."

He took several sharp, rattling breaths, his eyes holding the boy's as he struggled to speak. "Ahren?" Pen whispered.

"Promise me."

The Druid's eyes became fixed and staring, and he quit breathing. Pen could not look away, finding in that terrible gaze strength of purpose he would not have believed possible. He reached out and touched the Druid's charred face, then closed those dead eyes and sat back again. He looked over at Khyber, who was crying silently into her hands, then at Tagwen.

"I never thought anything like this would happen," the Dwarf said quietly. "I thought he would be the one to get us safely through."

Pen nodded, looking out over the burning lake at the flames licking at the twilight darkness, staining sky and earth the color of blood. The surface of the water burned silently, steadily, a fiery mirror reflected against a backdrop of shadow-striped trees. Smoke mingled with mist and mist with clouds, and everything was hazy and surreal. The world had an alien feel to it, as if nothing the boy was seeing was familiar.

"What are we going to do?" Tagwen asked softly. He shook his head slowly, as if there were no answer to his question.

Penderrin Ohmsford looked over again at Khyber. She was no longer crying. Her head was lifted and her dark features were a mask of resolve. He could tell from the way she was looking back at him that there would be no more tears.

The boy turned to the Dwarf. "We're going to do what he asked of us," he said. "We're going to go on."

TWENTY-SEVEN

Shadea a'Ru stalked from the Druid Council without sparing even a glance back at those fools who expected it, her eyes directed straight ahead. She would not give them the satisfaction. She would give them nothing. She was seething with rage and frustration, but she would not let even a hint of it escape. Let them suspect what they wished about her true feelings; their suspicions were the least of her problems.

Her stride lengthening, she shouldered past the few grouped by the doors leading out, using her size and weight to brush them aside, and turned down the hallway toward the stairs leading up to her rooms. It was a kindness she bestowed on them, leaving so abruptly. Had she hesitated longer, she might have killed one of them.

Surely that would have been more satisfying than anything else that had happened.

She had spent the entire afternoon trying to convince the Council of the necessity of taking a stand on the war between the Federation and the Free-born. She had insisted that no progress in the efforts of the Druid order could be made until the war was concluded. It was inevitable, she argued, that the Federation, superior in men and materials, would emerge as the eventual victor. Better that it happen now, so that the rebuilding could begin, so that the work of the Druids could commence in earnest. Callahorn was Southland territory in any event, inhabited mostly by members of the Race of Man and naturally aligned with the interests of the Federation. Let them have it. Make that the condition to ending the war. The Free-born were a rebel outfit at best, consumed by their foolish insistence on keeping Callahorn for themselves. Remove the tacit support of the Druids and the rebels would collapse.

She did not tell the Council, of course, that she had made a bargain with Sen Dunsidan to help him secure control over the Borderlands. She did not tell them that Federation control of Callahorn was the price of his support of her and her efforts to expand the authority and influence of the order. That wasn't something they needed to know. It was enough that she was proposing a reasonable, commonsense solution to a problem that had plagued the order since the day of its inception.

But the Council had balked at adopting her proposal, its members led in their opposition by that snake Gerand Cera, who had insisted that a thorough study of the consequences of such drastic action was needed first. The matter was not as simple as the Ard Rhys was trying to make it seem, his argument went. Elven interests would be impacted by the outcome of the Federation–Free-born war in a significant way, as well. Once he had mentioned the Elves, it was only moments before the Dwarves were insisting that their interests were important too. Soon, everyone was arguing. Clever of him. Without repudiating the suggestion outright, he had managed to defer any action on it until a later date, all with an eye toward his own special interests, she was certain.

Very well. He had won this day, but there would be another—although not necessarily for him. He was becoming something of a nuisance, one that she would have to deal with soon. If he could not be brought into line, he would have to be removed.

For the moment, she had more pressing concerns. Sen Dunsidan would arrive in three days, and he would expect to hear that she had secured the Council's approval for Federation occupation of Callahorn along with its open repudiation of Free-born claims to the land. He would be expecting a joint announcement of solidarity on the matter, one that would clearly indicate to the Free-born that their cause was lost. His expectations would not be met. She would have to tell him that the matter was not settled, that he would have to be patient. He would not like that, but he would have to live with it. He was used to disappointment; he would survive.

She began to climb the stairs to the tower, conscious of the darkness pressing in from without, filtering through the windows to cast its shadows in the flickering torchlight. Nighttime already, and she had not yet eaten.

She was halfway up when Traunt Rowan appeared at the top of the stairs on his way down. She could tell at once that something was wrong.

"You had better come, Shadea," he told her quietly, waiting until she had reached him, then turning back the way he had come. "The cold chamber."

She fell in beside him, angry without yet knowing why. "Has Molt failed yet again?"

"Someone has. The scrye waters indicate a massive collision of magics somewhere east of Anatcherae. The *Galaphile* is gone."

"Gone?" She stared at him. "Gone where?"

"Destroyed. Obliterated."

Her fists clenched in fury. "How could Molt allow such a thing to happen?" Her mind spun with possibilities. "When was our last report from him?"

"Yesterday." Rowan wouldn't look at her. "The message indicated he was in pursuit of the boy and the others and had caught up with them in Anatcherae. That would have been two days ago."

She forced herself to stay calm, to think it through. Courier birds released from the *Galaphile* brought her regular messages from Molt, indicating where he was and what he was doing. Nothing in yesterday's message suggested the Dwarf was in any trouble, let alone the sort that would cause a Druid warship to be destroyed. Magic of such power was unusual, and it would have to have been employed in just the right way. The Elfstones? Perhaps. But Ahren Elessedil was not a warrior Druid or trained in battle the way Molt was. It was inconceivable that he would have prevailed in a confrontation.

They entered the cold chamber to find Iridia Eleri standing at the basin, staring down at the scrye waters with haunted eyes, arms folded across her rigid body. Her eyes snapped up at their entry, and the haunted look gave way to one of rage.

"If you had sent me, this wouldn't have happened!" she hissed at Shadea, making no effort to hide her feelings.

Shadea ignored her, walking over to the basin and looking down. Heavy ripples emanated from a point at the eastern shore of the Lazareen, perhaps somewhere within the Slags. She knew that country. Dangerous to anyone, no matter how well armed or prepared. There was no mistaking what she was reading in the waters. The nature of the ripples clearly indicated a massive explosion, one instigated by a use of magic. The little blip that had served as a beacon for the *Galaphile* was gone. Traunt Rowan was not mistaken in what he had told her.

"There's no way of knowing who survived this," she said, mostly to herself.

"Not without sending someone to find out," Traunt Rowan said.

Iridia spun around the end of the basin and came face-to-face with Shadea. Although smaller of frame and stature, Iridia looked as if she intended to attack the bigger woman. Shadea took a step back in spite of herself.

"This is on your head," Iridia snapped, her words as sharp-edged as daggers, her voice freezing the air. She was shaking with rage. "You are responsible for this travesty, you and your insistence on doing whatever you choose to do. What do you need with the rest of us, Shadea? What have you ever needed with us? I thought you my friend, once. I thought we were sisters. But you are incapable of friendship or loyalty or caring of any sort. You are as much a monster as that creature you summoned to bear the Stiehl. And I am no better. I have been one of your monsters, one of those who act in your behalf. I have been your tool."

She shook her head slowly. "No more. Not ever again."

She held the other's gaze for a moment longer, then turned and walked from the room. Unimpressed, Shadea watched her go. She thought it unfortunate that Iridia could no longer sort things out in a reasonable manner. Her attachment to Ahren Elessedil had left her emotionally unstable, and Shadea found herself hoping that the Elven Prince had gone the way of the *Galaphile*. Then, perhaps, Iridia would come back to herself.

Shadea looked over at Traunt Rowan. "Are you of a like mind?"

The Druid shrugged. "I am no one's tool, and I do what I choose. Iridia's problems are her own. On the other hand, I question the wisdom of your decision to send Terek Molt after that boy. I don't see the benefit to it. It distracts us from what matters."

"What matters is making certain no one finds a way to bring the Ard Rhys back!" she snapped at him. "Why can't you see that? All of you are so certain it can't be done. But remember who she is. Others thought her dead and gone, as well, and lived to regret it."

"No one can go into the Forbidding—"

"Hssst! Don't even speak the word!" She leaned close. "It is bad enough that Ahren Elessedil and the boy know what has happened, and it would be a mistake for us to think that they do not. They will seek a way to reach her. Successful or not, they will not forgive us for what we have done. This matter will not resolve itself while they live. If you think otherwise, say so now!"

He stared at her in silence, then shook his head. "I think as you do."

Shadea wasn't sure she believed him, but it was enough of an affirmation for now. She looked back at the scrye waters. Another message would arrive by tomorrow if Terek Molt was still alive. If not, then she could only hope that he had taken the boy, the Elven Prince, and that sycophant Tagwen with him to the grave. Then she could stop thinking about all of them and concentrate on what was happening at Paranor.

It occurred to her suddenly that she had forgotten about Aphasia Wye, dispatched with the Stiehl, as Iridia had reminded her, to eliminate the boy and his protectors. What of him? Even if the *Galaphile* was destroyed, even if Terek Molt was dead, perhaps the assassin was still carrying through on his task. Nothing would stop him once he set his mind to it. The only character flaw she had ever discovered was his troublesome streak of independence. On a whim, he might abandon the whole project.

She stared down again at the scrye waters, studying the diminishing series of ripples that marked the passing of the *Galaphile*.

With Aphasia Wye, she thought, you never knew.

Iridia Eleri strode blindly from the cold chamber and down the hallway beyond, so furious she could barely make herself think. Tears leaked from the corners of her eyes, a series of ragged, glistening tracks on her perfect features. Had she stayed a moment longer, she would not have been able to hold them back. She stopped now, turning into a deep alcove in the empty hallway, and cried freely for several minutes, her body racked with sobs, her world collapsed about her. She knew what Shadea only suspected. Ahren Elessedil was dead. The voice had told her so.

When she stopped crying, she stood motionless in the alcove's darkness and forced herself to confront the truth. She had lied to herself, lied to them all. She was still in love with Ahren. She had always been in love with him and always would be. Shadea might sneer and the others might doubt, but it was so. It didn't even matter that he was dead. She loved him anyway.

What she could not bear was that he had not loved her in turn.

She stared into space, the words echoing in her mind. The voice had promised that this would change, that with time and patience, he would love her. The voice had promised from the very beginning, when it had first summoned her and offered its help. The voice was persuasive and comforting, and so she had listened and believed. Ahren could be hers, and for that she would do anything.

And had.

She closed her eyes against a wave of memories that paraded through her mind like specters. A flood of emotion followed on their heels. The sadness she felt for the man she had left in order to pursue Ahren. The emptiness she had experienced when she had given birth to and then abandoned the man's baby. The humiliation she had endured when Grianne Ohmsford had discovered what she had done. The terrible hurt she had suffered when Ahren had told her that in spite of everything, they could not be together, that his life was meant to go another way. The rage she had called upon to ally herself with Shadea and the others in their determination to rid the Druids of Grianne Ohmsford. The hatred she had nurtured for the Ard Rhys, the person most responsible for her misery.

The sense of devastation and irreparable loss she felt now, with Ahren Elessedil forever beyond her reach.

—But it need not be so—

Her eyes snapped open and she took a quick breath. The

voice was back, come to comfort her anew. She nearly began crying again, so grateful was she to hear it. How much she depended on it. Just the sound of it was enough to give her fresh hope, new strength.

—He can still be yours—

She nodded at the darkness, wanting it to be true. But how could it? Ahren was dead, the voice had already told her so. There was no way to bring him back, no way to restore life to his shattered body. She could join him, of course. She could end her own life and reunite with him in death. She believed that was possible and even preferable to what life offered without him. Maybe she would have that, anyway. Now that she had broken with Shadea, it would not take the other long to decide to eliminate her.

—You need not die to have him back—

She had always trusted the voice, and she had never had cause to regret it. From the beginning, when it had summoned her north to the ruins of the Skull Kingdom and she had built the fires and made the sacrifices that had brought it into being, she had known it spoke the truth. It was a small thing for her to help it, when it was doing so much to help her. Shadea had believed from the first that she was the guiding force behind the conspiracy to eliminate the Ard Rhys, that she was the one who had sought out and found the means to carry out the act through her connection with Sen Dunsidan. The Federation Prime Minister, in turn, believed that he was the one who was determining the course of events, that his promises and gifts to Iridia, after she had approached him, had subverted her and made her his spy within the Druid camp. But she was the one to whom the voice spoke. She was the one who had brought it out of the darkness and into the light. She was the one to whom it had given the liquid night and the means by which she could gain some small measure of revenge against the woman who had turned Ahren

Elessedil against her through scurrilous subterfuge and self-serving advice.

The others could think what they wished. She was the one who had made everything possible.

—I am here, Iridia—

She felt a surge of expectation and joy. She had waited for it, longed for it, the time when the voice took form, as it had promised it would, to give her back her place in the world. It would happen after the exile of the Ard Rhys, it had told her. Once the High Druid was gone, the voice could come out of hiding. It could take form and become for Iridia the friend and confidant she had once thought Shadea might be.

—I can be more than that, Iridia. I can be him—

Not quite willing to believe that she had heard the words correctly, she felt her heart lurch. She stood frozen in the darkness of the alcove, listening to their echo in the silence. *I can be him.* Was that possible? The voice was a chameleon, a changeling, capable of wondrous things. But could it bring back the dead? Could it make Ahren Elessedil whole again? Was the voice capable of that?

—Walk to me. In the cellars—

She left the alcove at once and proceeded to the main staircase, descending in a rush, her footfalls tiny and lost in the cavernous passage. No other Druid was abroad; most were gathered in the dining hall, the rest in their rooms or libraries. It felt to her as if she were alone in the world, free of its constraints and discriminations. She had never been well liked, never a part of anything, always alone. It was because of her childhood, where she had been set apart by her skills and the mistrust of those who recognized them. Even her parents had looked on her with growing suspicion and doubt, distancing themselves and their other children, sending her away early to study with an old woman who was said to understand such magic. The old woman did not, but living with her gave Iridia space and time to grow as she wished, to hone her talents, to gain a better understanding of what they offered. She needed no mentor to help her with this. She needed only herself.

Ten years she lived with the old woman, a crone of demands and false promises that would have eroded a less determined student. But Iridia only smiled and agreed and acquiesced to all, pretending obedience and waiting until she was alone to do what she wished. The old woman was no match for her, and when it was time, Iridia led her abusive and demanding benefactor to the well out back and pushed her in. For three days and nights, the crone screamed for help that never came.

Iridia turned down the lower hallway to the cellar doors at the north end of the Keep, knowing instinctively that was where she was meant to go, that was where the voice would be waiting. Shadows draped the heavy stones of the floors she passed across, her own the only one moving. No guards warded the passageways or walked the walls of Paranor now; the Druids alone kept watch, and theirs was a desultory, disinterested effort. In the time of the Warlock Lord, the keep would have fallen already.

At the heavy, ironbound doors leading down, the Elven sorceress paused to look back. No one was in sight; no one had followed. Shadea might have thought to try, but had not made the attempt. Just as well, Iridia thought. That would have complicated things. She wanted no one to intrude on her meeting.

Hurry, Iridia. I am anxious—

As was she, flushed with unexpected passion. She was like a young, foolish girl, filled with wild emotion and desperate need. The voice had never failed her, and now it was going to give her the thing she desired most. It made her feel heady, as if she could dare anything, as if anything were possible. She pushed through the cellar doors in a rush, taking one of the torches from the brackets just inside, lighting it with a sweep

of her fingers and a spray of magic, and started downward
once more.

This time, her descent was much longer and darker, the
stairwell windowless and narrow as it tunneled into the deep
earth beneath the castle foundation. The air was damp and
stale, smelling of long years of confinement and ageless dust.
Her footsteps on the stone steps matched the sound of her
breathing, quick and hurried. When this was finished, she
thought, she would leave Paranor and go far away, taking
Ahren with her so that they could build a life together free of
everything that had gone before. It was what she would have
done in the first place, had the Ard Rhys not poisoned Ahren
against her. Ahren claimed Grianne had nothing to do with
his dismissal of her, but Iridia knew better. His claim that he
had never loved her, did not feel for her as she did for him,
was a lie forged in the furnace of his anger at what *she*, who
would always be the Ilse Witch, had told him. For that alone,
she had deserved banishment to the Forbidding, and much
worse.

At the bottom of the stairs, a rotunda formed a hub for a
dozen passageways leading in different directions. Iridia
chose the one from which the voice was calling, certain of its
location, of its presence. Holding out the torch to chase back
the darkness, she went down the passageway, a silent presence in a silent tomb. The catacombs were used infrequently,
which had something to do with the past, with the history of
the Keep, though Iridia had never cared enough to find out
what that history was. It was the place she met with her coconspirators, but not a place she visited otherwise. It was
enough that she would do so for the last time tonight.

A hundred feet down the corridor, a door stood open, the
room beyond as black as pitch.

—I am here—

Iridia stepped inside, the torchlight flooding the room with its yellow glow. Her eyes searched swiftly. Four blank walls, a floor, and a ceiling. The room was empty.

"Where are you?" she asked, unable to keep the desperation from her voice.

—In the air, Iridia. In the ether you breathe. In darkness and in light. In all things. Close your eyes. Can you feel me—

She squeezed her eyes shut and exhaled slowly. It was true. She could feel his presence. He was there, all about her. "Yes," she whispered.

—It is time to give you what you were promised for helping me. To give you Ahren Elessedil, whole and complete again. To give you peace and love and joy. It is time, Iridia. Are you ready—

"Yes," she breathed, tears flowing once more, gratitude flooding through her. "Oh, please."

—Extinguish your torch and lay it on the floor—

She hesitated, not liking the prospect of being left in darkness. But her need for Ahren overcame her doubts, and she did as the voice had commanded. The torchlight went out and she was left standing in the heavy darkness.

—Close your eyes, Iridia. Stretch out your arms. I will come to you, into your embrace, no longer a voice, but a man. I will be him. For you, Iridia. Forever. Enfold me with your love and your desire. Accept me—

She would not have thought to do otherwise, though she still did not see how it could happen. But the persuasiveness of the voice was sufficient to make her believe. Again, she did as she was told. She closed her eyes and opened her arms.

Almost instantly, she felt a presence. It was only a faint sense of movement at first, a stirring of the air. Warmth followed, an infusion that spread through her like the flush of expectation she had experienced earlier. She felt a tingling, and her breath quickened at the prospect of what waited.

Then he was there, in her arms, Ahren Elessedil come back to life. Though she had never held him and did not know how it would feel, she knew at once that it was him. Her arms came about him gratefully, and she breathed in his smell and pressed her body against his. He responded at once, pliant and anxious, the part of her that was missing, the part that would make her whole.

"Ahren," she whispered.

He moved closer still, so close that it felt as if he were a part of her. She could feel them joining, becoming one. He was melting into her, entering her, becoming a part of her physically. She started in shock, then instinctively tried to resist what was happening. But it was too late, he was already fused to her as metals in a forge locked together to form a single skeletal frame.

Then the pain surged through her, so intense that when she began screaming she could not stop. Raw and sharp, pulsing with razors and knife points, it riddled her from head to foot, and her scream turned into a shriek that lasted until her voice gave out and her mind snapped.

Then she ceased to think or feel anything.

It was later that evening when Shadea a'Ru passed down the corridor of the north tower on her way to her chambers and encountered Iridia coming from the opposite direction. She approached the Elven sorceress warily, remembering how they had left things in the cold chamber earlier. One hand snapped free a dirk from the sheath bound to her wrist beneath her tunic sleeve. She had endured enough of Iridia's unpredictable behavior. If there was to be a confrontation, she wanted it to be done with quickly.

The other woman came right up to her, but there was no anger or resentment or challenge of any sort in her green eyes. Her perfect features were composed, and there was an air of new determination about her.

"I behaved poorly this afternoon," she said, coming to a stop several feet away. "I apologize."

Shadea was immediately suspicious. She didn't like the abrupt switch. It wasn't like Iridia to forgive so readily. Not her, not anyone. Nevertheless, she nodded agreeably. "We will put it behind us."

"That would be best for everyone," Iridia said as she turned away.

She walked past Shadea and continued down the hallway without looking back. Shadea stayed where she was, watching until the other was out of sight, all the time wondering what was going on.

TWENTY-EIGHT

They chose not to bury Ahren Elessedil's remains, but to burn them. A wetland was a poor place to dig a grave, and they had only their long knives to attempt the task. Besides, Khyber was not happy with the idea of leaving her uncle interred in a mud flat where rains and erosion might soon uncover him and leave him food for scavengers.

Working by light provided mostly from the still-burning swamp waters, they collected deadwood, piled it high on the mud bank where he had fought and died, and placed him on it. Khyber sang a Druid funeral song, one she had learned from her uncle, one that spoke of the purpose of a life well lived and an afterlife where hopes were fulfilled and rebirth possible. She used her magic to ignite the dry wood, and soon it was burning. They stood together, watching as it consumed her uncle's body, turning it to ash and smoke.

When it was finished, they moved into the trees and slept, exhausted physically and emotionally, not bothering to mount a watch against the things that dwelled in the Slags. They shared a sense of inevitability that night, that what would happen to them was not within their control, that if their strongest member could be taken from them so abruptly, their own efforts at protecting themselves would make little difference.

They woke unharmed and in a better frame of mind, the trauma of the previous day far enough behind them that they could think about what was going to happen next. The day was typical of the Slags, all grayness and mist and sunless, fetid air. The fires of the funeral pyre and the doomed *Galaphile* were extinguished finally, and only dark smears of ash remained to mark their passing. Looking out over the bay, Pen caught sight of heavy ripples that indicated the movement of something big beneath the dark surface. Life went on.

With nothing to eat or drink, the three companions huddled down in the chilly dawn light to discuss what they would do.

"Perhaps we should think about going back," Tagwen offered solemnly. "Don't misunderstand me. I'm not suggesting we give up—just that we not continue on as we are. After all, we are in a rather desperate situation. We are lost, grounded, and weaponless. I know what Ahren told us to do, but it might not be the best thing. We might be better off doing what I started out to do in the first place—finding Penderrin's parents and seeking their help. With Pen's father's magic and an airship, we will have a better chance of getting to where we want to go."

To Pen's eyes, the Dwarf looked a wreck. His clothes were hanging raggedly from his once stout frame, his face was haggard and worn, and his eyes had a jumpy, nervous look to them. The gruff, determined air he had brought with him to Patch Run had vanished in the chase across the Lazareen and through the Slags. There was more than a hint of desperation about him.

But, then, he might be describing any of them, Pen thought. He need only look at his own reflection in the waters of the bay to see that was so.

"I don't know where my parents are," he said to the Dwarf. "I'm not sure we can find them."

"Besides, it would take as much effort to go back as to go on," Khyber pointed out. "At least out here we are safe from the Druids who hunt us. With the *Galaphile* destroyed, the closest enemies are eliminated. Unless we give ourselves away again, the rest can't find us once we're out of the area."

"Oh, they can find us, don't you doubt it!" Tagwen snapped. "They are resourceful and skilled. I should know. And Shadea a'Ru is a demon. She won't give up, even with the *Galaphile* gone. Maybe *especially* with it gone, since she will blame us for its destruction. And for Terek Molt's death."

Khyber glared at him. "Well, they won't find us right away. If we can get out of this swamp, we can find help among the Trolls. Didn't you say that Kermadec lives in the Taupo Rough country? Surely he will help us."

"He will help us if he is still alive, but given the way things are going, I wouldn't say that's at all certain!" Tagwen was not to be placated. "I don't know how you expect to find him when you don't know where you are yourself! And you say we will be all right if we don't use the Elfstones, but if we don't use the Stones, we might not find our way out of here! And remember this—Ahren Elessedil thought he wouldn't have to use the Elfstones, either, but he did have to, didn't he?"

He was nearly in tears, the tough old Dwarf, and for a moment it appeared he would break down completely. He looked away in embarrassment and frustration, then rose and stalked down to the edge of the bay, where he stood for a time looking out into the mist. Pen and Khyber exchanged glances, but said nothing.

When Tagwen returned, he was calm again, his rough features composed and determined. "You're right," he announced without preamble. "We should go on. Going back would be a mistake."

"Will Kermadec help us if we can find him?" Pen asked at once.

The Dwarf nodded. "He is devoted to the Ard Rhys. He will do whatever he can to help. He is a good and brave man."

"Then we have our plan," Khyber declared. "But we will

be careful how we go, Tagwen," she assured the Dwarf. "We won't be careless. Uncle Ahren gave us a chance to complete this journey. We won't waste that gift."

"Then we'd better think about moving away from here right now," Pen declared. "If they can track us from our use of magic, they won't have much trouble finding us here. Not after the expenditure of magic used to destroy the *Galaphile*."

Khyber stood up. "Once we're back in the trees, we won't be so easy to track." She paused. "I just wish I knew how much farther we had to go."

"Then why don't you find out?" Pen asked. She stared at him. "Use the Elfstones. What difference does it make if you use them now? We've already given ourselves away. Before we set out, let's see where it is that we're going. Then maybe we won't have to use the Stones again."

"The boy is right," Tagwen said at once. "Go ahead. Let's see where we are."

They stood in a ragged group at the shore's edge while Khyber took out the Elfstones and balanced them in her hand. They stared at the glittering talismans for a moment, transfixed by their brightness and their promise. Without saying so, they were all thinking the same thing. So much depended on what the Stones revealed. If they were too deep in the Slags to avoid its snares and predators, then they might have to use the magic again, even if it gave them away. But if they were close to the wetland border, they might have a chance to escape undetected.

Khyber closed her fingers about the talismans and held them out in the direction of the sunrise. Long moments passed, and nothing happened.

"They're not responding," she said. Her voice was strained and rough. "I can't make them work."

"Don't be afraid, Khyber," Pen said.

"I'm not afraid!" she snapped.

"Yes, you are. But don't be. I'm frightened enough for the both of us."

She glanced over at him, saw the look on his face, and smiled in spite of herself. She dropped her arm to her side. "All right," she said. "Let me try again."

She took a deep, steadying breath, exhaled slowly, and held out the Stones. Her eyes closed. An instant later, the magic flared from her fist, gathered itself in a blaze of fire, and shot out into the gloom like a beast at hunt. Slicing through trees and brush and grass, through the whole of the Slags, it flared in sharp relief against a backdrop of hills leading into mountains, of green fields brightened by wildflowers, of streams and waterfalls, and of dazzling sunshine.

The picture shimmered bright and clear for a moment longer, then vanished as if it had never been, leaving them encased once more in mist and gloom. They stood looking off in the direction it had shown for a moment, savoring the memory, the promise, then looked at one another appraisingly.

"It's not all that far," Pen declared bravely, although in truth he had no idea how far it was. "We can make it."

"Of course, we can," Tagwen agreed, screwing up his worn countenance into a mask of resolve.

"It can't be more than another day," Khyber added, pocketing the Elfstones. "We can be there by sunset."

They began walking, turning back into the trees and leaving the mist-shrouded bay and its dark memories behind. It was slow going, their passage obstructed by fallen trees, heavy brush, and endless stretches of swamp water. They had to be especially careful of the latter because many hid patches of quicksand that would have swallowed them without a trace. Pen used his magic once more, reaching out to the life of the swamp to discover what it was thinking and doing. Though he couldn't see what he was hearing for the most part, he was able to detect the presence of small birds, rodents, insects, and even a smattering of water creatures. Each told him something of what was happening around them. He was able to discover more than once dangers that threatened. He was able to tell from moods and responses between species the paths they should follow and those they should avoid.

They walked all day, yet by sunset it felt as if they hadn't gone anywhere. Everything looked exactly the same as it had hours earlier. Nor was there any apparent end in sight, the gloom and mist and wetlands stretching on endlessly in all directions. If anything, the swamp had thickened and tightened about them, stealing away a little more of the light and air, eroding their hopes that they might get clear soon.

When they stopped for the night, Pen used his compass a final time to check their direction. It seemed as if they were going the right way, but he was beginning to wonder if the compass was working. His concerns were fostered in part by the way in which the light seemed not to change in any direction, the gloom and haze so thick that it was getting harder and harder to tell which way the sun was moving through the hidden sky.

"We might be lost," he admitted to them. "I can't be sure any more."

"We're not lost," Khyber insisted. "Tomorrow, we will be through."

But Pen wasn't convinced. He took the first watch and sat brooding while the others slept, replaying the events of the past few days in his mind, a nagging concern that he couldn't identify tugging at his already dwindling confidence. Something wasn't right about the way they were looking at things, but he couldn't put his finger on it. As the darkness deepened and the minutes slipped by, he found himself going further afield with his thinking, working his way back through the entire journey, from the moment Tagwen had first appeared with news of his aunt's disappearance. Remembering how he had been forced to flee his home triggered memories of his parents and made him aware of how much he missed them and wished they were with him. He had always been an independent sort, raised to be that way, but this was the farthest he had ever been from home. It was also the most threatened he had ever felt. He knew of the dangerous creatures that dwelled in the places he visited regularly on his skiff journeys, but most of those he was encountering now were entirely new. Some of them didn't even have a name.

And just like that, he realized what was bothering him. It was his inability to account for what had become of the mysterious hunter that had chased him through the streets of Anatcherae on the night he had fled Terek Molt.

He took a long moment to think it through. His pursuer had come after him outside Fisherman's Lie, when the little company had fled into the streets to reach the safety of the *Skatelow*. A man had died right in front of him, killed by a dagger thrown from the rooftops and intended for him. During all of this, he had caught only brief glimpses of the wielder, just enough to suggest it wasn't entirely human.

What had happened to it?

It would be comforting to think that it had died aboard the *Galaphile*, consumed in the inferno that had claimed the ship, the Gnome Hunters, and Terek Molt. But Pen didn't think that was what had happened. It didn't feel right to him. The thing that had chased him through the streets wouldn't have been caught off guard like that. If it was still with Terek Molt at the time the *Galaphile* had found them, it would have been off the ship and stalking him anew. It would have survived.

It would be out there now.

In spite of the fact that he was virtually certain it wasn't, he looked around cautiously, peering into the darkness as if something might reveal itself. He even took time to read his magic's response to the sounds of the night creatures surrounding him, to the insects and birds and beasts that inhab-

ited the swamp gloom, searching for anything that would
warn him of danger. When he had satisfied himself that he
was not threatened, that the hunter he feared might be lurking
out there, invisible and deadly, was not, he took a deep breath
and exhaled softly, feeling comforted for the moment, at
least.

He sat listening, nevertheless, through the rest of his
watch.

When his watch was finished, he took a long time falling
asleep.

On waking the following morning, Pen said nothing to Khyber and Tagwen of his concerns. There was nothing to be gained
by doing so. Everyone was already on edge, and adding to the
tension could not help the situation. Besides, the hunter of
Anatcherae's dark streets might have been a denizen of the
port city rather than a tool of Terek Molt's. If the hunter had
been the Druid's creature, then it stood to reason that it would
have been used in tracking them down and disposing of them
long since. The Druid wouldn't have confronted them himself when he had his creature to do the job for him.

It was solid reasoning, but it didn't make Pen feel any better and in the end it didn't convince him that his problems
with his mysterious enemy were finished. Just because he
couldn't account for its whereabouts didn't mean he was rid
of it. But he kept that unsettling thought to himself, knowing
that what mattered just then was getting clear of the Slags.

They worked all day at doing so, picking their way through
a quagmire of tangled roots, choking reeds, quicksand, sink-
holes, and mud flats thick with biting insects and gnats. They
still hadn't had anything to eat or drink since they had lost
their raft in the attack of those vines, and the lack of nourishment was beginning to tell. Tagwen was experiencing stomach cramps, Khyber was fighting off dizzy spells, and Pen felt

feverish. All three were weaker, and progress had slowed noticeably. If they didn't find food and drink soon, they were going to be in serious trouble.

It was midafternoon when they entered a sprawling wilderness of scrub-choked trees that stretched in both directions until it could no longer be seen. Threaded by tendrils of mist and layered with shadows, the woods were so vast that there wasn't any hope of finding a way around. In any case, they were too exhausted to do anything but go forward, and so they did. Pushing into the tangle, they soon found themselves forced to proceed in single file, the trees grown so close together and the spaces between so clogged with brambles and scrub that any other formation was impossible. Weaving between the trunks and stalks, they slogged through pools of swamp water and sucking mud, using roots and limbs for handholds. Overhead, flying squirrels and birds darted through the dank foliage, and on the uncertain ground snakes slithered and rodents scurried in silent, dark flashes. Now and then, they caught glimpses of larger creatures sliding ridgebacked and deadly through deeper water.

"I thought it couldn't get any worse," Tagwen grumbled at one point, his beard a nest of brambles. "Is there any end to this place?"

As they continued on, Pen began to worry about what would happen if they were caught in that tangle when darkness fell. If that happened, they would have to climb a tree and spend the night aloft. He didn't care for the prospect of watching the limbs for big snakes all night, but he didn't see that they would have any alternative. He began to make promises to himself about the sort of life he would lead if they could just reach better ground before dark.

It was gratifying when they did, if only momentarily. They slogged out of a heavy stretch of mud-soaked grasses and reeds and climbed an embankment to what seemed to be an island in the midst of the swamp, a low forestland amid the damp. Pen, leading the way, heaved a sigh of relief as he stepped onto the first solid ground he had felt beneath his feet in days, then immediately froze.

Directly to his left, not ten yards away, was the biggest moor cat he had ever seen in his life. He was not unfamiliar with moor cats, so coming on one unexpectedly was not in and of itself shocking. But that particular cat froze him in his tracks and sent a lurch through his stomach that he felt all the way to his toes. For starters, it was huge—not just big in the way of all moor cats, but gigantic. It wasn't lean and sleek; it was muscled and burly, a veteran of battles that had left its mottled, dark body crisscrossed with scars. It loomed up before him like a Koden gone down on all fours, the thick ruff around its neck giving it a bearish look. Its face was striking, as well, marked with a black band across its eyes that made it look as if it was wearing a mask.

Pen hadn't sensed it, hadn't detected it at all. He was searching for things that might threaten them, connected to the life around him, and still he hadn't known the cat was there. It must have been waiting for them, biding its time, letting them come to it.

Seeing Pen, the moor cat pricked its ears forward and its luminous eyes widened into amber lanterns. It made a coughing sound, deep and booming, and instantly the entire swamp went still.

Khyber Elessedil gave a strangled gasp. "Shades," she managed to whisper.

Pen's eyes were locked on the moor cat, trying to read its intentions. It didn't seem to have any, mostly finding them curious. Suddenly its eyes narrowed and its muzzle drew back in warning, and Pen glanced back to find Khyber slowly withdrawing the pouch with the Elfstones from her pocket.

"Put those away!" he hissed at her. "They're useless anyway!"

She hesitated. Then, slowly, the Elfstones disappeared back

into her clothing. Flushed and angry, she glared at him. "I hope you have a better plan, Penderrin!"

Tagwen looked as if he hoped the same thing, but the truth was Pen didn't have a plan at all beyond trying to avoid a confrontation. It appeared that the cat and the humans each intended to go through the same patch of ground. One or the other was going to have to give way.

The big cat growled, more a grunt than a cough. Though Pen could tell it was not intended as a threatening sound, it came across as one nevertheless, causing his companions to back away hurriedly. The boy motioned for them to stand their ground, not to make any movements that suggested they were trying to run. Movements of that sort would bring the moor cat down on them instantly. The trick was to appear unafraid, but not threatening. A neat trick, if they could figure out how to make it work.

The moor cat was growing restless, its huge head lowering to sniff the ground expectantly.

Better try something, Pen thought.

Relying on his magic to guide him, he made a rough, low coughing sound at the cat, a sound meant to communicate his intentions, one he knew instinctively would be understood. The moor cat straightened immediately, head lifting, eyes bright.

"What are you doing?" Khyber hissed at him.

Pen wasn't sure, but it seemed to be working. He made a few more sounds, all of them nonspecific but indicative of his desire to be friendly. *We're no threat,* he was saying to the cat. *We're just like you, even if we look and smell a little different.*

Intrigued, the moor cat answered with a series of huffing noises that came from deep within its throat. Pen was working furiously now, taking in the sounds and translating them into words and phrases, into deciphering the nature of the big animal's interest in them. The moor cat wanted reassurance that Pen and his companions were passing through to other places and had no intention of trying to usurp its territory. There was an unmistakable challenge in the sounds, a testing for antagonistic intent. Pen responded at once, doing his best to create a semblance of the coughing sounds, demonstrating that he and his companions were on their way to their own home, that a challenge to the moor cat's territory was of no interest.

He acted instinctively, almost without thinking about what he was doing. His magic guided him, leading him to say and do what was needed to connect with the moor cat. He was surprised by how easily the sounds came to him, at the certainty he had of what they were communicating to the cat. The huge beast seemed to be listening to him.

"Is he actually talking with that beast?" Tagwen whispered to Khyber.

"Shhhh!" was her quick, irritated response.

Then all of a sudden the moor cat started toward Pen, its great head swinging from side to side, its huge eyes gleaming. It stopped right in front of him and leaned in to sniff his face and then his body. It was so big it stood eye to eye with him, equal in height but dominant in every other respect. Pen stood perfectly still, frozen with shock and fright. Running or fighting never entered his mind. He swallowed hard and closed his eyes, letting the cat explore him, feeling the heat of its breath on his skin, hearing the sound of its breathing.

Finally, the cat stepped away, satisfied. It circled back the way it had come, then turned in the direction it had been going and disappeared into the trees without even a glance in their direction, and was gone.

Pen and his companions stood statue-still for long minutes, waiting for it to return. When at last it became apparent that it did not intend to, Pen exhaled heavily and looked from Khyber to Tagwen. The expressions on their faces almost certainly mirrored the one on his own, a mixture of heart-stopping awe and deep relief. With one hand he brushed nervously at his mop of reddish hair, which was finally beginning to grow out again, and realized he was coated with sweat.

"I don't care ever to have that experience again," Tagwen declared, doing his best to keep his voice from shaking. "Ever."

Khyber glanced in the direction of the departed moor cat. "We need to go that way, too," she pointed out.

Pen nodded. "Yes, we do."

Tagwen stared at them, horror-stricken, then straightened very deliberately. "Very well. But let's rest up a bit before we do."

And before they could object, he sat down quickly.

TWENTY-NINE

They trooped on for the remainder of the afternoon, fighting through scrub-growth woods and a new stretch of swamp laced with mud holes and waterways, everything encased in mist and gloom and crosshatched with shadows. The light lasted for another three hours and then began to fail rapidly. Still, they slogged ahead, reduced to putting one foot in front of the other, to pushing on when it would have been much easier not to.

It was almost too dark to see when Khyber realized that the feel of the ground had changed and the air no longer smelled of damp and rot but of grass and leaves. She stopped abruptly, causing Tagwen, who was walking behind her with his head down, to bump into her. Ahead, Pen heard the sudden oaths and quick apologies and turned around to see what was happening.

"We're out of the Slags," Khyber announced, still not quite believing it. "Look around. We're out."

She insisted they stop for the night, so bone weary and mentally exhausted from the events of the past few days, so in need of sleep that she barely managed to find a patch of soft grass within a stand of oaks before she was asleep. Her last memory was of the sky, empty for the first time in days of mist and clouds, clear and bright with moonglow and stars.

She dreamed that night of her uncle, a shadowy figure who called to her in words she could not quite make out from a place she could not quite reach. She spent her dream trying and failing to get close enough to discover what he was saying. The dream world was shadowy and uneven in its feel, the landscape misty and changing. It was filled with dark creatures that hovered close without ever quite coming into view. It was a place she did not want to be, and she was grateful when she woke the next morning to bright sunlight and blue sky.

Pen was already awake and returned from foraging for food, and it was the cooking fire he had built that brought her out of her dream. Somehow, the boy had snared a rabbit, which he was skinning, dug up some root vegetables, and picked several handfuls of berries. Added to the fresh stream water he had collected, it made the best meal Khyber could remember in years and gave her a welcome and much needed sense of renewal.

They set out shortly after, heading east and north into the hilly country that fronted the Charnals, determined to find Taupo Rough and the Troll Maturen, Kermadec. None of them had ever been in that part of the world or knew enough about it to be able to discern much more than the general direction they should take. Taupo Rough lay at the foot of the mountains somewhere north of the Slags. The best they could do was to use the pocket compass and head in that direction, trusting that sooner or later they would come across someone to help them. The Rock Trolls were a tribal people and there was some animosity between tribes, but the Trolls were not at war with the other Races just then and there was no reason to think they posed a threat to travelers in their country. At least, that was what Khyber hoped.

She gave it some thought on setting out, but they had little choice in the matter and therefore little reason to dwell on the unpleasant possibilities if they were wrong. Tagwen seemed to think that whatever Rock Trolls they encountered would be of help once they heard Kermadec's name. Maybe that was so. Khyber was so grateful to be clear of the Slags that she was willing to risk almost anything. Even the simple fact of no longer being shrouded by the wetland's gloom and mist gave her a large measure of relief.

But it was more than that, of course. It was the leaving behind of the place in which Ahren Elessedil had died. It was the sense that maybe she could come to terms with his death if she could put time and distance between herself and its memory. She had persuaded herself to continue on without him, but accepting that he was really gone was much more difficult. Losing him had left her devastated. He had been more than an uncle to her; he had been the father she had lost when she was still a child. He had been her confidant and her best and most dependable friend. As compensation for her anguish, she told herself that he was still there, a spirit presence, and that he would look out for her in death even as he had in life. It was wishful thinking, but shades were real and sometimes they helped the living, and she needed to think it could happen here because she had serious doubts about herself. She did not believe that her meager talents with Druid magic were going to be enough to see them through the remainder of their journey, no matter what reassurances Ahren had offered her. Even her use of the Elfstones was suspect. She had managed to bring the magic to bear in the battle against Terek Molt, but that had been facilitated by her uncle's sacrifice. She still shivered at the memory of the Elfstone power coursing through her, vast and unchecked, and she did not know that she could make herself summon it again, even to defend herself. In truth, she did not know what she might do if she was threatened, and the uncertainty could prove as dangerous as the threat itself. It was one thing to talk as if she possessed both resolve and confidence, but it was something else again to demonstrate it. She wished she had a way of testing herself. But she didn't, and that was that.

They walked on through the morning, and she felt a little

better for doing so. Time and distance helped to blunt her sadness if not her uncertainty. Given the nature of their journey thus far, she would take what she could get.

"Did you see him?" Pen asked her when they stopped at midday to drink from a stream and to eat what remained of the roots the boy had foraged that morning.

She stared at him. "See who?"

"The cat. It's tracking us."

"The moor cat?"

Tagwen, sitting a little bit farther away, turned at once. His eyes were big and frightened. "Why would it be doing that? Is it hunting us?"

Pen shook his head. "I don't think so. But it is definitely following us. I saw it several times, back in the trees, trying to keep out of sight, following a course parallel to our own. I think it's just interested."

"Interested?" the Dwarf croaked.

"You can't mistake that masked face," Pen went on, oblivious to the other's look of terror. He grinned suddenly at Khyber, a little boy about to share a secret. "I've decided to call it Bandit. It looks like one, doesn't it?"

Khyber didn't care what the moor cat looked like, nor did she care for the idea of it tracking them into the mountains. She had always thought moor cats pretty much stayed in the swamps and forests and clear of the higher elevations. She hoped theirs would lose interest as they climbed.

They trekked on through the remainder of the day, through hill country dotted with woods and crisscrossed by streams that pooled in lakes at the lower elevations, bright mirrors reflecting sunlight and clouds. The hours drifted away, and although they covered a fair amount of ground, they did not encounter any of the region's inhabitants. Darkness began to fall and the shadows of the trees to lengthen about them, and still they had not seen a single Troll.

"Is that moor cat still out there?" Khyber asked Pen at one point.

"Oh, sure," the boy answered at once. "Still watching us, sort of like a stray dog. Do you want me to call it over?"

They made camp in the lee of a forested bluff, finding shelter in a grove of pine by a stream that tumbled down out of the rocks. Behind them, the hill country they had trekked through all day sloped gently away through woods and grasslands until it disappeared into the twilight shadows. Although Pen made a valiant effort to catch something, he was unsuccessful; there was nothing to eat. They drank stream water and chewed strips of bark from a small fig tree.

"Don't worry," Pen reassured his companions. "I'll go hunting at sunrise. I'll catch something."

They sat back to watch the stars come out, listening to the silence fill with night sounds. No one spoke. Khyber felt an emptiness that extended from the darkness down into her heart. She could not put a name to it, but it was there nevertheless. After a moment, she rose and walked off into the trees, wanting to be alone in case she cried. She felt so unbearably sad that she could hardly manage to keep from breaking down. The feeling had come over her insidiously, as if to remind her of how badly things had gone for them and how desperate their circumstances were. She might argue that they were all right, that they would find their way, but it wasn't what she felt. What she felt was utter abandonment and complete hopelessness. No matter what they tried or where they went, things would never get any better for them. They would struggle, but in the end they would fail.

Away from her companions, unable to help herself, she sat down and cried, bursting into tears all at once. She wished she had never come on the journey. She wished she had never left home. Everything that had happened was because of her insistence on looking for a stupid tree that Pen thought he had been sent to find but might well have simply dreamed up. Uncle Ahren was dead because of her intractability and her foolish, selfish need to find a way out of her pointless life. Well, she had accomplished her goal. She could never go back to Arborlon, never go home again. Not after stealing the Elfstones. Not after letting her uncle die. She bore the burden of her guilt like a fifty-pound weight slung across her shoulders, and she had nowhere to set it down. She hated herself.

In the midst of her silent diatribe, she realized that someone was looking at her.

Or something.

Huge, lantern eyes peered at her from out of the blackness. It was the moor cat.

"Get out of here!" she snapped in fury, not stopping to think about what she was doing.

The eyes stayed where they were. She glared at them, hating that the cat was watching her, that it had seen her break down and cry, that it had caught her at her worst. For no reason that made any sense at all, she was embarrassed by it. Even if it was only an animal that had witnessed it, her behavior made her feel foolish. She took several deep breaths to steady herself and sat back. The cat wasn't going to move until it felt like it, so there wasn't much point in railing at it. She found herself wondering once again what it was doing there. Curiosity, Pen had thought. Could be. She kissed at it, whispered a few words of greeting, and gave it a wave. The cat stared without blinking or moving.

Then all at once, it was gone again. Like smoke caught in the wind, it simply disappeared. She waited a moment to be sure, then rose and walked back to where Pen and Tagwen were already asleep. The first watch was hers, it seemed. Just as well since she wasn't at all tired. She sat down next to them and wrapped her arms about her knees. It was chilly so high up, much more so than in the Slags. She wished she had a blanket. Maybe they could find supplies in the morning. There had to be a settlement somewhere close by.

With her legs drawn up to her chest and her chin resting on her knees, she listened to the sounds of Pen and Tagwen breathing and stared out into the night.

Intending to wake one of her companions to share the watch, but failing to do so, she dozed off sometime after midnight. When she came awake again, it was with the sudden and frightening realization that things were not as they should be. It wasn't the silence or the darkness or even the sound of the wind rustling the leaves like old parchment. What caught her attention as her eyes snapped open and her head jerked up was the dark movement that crept like a stain across the forest earth in front of her. For a moment, she thought it was alive, and leapt to her feet, backing away instinctively. But then she recognized its flat, fragmented shape and realized it was a shadow cast from something passing overhead.

She looked up and saw the *Skatelow*.

She couldn't believe it at first, thinking that she must be mistaken, that her eyes were playing tricks on her. It wasn't possible that the *Skatelow* could be there, flying those skies, so many miles east of where it should be. But the shape was so distinctive that Khyber quickly accepted that it was her, come after them for a reason that was not immediately apparent. For come after them she had, the Elven girl reasoned, or she would not be here at all.

Particularly since she was flying straight toward them.

But there was something not quite right about her, a look to her that was foreign and vaguely frightening. She carried only her mainsail; its canvas billowed out in the rush of the wind, yet there were yards of rigging stretched bare and stark from decking to spars like spiderwebbing.

Khyber stared, transfixed, not yet fully awake and not yet come to terms with what she was seeing.

The *Skatelow* passed overhead and when she had gone a short distance beyond where the Elven girl stood watching, somewhere above the bluff east, she wheeled back and slid across the star-scattered firmament a second time, more slowly, as if searching.

Then, abruptly, she started to come down, making a slow and cautious descent toward the grasslands that lay just beyond the woods in which Khyber and her companions slept. As she did so, Khyber saw what she had missed before. Three ropes dangled in a ragged line from the yardarm, pulled taut by the weight of the bodies attached.

"Pen!" Khyber hissed, reaching down quickly to shake the boy awake, galvanized by sudden shock and a rush of fear.

Penderrin Ohmsford jerked upright at once, eyes darting in all directions at once. "What is it?"

Wordlessly, she hauled him to his feet and pointed, leaving Tagwen still stretched out and asleep at her feet. Together, they watched the *Skatelow* settle toward the grasslands, a ghost ship dark and ragged against the moonlit sky, the bodies at the ends of the ropes swaying like gourds from vines. The light caught those bodies clearly by then, illuminating them sufficiently for Khyber to identify Gar Hatch and his crewmen, faces empty, mouths hanging open, eyes wide and staring. There was a wizened, drawn cast to their features, as if the juices had been drained from them, leaving only skin and bones.

"What's happened?" Pen breathed.

Then his fingers tightened sharply about her arm, and he pointed. She saw it at once. Cinnaminson stood in the pilot box, a thin, frail figure against the skyline, her head lifted into the wind, her clothing whipping against her body, her arms hanging limply at her sides. One end of a chain was attached to a collar about her neck; the other was wound about the pilot box railing.

Khyber scanned the decks of the sloop from end to end, but

no one else was visible. No one was sailing the airship, no one acting as Captain and crew, no one visible aboard save the three dead men and the chained girl.

Then Khyber saw something move across the billowing mainsail, high up in the rigging, a dark shadow caught in a swath of moonlight. The shadow skittered down the lines like a spider over its webbing, limbs outstretched and crooked as it swung from strand to strand. Nothing more of it was visible; its head and body were cloaked and hooded, its features hidden. It was there for just an instant, then gone, disappeared behind the sail and back into the shadows.

Khyber took a deep breath. It was the thing that had chased them through the streets of Anatcherae—the thing that had tried to kill Pen.

A shiver ran down Khyber's back when Cinnaminson turned her head slightly in their direction, as if seeing them as clearly as they saw her. In that instant, her features were clearly revealed, and such anguish and horror were mirrored there that Khyber went cold all the way to her bones. Then the Rover girl looked away again and pointed north. The thing that hung from the mainmast moved quickly in response, leaping through the rigging, changing the set of the sail, the tautness of the radian draws, and thereby the direction of the airship. The *Skatelow* began to lift away again, turning north in the direction Cinnaminson had pointed. The crooked-legged thing darted back across the moonlight, then fastened itself in place against the mast, hunching down like a huge lizard on a pole.

Seconds later, the airship disappeared behind the rise of the bluff, and the sky was empty again.

In the dark aftermath, Khyber exhaled sharply and exchanged a hurried look with Pen. Then she jumped in fright as Tagwen stood up suddenly next to her, rubbing at his bleary eyes. "What's wrong?" he asked.

"Don't do that again!" she snapped furiously, her hands shaking.

They told him what they had seen, pointing north at the empty sky. A look of disbelief crossed his rough features, and he shook his head, blinking away the last of his sleep. "Are you certain of this? You didn't dream it? It wasn't just the clouds?"

"It's tracking us," Pen answered, his voice dismal and lost-sounding. "It's killed Gar Hatch and his Rover cousins, and now it's using Cinnaminson to hunt us."

"But how did it get aboard the *Skatelow*?"

No one could answer him. Khyber stared at the empty sky, trying to reason it through. Was there a connection between the creature and the Druids? Could it have gotten aboard the *Skatelow* while the *Galaphile* had the Rover airship in tow? That would mean Terek Molt had deliberately lied to them about sending the *Skatelow* safely on her way. But why do that? For that matter, why bother to put the creature aboard the *Skatelow* at all if the Druid intended to hunt Penderrin on his own anyway?

Whatever the answer, someone was going to an awful lot of trouble to prevent the boy from attempting to rescue his aunt. So someone must think he had a very good chance of succeeding, even if the boy himself thought he had very little. It was an intriguing conclusion, and it gave her unexpected reason for hope.

Pen was staring at her. "Do you think the Elfstones could be used against whatever's got Cinnaminson?"

She gave him a doubtful look. "We don't even know what it is, Pen. It might be human, and the Elfstones would be useless."

"It doesn't look it."

"Whatever it is, we're not going to fight it if we don't have to." She motioned toward the bluff. "Let's get out of here. We can stop and eat when it gets light. I don't want to chance it coming back again."

Pen stood his ground, his mouth a tight line. "Did you see the way she looked at us?"

Khyber hesitated.

"She saw us. She knew we were here. Yet she turned the ship the other way." His voice was shaking. "She's being made to track us, Khyber. Maybe her life depends on whether or not that thing finds us. Yet she steered it away. She saved us."

Tagwen shook his bearded head. "You don't know that, young Pen. You might be mistaken."

The boy kept staring at Khyber. She had a sinking feeling in her stomach as she realized what he was about to ask. She had to stop him, even if it meant lying to him about what she had seen. But she could not bring herself to do that. That was the coward's way out. Ahren would not have lied in that situation. He would have told Pen the truth.

"We can't do this," she said.

"We have to!" he snapped. His face had an angry, almost furious look. "She saved us, Khyber! Now we have to save her!"

"What are you talking about?" Tagwen demanded. "Save who?"

"She's not our concern," Khyber pressed. "Our concern is with your aunt, the Ard Rhys."

"Our concern is with whoever needs our help! What's wrong with you?"

They faced each other in stony silence. Even Tagwen had gone quiet, looking quickly from one face to the other.

"We don't have any way of saving her," Khyber said finally. "We don't know anything about that creature, nothing about what it will take to overcome it. If we guess wrong, we'll all be dead."

Pen straightened and looked off to the north. "I'm going,

whether you go with me or not. I'm not leaving her. I have to live with myself when this is over. I can't do that if something happens to her that I might have prevented." He glanced back at her, the angry look suddenly pleading. "She isn't the enemy, Khyber."

"I know that."

"Then help me."

She stared at him without answering.

"Khyber, I'm begging you."

He wasn't asking Tagwen; he was asking her. With Ahren Elessedil dead, she'd become the unofficial leader. She was the one with the Elfstones and the magic. She was the one with the lore. She thought about the choices she had made on the journey and how badly many of them had turned out. If she made the wrong choice here, it might cost all of them their lives. Pen's heart ruled his thinking; she had to remember to use her head.

She found herself wondering what Ahren would do in that situation but was unable to decide. The answer would have come quickly and easily for him. It would not do so for her.

She looked off into the trees and the night, into the shadows and darkness, searching for it in vain.

THIRTY

When Grianne Ohmsford reached the rim of the Forbidding's version of the Valley of Shale, Weka Dart was gone. Fled out of fear, she decided, too terrified to remain once the Warlock Lord appeared. Even so, she took a moment to look for him, thinking he might be hiding in the rocks, his sharp-featured face buried in his hands. But there was no sign of him.

He would be back, she told herself. No matter what happened, he would be back.

She wondered at her certainty about this, and decided rather reluctantly that it was fostered in part, at least, by the comfort she found in his presence. In a better world, such as the one from which she had come, she might not have tolerated him at all. Here, she had to take what friendship she could find.

She started back down the mountainside. Silence enveloped her, a hush that felt strange in the wake of the disappearance of the shades that had tormented her on the way in. They had all vanished, drawn back down into the netherworld with the Warlock Lord. Yet the memory of them haunted her, voices whispering at the back of her thoughts, damp fingers trailing lightly across her unprotected skin, an insidious presence.

The sun was rising, turning the eastern horizon the color of ashes, gray and damp against the departing night. Another day of low clouds and threatening skies. Another day of colorless gloom. She felt her already battered spirits sink at the prospect. She wanted out of this miserable place, out of this world of savagery and despair. She pondered on the words of Brona's shade. *A boy is coming.* The pronouncement confounded her, no matter how often she repeated the words in her mind. What boy? Why a boy in the first place? It made no sense to her, and she kept thinking that it must be a puzzle of some sort, the secret to which she must find a way to unlock. Shades were famous for speaking in riddles, for teasing with half-truths. Perhaps that was what had happened here.

She stopped for a moment and closed her eyes, feeling dizzy and weak. Her encounter with the Warlock Lord's shade had left her battered of mind and body, light-headed and unsteady. She could feel an aching not only in her muscles and joints, but also in her heart. Just standing in the presence of the shade had left her sickened. Its poison had permeated the air she breathed and the ground she walked. It had infused the entire valley, though she had not been aware of it until now. Evil—in its rawest, most lethal form—had infected her. Though she had resisted the Warlock Lord's offer to embrace it, it had claimed her anyway. She wouldn't die from it, she thought, but she would be a long time ridding herself of its feel.

The dizziness passed, and she walked on. A boy, she kept thinking. And she must wait for him. She could do nothing from this end, nothing that would set her free. She did not believe it; there was always something you could do to help yourself in any situation. There was always more than one way in or out of any place, even this one. She need only find what it was. But even as she told herself it was so, she found reason to doubt the words. No one—until now—had ever found a way out of the Forbidding, not after thousands of years. No one had ever found a way in, once the wall of magic was set in place. It was a prison that did not allow for escape.

It was light by the time she reached the base of the mountains: the same sooty gray light that seemed to mark every day, the clouds slung low against the earth, fused with mist and darkened by the threat of rain. Weka Dart was sitting on a rock at the trailhead, chin in his hands, looking south across the flats, but he leapt to his feet on hearing her approach and was waiting eagerly as she came up to him.

"I thought you weren't coming back, Straken," he announced, not bothering to hide the relief in his voice. "That shade, so terrible, so threatening! It didn't want you?"

She shook her head. "Nor you, so you needn't have run away."

He bristled with indignation. "I didn't run! I chose to wait for you here!" His cunning features tightened as he prepared to lie. "I realized that you could not afford to be disturbed during your summoning and decided to come back down here to keep watch against . . . whatever might intrude." He spit. "It worked, didn't it? Were you bothered in any way? Hah! I thought as much!"

She almost laughed. The truth wasn't in the little Ulk Bog, but she didn't find herself angry or even disappointed. It was simply his nature, and there was no point in hoping for anything else. Candor was not a quality she was likely to see much of in Weka Dart.

"If I had thought you needed protection from that shade, if I had not believed you to be a Straken of great power and experience, I would have stayed to see that you were kept safe!" he continued hurriedly, clearly not knowing when to stop. "But since there was no reason for worry, I came down here, where I knew I could be of more use to you. Tell me. What shade was it you spoke with?"

She sighed. "A warlock of immense power."

"But its power was no greater than yours or you would not have dared summon it. What did it tell you?"

She sat down next to him. "It told me I must go back to where you found me."

Instantly, his demeanor changed. "No, no!" he insisted at once. "You mustn't go back there!"

She stared at him in surprise. His distress was reflected on his rough features, revealed by the way the furrows on his brow deepened and knotted and his mouth tightened.

He seemed to realize he had overreacted. "What I mean to say is that you've already barely escaped a Dracha. What reason would you have to risk another encounter? I thought we had decided we would go to . . . I thought . . ."

He trailed off. "What did we decide, exactly? Why did we come here? You never said."

She nodded, amused by his confusion as much as troubled by his distress. "We came here so that I could speak with a shade, Weka Dart. I was not given a choice as to which one."

The Ulk Bog nodded eagerly. "But you did speak with one. What did you ask it? Why did it tell you to go back to where you had come from? What was its reason for doing so? It must be trying to trick you, perhaps to see you hurt!"

She considered her answer carefully. "I don't think it wants me hurt. Not in the way you suggest. What I asked was how to find my way home again."

Weka Dart bounded up from the rock to face her. "But you won't reach your home from there! You were lost already when I found you! Anyway, that place is too dangerous! There are dragons everywhere, some worse than that Dracha you encountered!" He was practically jumping up and down now, his hands balled into fists. "Why do you have to go back there to find your way home? Can't you find it from somewhere else?"

She shook her head, watching him carefully. "No, I can't.

Why are you so upset? Are you frightened for yourself? If so, don't come with me. I can find my own way. Go west, where you were headed when you met me."

"I don't want to go west!" He practically screamed the words at her. "I want to stay with you!"

"Well, if you want to stay with me, you have to go back to where you found me. What's wrong with you? Are you afraid I can't protect you from those hunting you? Is that what this is all about?"

He flew at her in a rage, catching himself just before he got within reach, wheeling away again, then stamping the earth with both feet until she thought he was in danger of breaking his legs. "Aren't you listening to me?" he screamed at her. "Don't you believe me? You can't go back there!"

She came to her feet, ready for another attack. "Are you coming with me or not? Make up your mind."

He hissed at her like a snake, his face twisted into a grotesque mask, and his fingers extended like claws. She was so astounded by the transformation that for a moment she thought she had better summon the magic and immobilize him before he lost all control. But then he seemed to get hold of himself, going so still that he was frozen in his bizarrely aggressive pose. He took a deep breath, blew it out, wrenched his fiery gaze away from her and directed it out onto the flats.

"Do what you want, Grianne of the foolish heart," he said quietly. "Go to whatever doom awaits you, whatever fate. But I will not be caught up in the net, as well. No, I will not come with you."

Without another word, he stalked away, moving off at a rapid pace, no longer darting from side to side as he had done all the way there, but proceeding straight ahead, south into the Pashanon. She watched him incredulously, not quite believing he was giving up so easily, certain he would turn around and come back after he had gotten far enough away to make his point.

But he did not turn around or come back. He kept walking, and she kept watching him until he was out of sight.

She found a stream from which to drink, then began retracing her steps west. She was near exhaustion from her encounter with the shade of Brona, but she didn't think she should try to sleep until she reached less open country. She was hungry, as well, but as usual there was no food to be found. She thought she might find some ground roots when she reached the forests again, but there was no way to be certain. Grudgingly, she admitted that having Weka Dart along would have solved the problem, but the Ulk Bog just wasn't worth the trouble. It wasn't entirely his fault, of course. He couldn't understand what she was trying to do, and that frustrated him. It was better that he was gone.

Nevertheless, she couldn't help puzzling over his extreme reluctance to return to where he had found her. He was adamant about avoiding that place, and she thought there was more to it than his fear of encountering the tribal members he had fled. Something else was going on, something he was keeping to himself. Had she wanted to, she could have used her magic to force it out of him, but she no longer did things like that just to satisfy her curiosity. That approach to problem solving belonged to the Ilse Witch, and she was careful to keep it in the past.

Her trek, though across open, mostly unencumbered ground, quickly tired her, and by midday she was having trouble concentrating. The oppressive grayness closed about her in a deep gloom, and tracking the sun through the screen of clouds took more than a little effort. Sometimes, there was no indication of where it was in the sky, and she could only guess at its progress. Sometimes, she felt as if there were no sun at all.

It was wearing on her, this prison to which she h
consigned. It was breaking down her confidence and ... determination. The erosion was incremental, but she could feel
it happening. Even the prospect of rescue seemed remote and
gave her no real encouragement. Too much relied on chance
and the efforts of others. She didn't like that. She had never
trusted either.

She was approaching the hill country where they had encountered the Furies two days earlier, and she decided to turn
north toward the mountains again. Her memories of the death
of that ogre were too fresh to ignore, and she thought that if
she stayed close to the base of the cliffs, she might have better
luck escaping notice. She didn't know enough about Furies
to have a clear idea of how to avoid them, but she suspected
that staying out in the open was not wise. Better to take her
chances where there was a chance for finding cover if the
need arose.

Her choice yielded unexpected benefits. She found fresh
water and an odd tree that bore a round orange and yellow
fruit that, while bitter, was edible. She ate the fruit, sitting by
the stream in the shadow of the tree and looking out into the
blighted landscape. She felt light-headed and heavy-eyed afterwards, a condition she attributed to lack of rest. She would
feel better by the next morning. At least, she reminded herself, she was still alive.

Did any of those she had left behind believe her so? Or did
they think her dead and gone?

She took a moment to picture what it must have been like
when she disappeared. Tagwen and Kermadec would have
been frantic, but there would have been nothing they could
do. Nothing anyone could do, the Druids included. Only a
handful, at most, knew what had really happened, those few
who had orchestrated her imprisonment. But how much did
they understand of what they had done? Not as much as th

thought, perhaps. The shade of the Warlock Lord had called them pawns. It was the creature from the Forbidding who controlled them all.

A creature of immense power and great cunning, an enemy perhaps even more dangerous than the Morgawr, it had found a way to reach across the barrier of the Forbidding and subvert at least one of her Druids to its cause. It had tricked that Druid into helping it make possible the exchange of an Ard Rhys for a monster. Perhaps she had been party to the effort, as well. It was possible that her journey to the ruins of the Skull Kingdom with Kermadec was prompted by the thing's need to connect with her. It was possible she had been lured there to make that happen. She could remember the malevolent, dark look of it when it had shown itself. She could still feel the evil that emanated from it. It was not difficult to believe that it had gained a hold over her just from that single, brief encounter.

What did it intend to do, there in the Four Lands, outside the Forbidding for the first time in thousands of years? That it had escaped would not be enough. It was after something more.

Before she set out again, she used her magic to probe the surrounding countryside. It was a precaution, nothing more. She hadn't seen anything move all day, not even in the sky. She felt alone in the world, and the thought was immensely depressing because for all intents and purposes, that was exactly what she was. It didn't make any difference who or what she encountered; the best she could hope for was another Weka Dart. Everything locked within the Forbidding was a potential enemy, and that wasn't going to change.

She walked on through the remainder of the afternoon without incident, and her spirits lifted marginally. Perhaps she would find a way out of this situation in spite of her doubts. Perhaps someone really was coming to rescue her.

Nightfall was approaching when she heard a strange met
chirp that reminded her of birdsong. She was so surprised
by the sound that she stopped where she was and listened
until she heard it again, then started to walk in the direction from which it had come, curious. She reached a grove
of shaggy, moss-grown trees when she heard it a third time
and saw a flash of something bright red within the shadows.
She didn't care for the sickly color of the gnarled trunks, almost a fire-scorched black and gray, or for the way in which
the moss draped the limbs like a badly torn shroud, but the
sound and the flash of red were simply too intriguing to
ignore.

She moved into the grove warily, and almost at once she
caught sight of the bird, a fiery crimson splash in the gloom.
What was it doing here? It was tiny, too small to be obviously
dangerous, but she knew better than to take anything for
granted. She eased closer, probing with her magic for hidden
dangers. The bird sang again, a quick, high note that was so
pure and true she almost cried at the sound.

She was right underneath it, peering up into the branches,
when the ground beneath her feet was yanked out from under
her and a net whipped tightly about her flailing arms and legs
and hauled her up into the trees in a collapsed, gasping bundle. She fought to break free, tearing at the netting, screaming
in rage and frustration. But almost instantly fumes flooded
her nostrils and mouth, thick, toxic and mind numbing.

Her last thought before she lapsed into unconsciousness
was that she had been a fool.

She woke to a rolling, shaking motion that jerked her back
and forth against the chains that secured her arms and legs to
wooden walls and iron bars. The chains allowed her to move
just enough to turn from side to side, but not completely
around. Nor was there enough play in the lengths to allow her

to reach her head or body. She rested on a bed of straw inside a wheeled wooden cage being pulled by two huge, broad-back horned animals that looked a little like bulls but were clearly something more. A second cage preceded her own and a third jolted along behind. There might have been more; she couldn't see.

Her joints ached and her head throbbed. When she tried to clear her mouth of its dryness, she found she was securely gagged.

She closed her eyes, gathering her strength, taking a moment to remember how she had come to this. The birdsong. Then the bird itself. A lure, she realized now, clever and seductive. She had let herself be trapped by one of the oldest tricks in the world. Her magic had failed to detect the snare. That was odd, but not impossible. The snare was sophisticated. Whoever had set it had taken great pains to hide it. That suggested that the trapper was expecting its prey to have the use of magic, which in turn suggested the trapper was looking for someone like her.

She opened her eyes and peered around. The landscape was blighted and gray with shadows, and the air smelled of deadwood and old earth. Through the bars, she could see a handful of lupine forms loping silently through the graying daylight, massive four-legged beasts with shaggy ruffs. Tongues lolled and breath steamed, even though the day was warm. When one of them caught her looking, it lunged at her, snapping at the iron bars and snarling furiously when it failed to reach her.

A tall, rawboned creature wearing leather half-pants and a tunic appeared suddenly at the side of the cage, peering in at her. Coarse black hair formed a topknot on a nearly pointed head, and a beard fringed a face that was as elongated and sharp-featured as a child's drawing of a Spider Gnome. It chattered at her with high-pitched sounds that reminded her vaguely of Weka Dart. But the language was different. She stared at it mutely, and the creature stared back. Then it was gone.

She glanced around, trying to get her bearings. To her dismay, she saw the Dragon Line fading into the gloom and mist behind her. She was headed south, away from her original destination.

Away from the mysterious boy who was coming to save her.

Here ends BOOK ONE of
HIGH DRUID OF SHANNARA.

In BOOK TWO, *Tanequil,* Pen Ohmsford and his
companions continue to search for the strange
tree that will provide access to the Forbidding and
a chance to rescue the increasingly threatened
Ard Rhys, while on the Prekkendorran, the war
between Free-born and Federation enters a
dangerous new phase.

Read on for a taste of

Tanequil

Book Two
of

HIGH DRUID OF SHANNARA

by

TERRY BROOKS

It was late in the day. The assignment of duties had been given out and the members of the Druid Council dismissed to their rooms when Traunt Rowan and Pyson Wence appeared at the door to Shadea's chambers. She had not seen them since that morning, when she had advised them of the message from Aphasia Wye. Their response had been guarded, perhaps out of a sense of resignation that the unpleasant task of capturing the young boy was going to be carried out after all, perhaps out of a sense of futility regarding the whole business. Neither had been overly supportive of the endeavor. It was as if they believed that eliminating Grianne Ohmsford was all that mattered, that beyond her removal lay green pastures and blue skies. They lack the fire of old, she thought, the passion that had brought them into her circle of influence. But she didn't worry. They were still committed enough to do what was needed and not likely to disappear in a pointless rage as Iridia had done.

Besides, she was already making plans for new alliances that would eliminate the necessity of maintaining the old.

"A message just reached us, Shadea," Traunt Rowan began as soon as he had closed the door behind them. "We have found the boy's parents."

She felt a surge of elation. Everything was finally falling into place. Once they had the parents under their control, they could rest easy. There was no one else who would pursue the matter of the Ard Rhys's disappearance, no one who cared enough to become involved. Kermadec might still be out there, or Tagwen, but neither possessed the magic of Bek Ohmsford. He was the one who was dangerous.

"Where?" she asked.

"In the Eastland. We have been searching that area ever since Molt discovered from the boy that his parents were on an expedition in the Anar. But no one had seen or heard anything until two days ago. Then a trader working the supply route along the Pass of Jade on the lower edge of Darklin Reach sold some goods to a man and woman piloting an airship bearing the name *Swift Sure*. They would be the ones we seek."

"A week ago?" Shadea frowned.

"Ah, but here is the thing," Pyson Wence interrupted eagerly. "All this time we have been searching for them in the Wolfsktaag Mountains, because that is where we assumed they were going. But that isn't where they have been! They have been exploring the Ravenshorn, farther east and so deep into the Anar that no word at all has reached them of our search. We are fortunate, Shadea, that they still have no idea of what has happened to their son, or we would have lost them for sure."

"Have they no idea now?"

Wence shook his head. "None. We learned of their location by accident, our spies making inquiries everywhere. The trader had no idea of the value of his information and gave it willingly to those who did. So now we know where they are. What do we do?"

She walked to her window and stood looking out, thinking it through. She must be careful; unlike the boy, Bek Ohmsford was possessed of enough magic to incinerate anyone foolish enough to give him reason to do so. He would not be easily disposed of. He must be brought to Paranor if it was to be done properly.

She turned back to them and gestured at Traunt Rowan. "Take the *Ballendarroch* and go east. Find our spies and get what additional information you can. Then find the boy's parents."

"Am I to kill then as well?" the other asked, not quite managing to keep the disdain from his voice.

She walked over to him and stood close. "Do you lack the stomach for it, Traunt? Are you too weak to see this matter through?"

There was a long pause as she held his gaze. To his credit, he did not look away. He was conflicted, perhaps, but determined, too.

"I have never pretended to support what you are doing, Shadea," he said carefully. "I would not have bothered with either the boy or his parents, but the decision was not given to me to make. Now that we are committed, I will do what is needed. But I won't pretend that it makes me happy."

She nodded, satisfied. "This is what you do then, and you are the best one to do it. Tell them that the Ard Rhys has disappeared and we are seeking her. Tell them that their son has gone looking for her and that we are seeking him, too. If they come with you to Paranor, perhaps they can help find both. None of this is a lie, and in this instance, the truth is preferable. No one is to die outside these walls if we can help it."

Traunt Rowan nodded slowly. "You would keep them alive just long enough to help you do . . . what?"

"To help us find the boy, if it becomes necessary, and perhaps to help us make certain that Grianne Ohmsford is safely locked away within the Forbidding. Bek Ohmsford's magic is very powerful, and if properly applied, it may serve us well."

"I think we should kill him and be done with it," Pyson Wence declared, brushing her suggestion aside. "He is too dangerous."

She laughed. "Are you such a coward, Pyson, that you now fear to take any risk? We have eliminated our greatest enemy, our most dangerous foe. What do we care for someone as unskilled as her brother? He isn't even a Druid! He doesn't practice his magic. He chooses to ignore it entirely. I don't think we need spare too much concern for his abilities. We are Druids of some power ourselves, as I recall."

The small man flushed at the rebuke, but like Traunt Rowan before him, did not look away. "You take too many chances, Shadea. We are not as powerful as you pretend. Look at how things stand with the Council. We barely control it, our grip so tenuous that it could slip away entirely on the taking of a single misstep. Instead of hunting down Grianne Ohmsford's relatives and playing games with them, we should be consolidating our power and strengthening our hold on the Council. With Molt dead and Iridia gone off on her own, we need allies if we are to keep control. There are allies to be had, of that I am certain. But they won't come without persuasion and enticement."

"I am aware of this," she replied evenly, keeping her anger in check. He was such a fool. "But watching our backs is our first order of business just now. We mustn't let any of those who have strong feelings for the former Ard Rhys get behind us."

There was a strained silence as they faced each other. Then Pyson Wence shrugged. "As you wish, Shadea. You are our leader. But remember—we are your conscience, Traunt and I. Don't be too quick to dismiss us."

I will do worse than that soon enough, little rat, she thought to herself. "I would never dismiss you without first listening carefully to what you have to say, Pyson," she said. "Your advice is always welcome. I depend on you to offer it freely." She smiled. "Are we done?"

She waited until they had departed before sitting down to write the note, Traunt Rowan having agreed to leave aboard the *Ballendarroch* at first light, Pyson Wence to accept her decision on the fate of the Ohmsfords. In truth, they didn't care one way or the other about the Ohmsford family, so long as they could feel they had put some distance between themselves and any bloodletting. They were strong enough when it came to manipulation and deceit, but not so good when it came to killing. That was her province—hers and Aphasia Wyc's.

She sometimes thought how much easier her life would have been if she had never come to Paranor. Perhaps that would have been the wiser move. She would not be Ard Rhys of the Order, but neither would she be forced to bear the burden of its members' confusion and indecision. She could have practiced her magic alone, or even with Iridia as her partner, and accomplished much. But she had been desirous of more than that, greedy for the unmatchable power that came from leading those who could most affect the destiny of the Four Lands. Sen Dunsidan might think that the Federation was the future of the world, but she knew differently.

Nevertheless, there were times when she wished she could simply eliminate all the Druids and do everything herself. Things would be accomplished more quickly and efficiently. Things would happen with less conflict and argument. She was tired of shouldering the responsibility while being questioned at every turn by those she depended on to support her. They were a burden she would gladly shed when the time was right for it.

She wrote the note swiftly, having already decided on its contents while listening to the prattling of Pyson Wence. The time for hesitation was over. If they weren't strong enough to do what was needed, she would be strong enough for them.

When the note was finished, she read it back to herself.

When you find the boy,
don't bother with bringing him back.
Kill him at once.

She rolled up the message and placed it into the tube she had retrieved from the arrow swift earlier in the day. Walking over to the window, she reached into the bird's cage and refastened the tube to its leg. The sharp-beaked face turned, bright eyes fixing on her. *Yes, little warrior,* she thought. *You are a better friend to me than those who just left. Too bad you can't replace them.*

When the tube was securely fastened, she lifted the swift and tossed it into the air. It was gone from sight in moments, winging its way north into the twilight. It would fly all night and all the next day, a durable, dependable courier. Wherever Aphasia Wye was, the arrow swift would find him.

She took a moment to think about what she had done. She had imposed a death sentence on the boy. That had not been her original intent, but her thinking about the Ohmsfords had changed since she had begun her search for them. She needed to simplify things, and the simplest way of dealing with the Ohmsfords was to kill them all and be done with it. She might tell Traunt Rowan and Pyson Wence otherwise, might suggest there was another way, but she knew differently. She wanted all doors that might lead to Grianne Ohmsford permanently locked and sealed.

By this time next week, that job would be done.

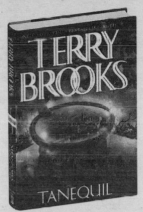